Dynamic . . . Pas
High adventure

Under the tyranny of Oliver Cromwell,
the Irish continue their fight for freedom . . .

. . . freedom to live and to love . . .

. . . freedom from religious persecution . . .

. . . freedom to declare political sovereignty.

It was a mortal clash of wills in a timeless struggle.

Against the backdrop of a ruthlessly waged war,
an English army captain set out with deadly
efficiency to take the O'Hara lands in Ireland.

Meanwhile Conor O'Hara and the beautiful Maggie
fought desperately to keep themselves, their love,
and their heritage alive.

THE CRITICS CONTINUE TO RAVE

This is the third volume in the international bestselling
saga of the O'Haras—a tale that has been called
"impressive and compelling,"[3] "captivating . . ."[4]
"an epic account"[5] that "grips your heart and soul."[4]

[1]*Romantic Times*
[2]*Glamour Magazine*
[3]*Good Housekeeping*
[4]*Affaire de Cœur*
[5]*The Sunday Denver Post*

THE O'HARA DYNASTY

THE O'HARA
DYNASTY

The Renegades

by MARY CANON

WORLDWIDE

TORONTO•LONDON•NEW YORK•SYDNEY

TO JEAN AND JACK PETTIT
WHO CAME THROUGH THE WARS WITH US

Published September 1982

ISBN 0-373-89003-6

Printed in U.S.A.

Cast of Characters

THE O'HARAS OF BALLYLEE

RORY O'HARA (THE O'HARA): Head of his clan, he is one of the leaders of the Irish Rebellion, a renewed bid by the Irish to regain lands usurped by the English and to free themselves from English rule. Ancestral home is Ballylee.

AILEEN O'HARA: The beautiful wife of Rory, mother of Conor and Brian.

CONOR O'HARA: Elder son of Rory and Aileen, he defies The O'Hara's order to flee to France at the beginning of the Irish Rebellion and grows into young manhood as a warrior at his father's side.

BRIAN O'HARA: Younger brother of Conor, he is a scholarly youth with no love for war. Sent to France by his father at the beginning of the Irish Rebellion, he pursues his academic ambitions in peace.

THE O'HARA TALBOTS

SHANNA O'HARA TALBOT: Sister to Rory and widow of The Scot, Sir David Talbot, assassinated in France some years earlier. Proud and defiant, she elects to remain at her beloved home, Ballylee, rather than flee Oliver Cromwell's New Model Army.

MAURA O'HARA TALBOT: Beautiful daughter of Shanna and David, she grows into young womanhood at Ballylee. She marries Donal O'Hara of Ballyhara and was ordered to France as chaperone to younger family members at the beginning of the Irish Rebellion.

PATRICK O'HARA TALBOT: Son of Shanna and David and younger brother of Maura, he falls in love with Elana Claymore. A great warrior, he is captured by the English at the massacre of Drogheda, but escapes.

THE O'HARAS OF BALLYHARA

DONAL O'HARA: Distant cousin to Rory, he arrives at Ballylee after his ancestral home of Ballyhara in Antrim is taken from him by the English. Marries Maura.

MARGARET (MAGGIE) O'HARA: Comes to Ballylee as a child with Donal. Sent to France with Brian and Maura at the beginning of the Irish Rebellion, she returns to Ireland at thirteen, already blossoming into a young beauty. Falls in love with Conor, her childhood companion.

THE O'HANLONS

KATHLEEN (KATE) O'HANLON: A bonny young woman, she struggles to make a living for herself and her younger brother and sisters as tenants of Lord Claymore. Falls in love with Patrick.

TIMOTHY O'HANLON: Younger brother of Kate.

*　　　　*　　　　*

ELIZABETH, LADY HATTON: A highborn Englishwoman and beauty of her time, she survives her two husbands and her daughter, Brenna Coke Hubbard, to raise her grandson, Robert Hubbard.

ROBERT HUBBARD: Illegitimate son of Rory O'Hara and Brenna Coke Hubbard, Viscountess Poole. Aware of his O'Hara blood, he is ruthlessly determined to take Ballylee and claim that heritage.

BYRON CLAYMORE: An English lord granted Claymore Castle and its lands under the plantationing schemes following England's defeat of the Irish Rebellion of 1603. A Catholic, he agrees to side with the Irish Catholics against the Scots Presbyterians and English Puritans.

ELANA CLAYMORE: Beautiful, willful and scheming daughter of Lord Claymore, she becomes a spy in the employ of John Redding to further her ambitions for wealth and station.

LORD GORMANSTON: A Catholic colleague of Lord Claymore, uncle of John Redding.

LORD ANTRIM: A Catholic colleague of Gormanston and Claymore.

SIR JOHN REDDING: Nephew of Lord Gormanston, he becomes a valuable spy to the Protestant forces in Ireland.

OWEN ROE O'NEILL: Nephew of Hugh, The Great O'Neill, and cousin to Rory O'Hara. After thirty-five years of exile in Europe, returns to Ireland to lead the Irish Rebellion.

SIR PHELIM O'NEILL: An Irish lawyer, he receives his training in London. One of the leaders of the Irish Rebellion.

JAMES BUTLER, EARL OF ORMONDE: Lord Lieutenant of Ireland. A fervent royalist, he sides with the Irish Catholics in their fight against England's Puritan forces.

JOHN PYM: Acknowledged leader of England's Puritan Parliament and one of the instigators of the civil war.

ROBERT DEVEREUX, THIRD EARL OF ESSEX: Although a lord, he favors Parliament and he assumes command of the Parliamentary army at the beginning of England's civil war.

OLIVER CROMWELL: A former squire, he rises to power as an officer in Parliament's Puritan army. Eventually replaces Essex as its general and develops his New Model Army that later conquers Ireland.

KING CHARLES I: Son of James I, ruler of England from 1625 to 1649, and husband of Henrietta Maria of France. Finally defeated by Parliament forces at Naseby in 1645 and beheaded in 1649.

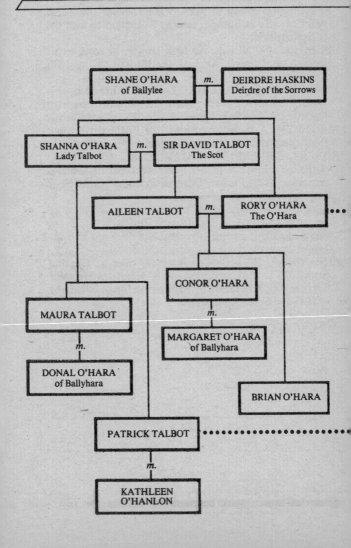

THE O'HARA DYNASTY

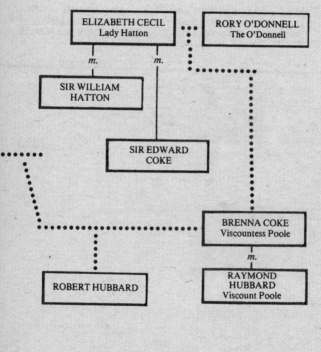

ELIZABETH CECIL
Lady Hatton

m.

SIR WILLIAM
HATTON

m.

RORY O'DONNELL
The O'Donnell

SIR EDWARD
COKE

ROBERT HUBBARD

BRENNA COKE
Viscountess Poole

m.

RAYMOND
HUBBARD
Viscount Poole

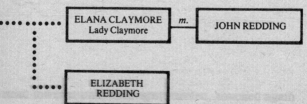

ELANA CLAYMORE
Lady Claymore

m.

JOHN REDDING

ELIZABETH
REDDING

"SURE AN' ALL ULSTER'S A TRAGEDY, AND HASN'T IT
ALWAYS BEEN? BUT I THINK THE REAL TRAGEDY IS NOT
THAT IRISHMEN HATE EACH OTHER SO MUCH IN THE NORTH,
IT'S THAT THEY DO IT IN THE NAME OF CHRIST."

A BARMAID IN DONEGAL

Prologue

Fall 1649

DROGHEDA, IRELAND

A STENCH OF DEATH hung over the city like a pall. The booming cannon had long since been stilled and the sharp ring of steel on steel no longer echoed through the streets. The annihilation of Drogheda was complete. A terrible stillness had settled over the town, broken only by the agonized cries of the wounded, the solemn cadence of soldiers' boots on the cobbled streets, the occasional wailing cry of a motherless babe, a muffled roar as yet another building succumbed to the flames and toppled to the ground.

Twenty thousand strong, the soldiers had landed in Dublin harbor and marched inexorably northward on nonexistent roads, past ruined castles and burned-out forts. None in their path had dared try to stop them. Their reputation had preceded them, and all had cowered before the awesome spectacle of the bloodlike red of their uniform tunics vivid against the blinding green of the countryside. Unchallenged, they had reached the southern gates of Drogheda, and although the city was defended by three thousand of the flower of Irish royalists, the soldiers had breached the ramparts on their third attempt.

The ensuing massacre had been swift, merciless and all encompassing.

Now, Captain Robert Hubbard of Cromwell's English New Model Army stood on the arch of Duleek Gate, above the courtyard of St. Mary's Church. Flickering light from the still-burning fires of the city played over his gleaming breastplate and visored helmet. The strong jaw of his handsome, swarthy face was set in a hard, grim line, and beneath heavy, dark brows his eyes burned like two ebony coals.

But they burned coldly, impassively, as Robert Hubbard watched the defeated Irishmen file through the gate and mill like cattle in the courtyard. "'Tis done," he murmured aloud, his bass voice a low rumble. "And yet, 'tis just the beginning."

The governor of the city, Sir Arthur Ashton, had said, "He who could take Drogheda, could take Hell." *Well,* Hubbard thought, *hell has been taken.* It was but a matter of time before the rest of Ireland fell under the Puritan sword.

Drogheda would be a lesson to rebellious Irish garrisons of lesser might. Surely few, if any, would try to withstand a siege knowing that Cromwell's army would give no quarter. For in Drogheda, friars and priests had been put to the sword as quickly as they had been found. No man in uniform or bearing arms had survived, and civilians who had found themselves in the way had been cut down with equal lack of mercy. All corpses had been ransacked for valuables and those who had thought to escape by hiding had been ferreted out and slaughtered like cattle.

No quarter. That was the rule of war—and the bloody harvest reaped by those who would sow rebellion.

"Think not of what we do as monstrous," General Cromwell had proclaimed, "for all the blood we spill is done as God's work and in God's name!"

Robert Hubbard smiled at the thought. *Let them all do God's work,* he mused. *I'll do mine.*

Once again his eyes surveyed the wretched crowd in the courtyard and roved over the long line that stretched from Duleek Gate almost as far as the River

Boyne. One by one the prisoners—men, women and children—moved up to stand before a table at the gate's entrance. Behind the table sat an English sergeant, draped in a heavy black cloak. In front of him lay a huge open book.

The process seemed unending. Each Irish rebel's name, age, place of birth and religion was demanded and recorded. Then, in a bored, sonorous voice the sergeant ordered the prisoner to "Step on," and join the others in the courtyard.

As Hubbard watched impassively, a toddling child of five, perhaps six, stood before the table. Idly, without guilt or remorse, Captain Hubbard wondered how this "rebel" would die: by sword or starvation.

"Do away with their young today, and you'll have no rebels to fight tomorrow!" his superior officers had often said.

Their reasoning was sound, Hubbard thought, as the child walked under the arch and disappeared in the mass of milling bodies.

He was about to retire to his quarters when a broad-shouldered youth with a full head of rust-colored curls stepped up to the sergeant.

"Name."

"Conor O'Hara," came the lad's voice in a booming baritone that arrested Hubbard in midstride.

"Place of birth?"

"Ballylee."

"Age?"

"Seventeen."

"Religion?"

"Irish."

"Irish what?" the sergeant growled.

"Irish free man," came the insolent reply.

The sergeant's arm whipped out and viciously struck the youth's face, sending him sprawling.

At that instant a girl of about the boy's age, with

flaming red hair and sharply drawn, beautiful features ran up and knelt beside him. Tenderly she cradled his head in her arms while the youth blinked and tried to regain his feet.

Ruthlessly, the two were dragged apart. O'Hara wrestled himself free from the grasping arms of the English soldiers and leaped toward the sergeant.

It was a foolhardy move, despite the youth's width of shoulder and heavily muscled arms and thighs. The burly sergeant merely stepped aside and cuffed him to the ground. A dagger appeared in the soldier's hand and the girl screamed.

"Sergeant!" Robert Hubbard called down from his vantage point.

"Sir," the sergeant answered crisply, halting the downward motion of his arm and managing to turn the movement into a salute.

Hubbard then shifted his attention to the girl. Her face was clearer now, illuminated by the torches overhead. He could see that it was indeed beautiful, with high cheekbones and wide, sparkling green eyes under heavily shadowed lashes.

"Your name!" Hubbard demanded.

"Margaret O'Hara," she replied proudly, flashing her emerald eyes upward.

"Are you sister to the lad?"

"Nay, cousins. I am of the Antrim O'Hara clan, of Ballyhara."

Hubbard's lips curled into a thin smile and a chill of anticipation rippled through his body. He could hardly believe his good fortune.

"This lad, Conor. Is he the son of Rory O'Hara of Ballylee?"

"Aye," Margaret replied, although a puzzled frown now creased her forehead.

"Sergeant!" Hubbard barked. "Put the boy in irons and bring the girl to my quarters!"

She was shouting at him now, but Hubbard, already descending the stone stairs to the courtyard, paid no heed. His mind was racing ahead to the day when Cromwell's Puritan army would reach Ballylee.

On that day he would take what he considered his birthright, and the youth, Conor O'Hara, would be on his way to Barbados as a slave.

How much easier, Hubbard thought, *to claim Ballylee without a half brother on the land to challenge me!*

Part I

July 1641

CHAPTER ONE
BALLYLEE, IRELAND

THE WEATHER WAS KIND to western Ireland that summer eight years before the massacre of Drogheda. Bathed in a warm summer sun, the land was like a reclining woman with a smooth skin of green grass. Her bones were of polished marble and her hillocks rose like firm breasts toward the cloudless sky.

Above the arc of her hips lay the fertile rolling hills of Ballylee, ancestral home of the O'Haras. Here the sun seemed to shine its brightest, the grass seemed more lush and the fields of oats and barley grew higher.

The mansion of Ballylee—half Norman castle, half manor house in the Tudor English style—lay in the curve of the woman's waist. It sparkled like a gray stone-and-glass jewel, with the sea to its back and over twenty thousand O'Hara acres stretching inland beyond its high protective walls.

From the open windows of a third-story corner room, the cheerful sound of feminine laughter filled the air above perfectly tended orchards and gardens lush and colorful with blossoming flowers. Carried by a light refreshing breeze, it reached beyond the outer walls to workmen who labored at digging and shoring a moat that had been filled in years before.

Pausing in their work, two of the men raised their heads as a tall blond young woman in an emerald green dress appeared at the window. The sun turned her straw-colored hair a shimmering gold and high-lighted her skin to the hue of a pale pink rose.

She saw the men's upturned faces and waved.

Returning the salute, they openly admired her fine-featured face and full figure.

"And when's the great day, m'Lady Maura?" one of them called up to her cheerfully.

"A month today," she replied, her pursed lips breaking into a wide smile that revealed even white teeth.

"Ah, she's a beauty she is," the workman said in a low voice to his comrade.

"Aye, like her mother, the Lady Shanna."

"'Tis a good thing, this wedding uniting the O'Hara families of Ballylee and Ballyhara."

The second workman nodded and let his eyes rest in open approval on Maura O'Hara Talbot's full, firm hips and the arching swell of her breasts visible above the gold embroidery on her bodice.

"She has the hips for babies, she does, and the breasts to make 'em grow. Soon there'll be more O'Haras than Castle Ballylee can hold!"

"Pray God there'll be enough O'Haras to hold it and Ballylee doesn't go the way of Ballyhara," remarked his companion fondly.

Both men crossed themselves in agreement and returned to their tasks. They never saw the slight frown that furrowed the young woman's high fore-head as her deep blue eyes moved from them to the score of other men toiling just beyond the castle's outer wall.

Years before, when Maura had been still a child, her father, Sir David Talbot, had filled in the moat. "There will be no more need for it," he had said. "Times have changed since the bloody British cooped us up in stone towers behind moats and slit-ted windows. The O'Haras and the Talbots are on

Ballylee, and as long as we are, I would have us live with graciousness like the lords of England."

Old Shane O'Hara's beloved Ballylee had been but rubble when his son, Rory, and daughter, Shanna, had returned more than a decade before from exile in France. Drawn together by their mutual love of Ireland, Shanna and the Scottish adventurer, Sir David Talbot, had fallen in love and married. Together with Rory they had rebuilt Ballylee to its present power and magnificence.

After David Talbot had been murdered by an assassin's bullet in Paris, Rory O'Hara had carried on. The lands of Ballylee had increased from ten to fifteen and then blossomed to twenty thousand acres. The O'Hara wealth had multiplied tenfold until the name had become a power to be reckoned with and was feared and envied by many. And during the whole of Maura's childhood there had been peace.

But now her uncle, Rory O'Hara, the master of Ballylee, had ordered that the moat be redug and filled. There could be only one reason: like everyone else in Ireland, O'Hara expected war.

A shudder passed through Maura's body as she thought of the possibility of war. She had been born in 1621, eighteen years after the last battle of the Great O'Neill's rebellion and fourteen years after the flight of the earls into exile in Spain, France and Italy. Her mother, Shanna, and The O'Hara, had been no more than children at the time of the 1603 rebellion and the earls' flight in 1607 and they had never forgotten either. How often Maura and her younger brother, Patrick, had sat before a warm turf fire while the Lady Shanna had regaled them with tales of battles, of Irish bravery and of exile.

But for many years now there had been peace, and it was hard for Maura to imagine that it might end, particularly when her wedding was just a month away.

Her wedding.

Would the sons and daughters she hoped to bring forth from her womb have the same love and care and joy of living she had enjoyed? Or would they go through the same trials and tribulations of past O'Haras caught up in the winds of war and rebellion?

An undercurrent of anxiety between Protestant and Catholic had always existed in Ireland; the English and the Irish refusing to trust one another fully despite the years of peace. But never could Maura remember it being as bad as it had been during this past year. Anxiety had now given way to real alarm, and it seemed as though the old fires of hate would be rekindled under the cauldron that was Ireland.

Was this, then, a time for her to contemplate marriage and, she hoped, children soon after?

Maura knew it wasn't. But neither did she care. She was in love, and each day that brought her closer to the consummation of that love made her heart swell with tenderness and her body quiver with desire.

Her gaze lifted to the hills to the south and east. Soon, perhaps even today, her brother, Patrick and her husband-to-be, Donal O'Hara, would come riding over those hills. What news, she wondered, would they bring?

The two youths had been sent by Rory O'Hara to Dublin Castle in response to a request from James Butler, Earl of Ormonde, for a meeting. Maura's knowledge of the mission didn't extend to its details, but she had been privy to enough of the conversations in Ballylee's great hall to understand the reasons.

King Charles of England was on the verge of war with his Parliament. If civil war erupted in England,

Charles would need the assistance of Irish troops to hold his crown. But the king had little hope for such aid if Irishmen seized on Charles's troubles to rebel in their native land.

For years, both Irish landowners and others who had been stripped of their lands through plantationing schemes had petitioned the king for guarantees of their birthright and religious toleration. Characteristically, Charles had vacillated, unwilling to bow to the demands of Irish Catholics for fear of alienating English Protestants.

Now, however, the threat of civil war was forcing him to make a decision.

Ulick de Burgh, Earl of Clanricarde, had recently hastened to England to speak to the king on behalf of the Irish nobility and the Old English gentry alike. His mission was to urge Charles to grant religious toleration to both Irishmen and English Catholics and to insure their rights of land. If de Burgh succeeded, there was every reason to believe that rebellion in Ireland could be stemmed and the nobility would support the king in any confrontation with Parliament and the Puritans.

Would the king meet their requests? And even if he did, would the Irish leaders believe him? Charles Stuart, like his father, King James, was not known for keeping his word, especially in matters concerning the Irish.

Maura was proud that her uncle, The O'Hara, had chosen Donal to be his emissary. But she was also fearful.

A full year had passed since Donal O'Hara had ridden into the courtyard of Ballylee with his copper-haired little sister, Maggie, riding pillion behind his saddle. Even now, Maura could remember that day in vivid detail.

Donal's worn and faded mantle, his heavy, scuffed

brogues and mud-caked trews, had made him appear more like a peasant than an Irish lord. His dark eyes that peered from deep hollows in his angular, handsome face had been filled with sadness and despair.

"God bless all here," had been his first words as Rory O'Hara had stepped forward to meet him.

"And may His grace shine on you and the little one as well," O'Hara had replied to the traditional greeting.

"I am Donal O'Hara, son of Cormac, Lord of Ballyhara, and this is my sister, Margaret."

Shock had registered briefly on Rory O'Hara's face but had passed quickly as he had hastened to make the visitors feel at home. "Welcome, cousin. Stand down and the O'Haras of Ballylee will show you their hospitality."

The entire family had gathered in the castle's great room to hear the travelers' tale. But it wasn't until the newcomers had both been fed and his sister put to bed, that Donal, in short, clipped sentences full of anguish, told his tale.

Many years earlier, during Queen Elizabeth's reign, the Scots had come into Antrim with crown powers to requisition lands. Donal's father, Cormac, had been powerless to stop them and little by little the property belonging to Ballyhara had been taken away. All Donal's older brothers had taken to the hills and joined the reparees, the brigands and highwaymen who preyed on travelers. His older sisters had left the land as well, some to marriage, others to the streets of Dublin.

Two years earlier, in 1639, old Cormac O'Hara had died. At about the same time, the Lord Lieutenant of Ireland, Thomas Wentworth, had appeared with a grant on Ballyhara that had been given by King James to one William Parsons. To retain the land, Donal had been required to pay off Parson's demand of fifteen thousand pounds.

It had been impossible, and what had been left of Ballyhara had gone to Wentworth.

At the conclusion of Donal's tale, several of the women had openly wept. Rory O'Hara had only nodded, for he had known the scheme well. Wentworth had done the same to the O'Byrnes and O'Tooles of Wicklow, to the O'Briens of Cahir, and the O'Hanlons of Armagh and to many others. It had been a foolproof scheme that had allowed the Lord Lieutenant to line his pockets with profits from Irish lands. And the ambitious man who had once been no more than a Yorkshire squire and a champion of Parliament before switching his allegiance to the king, had played it for all it was worth.

"And so we are all that's left of the clan O'Hara of Antrim," Donal had concluded sadly. "I would ride the highroads and, like my brothers, die on a gallows, but 'tis no life for my sister Maggie. Tales are told in all of Erin of the prosperity of Ballylee. I ask you, Cousin Rory, for a tiny bit of tenant land, for I would become your kern and raise sweet Maggie to something besides the streets of Dublin."

Rory's response had been immediate and sincere. Rising to his feet, he had dropped his huge hands on the younger man's shoulders. "My cousin, you'll not be a tenant," he had vowed. "You're an O'Hara, and as such, you'll share in all we have under this very roof."

One by one, Rory O'Hara had then introduced Donal to his distant kinsmen.

Maura smiled when she remembered those deep, brooding eyes meeting hers for the first time. Her heart had thundered in her breast, for she had known even then that Donal O'Hara would one day be more to her than a distant cousin.

And now, a year later, that day was only a month away.

During that year much of Donal's bitterness had faded. As his love for Maura had grown, so the wildness had faded from his eyes and his constant call for war and rebellion to regain Ballyhara had ceased.

Would Donal's and Patrick's trip to Dublin Castle and the growing talk of rebellion rekindle all his old bitterness?

Pray God that it doesn't, she thought fervently. *Let them rail and argue and even kill each other in Ulster and Munster and in the Pale, but here in the west, in Ballylee, let us remain in peace.*

"Here now, lass, stop your daydreaming. It will bring the lad back no sooner. Turn around and see what we have for you!"

Her mother's voice stilled her, bringing her thoughts back to the room and the reason she had been told to turn away from her half sister, Aileen, and her mother as they unveiled their surprise.

Maura whirled around, only to stop short with a gasp. "Oh, mother...Aileen! 'Tis truly the most beautiful wedding gown in Christendom!" Maura's fingers trembled as they ran lovingly over the fine, petit point lace. It covered the white satin of the gown completely, from bodice to hem. "And the cut— Oh, 'tis so new. I'll feel like a Paris bride!"

"Nay, not quite so risqué as that," Aileen laughed. "Unlike the French pattern, this will leave some mystery to your husband's eyes before the bedding comes."

The sleeves were short, gathered into two high puffs at the shoulders. The bodice, though cut exceedingly low, was meshed by more lace ending in a ribboned choker at the throat. The streamers, like the bodice, were embroidered with white thread just a shade off-color from the stark white sheen of the dress material.

"You'll be a beautiful bride, my darling," Shanna Talbot said, her dark eyes beaming as she watched the joy spread over her daughter's face.

"A bride fit for any O'Hara," Aileen said. "Were father only here to see it."

Aileen saw the brief cloud pass over Shanna's face and bit her tongue. Maura saw her mother's distress, too, and quickly embraced her.

"He will see the wedding, you know," she said, kissing her mother lightly on the cheek, "for there is not a day that passes when he is not with us everywhere we look at Ballylee."

Shanna's mood passed quickly and her dark features broke into a smile. "Indeed he is, and if he were here in the flesh, he would be the gaiest of us all. It was his life's desire that there would always be O'Haras on Ballylee. What better way than to have the daughter of an O'Hara Talbot marry another O'Hara?"

Maura blushed. "Mother, you make our union sound incestuous," she protested.

"How so?" Shanna cried indignantly. "I've done the pedigree. You and Donal are fourth cousins at least!"

"I know, but—"

"Oh, hush, the both of you," Aileen laughed, tossing her head of rich blond curls and shaking out the voluminous skirt of the wedding gown. "Come, Maura, out of that green thing and let us see how true my eye guided my needle."

"Ah," Maura chirped, "now she sounds more like the aunt than the sister!"

All three women laughed at this, for the relationship between Maura and Aileen was indeed unusual. Maura's uncle, Rory, The O'Hara, had married

Aileen Talbot, who was the daughter of David Talbot through an alliance in his youth. This made Aileen Maura's aunt as well as her half sister.

At times it was confusing, especially for the younger children, but always humorously so, for they were all of the family O'Hara, and that was what really mattered.

While Aileen helped Maura change, Shanna took up her fan and moved to the open windows. Aileen's reference to David had brought more than just a tug to her breast.

How Shanna had missed him these past years, missed the warmth in his gray eyes when he looked at her, missed the gentle yet insistent touch of his fingers on her body. Even now, when she was well past forty, Shanna still experienced a pang of desire when she thought of his touch.

She had always been a passionate woman, but David Talbot had brought a flowering to that passion beyond anything she had dreamed of as a young girl. It was a true test of Shanna's love for David that she had felt passion for no other man since his death.

He had been a fine man who had given her a beautiful daughter and a handsome if somewhat wild-natured son. And he had given her something that she valued more than life itself: a return from exile in France to Ireland and her beloved Ballylee.

The O'Haras now had a small empire in the west of Erin. Five hundred tenants worked the land. Cattle and sheep were abundant, and the crops were so plentiful that they could be sold for export.

It is good, Shanna thought, with a smile and an upward tilt of her defiant chin, *that no matter how many O'Hara and Talbot mouths there are to feed, Ballylee can provide.*

A squeal of childish laughter suddenly reached her ears and shifted her attention to the orchard below.

There she caught sight of Aileen's and Rory's two sons, Conor and Brian, who looked like tiny deer as they ran through the trees. Close behind them was Maggie O'Hara, whose coppery hair glinted brilliantly in the sunlight.

Back and forth the figures darted among the trees. As usual, Conor, the oldest of the three, quickly outdistanced the other two. But even with the burden of cumbersome skirts and petticoats, Maggie was closing the gap between herself and Brian. Finally, with a shout of triumph, she leaped upon the boy's back.

Although Maggie and Brian were the same age, eight, she was the larger of the two. She rode Brian to the ground as if she were a boy herself.

The chagrin on Brian's face brought a chuckle from Shanna. Brian, a year younger than Conor, was always the first to get caught in any games the children played. Unlike his brother, whose young body was already developing like a thick trunked tree, Brian was thin and almost frail, with the porcelain-pure features of his mother, Aileen.

As an adult, thought Shanna, Conor would be built much like his father, Rory, with powerful arms and broad, sinewy shoulders. Brian would be taller, with the lithe and wiry body of his grandfather, David Talbot. Already the boy's hooded gray eyes seemed to emulate his grandfather's when he was deep in brooding thought.

Brian had inherited David's keen mind as well. Brian might be last in physical games, but he was always first at his lessons. He was already well on his way in the study of philosophy, divinity and mathematics as well as the mastery of three languages.

Conor was the exact opposite. Completely at one with a horse when he rode, he brought many a gasp of dismay to Shanna's and Aileen's lips when he thundered at breakneck speed across Ballylee's fields and over its fences. Rather than sit at lessons, he preferred to seek out a tenant who had once been a soldier and swordsman. Then, hour after hour, the clang of steel meeting steel could be heard from some distant glen.

"Aye, different they are, and 'tis good," Rory O'Hara often declared, in his thundering voice. "For it will take brains as well as brawn—and a feel for people as well as a knowledge of soldiering—to run Ballylee one day!"

They were both fine boys, Shanna mused. Pray God Ireland would not erupt into war so that they might grow into strong men and have sons of their own.

"What think you, mother?" Maura asked shyly, breaking into her mother's reverie.

Shanna turned, and a film formed in her eyes the moment she saw how radiant her daughter looked in her wedding gown. "You are truly beautiful, my darling," she breathed, and then could say no more as a lump formed in her throat.

The mood struck the three of them at the same time. Hands quivered and eyes misted as they all moved forward to embrace each other. "We are so lucky," Shanna whispered, tears flowing down her cheeks, "to have love...."

"And love," Aileen murmured, "is life to a woman."

IN THE GRASS BESIDE BRIAN LAY MAGGIE, her chest heaving from their recent exertion. Nearby, Conor's strong young body was perched seemingly precariously but with perfect balance in a tree.

"She caught you again, Brian!" he gibed his brother with a grin.

"Aye," the dark-haired boy replied good-naturedly. "And doesn't she always?"

Maggie sat up with a toss of her coppery mane and glowered at Conor. "He tripped," she corrected.

Her defense of Brian brought a bubbling laugh from Conor's throat. That was always Maggie's way, he thought. She would do all she could to best Brian and then make excuses for him when it was done.

"Did he now?" Conor asked innocently, his eyes taking on a mock seriousness as they met his cousin's. "Did you trip, Brian?"

Brian shrugged, his lips forming a wan smile. "I might have. The truth of it is. . . I don't remember."

"B'gar!" Conor howled, rolling out of the tree and landing lightly on his feet like a cat. "You two plot against me in every game. Come! Let's have at pirates. I'll kidnap the damsel—" So saying he bent forward and before Maggie could stop him, planted his shoulder in her belly and heaved her into the air. "And you, Brian, come rescue her from my lair!"

"Nay, my chest still hurts from the last run."

Brian's voice could barely be heard above Maggie's screeching from her perch atop Conor's shoulder. He held her like a writhing sack of potatoes as her legs kicked and her small fists beat upon his back.

Laughter and screeching alike came to a sudden stop as a hunting horn sounded its eerie wail in the distance. Conor set Maggie's booted feet to the ground and three pairs of eyes scanned the shimmering haze beyond the heath.

In the distance a knot of horsemen grew steadily larger.

"'Tis The O'Hara!" Maggie said.

"Aye, 'tis father," Conor cried. "Come!"

They set off as one and as before, Conor quickly outdistanced his brother and Maggie. He sprinted through the heather, his knees high and his shoulders moving in perfect unison with his legs. Without pause he bypassed the stables and, picking up speed on a hard-packed mud path, headed on toward the riders.

The group of horsemen was less than five hundred yards away now, and Conor could discern the riders' faces. His father was in the lead, his gray-streaked heavy black curls dancing in unison with his horse's trotting steps.

"Papa, papa!" Conor cried.

O'Hara smiled broadly, his even white teeth gleaming through the heavy black beard when he saw his son. Lightly he put spurs to the stallion and the big horse broke obediently into a canter.

Only then, when his father's massive frame moved away from the group, did Conor see the two horses in the center of the riders. A body was slung, facedown, over each of the hide-covered, wooden saddles. Under the animals' bellies the men's wrists were tied to their ankles.

"Hola, my son!" O'Hara called, in his rumbling bass.

"Papa!"

The father leaned low and extended a heavily sinewed, leather-covered arm. Conor lifted his arms as if in greeting but, in the last second before his father passed him, gripped his powerful arm. O'Hara swung the boy upward; and with a grace beyond his years, the lad settled astride the horse's rump.

"Hola, my son," O'Hara greeted him once more. "And what mischief have you been at today?"

"As much as I could find," the boy replied with a gleeful laugh.

O'Hara half turned to stare at his son. Another smile spread across his wide-jawed face at the sight of Conor's open, boyish features. He had a look of mischief that brought clucking sounds from the women and dire predictions of future doom from the priests. With his curly, rust-colored hair and his darting, deep-blue eyes that conveyed beguiling innocence, O'Hara felt his son looked more like an aged barrel-chested imp than a nine-year-old boy.

"If you've given your mother a time, I'll turn your hide the color of your hair," he threatened.

"Nay," Conor replied, the mischief in his blue eyes gleaming even more brightly. "Only to Brian and Maggie...and maybe a wee bit to old O'Higgin."

O'Hara chuckled to himself at the thought of Conor teasing his old bailiff, Dermott O'Higgin. One of Conor's first acts when barely sprung from his mother's womb had been to tug at O'Higgin's wild red beard, and the boy had been doing it ever since. And no matter how much O'Higgin might grumble, Rory knew he reveled in the love and attention, even in the childish pranks his master's sons inflicted on his daily life. For O'Higgin saw in Rory's offspring his own sons who had died in the fighting so many years before.

"Have you killed some reparee sheep stealers, papa?"

"Aye," O'Hara said, his lips losing their smile. "They chose to fight rather than run."

"Damn fools," the boy said matter-of-factly.

O'Hara was about to reprimand his son for such callousness but held himself in check. He cursed inwardly the times that made a nine-year-old boy think so little of death, and aloud he admonished the child in a different way. "Think not too ill of them in death, lad, for they are still Irishmen."

But Conor persisted, "O'Higgin calls 'em rogues when they steal from a fellow Irishman."

"A man knows not his enemy from his friend, son, when his belly button meets his spine. Ah, me Brian and darling Maggie!"

Breathless from their exertions, the other two chil-

dren had reached the center of the heath. O'Hara
didn't whisk them into the saddle at a dead run; instead he reined in and lifted them one by one.

Conor made room between himself and the saddle
for Brian, while Maggie threw both her legs over
O'Hara's lap, her smiling face inches from his thick
black beard.

"Have your brother and Patrick found their way
home yet, sweet Maggie?"

"Nay," the girl replied, her eyes darting over
O'Hara's shoulder to the two horses in the midst of
the group. "Are they dead?"

"Aye, lass, they are," The O'Hara answered reluctantly.

"And they be Irishmen?"

And again, Rory responded quietly, "Aye."

Maggie's sea-green eyes misted and her delicate
mouth trembled. "'Tis so sad. Know you their
names?"

"Nay, little one."

"I shall say my beads tonight for their poor
souls," Maggie whispered.

O'Hara's throat tightened as he saw the girl's wide
eyes fill with tears and twist her pretty features. Since
she and Donal had arrived at Ballylee nearly a year
ago, O'Hara had grown to love her as he loved his
own children. He hated for her to be exposed to the
brutality of the world outside his lands, but he knew
it was necessary, for one day soon that world might
well come crashing in on them. And when that day
came, Maggie, as well as his two sons who now clung
so tightly to him, would have to face it like adults if
they were to survive.

"Aye, pray for them, lass," O'Hara urged gently.
"And remind God that their sins were not all of their
making."

O'Hara slowed the big stallion to a walk, and the

four of them rode into the cobbled courtyard of
Ballylee and the welcoming arms of the women of the
O'Hara clan.

AILEEN BREATHED THE COOL NIGHT AIR sweetened by a
lightly falling rain and raised a trembling hand to
close the shutters. They were barely latched when she
heard O'Hara's heavy tread on the stone floor outside their bedchamber door.

Quickly she moved to her vanity table and sat
before the mirror on a tiny velvet-covered stool. The
outer door opened, then closed. By the time Rory's
huge bulk filled the arch between foyer and inner
chamber, she was brushing her long blond tresses as
if it had been her only occupation for these past two
hours.

But when she lifted her eyes to meet her husband's
dark stare in the mirror, Aileen knew he could guess
her fears. From the beginning it had been that way
with them. Words had never been needed to convey
their emotions. A look—even the merest lift of an
eyebrow—could communicate mood and feeling one
to the other. As it did now.

Donal and Patrick had returned just before the
evening meal. The warmth of greeting had soon been
chilled by the brooding look on Donal's dark face.
The word from England was not good. All at the
table could sense it, but tongues were held until the
lads could be questioned by The O'Hara.

At the meal's conclusion O'Hara had motioned
them to follow him to the upper reaches of the house
where O'Higgin would be awaiting them in his tiny
office.

For two hours they had been talking and planning.

"The news?" Aileen asked now, her eyes never
leaving Rory's bearded and weather-seamed features.

Wearily he replied, "Not good, lass...methinks far from palatable to the hotheads."

He took off his leather tunic, tossed it aside and eased his aging but still powerful body into a high-backed, wide-armed chair near the fire. "Blessed Ireland," he sighed, his fingers tugging at the leather ties of his broadcloth shirt. "Even in the dead of summer we need a fire to take away the dampness."

"Would that dampness were the only thing we have to chill an Irishman's bones," she replied, kneeling and reaching out to unfasten his rolled Spanish boots. O'Hara removed his shirt and then aided his wife as she tugged at his boots. Finally he was clad in just a pair of trews that fitted his muscled thighs like a deeply tanned second skin.

Aileen handed him a goblet of brandy and then stood with her back to the fire, surveying the man she loved. Her whole life had revolved around this man who had given his love to another so long ago and yet had then allowed himself to find happiness in her own youthful arms.

A shudder passed through her as she remembered that night many years before, when she had stood on the parapets of Ballylee high above. Her thoughts—and her love—had been as clear then as they were now.

O'Hara had come back to Ballylee for good, leaving France and the woman he had loved there behind him. He had regarded the daughter of his friend David Talbot as no more than a child but Aileen had known differently. And as she had gazed at him that night her heart spoke.

I am no longer a child, Rory O'Hara. I am a woman with passion in her body and love in her heart. I know the tears you have shed and the heartaches you have endured. And believe me, O'Hara, when I say I can mend them.

Aloud, she had told him, "I'll never make you forget her, but you'll never regret that I replaced her."

Now, staring at his ruggedly handsome features that age had only enhanced and at his still-powerful, near-naked body Aileen felt secure in the knowledge that she had accomplished everything she had set out to do, and more. Rory O'Hara loved her with all his heart and soul. If he did remember his first love, the raven-haired English beauty, Brenna Coke Hubbard, the Viscountess Poole, it was only because of the child they had created out of their love.

Young Robert Hubbard would be fifteen now, and Aileen knew that there were times when Rory would muse on the son he had sired but never seen. But those musings had never for one moment disrupted their life together on Ballylee, for Aileen had given The O'Hara two strong, handsome sons, and he loved them with his life.

"The firelight shines through your chemise," Rory said, his rumbling voice pulling Aileen back from her reverie.

She smiled. "And to think I mistook that look in your eyes for weariness."

"'Tis both desire and weariness," he chuckled. "Desire for you, my love, and weariness of the stupidity I see in my fellow man."

Aileen wanted to move to her husband's side and dispel his burden with her caresses. But the tone of Rory's voice told her that he wished to talk, so she held her place.

"Our weak king has at last turned the full brunt of his tyranny on his own people and would forfeit those nearest to him to save himself. Charles signed Wentworth's order of execution."

Aileen gasped, "You mean—"

"Aye, Wentworth is dead. 'Tis the first telling

blow dealt by John Pym and Parliament to the crown, and methinks far from the last.''

O'Hara's dark eyes clouded and his broad forehead furrowed in deep concentration. Aileen both knew and understood his unvoiced thoughts. There was not an Irishman in Ireland who had not hated Thomas Wentworth, Earl of Strafford, the ruthless Lord Lieutenant of Ireland until his recall to London a year earlier to become the king's first minister. Nevertheless, those among the Irish gentry with cooler heads knew that during his rule in Ireland, he had at least held Ireland for the crown and kept rebellion in check.

Rory O'Hara was one of those cooler heads. The reasoning of his astute mind told him that if civil war broke out in England, Ireland's only hope was to declare its support for the king. For if the king should lose, Irishmen, Catholics to a man, would fare even worse under the rule of the Puritans in Parliament. Their leader John Pym, a former Somerset man and a lawyer, was known to be both adamant and ruthless in his cause against king and Catholic alike.

There were many, O'Hara knew, who disagreed with him. They would say be off with king and Parliament and declare open rebellion against both.

Aileen held her quivering hands behind her back to hide from her husband's weary eyes the fears they spoke. But in her mind the thunder of a coming storm rumbled and she was forced to speak her thoughts. ''Then King Charles refused to grant our requests for religious toleration and a guarantee of lands that were sent through de Burgh?''

''Nay, Charles is true to himself and the reign of James, his father. He would say yes in one moment and refuse to put pen to paper in the next. He would ask for the Irish to aid him in his struggle with Parliament today and refuse them payment tomorrow.''

O'Hara paused to take a sip of brandy from the goblet in his hand. Then he continued, a rumbling laugh marking his words. "Good King Charley would bribe me with a baronetcy. What think you, lass, to be Baroness of Ballylee?"

"I think as you," Aileen replied, lifting her chin and squaring her shoulders. "An English title may one day be as worthless as the crown that granted it. I would have none of it."

Again O'Hara laughed, raising his eyes to meet hers. "Aye, but you must admit 'tis a wily gift Charles offers."

"Oh, he's a cunning man, for as Baron of Ballylee you would have no choice but to declare for the crown. But 'tis a stupid supposition to think O'More, Phelim O'Neill and the others would follow you."

O'Hara nodded. "Such a gesture only shows how little Charles knows of an Irishman's heart or mind." He sighed, pulling himself to his feet and crossing to the shuttered window. "I would be tempted if I thought it would keep the peace."

"But it would not," Aileen countered. "It would only lose you the respect of other Irishmen and the Old English Catholics alike."

"Aye, I know." O'Hara unchecked the lattice and opened the louvered shutters. At once a brisk wind ruffled his gray-flecked black hair and droplets of light, warm rain dotted his seamed face.

Beyond the bailey and the edge of the castle's parapet, he could hear the sea pounding the rocks at the base of the cliff below Ballylee's walls. Now and then a wave would curl high enough so that its foamy white tip could be seen in the darkness.

"How often my father, old Shane, must have stood and looked from this place and dreamed of war. And now I stand, not dreaming of it but dreading it."

Aileen shivered despite the warmth from the fire crackling so near behind her. When she spoke her voice seemed to echo in the stillness of the room. "The body of Ireland is—as it seems it has always been—chained. But, Rory, my love, here on Ballylee we live in peace and our souls are free. Is there no way to temper our countrymen and play a waiting game with the crown?"

"I think not. For whether we declare war for the king or war for ourselves and Ireland, there will still be war," he replied, his voice heavy.

A sob escaped Aileen, and suddenly the chill she felt forced her into his arms. "All our fathers knew was the grief of battle, and now we are to endure the same. Must we forever be fleeing or fighting? Can men's minds never find peace and settle their lives in what it offers? Must all men test their mettle eventually as warriors?"

"It would seem so," O'Hara replied, encircling her body with his huge arms. "The Scots pray, we pray, the king prays, and Pym sits primly in Parliament praying. And we all pray for God's grace in defeating each other. I wonder if there were as many wars before the Bible was written."

Aileen's head jerked upward, her eyes wide, her face a mask of sudden ire. "Do not blame God for man's deceits! Blame men for the way they interpret His word!"

Perfect, even white teeth gleamed through the blackness of Rory's beard in a disarming smile. "I do, lass. But it still doesn't seem to make any difference."

Again Aileen burrowed her cheek into the wiry mat of black hair on his barrellike chest. She knew his thoughts and, to herself, admitted the truths he spoke, even though they doubled the fear in her breast and intensified the pounding of her heart.

"Happy we've been, here in our corner of Ireland," he murmured, his voice a soothing rumble. "Not many men have had the love I've enjoyed. You fill me with love, and my children fill my days with pleasure. 'Tis only a war that could change the way we live, what we've had."

"Must we be satisfied just with what we've had?" she rejoined, combing her fingers through the hair on his chest. "Must you be a warrior, your father's son?"

"'Tis changed from my father's day, from the days of the mighty clan chiefs."

Gently he curled the fingers of one hand under her delicate chin and tilted her face so that their eyes met. "Ah, Aileen, my lass, my love...I've had so much more than my father had. In old Shane's day men lusted more for battle than for their bed, because it was all they knew—how to be warriors. Then, pride and honor was all a warrior really had. He rarely saw his woman long enough to bed her, and his children knew not what to call him. In my time I've been lucky enough to realize that it's a foolish man who needs more than his land and the love of his woman."

A tear formed in the corners of Aileen's limpid eyes, built to overflowing and rolled down her cheeks. "But you will to war?" she asked, her voice little more than a half-fearful whisper.

O'Hara made no reply but caught her fiercely in his arms and buried his face in the golden mist of her scented hair. For many moments they stood immobile, locked in each other's arms. Then, as suddenly as she had been locked in his arms, Aileen felt her feet leave the floor. Against his massive chest her breasts throbbed with both despair and anticipation as he carried her to the great postered bed. Tenderly he laid her on the eiderdown puff, and she heard the scuffling sound of his bare feet as he struggled to remove his trews.

Her hands tugged deftly at the bodice string of her chemise. But as she began to remove the garment his hands stopped her. "No—let me!"

Aileen sighed and gasped in turn as she felt his fingers, gentle in their great strength, trickle over her body. Tenderly he kissed her cheeks and lips and stroked her hair with his cheeks and nose. She felt her body respond to his touch and covered his hands with her own, guiding them over her flesh to the places she knew would arouse her more.

"How kind you are, my love. . .in all you do. 'Tis a pity to turn such a man into a warrior."

Rory stiffened, and for a moment she thought she had broken the spell. Relief flooded through her as she felt the down-filled mattress lower and his warmth meet hers.

"Rarely do gentle warriors last through a battle, lass. Because I love you and ours so much, know that when the time comes I will be a wolf in the field in order to return to you."

"Then Ireland will to war?" Aileen asked again softly.

"Aye, but that is tomorrow, and this is tonight."

As if his huge bulk were but a pound, he gently covered her body with his own. The firm, hard maleness of him washed away her despair and fanned her desire.

And the words she spoke when her body rose to meet her husband's came from the depths of her heart. "No matter tomorrow. Tonight, and all the nights that have ever been, are full of my love for you."

Aileen felt herself respond as only a woman sure of herself, sure of her man and sure of their love, could respond. And then they were one.

THE RAIN was little more than a warm, gentle summer shower. Oblivious to it, Maura stood, her spine straight, the weight of her upper body supported by her hands, balled into fists and resting on a stone tooth of the parapet before her. A dark cloak, its cowl covering all but a few wisps of her golden hair, made her nearly invisible against the blackness of the night.

Her usually rose-hued face was white now. To Donal, standing beside her, she looked inscrutable. But he knew that inside this girl he had grown to love so deeply there was a passion that could match the rage of the storm that was centered somewhere over the sea before them.

For just as Rory O'Hara was giving the news from England to his wife of so many years, Donal had said nearly the same words to his wife to be. Maura had taken it calmly, her softly curving lips thinning ever so slightly and her body trembling imperceptibly.

Now she was silent, her thoughts turned inward. Donal, too, remained silent, preferring to let Maura speak when all he had said and intimated had been digested by her quick and thoughtful mind.

Maura sensed that the man she loved and was soon to marry awaited some reply, some comment, but she knew not how to respond. The fact that rebellion was almost a surety and that Donal would join the rebels' camp no matter what Rory O'Hara chose to do, had stunned her nearly as much as his last pronouncement.

"So, my darling Maura, no matter how much I love you it is an O'Hara and an Irishman I have to be. If war comes I must go—to fight not for any king but for Ireland."

And then he had spoken the words that had chilled her heart.

"If we should be married first... and anything

should happen. . . I could not forgive myself, even in death—especially if you were with child. It would not be fair, Maura. Perhaps we should postpone. . . ."

No wedding. That was what he was suggesting, she thought with a lurch in her heart. That the wedding that had occupied her every thought these past few months be put off, in case. . . .

Death? Donal with the brooding eyes and the sad, handsome face that brought a wrench to her heart every time she looked at him?

Donal. . . dead? Lying asleep forever in the midst of some far-off battle?

It was unthinkable. . . impossible!

Maura had never really thought about death, at least not in terms that deeply concerned her. Death and dying had always seemed too far away to contemplate seriously. It was something she associated with withered bodies and the infirmities of old age. Death had claimed Shane O'Hara and his beloved Lady Deirdre, Rory O'Hara's parents, as well as Maura's father, David Talbot. They lay in the crypts of Ballylee's chapel more like legends than corpses.

She shivered slightly, and impulsively Donal drew her into his arms. Her cloak parted and her breasts, budding above her bodice, pressed against the dampness of his doublet. But even through the thickness of its material she could feel the warmth and hardness of his young and vibrant body.

Death—for Donal and Maura? Nay, they would live together and they would live forever.

"Donal," she whispered.

"Aye, my love?"

Maura looked pleadingly into his eyes and urged, "Touch me. . . kiss me!"

The fingers of his strong hands spread in the small of her back as he lifted her to her slippered toes. His head lowered until their lips brushed, touched again and then came gently together. The kiss was long and tender, its sweetness sweeping all from her mind like a gentle spring breeze moving clouds to a faraway place.

At last their lips parted and Donal looked down into the shimmering jewels of her eyes. The tiny droplets of rain seemed to highlight the firm and perfect line of her jaw as well as the prominent cheekbones that gave such strength to her features.

"Maura..." Donal began, but a claw seemed to clutch at his throat as he looked down into the radiant love and innocence he saw shining from her upturned face.

"There will be a wedding, my love," she whispered, pressing the fullness of her yielding body against him. "No matter what."

"And you are sure?" he said at last.

"As a young girl—perhaps not too young—I always thought that when the time came to love a man, to make love to a man, it wouldn't be anything that I would be able to ponder about. There would be no time for a great, momentous decision; it would just happen. Then as I grew older, thoughts of passionate moments shared with a man came more often, but they were like reveries of idle curiosity—Why, Donal O'Hara, I do believe you're blushing!"

He hoped she wouldn't notice, but he could feel the heat rising from his collar and could not prevent it from adding color to his face.

Her eyes sparkling, Maura exclaimed, "You never cease to amaze me."

Donal gave a sheepish chuckle, and it was answered by Maura's tinkling laugh as she melded her body even closer to his.

"I have known since the day you and your sister, Maggie, rode into the courtyard of Ballylee that all my reveries would come true. And I have worked toward that end each day since, have I not?"

Now the smile that lit his face was genuine as he brushed his lips across the tip of her nose. "You bewitched me."

"Evidently not enough," she teased. "How many secret trysts have we had that came to naught?"

"They came to naught, my sweet, because you are a lady. And how dare you call a simple afternoon ride a tryst?"

"Because," she chuckled, "that's what I wanted such rides to be! Oh, Donal, how many of those afternoons in shaded glens by clear-running streams, lying side by side in the tall heather, have I wanted you to take me as you must have taken so many wenches. You have had a chambermaid or three, haven't you, Donal? Come, admit it!"

The flush heightened in his cheeks, and to hide it he pushed back the cowl and buried his face in the silk of her hair.

"Beware, wench, or I shall take you at your word."

"And...?"

"And take you here and now!"

"Do! Take me here and now, in the gentle rain, with the sea pounding the rocks below and God smiling down through the dark clouds at two lovers who truly love!"

Deftly she unlaced her bodice and shrugged until both dress and chemise fell away to bare her breasts. Just as deftly she brought his hands from the small of her back to cup their rounded softness.

"You are so very beautiful," he murmured, gently moving his palms upward to caress the hardened nipples. "And so much the wanton."

"Not wanton—a woman," Maura whispered seductively. "'Tis you who make me so."

"There will be a wedding. And on that night I'll take you...as a wife, in a soft down bed, with nothing between us, as it should be."

"I love you, Donal O'Hara," she declared.

"And I you, my Maura, for all the time God gives us."

August 1641

CHAPTER TWO
STOKE POGES, ENGLAND

A LIGHT RAIN, no more than a chill vapory mist, fell from a gray overcast sky onto the mourners' shoulders. In pairs they filed from St. Giles Chapel and down a graveled path to the tiny graveyard. The mourners were few, and all but two had been paid for their silent wails and feigned tears.

In her sad life Brenna Coke Hubbard, the Viscountess Poole, had made few friends and more than a few enemies. Her eventual conversion from the Anglican Church of England to the popish faith had alienated her from court society and driven a wedge of ill-feeling between the lady and what family she could claim.

Moments earlier, the mourners had gathered in the chapel to gaze for the last time on this woman who had endured so much. In her life she had been a woman of dark, transcendent beauty. Now, even in death, her face seemed Madonna-like, revealing the haunting, fragile quality that inspired the dreams of poets. The telltale lines of care, worry and despair that had marked her olive-skinned features in life seemed to have disappeared in the peaceful rest of her final and everlasting sleep.

The signal was given to close the coffin, and in another moment the Lady Poole would be deposited in her last resting place.

A year before, Brenna had been the only one present to mourn the passing of her husband, Raymond

Hubbard, Viscount Poole. Now she herself was being mourned by her only surviving blood relatives, representatives of the generations before and after her. They walked with bowed heads behind her simple, undraped coffin, their thoughts turned inward.

Lady Hatton moved with faltering steps. Her frail and slightly stooped body was aided in its progress by a cane in her right hand and the strong, steady hand of her grandson, Robert Hubbard, under her left elbow. Despite her age, there could be no doubting that the elderly woman clothed entirely in black satin was the mother of the raven-haired beauty, Brenna Coke Hubbard.

Lady Hatton was sixty-seven years old, yet the waxen features of her lined face could not hide the beauty that had made her the toast of London in her youth. Her eyes were still sharp and clear emerald green as they searched the damp ground before each step. Her hair, once a fine auburn, was now completely gray, but still there was majesty in the carefully rolled and piled shape of its coif.

She had outlived two of England's rulers, Queen Elizabeth and King James, both of whom she had fought with bitterly during the length of their separate reigns. She had survived nearly all her own family and two husbands, Sir William Hatton and Sir Edward Coke. Nor had she ever really loved either of them. She had lived a life fueled by ambition and had garnered notoriety, great wealth and status from it. She had known the sorrow of hatred and the exquisite joy of one great love.

Now she was laying to rest her only child, the child of that love.

The procession finally reached the graveside, and the hired pallbearers gingerly set the casket on the waiting scantlings. Lady Hatton stepped aside to allow the Puritan rector to take his place at the head of the grave.

As the rector opened a Bible and began to read in a sonorous voice, a slight smile played around the corners of the lady's lips beneath her dark heavy veil. *'Tis all right, Brenna, my sweet,* she thought. *Though they may war here on earth, priest and Puritan do pray to the same God. Methinks either can send you on your way, no matter how much they may deny it to themselves.*

The smile broadened as Lady Hatton remembered the rector's words when she had asked him to perform the service.

"Nay, madam, 'tis blasphemy to speak over a woman who has sinned by taking the popish faith as her own. I cannot and will not do it. It would be sinning myself!"

The rector was now sinning, but Elizabeth was sure his conscience had been properly salved by her donation of two hundred pounds that currently swelled his purse.

She tried to listen to the droning voice but found other voices, voices from the past, pushing it from her mind.

What lives they had led, she and her willful daughter. They had both shared moments of glory and greatness with the powerful and those who would be powerful. They had both lived and loved and laughed with men who would move mountains and make nations.

And where were they now, those men who had aspired to such power and glory?

Most had bent like saplings before the winds of time until they had broken and, like Brenna, had returned to the earth that had given them birth.

How odd it is, Elizabeth mused, *that you, sweet Brenna, should perish before me.*

Brenna had always been gently soft where Elizabeth had been hard. The daughter had found goodness where the mother saw only deceit. Brenna would believe when Elizabeth denied, cajole while her mother would rant and demand. So early a death seemed a strange way for God to repay so kind and loving a servant.

Memories. At times Elizabeth found them soothing, but more often they stabbed at her heart like sharp spears and made her temples throb with the ache of regret.

It was rare now that she spent time in London at her beloved Hatton House. She had been married there, more than a half century earlier, to Sir William Hatton, a man much more than twice her age. Sir William had been kind, but far too advanced in years to inspire passion in a beautiful young girl. Indeed, for a long time Elizabeth had wondered if there was ever to be passion and love in her life.

All that had changed when she met Rory O'Donnell, a prince of the warring Irish clans. With him had come love, passion—and Brenna. A widow at the time, Elizabeth had been forced to avoid scandal by choosing a second husband before Brenna's birth.

She had, in the person of Sir Edward Coke. The marriage had soon proved to be a sour experience, but it had been too late. O'Donnell had chosen to return to his Ireland, and Elizabeth had been too much a part of London and English society to give up wealth and her ambition for love.

Did she regret it now? Only when she remembered how the tempests of her own life had been repeated in the life of her daughter.

For Brenna, too, had foolishly succumbed to the charms of a wild Irish rogue, and for the rest of her life she had paid the price. Forced by King James's favorite, the Duke of Buckingham, into an unwanted marriage to the weak but kindly Sir Raymond Hubbard, she had tried to make the best of a life beyond her control. But her chosen path had been fraught with difficulties. True, Sir Raymond Hubbard had loved her dearly, but although she had held him in great respect, she had never been able to return his deep and abiding adoration. During the last few years of her marriage it had grown even worse. As the child of her one great love had grown into manhood, Brenna had scarcely been able to look at him without remembering the father. For in Robert Hubbard even a blind man could see the seed of the Irishman, Rory O'Hara. Mother and son had never been close, but this living reincarnation of her past had driven them even further apart.

It had fallen to Brenna's mother to raise the boy. As she stood in a light rain under the gloom of gray clouds at her daughter's graveside, Elizabeth Hatton wondered about the character of the man she had molded from the boy.

For a man he had become, far beyond his years both physically and mentally. Had she implanted in the lad's heart too much of the bitterness and hatred she held in her own? Had she instilled too much of a sense of purpose and ambition in Robert, imbuing in him a nature that was more like her own rather than that of his gentle mother? And if she had, would Robert one day experience the same cruel gusts of memory that now plagued her—the same doubts about his life that Elizabeth felt about her own?

Much of the turbulence and unhappiness in her younger years had been caused by the kings and queens who had ruled her life. Her bitterness toward the monarchy had steadily grown until it had gradually become an obsession. Blindly, she had come to believe that the emancipation of the English people, rich and poor alike, was of more importance than the aspirations of Charles, the Stuart king who steadfastly believed that his right to rule was God-given.

When in Parliament the Puritans began their rumblings against Charles, Elizabeth Hatton had been one of the first of the gentry to sway toward their side. Infuriated by the Lady Hatton's support, the queen had ordered that Elizabeth be ousted from court. To make matters worse, her political leanings had given the king reason to confiscate a great deal of her rents and holdings.

Such high-handed methods had only driven Lady Hatton further into the Puritan camp, so much so that the court beauty during the reigns of James I and Elizabeth Tudor had quickly become a friendly matriarch to the renegade Parliament of James's son, Charles I.

She lent her country home, Stoke Poges, to the king's enemies when a secret place was needed for their meetings. It was not uncommon to see the earls of Northumberland, Essex and Warwick, the lords Holland and Saye, and the nominal leader of the Puritan movement, John Pym, pass through the huge gates of Stoke on any dark night. Elizabeth knew young Robert was aware of their comings and goings, but he had never revealed his thoughts on the subject, preferring to remain moodily silent.

It was for Robert's sake that Elizabeth had the only misgivings about her current political path. Because of Brenna Coke Hubbard's conversion to the popish faith and the rumor of his own illegitimacy, doubt had been cast on Robert's claim to the title of Viscount Poole. If that claim should be eventually denied, young Robert Hubbard's only means in life would be his grandmother's estate. And now, thanks to Lady Hatton's Puritan leanings, what was left of that estate was dwindling rapidly.

What did Robert think, Elizabeth wondered. Was he angry, bitter? She had no idea. From the time her grandson was a child, she had been unable to fathom the workings of his mind.

Sometimes he amazed her: more often he frightened her. She found his habit of riveting the twin coals of his black eyes on one disconcerting. Even as a young boy, he had had the ability to send a chill of foreboding up one's spine.

There was no doubt that Robert's eyes were his most arresting feature. They could flash with anger in one moment and sparkle with gaiety the next. But Elizabeth knew it was often a false gaiety, a sham to charm those around him. There was a coldness, even a cruelty, in their depths that never quite seemed to disappear.

Ever since she could remember he had had a haughty, insolent air about him, but he nevertheless managed to appear graceful in public, charming all who came into contact with him. Despite his youth, Robert was not above encouraging friendships simply to gain whatever advantage he could from them.

These disturbing aspects of his character his grandmother chose to ignore, attributing them to the chaos of his childhood. Only now and then, in brooding moments of her own, did Elizabeth wonder if the cruelty expressed in Robert's eyes had been instilled in him by her.

Thinking of him, Lady Hatton's gaze lifted, straying to the edge of the grave and the tall, darkly clad form of her grandson.

How handsome he is, she thought, *with his olive skin, ebony hair and piercing black eyes. Only fifteen, and already a young giant towering over those around him.*

What will become of him, she wondered. *In the*

time left to me I must do everything possible to secure his future.

The grating sound of the scantlings brought Elizabeth's attention back to the grave. She watched as with nimble, experienced hands, the pallbearers slowly lowered the coffin into the damp earth. There was a final, thudding sound, and Elizabeth fumbled in her sleeve for a lace kerchief. Her hand trembled as she brought the thin fabric up under her veil to dab at the sudden wealth of tears that filled her eyes.

A slight cough arrested the movement and made her turn to face Robert, who had moved to her side. The only thing she saw in that instant were his eyes, totally dispassionate and devoid of any tears.

ROBERT HUBBARD STOOD at the library window, his doublet open, his hands thrust into the front of his breeches. Outside, day was swiftly turning into night and the dreary rain continued unabated. Behind him a large log burned cheerily, throwing dancing shadows on the book-lined walls.

Beneath his wide forehead and mane of curly black hair his dark eyes glowed, probing beyond the grayness enveloping the grounds to the tiny graveyard and the newly erected stone in its center. His thoughts, as usual, were clear and precise. Neither regret nor sorrow clouded the musings of his mind about his mother's death. He weighed her passing only in terms of how its consequences might affect him.

At times during his young life he had felt sorry for her, perhaps had even pitied her, but he could never remember having loved her. Now that she was gone he was conscious only of relief, a sense of absolute freedom. It was a feeling that had begun a year before when his father, Raymond Hubbard, the Viscount Poole, had died. Now, with his mother's death, it was complete. It was as if the shades that had plagued his youth had disappeared at last. No longer would he be forced to display a loyalty that he didn't feel, a respect that was hollow.

In life his parents had given him little; in death they had left him nothing. This he accepted without complaint, for it was no less than he had anticipated. Early on, his grandmother had taught him to expect the worst from everyone. She had schooled him in the ways of kings and commoners alike, pointing out their perfidy and showing him how to overcome it and prosper.

Robert had learned his lessons well. To survive and to prosper had become his creed; all other emotions and yearnings were suppressed until they lay dormant in his fertile mind or disappeared altogether. Now he was free to pursue his ends, without the charade of paying lip service to the God of scriptures so adored and feared by his father and mother.

The sound of glass and liquid being poured into goblets stirred him. He turned and accepted the drink from his grandmother's thin blue-veined hand. For a few moments they remained silent, she sitting, he standing tall and straight, staring down at her gray head and slightly stooped figure.

At last Lady Hatton raised her eyes to his and spoke. "And so there are just the two of us."

"It would seem so, madam."

Elizabeth winced slightly. If Robert saw the reaction he chose to ignore it. As a child, he had called her grandmama. But after Sir Edward Coke's death in 1634, he had changed the form of address. Indeed, the vulturelike way in which Lady Hatton had swooped down on Stoke Poges, loudly proclaiming the estate to be hers on the very day of her husband's death had caused him to change his attitude toward many things.

He had been in the room when Elizabeth had raged at the solicitor to be gone, declaring furiously that she had no need of his help. There could be no doubt that Stoke was hers, since Sir Edward had seen fit to plunder her inheritance from her first husband, Sir William Hatton, to pay for it.

The solicitor's features had quivered with outrage at what he considered unseemly conduct on the part of a widow. "Surely, madam," he had protested stiffly "if you did not love or respect the man in life, you could at least do so in death."

"Damme if I will! My husband died as he lived— the most disagreeable man of his times. I see no reason to change my opinion toward him now that he is dead at last!"

When the solicitor had given up and departed, young Robert had looked up at her with narrowed eyes and asked, "Why is it that mother declares so much love for father while you declare only hatred for grandfather?"

"Because love has nothing to do with marriage," Elizabeth had replied curtly. "You will learn one day, Robert, that marriage is a thing foisted upon women to rob them of everything but their souls. And, in any event, Sir Edward was not your grandfather, so you needn't revere him."

"But I want to, grandmama."

"You won't! He never claimed you; you shall not claim him!"

The boy hadn't understood and Elizabeth hadn't elaborated. Indeed, she had been uncertain of how to explain to a lad of eight, the supposed son of the Viscount Poole, that both he and his mother were no more than bastard offspring of Irish rebels and therefore unrelated to the man he had called grandfather.

But her admonition had been so strong, so loud and vehement, that it had thrown the boy into momentary shock laced with fear.

More than a little confused, he had at last untangled the web in the only way his childish mind would allow. If Sir Edward had not been his grandfather, then the Lady Hatton could not be his grandmother. "As you wish, madam," he had replied, and had never called her grandmama again.

Elizabeth toyed with her wineglass, preferring to focus her eyes downward rather than face the coldness of her grandson's glare. "As you know," she ventured, almost hesitantly, "your mother left very little means."

"I expected none," Robert replied evenly.

"But that does not mean you are without expectations. I am not as wealthy as I once was, but what I have left is more than enough to make you a gentleman of future means."

A mirthless chuckle slipped from Robert's lips as he moved around to stand directly in front of her chair. "Should this strife between king and Parliament continue, madam, I daresay it will turn into war. If that happens and Parliament loses, I doubt that you will have anything left."

The cold logic in his voice chilled her. How could he be but a youth of fifteen, she thought, yet think and act like a man twice his years? And yet, if she admitted the truth to herself, Elizabeth knew only too well. It was she who had taught him.

Ignoring the doubts that had begun to plague her mind more recently of late, she went on in a firm voice, "For that very reason, Robert, you must make a choice. I suggest you choose the Puritan cause, whether you truly accept it or not."

Robert groaned and returned to the window. He cared little for any religion and less for the men who would exhort others to follow their chosen path. But most of all he despised the Puritans.

Robert thought of himself as a member of the gentry, a man with education and breeding, a product of the aristocracy and to the manner born. He had no taste for the drab, black-clothed and ill-mannered men and women who thumped their Bibles and sang their psalms day and night. Nor did he have any respect for them. How often his cynical mind had mused on their desire for the very things of class that they claimed to despise: sumptuous clothes, good manners, fine homes and servants lower than themselves.

"Do you honestly believe in this faith of theirs, madam?"

"Nay, I do not, and you know it," Lady Hatton replied, with a fervor in her voice. "But I believe that they would control the king—aye, even bring him down. His divine rule is blind and unjust, as was his father's before him."

"I agree with your thoughts on the king, madam, but I do not agree that the Puritans can win. They are rabble—base fellows without breeding or refinement. Nay, the king will win in the end. I will find some way to ingratiate myself with his person and secure the peerage that is my birthright."

So heavy was the sigh Elizabeth uttered that it caused him to turn in surprise.

"Robert," she said wearily, "no matter how England's troubles are resolved you will never be the Viscount Poole."

"Madam, I will not listen. As a child, the taunts and rumors—"

"They are true, Robert. Sit down!"

Elizabeth almost smiled at the sudden whiteness of her grandson's face. As he lowered himself slowly into a high-backed chair across from where she sat, she could see that she had struck the only chord that could reach him. No longer was his face full of insolence. The self-assured man of the world so far advanced beyond his years was gone, replaced by the youth he was, his face a mask of disbelief and fear.

"True...?"

"Yes. Your mother kept a journal of her life and, sad as it is for me, a journal of mine as well. I promised her that I would give it to you when she was gone. I never intended to keep that promise, but now I know that I must."

"How s-so?" he stammered.

"Because I see that I must prove to you that you have no choice in this matter. I must show you that the cause of Mr. John Pym and Parliament is the only way open to you."

"No! I will not listen! I am the son of Viscount Poole, a peer. A seat in the House of Lords is my right!"

Painfully, Elizabeth stood and crossed the room. Slowly she unlocked a drawer in a huge chest and from it extracted a worn leather book several inches thick. Wordlessly she handed it to Robert and, with the aid of her cane, shuffled from the room.

When at last she returned, all light had disappeared from the window and outside it was as dark as a tomb. Robert sat in the chair he had been occupying when she had left, his shoulders sagging, his head in his hands. The journal lay open on the carpet at his feet.

"So now you know," she murmured. "Sir Raymond Hubbard, Viscount Poole, was not your natural father. If you press for your peerage the old scandal will come out, and the lords will know it as well."

His face when he looked up was whiter than ever, and for the first time in years Elizabeth saw tears in his eyes.

"Tell me—" he gasped, with great difficulty "—tell me what is not in this book. Tell me about Rory O'Hara of Ballylee."

Late August 1641

CHAPTER THREE
BALLYLEE, IRELAND

THE MORNING of Maura's and Donal's wedding dawned brightly, with the smell of hawthorn filling the air. The sweet scents of fading summer were everywhere. As the sounds of the nightingale gave way to the cuckoo and the sun rose over the tart greens and purples and reds of Ballylee's gardens, the castle came alive. Below, in the buttery and in the kitchen, voices hummed as happy faces bustled about, preparing mountains of food.

Long tables were arranged beneath the spreading yew and oak trees. By the time the first guests began to arrive, the table had been laid with fine linen napery and decorated from one end to the other with flowers. Elegant venetian glass stood at each place, and even a fork had been placed at every setting, although everyone knew that few would be used. As O'Hara had commanded, pewter was the only metal displayed on the tables.

"Even if we had such a vast amount of silver plate, it would be unseemly to appear so rich when many of our guests are so poor."

On this day Gaelic gentry would mix with the old English nobility. For every O'Reilly, O'More and O'Neill, firebrands of Erin, there would be a Lord Gormanston, a Lord Antrim and a Lord Claymore faithful to the English crown.

Nevertheless, O'Hara expected no flaring of tempers, for much as these men might differ in their political views, they all had one thing in common. They were Catholic, and this was to be a Catholic wedding. Of course, the crown-appointed Protestant minister would have to be paid his fee, but it would be a priest, Heber MacMahon, Vicar-General of Clogher, who would actually perform the ceremony.

O'Hara was one of the few wealthy Irish nobles on good terms with the old English lords, although his invitation to them to attend the wedding hadn't been extended solely out of friendship or respect. In part, it had been a political move, for he hoped their presence would allay any suspicion about the meeting planned for that day among the men intent on rebellion in Ireland.

O'Hara was not entirely in favor of the meeting, as he told his old bailiff, Dermott O'Higgin, early that morning. "I've no taste for war—and less for rebellion, my old friend."

"But 'tis you they will turn to, m'lord," O'Higgin rejoined.

The bailiff's expression of loyalty had brought a smile to Rory's lips. Since their first meeting so many years before on a quiet heath, O'Higgin had insisted on using the old title. No matter how much he might object, to O'Higgin he was and always would be The O'Hara, son of Shane and lord of Ballylee.

"Aye, I know, O'Higgin," he sighed. "But I, like you, remember the hordes Queen Elizabeth sent into Ireland. The others—O'Neill, O'More—they are too young to remember those times. One day again, as it was in the days of the queen, there will be prices upon our heads the same as there be on the heads of wolves."

"So be it," growled the old man. "Better to die fighting with fangs bared than to starve toothless. 'Tis your destiny, m'lord. You are The O'Hara."

His words brought another smile to Rory's lips.

O'Higgin was no politician; he was an Irishman to
the core. "Destiny, O'Higgin? 'Tis a heavy word,
meant for kings. I would be merely a planter and live
in peace."

The old man shrugged. "If all of Ireland could live
and prosper as we do here in Ballylee, there would be
no need for rebels. But as sure as the rain makes Ireland green, the fires will burn in Ulster. From there
they will move south and eventually west. Ballylee is
no island within an island, m'lord."

O'Hara nodded. *Aye,* he thought wearily, *no matter how much David Talbot had dreamed it to be so.*

O'Higgin moved away, leaving O'Hara to his musings.

Destiny. Even the word was distasteful. When
Rory was but a boy, his uncle, The O'Donnell, had
used it, as had his sister, Shanna, when she had
begged and cajoled him to return to his native land
and Ballylee. At that time, he had neither wanted to,
nor thought it possible. In France, as a youth in the
service of Richelieu, he had thought his destiny a
nightly round of brothels and taverns. What better
life could an exile with no means save a strong sword-
arm have?

In England he had thought his destiny would be
death. Instead, it had become love. How long ago
that had been, and how tumultuous those times.

Rory closed his eyes, but no matter how hard he
tried he could not conjure up the image of Brenna
Coke's darkly beautiful face.

The wound caused by their parting had been
healed many times over by Aileen, and it had been
with his beautiful blond-haired wife that he had
again claimed his land and found peace. For years
now, he had thought that to be his destiny, but now,
on the day of his niece's wedding, he knew his dream
of peace was false.

*Now I know that, like O'Donnell, the Great
O'Neill and my father, Shane, before me, my destiny
is war. It would seem that is the destiny of all
Irishmen.*

"So be it," he said aloud, buttoning the dark blue
satin doublet he had chosen to wear for the wedding
and walked resolutely into the sunlit garden.

MAURA RESEMBLED A PAINTING as she walked down
the bridal path with her hand steady on the strong
arm of her uncle, Rory O'Hara. The chiaroscuro of
sun and shadow passing across her face from the
trees overhead gave it a radiance that brought gasps
from many of the guests as she passed.

Her thick blond hair was swept up and back from
her forehead and gloriously curled at the back and
sides. It fell in ringlets to her shoulders, framing her
strong yet delicate features and her large, luminous
blue eyes. Two strands of pearls the hue of a pale
rose sat atop her coif like a crown.

The wedding dress of white satin was all that
Shanna and Aileen had dreamed it would be. Now a
collar of exquisite Irish lace had been added, as well
as tiny pearls sewn into the bodice and the cuffs of
the long sleeves. The veil, too, was of fine lace, and
so sheer that every feature of her smiling face could
be discerned.

From behind her veil Maura saw a few frowning
faces, but she chose to ignore them. Today she would
see only joy for politics, the problems of men and the
perniciousness of nations had no part in this, the
happiest day of her life.

Her glance fell on Donal O'Hara, who stood
waiting for her, tall and handsome in a suit of deep
green with a half-cloak of gold satin. The sight of her
husband-to-be brought a slight flush to her cheeks
and a pounding to her heart.

How I do love you, Maura thought. *And how very fortunate I am.* Most women of her station were forced into arranged and unwanted marriages. For them, love was nothing more than a word bandied about in songs, letters and speeches. But she was to be married to a man she adored.

As she took her place beside Donal the plaintive, traditional Irish music filtered through the still air. Softly, Heber MacMahon began to intone the solemn yet joyous Latin words.

Maura barely heard him. Oddly, her mind was filled with the conversation of her maids while they had dressed her hours before.

"'Tis a good omen, m'lady, that we did not meet a funeral on the road today."

"Ah, m'lady, hear the sound of the cuckoo—'tis a fair sign!"

"...an' see how the sun shines down—could be nothing but a fine wedding day!"

Omens, folklore, anxieties...she pushed them all from her mind. Concentrating on the priest's words, she echoed each vow in a firm, clear voice and silently repeated Donal's words to herself as he, in turn, echoed the vows required of him.

As the ceremony ended, the priest blessed the newly married couple, and turning to Donal, said, "Give your wife the kiss of peace."

Maura's veil was lifted. Donal barely had time to brush her lips lightly with his own before everyone was suddenly crowding around them.

"Slainte!"

The bride and groom turned at the sound of her brother's voice. As a man and Maura's only sibling, Patrick Talbot had to be the first to wish her joy. Lithe and graceful, he stood with a cup of wine raised in his right hand. As usual, his lips were curved in a carefree reckless smile, but his heavy-lidded smoke-

gray eyes were warm and kind as he gazed happily at
his sister.

"Health and long life to you both. Land without
rent to you both. A child every year to you both. And
death in old Ireland!" Patrick cried. A cheer went up
from the crowd around them as Patrick ended his
toast and embraced both his sister and new brother-
in-law.

A huge cake was brought to the priest by four
white-aproned women. It was blessed and immediately cut. Donal and Maura were given a plate of oatmeal and salt. According to tradition, they each took
three mouthfuls. When the third had passed their
lips, another cheer filled the air, quickly drowned out
by the sound of music as the fiddlers took up their in-
struments and began to play.

With this signal to begin the feasting and dancing,
Maura and Donal were escorted to a raised dais at the
head of the first table. Over it was a canopy of white
satin trimmed in green and gold and emblazoned
with the rampant lion of the O'Hara crest. There
they sat while dancers reeled around them, men and
women drank and feasted, and lively music and gay
laughter swirled around their heads.

But they seemed neither to see nor hear any of it,
for they were totally preoccupied with each other.
Maura's happiness overflowed, her face as animated
as that of an excited child. Beside her, Donal stole
sidelong glances at her radiant beauty with un-
abashed love and adoration in his eyes.

At the foot of the same long table was the second
place of honor. Here Rory O'Hara sat, with his wife,
Aileen, on his left and his sister, Shanna, on his right.
All three were beaming as they watched the dancing
and general merrymaking. From one corner of the
garden came the furious and fast-paced jig and reel
music of the fiddlers. Nearer to the table, a harpsi-

chord blended with Italian flutes in the more subdued
rhythms of the pavane.

The dancers moved gracefully through the elegant
steps, each gallant posing to his partner and she, in
turn, to him. The women were arrayed in brightly
colored silks and satins, bedecked with ribbons and
jewels. The men wore dark velvet coats with satin
breeches. Most wore low shoes with silver buckles instead of the high, rolled cavalier boots so much in
vogue. And virtually all of them dripped embroidery
and lace at the throat and wrist.

"I wonder," Rory sighed. "If London society
could see this, would they still call us savages?"

A low, throaty chuckle came from his right and he
turned to see Shanna cover a smile with her fan.

"I daresay nearly everyone performing the pavane
was a part of that society at one time," she reminded
him. "I would rather be over there, doing a jig with
O'Higgin."

"Our English guests will hear you," Aileen whispered. "Look there at Patrick. Your son seems to
have made a conquest!"

Shanna peered through the moving, colorful figures until her eyes found Patrick. A cloud passed
over her face as her gaze fell upon her son's partner.

Patrick was dancing with Elana Claymore, only
daughter of Lord Byron Claymore. Shanna bit her
lip as she watched the young couple sway and circle
and curtsy as they shifted their feet in unison. "'Tis
more likely Patrick will be the conquered," she
hissed.

Rory saw the furrowing of his sister's brow and
squeezed her arm with a low chuckle. "Do not fear,
lass. Your Patrick is a wild lad, reckless and sometimes rash, but stupid he is not."

"Beauty such as that possessed by Elana Claymore
has been known to make the most intelligent of

grown men become simpering fools," Shanna retorted. "And Patrick is but eighteen."

"Aye, eighteen, perhaps," O'Hara agreed, laughing aloud now. "But when it comes to women and affairs of the heart, our Patrick is far from a boy!"

O'Hara's words failed to calm Shanna. Certainly, her son was far from an angel. With his sensuous eyes and elegantly handsome features, he had already gained a reputation with women, news of which had long since reached Shanna's ears. His rakehell escapades with women of every class—from Sligo to as far away as Dublin—made ample gossip for the servants of Ballylee.

But none of those women had been the daughter of an English lord. Even though she was the same age as Patrick, Elana Claymore had lived a more cosmopolitan life, having received her schooling in England and, more recently, in France. According to rumor, it had been during her stay in Paris that she had begun a scandalous affair with an Italian duke in Louis XIII's court. Once her father had learned of the affair, he had ordered Elana home and then virtually closeted her at Claymore Manor to repent her sins.

It was clear to Shanna, who had herself spent a great deal of time at the French court during her youthful exile from Ireland, that Elana Claymore had done little else in Paris but sharpen her feminine wiles. It also appeared that Elana had repented little since her return to Ireland.

At eighteen she was every inch a woman, tall, with an imposing carriage and beautiful shoulders sloping languidly from the long column of her aristocratic neck. As she danced every movement of her body and tilt of her head conveyed the message that the most important thing in the world to Elana Claymore was her own beauty.

The exquisite features of her finely sculpted face had been enhanced by cosmetics applied with the skill of an experienced artist. Her cheeks had been meticulously brushed with rouge to highlight her prominent bones. Her lips were perfectly lined and reddened with carmine, and just the right amount of blue shadow had been pressed on her eyelids.

Judging by the dress Elana had chosen for this occasion, Shanna knew there was no new style so daring that Elana wouldn't wear it. A sea-green satin skirt was trimmed with saffron ribbons. Her bodice, with its basque and stomacher snugly fitting her slender waist, was cut so low that the dark hue of her nipples was visible against the alabaster white of her high firm breasts.

Her hair, dark brown and lushly thick had been coiled into a bun and pinned high, with the sides falling in thick ringlets and a curling fringe coquettishly masking her forehead.

As well as her slightly scandalous reputation, Elana Claymore was also well known for her charm and wit. It came as no surprise to Shanna that most men who met her fell hopelessly in love with her. She didn't relish the thought of her son, Patrick, doing the same.

Concerned, she continued to watch the young couple closely as Patrick leaned his head forward and whispered in Elana's ear. The woman's proud chin lifted and a bell-like peal of laughter came from her lips. Then she curtsied and leaned forward until it seemed that her heavy breasts would slip from her bodice.

Outraged, Shanna gasped and was about to get up when O'Hara grasped her forearm in a viselike grip. "Shanna—pray do not make a scene that will further embarrass m'Lord Claymore. Look you there, the man suffers enough."

Shanna's glance traveled to a small table on the other side of the dancers. There Lord Claymore sat in conversation with two gentlemen, but it was obvious that he heard very little of what was being said. From the hurt in his kind old eyes and the flush that had spread across his aging face, there could be no doubt that he, too, had witnessed his daughter's brazen conduct.

"Aye," Shanna agreed, with a sign of sympathy. "It would be unjust to make the poor man suffer openly in front of our guests."

A tense silence developed between the three at the foot of the head table. Finally, it was broken by a trilling laugh from Aileen. "Look there, husband, at your own brood and pretty Maggie!"

On the fringe of the dancers, Conor, Brian and Maggie were making mockery of the pavane. While Brian mimed a violin with two sticks, his brother and Maggie bobbed and weaved with exaggerated steps and gestures. Their playful maneuverings made a posturing sham of the graceful ballet.

"Imps they are!" exclaimed Shanna, joining in the laughter as the children's antics took her mind away from her son and Elana Claymore.

"Look at Conor," Aileen said, suppressing a giggle. "He looks like a miniature bull at some pagan rite."

"And Maggie," O'Hara added with a chuckle. "Each time she feigns a trip, her concentration increases. Methinks if she did the dance correctly she would be more graceful than the older women!"

They watched and laughed until the children tired of their game and went off to join O'Higgin at a jig and reel. Soon the toasts and blessings to the bride and groom began.

"May the sons of your sons smile up in your face!"

"God grant you to be happy as the flowers in May."

"Health and long life to you!"

On and on the guests went, with Donal and Maura acknowledging the blessings of each and every one. And as they did so, the glances they exchanged made it clear to everyone present that the love they shared was tremulously beautiful.

As he watched their happiness, O'Hara sought his wife's hand and clasped it firmly.

"They are lovely," Aileen murmured.

"Aye," Rory nodded. "A much grander wedding than ours."

"The times have changed," she said, and noticing the frown her words brought to her husband's forehead, immediately wished she hadn't.

"Aye, lass, I'm afraid they have." He released her hand and stood up. "I'll be slinking off now. Keep a sharp eye and a bright smile toward our English guests."

Aileen could only nod and try to hold back the tears that suddenly filled her eyes as she watched Rory's broad back move through the trees and disappear behind a hedge.

"WHY IS IT, Patrick O'Hara Talbot, that you have never called at Claymore Manor? After all, we are neighbors."

"Aye, we are," Patrick replied, baring his teeth in a wicked smile. "But 'til now I've seen no reason."

"So now you do?" she queried archly.

"Can you have any doubt?" he countered, his eyes dropping boldly to her bodice. "Such beauty would make a man ride three horses into the ground to be near it."

"Damme," Elana laughed, "but the man is a rustic poet!"

"I am many things, m'lady."

The more they danced, the more Elana sensed that the handsome young Irishman was completely taken by her beauty and other obvious feminine attributes. Normally she would pay little heed to the lustful looks of a man so young. But Elana had been long without such looks from any man and this lad, Patrick O'Hara Talbot, was by far the best looking and most appealing of any dancing partner she had had that day.

His smoky gray eyes held an insolent boldness that thrilled her as he ran his gaze over the bareness of her bosom, up to her neck and face, only to return and look with open desire at her breasts. Don Peduardo had behaved like that upon their first meeting in Paris, and shortly thereafter she had made of him putty in her hands and given herself an entrée into the gay life of the French court. But, of course, Don Peduardo had not been her first lover...only her last since her father had forced her to leave Paris and return to this wretchedly boring country of Ireland.

"M'lady...." Patrick leaned forward until his lips were at her ear.

"Yes?"

"Your dress...."

"What of my dress?" Elana asked, with a slight smirk, knowing full well his meaning.

"Methinks it a seamstress's marvel...the way it defies nature by staying in place."

"Sir, you are too bold!" she retorted, feigning an air of shock that was masterful in its execution. In the next instant she laughed coquettishly and then curtsied low, leaning her shoulders forward once more to make her breasts swell alarmingly against the fringe of lace at her bodice.

"Ah," Patrick grinned when she again stood straight before him. "Now I know that boldness does indeed have its rewards."

straight before him. "Now I know that boldness does indeed have its rewards."

Instead of reddening, she only nodded, as if his words had been expected and no more than her due. To Elana, a man's adoration was a sign of his weakness and her superiority. She would have liked Patrick Talbot to praise her beauty with a little less mockery in his voice, but then she felt attracted to this brash youth whose sardonic wit and cynicism was not unlike her own. Manipulating men with her body amused Elana. Manipulating Patrick Talbot, she sensed, could be highly entertaining, and giving him an ample view of the deep valley between her breasts only made the game more dangerous and exciting.

As they moved through the dance she remembered her first introduction to the game of love. It had begun in Paris, with the advice of her older and wiser friend, Marcella, on the evening of their first ball. Intent on her reflection in the mirror, Elana had been adjusting her gown of rustling shot-silk when Marcella's tinkling, naughty laughter had sounded behind her.

"Oh, my darling Elana, you look so wan! Here, try some of my paint. And my dear, must you be so demure? Tighten your stomacher more and lower your collar!"

"Lower?"

"Of course, darling. If you would enjoy Paris, you must learn certain things. For instance, when you converse with a gallant who especially intrigues you this evening, don't forget to lean over when he speaks to you."

"Lean over?"

"So he can look down into your bodice, silly! It never fails. My dear Elana, if you appear untouchable you will remain untouched!"

That evening Elana had made a choice and had leaned over quite far and quite often. In the wee hours of the morning she had lost her virginity but had gained her first conquest. And she had been leaning over quite often ever since.

Her turquoise eyes were nonchalant as they strayed from Patrick's and lighted on the other dancers. They widened slightly, and a faint smile of amusement curled the corners of her lips when she saw that she and her partner were the center of nearly everyone's attention.

And then, quite suddenly, she felt herself being deftly maneuvered away from the dancing area. Before she fully realized it she found herself in Patrick's arms, out of sight behind a hedgerow.

"Pray you, sir, would you become even more bold?"

"Aye, m'lady," Patrick chuckled, "I would, for I find you not an ordinary woman."

"Oh?"

"You are blunt in your sensuality, quite frank in your invitation...."

His arms tightened at the small of her back and his eyes seemed to shift from gray to silver in the dimming light beneath the trees. Something in their flinty color alarmed her. Had she gone too far in her teasing?

"You are like a high-spirited, unbroken mare that would be a challenge to tame," he crooned, the pressure of his arms insistent.

Elana wrinkled her nose at the analogy and slid from his grasp. "I don't think I feel like being tamed just yet," she said haughtily, fully expecting him to continue the game and attempt to take her again into his arms.

But he declined the invitation. Stepping back, he took her hand in his. "So be it, m'lady," he said, lifting her hand to his lips and smiling up at her without a trace of rancor in his eyes. "Perhaps it is just as well. Methinks I remember a bit of business that needs my attention."

In an instant he had passed his lips across the scented smoothness of her hand and was gone.

Elana suddenly boiled with anger. Her hands balled into fists at her hips as she stomped one foot petulantly. How dare he! He was but an inexperienced lad. What gall he had to lure her away from the others with the theft of a kiss in mind, and then stalk off and leave her stranded. It was she, Elana, who was supposed to do the leaving. Only then would the hook be properly baited for another day.

With her eyes blazing and her heart pounding furiously in anger, Elana flounced down the graveled path in the same direction Patrick had taken.

We shall just see, she thought furiously, *what bit of business is so important that it would take him away from me!*

CURTAINS FASHIONED HASTILY from oat sacks had been thrown over the windows. They were intended to block out the sunlight as well as any uninvited, inquisitive eyes. The dimness within added a somber mood to an already somber gathering.

One by one the men had slipped away from the wedding festivities and made their way through the trees and hedgerows to Ballylee's sprawling stables. Now, seated in the dusty loft above the stalls and among the servants' pallets, they looked oddly out of place still dressed in their wedding finery.

From beyond the curtained windows came the sound of music and laughter. Below them issued the call of a stallion as he pranced and snorted for his mares. And in the room itself angry voices were raised in dissension.

"And I say it is God's grace that the former Lord Lieutenant of Ireland has left us and his head has left his body. During Wentworth's rule not a man of us could go to his bed at night and be sure he wouldn't wake up in the morning a landless outcast!"

"Aye, in that cur's eyes Ireland was a conquered country, and we had no rights but such as he was inclined to allow!"

"'Tis said that when Wentworth's head fell the cheer from the crowd could be heard clear to Whitehall! Methinks Master Pym and his Parliament have done us the greatest of favors."

"And what think you, O'Hara, of our great fortune to be rid of Wentworth?"

The speaker was Philip O'Reilly, a young lawyer who had gained a reputation as a speaker for Irish and Catholic causes in the Dublin Parliament. He was a small, wiry man with a mane of wild, unruly black hair and the high broad forehead of a scholar. Imbued with great strength of will and determination, he was a zealot who would stop at nothing to return all of Ireland's land back to the Irish.

Such a man, Rory O'Hara knew, could be a powerful influence on others, as well as a dangerous ally to those more cautious than himself.

O'Hara was sitting silently in the room's only chair. With a careful ear he listened to the words of his companions and with a slightly jaundiced eye he studied their faces in the flickering candlelight.

"Like you, O'Reilly—and the rest of you—I had no stomach for Wentworth's greed and underhanded manipulations. But the man was at least a statesman, a leader. Let me ask you this— While he was lord lieutenant, did not Ireland begin to prosper?"

Here O'Hara paused and smiled, then added, "And under Wentworth were we not all unified?"

"Aye, that we were," O'Reilly retorted with a

grunting laugh. "Scots, Irish and Old English alike hated him."

"Precisely. He spared no one. His only interest was in furthering the crown's power. And in so doing, he kept peace."

"I don't follow you, O'Hara," the young lawyer sneered.

"You should. Who have we in Wentworth's place?"

"Parsons."

"Aye, Parsons. And what is his creed, in his own words? 'Within the coming twelve months, no Catholic shall be seen in Ireland!' Those, gentlemen, are the words of a Puritan."

Rory O'More moved out of the darkness to stand near O'Hara's chair. He was a tall, spare man who spoke with thoughtful deliberation. "If I understand your meaning, O'Hara, you are saying that no matter how much we distrust King Charles and hated Wentworth, the prospect of an England ruled by Puritans is even more odious."

"Aye," O'Hara nodded. "That is indeed what I believe. If Charles falls, what have we then in place of the crown? Puritan rule. Would you have that?"

O'More's serious, almost sorrowful eyes locked on O'Hara's. "Your own David Talbot said it once in Irish Parliament, and I've said it since. If we are to be subjects of the Kingdom of England, then let us be ruled as a free people, governed by the laws of the kingdom and not by the crown's swords. We have asked, but the king has not listened."

"Perhaps one day soon he will be forced to listen. They say Queen Henrietta has a great influence over her husband. Might it not happen one day that she will sway Charles to her own—and our—Catholic faith?"

"'Tis an idle thought!" O'Reilly roared. "For

even if she does, a king of England, Catholic or not, is still an English king. The English government is and always will be but a yoke of slavery about our necks. Gentlemen, I say let England's difficulty be Ireland's opportunity. The war between Charles and his Parliament is but tomorrow away. When it happens, neither side will have time to fight in Ireland!''

O'More tried to arrest the man's fervor by placing a hand on his shoulder. Angrily, O'Reilly shook it off and continued. His eyes were bright with some inner flame, and he enunciated each word as if he had mentally rehearsed it a thousand times before its utterance.

"Who has robbed us of our lands, our liberties and our faith? 'Tis the Protestants—whether Scotch or English—and the Anglicans and Puritans alike. They are our enemies, and before Ireland can be ours again they must be put to the sword!''

"Odd," O'Hara mused in a quiet voice. "It seems that Protestant, papist, and Puritan held a similar view of such matters. Methinks I remember Parliament's man, Sir John Clotworthy, saying much the same thing. 'The conversion of the Irish papist can only be affected by the Bible in one hand and the sword in the other.' ''

"Then all the more reason to meet sword with sword," O'Reilly growled. "Pluck out thine enemy's eye before the point of his sword reaches yours!''

O'Hara shrugged in disgust and made to rise. O'More gently placed a hand on his shoulder to stay him and started to speak. But before the first word came another voice, that of Patrick Talbot, sounded from the dimness near the window.

"Being the youngest here, mayhap I should hold my tongue," he said in low, ominous tones. "But I find it impossible. I have been taught to listen and respect the words of those older and wiser than myself. I suggest, O'Reilly, that you do the same.''

Silence filled the room, broken only by the men's steady breathing. Philip O'Reilly dropped his hand to the hilt of his sword and drew himself up to his full height. His face was florid as he licked his lips.

"Your words are those of a rash youth, Talbot," he growled harshly. "But since it is you who have spoken them, I take them as an insult from a man."

To the surprise of everyone except O'Hara, Patrick chuckled. "And aren't we now—as my uncle tells me we always have been—fighting among ourselves to no good end?"

O'Reilly bristled further. "Then I take it, sir, that you don't press the conviction of your words with your sword?"

O'More made a move to put an end to their foolishness, but O'Hara stopped him with a look and a touch.

Patrick stepped forward into the light. A sardonic smile creased his lips, revealing even white teeth and, beneath their hooded lids, his gray eyes could hardly be seen.

"You take it quite correctly, sir, for I'm not a man who lives by some chivalric code. Nor am I a man taken with elaborate show. If you wish to draw your sword, O'Reilly, I will merely settle the matter by putting a ball between your eyes before your blade clears the sheath."

O'Reilly gasped at the threat. Snickers could be heard from some of the others.

Patrick continued, his voice low and deadly, "Winning is everything. Losing is nothing. I consider death no honor, therefore I would stay alive using any means at my disposal. I suggest, O'Reilly, you do the same and listen to the wisdom in my uncle's words.''

The point was made and all in the room knew it. They also knew that, even in youth Patrick Talbot was at heart an O'Hara, and a man to be reckoned with.

Hugh MacMahon, brother of the priest, Heber, had thoughtfully spirited a large leather jack of wine from the wedding tables. Now he broke the impasse between Patrick and O'Reilly by splashing the liquid into several tankards. When they were passed around he raised his in a toast.

"God save Ireland!"

The others echoed his words and sipped their wine.

"'Twill take more than God," said Sir Phelim O'Neill from his perch atop a table.

"What more than God do we have, O'Neill?" O'Hara asked, leveling his stare on the rangy knight from Dungannon in County Tyrone.

"We have strong hearts, strong hands and keen eyes," O'Neill replied, in a rasping voice.

O'Hara shrugged, "Aye, perhaps we have that. But what we need are powder, shot and muskets."

"And there may be a way to obtain those," Rory O'More proclaimed, taking the floor as if on cue. "Right now, there are eight thousand disbanded Catholic soldiers in Ireland. 'Tis the army mounted by Wentworth to help Charles in his foolish battle with the Scots Calvinists. If they were to be called up under an Irish leader and armed to go to war in the name of the king—"

"The king?" O'Hara interrupted.

"In name only." O'More turned and gestured to Phelim O'Neill, who took the floor. Withdrawing a sheaf of documents from beneath his doublet, he handed them to O'Hara and stepped back.

It took only a glance for Rory to recognize their content. They were commissions signed by King Charles to outfit an Irish army in the name of the king against the Parliament in Ireland. In quiet, even tones he asked, "Forged?"

"Aye," O'Neill replied. "But they'll do until they're no longer needed."

Rory sighed. He knew now that their plotting had gone much further, much faster than he had thought. Again he looked at the papers in his hand. There were four commissions made out, in the names of Connor Macguire, Sir Phelim O'Neill, himself and Owen Roe O'Neill.

"Owen Roe?" he questioned aloud.

For the first time O'More smiled. "We've been in contact for months. He chafes to return from Flanders to Ireland. He has given his word that if the Gaelic natives in Ulster—particularly in his native Tyrone—revolt, he will sail with a force of men and arms the same day."

O'Hara's thoughts moved backward in time to a ship sailing to France with all the princes of Ireland on board. When the earls had fled in 1607, he had been a lad of fifteen, as had been Owen Roe, nephew of Hugh, the Great O'Neill. Since then Owen had distinguished himself as a general in the Netherlands' Spanish wars. Only a year before he had made himself a legend in the defense of Arras against the French.

O'More was no fool, O'Hara thought. If Owen Roe returned, thousands would flock to the banner bearing the O'Neill's Red Hand of Ulster.

"We need but your hand in it, O'Hara, to make it complete," O'More coaxed.

O'Hara looked up, his glance lighting on each man's face in turn, his mind weighing their worth in a war of rebellion.

Sir Phelim O'Neill, a lawyer trained at Lincoln's Inn, London, who would turn himself into a general. O'Hara knew that Phelim lived extravagantly and was forced to mortgage his estates heavily. Was that his reason to rebel?

Hugh MacMahon, a thick-bodied fighter with a wizened face that conveyed cunning and could easily be distasteful to other men. He spoke in a thick, Scots accent that became nearly unintelligible when he drank, his most frequent occupation. Could he be depended upon if the tide turned against them, O'Hara wondered.

Then there was his brother, Heber, who had performed the wedding ceremony. Although a priest, his ambition made him dangerous. Rory was convinced that, given the power, Heber would rid the world of any man, woman or child who didn't believe in the leadership of Rome. Such a man had the determination to lead other men, but would they follow?

Philip O'Reilly—a hothead, but dependable. Once committed, O'Hara knew he would be loyal to the death. But he was not a soldier who could fight battles that went further than words.

And, finally, Rory O'More. Of all the men in the room he was the organizer, the strategist. It would fall on O'More's shoulders to keep the peace among the Irish when they started feuding over the spoils.

Could O'More do it? Could any man? None had accomplished it yet. Were these men the saviors of Eire? O'Hara thought not.

But then there was Owen Roe. Most of the Irish who had been driven from their lands to fight in the service of Spain, France and a dozen other countries would be drawn back to Ireland by the magic of Owen Roe O'Neill's name and reputation. Would that be enough?

O'More read the doubt on O'Hara's face and urged the others on. "In the armories of Dublin Castle there are arms, powder and shot for nine thousand men. Take Dublin Castle and we have the arms and command over Parliament and country!''

As O'More spoke, the passion of his words inflamed his listeners, and they all gathered around O'Hara.

''Phelim and Macguire will strike simultaneously in the north, and you in the west,'' O'More continued excitedly. ''Within days the rebellion will spread to the south, and all in the king's name, until Ireland is ours!''

The heated talk continued. O'Hara barely heard it, preoccupied as he was with his own thoughts. Then, with heavy steps he made his way to the window and parted the makeshift curtain so that he could look out across the garden.

Dusk was settling in and torches had been lit. Their flames danced gaily over the merrymakers. ''When?'' he asked softly.

Several voices answered his question almost at the same time.

''Rents and taxes are to be paid to Dublin the first of November. During the last week of October the tenants' half-year's rents will still be in their hands.''

''As will all our taxes—more than enough to fill a war chest.''

''And during that time the high winds will come. Few ships, if any, will dare the crossing from England.''

''When?'' O'Hara repeated. ''The day.''

''October twenty-third. 'Tis market day and strange faces on the streets will attract little attention.''

''We need you, O'Hara.''

''Ireland needs you.''

Aye, O'Hara thought wistfully, *and what of the needs of Ballylee?* Looking across at the stately outline of the manor house built over the ruins of the old keep and castle, O'Hara could once again hear the thunder of the siege guns and the agonized cries of dying men he had heard so many years before in another rebellion.

His eyes clouded, and he saw David Talbot's dream turned once more into rubble. But he knew he had little choice in the matter. Once again, events in England ruled the fate of Ireland. Charles's trouble with Parliament was too tempting an opportunity. Now was their chance to give every Irishman a path to freedom and even had he wished to, O'Hara was powerless to prevent his countrymen from rebelling.

Rory thought of the newlywed couple and saw again the smiles of happiness on the faces of his wife, Aileen, and his sister, Shanna. A vision of sweet Maggie's youthful beauty and innocence swam before his eyes, and with little effort he could see his own young sons, Conor and Brian, grown into breastplates and visors, with cavalry swords at their sides.

"October twenty-third," he said. "Less than two months."

"Aye," O'More replied. "But a hundred years in the making."

And mayhap, O'Hara thought, with a heavy heart, *another hundred years in the settling.*

THE FEASTING AND DANCING WOULD GO ON for many more hours, perhaps even beyond dawn's first light. But the impatient lovers were neither asked nor expected to linger that long.

Patrick, together with several close friends, escorted Donal to his chamber where, amid good-natured bantering and many toasts they undressed him and aided him into his nightshirt. This done, they accompanied him to the door of his wife's chamber and bid him good health, long life and a fertile wife.

In that room Aileen and Shanna performed nearly

the same rituals for Maura. Their tasks completed, they stole discreetly away to allow her to greet her husband and lover alone. She lit four candles, one at each corner of the huge canopied bed, then stood at its foot and waited.

Moments later Donal stepped into the room. Outwardly calm but inwardly trembling before this golden-haired beauty who was now his wife, he stood and gazed at her silently.

For Maura there was nervousness and trepidation, but there was also exhilaration. Throughout her youth she had thought many times of this moment and during the past year had dreamed of it almost nightly.

She knew the picture she made, standing before him in a white chemise and overgown of the finest satin, with her blond hair flowing free around her shining face and down to her shoulders. She could see it in Donal's eyes.

"You are so beautiful that it is almost unreal," he whispered, finding his voice at last.

"I am very real, my darling, flesh and blood . . . and yours," she said, her voice low and tremulous.

Impulsively she flung herself forward, catapulting her body into his arms and burrowing her face against his chest. He swept her up into his arms and, covering her face and neck with tender kisses, whispered her name over and over as though in disbelief that she was finally his.

Moving up from the base of her throat, his lips found hers. It was a slow, sensual kiss filled with both tender love and burning desire. His tongue slipped between her lips, tracing their outline, arousing her as never before and she felt herself grow weak with desire. When she thought she could stand it no longer, he moved to the bed. She felt her bare feet touch the floor, and then the overgown whispered from her body.

With her eyes closed she floated backward to the bed and settled into it as if its down-filled mattress were a sleepy cloud. Only by sound could she tell that Donal had removed his nightshirt. The mattress gave under his weight as he joined her on the bed, his warm flesh searing hers through the chemise.

A groan escaped his lips before he said, low and clear, "Maura, I love you as man was meant to love woman."

"And I you, my darling."

His lips found her throat and moved to her breasts. Deftly his hands worked at the laces of her chemise and then slipped it from her body.

"Beautiful...so beautiful," he breathed.

"For you, Donal, my love...love me—love me now," she implored.

His hands traveled over her body with a warm firm touch as his lips caressed her nipples. A flame seemed to grow deep within her and expand until her flesh was on fire. Suddenly she was caught up in a fit of passion that brought a low moan from her lips. The more gentle his kisses and the touch of his hands, the more desire filled her body. She reached out to him, urging him to cover her body with his own. "I want you so much...so desperately," she whispered.

She felt herself expand toward him in her nakedness. Gently but firmly his hips spread her thighs. Her breasts burned hotly against the coarse mat of hair on his chest.

And then he was against her, parting her, his body becoming one with hers. As his arms encircled her tightly, she lunged upward with all the rampant fire in her body.

For a single second her body stiffened with resistance, and then he was deep within her, his flesh burning through her instant of fear. He was hurting her, but she willed him on, not wanting him to stop.

The sweet burst of piercing pain was nothing compared to the joy of fulfillment she felt.

Together they reached the peak of a storming mountain and then, as one, tumbled from its precipice in ecstasy.

Slowly, as his massive strength ebbed from between her thighs, Maura felt the storm in her own body pass on. He slid to her side, and she caught his hands and brought them to her breasts. She felt weak, drained, as if her soul had left her body to float somewhere in the air above them. Gently, wordlessly, Donal continued to stroke her body until her eyelids fluttered and she fell into a light sleep.

Without waking her, he pulled her body in close to his, entwining it in the cocoon of his arms and legs. So beautiful, so peaceful and still so innocent was her face framed in its halo of golden hair that it brought a choke to his throat.

Soon, perhaps even tomorrow, he would have to tell her of The O'Hara's decision. Somehow, and as gently as possible, he would have to break it to his bride that in less than two months' time he must leave her.

Maura stirred in his arms and her leg moved against his thigh, exciting him anew.

"Again, my darling," she whispered, reaching for him. "Again...."

Tomorrow he would tell her. Tonight he was hers.

September 1641

CHAPTER FOUR
STOKE POGES, ENGLAND

A LIGHT SUPPER WAS SERVED by Lady Hatton herself. It would not be prudent for any of the servants to overhear the tidbits of information being exchanged at Stoke that evening. Her guests had even suggested that Robert Hubbard be excluded from the meal and the fireside conversation that followed. But this Elizabeth wouldn't allow. Since Robert was now sixteen and her only heir, she insisted he be included in the discussions that could well determine his future.

In the month since the facts of his birth had been revealed, Robert had evaluated all the avenues open to him with his usual cold, calm deliberation. He had spoken with men of all classes in both London and the countryside and had heard their views on king and Parliament. From those conversations he had learned that Charles was a man of integrity but also a king with a narrow, unbending will.

So sure had Charles been of is divine right that he had thought to rule England without Parliament. But without that body to vote him money he had been forced to levy arbitrary taxes on an already heavily burdened populace. Other kings had done the same before this Stuart had come to the throne, but times had changed in England. Power had shifted to the merchants.

In response to oppressive measures, the Protestant Puritans had allied themselves with Parliament. Many claimed that if civil war broke out, its cause would be religion. The queen, Henrietta, was staunchly Catholic. Charles was accused of favoring her friends and perhaps even her religion. No Englishman would willingly consent to be ruled by a king who was ruled by Rome.

On the religious question, Robert was well aware that both sides had committed excesses. Objecting to the manner in which the Archbishop of Canterbury, William Laud, in an effort to lend the clergy more dignity, leaned the Church of England toward the pomp and ceremony of the Catholic Church of Rome, the Puritans began holding prayer meetings of their own.

Seeing his own power and the power of the church being questioned, Laud moved to put a stop to the practice. At the same time, he found a new source of revenue for the king. Invoking on old Elizabethan statute that had fallen into widespread disuse, he decreed that everyone was obliged to attend church. Those who did not do so were hauled before the justices and fined one shilling a time. The Puritans saw it as persecution, but so unpopular was Laud's decree among the populace that it rallied many to the Puritan cause. Laud increased the pressure.

A Puritan woman who insisted on keeping Saturday as the Sabbath was imprisoned for eleven years. Puritan men who spoke out against Laud were pilloried or branded, and the cropping of ears became a common punishment. Many were tied to stakes and received thirty or more stripes on their naked backs.

The Puritans retaliated by storming churches, destroying altar rails and papist images. They smashed stained-glass windows and crucifixes. Church vestments and linen were taken, and it was said that on one occasion a painting of the Virgin Mary was paraded around on a pole.

So taken with the Bible as absolute truth, so fanatic were the Puritans in their belief, that their daughters bore such names as Grace, Prudence, Faith, Hope and Charity. Male offspring were even more unfortunate; Lament, Sorry-For-Sin, and Flie-Fornication were names inflicted on many sons.

But Robert Hubbard's decision to throw his lot in with Parliament and the Puritans had not been made on the basis of religion. Their belief that all men were the children of wrath, doomed before birth to everlasting hell by the arbitrary will of a relentless deity meant little to him. What did strike a responsive chord in the young man was the Puritan belief that poverty—not wealth—was a sin. For Robert had seen only too clearly that power and where it lay were all that mattered in society. And power automatically followed the accumulation of land and wealth.

Now, in the oak-paneled and book-lined study that had once been the private reserve of Sir Edward Coke, Robert sat quietly studying these men who would overthrow a king.

A lust for power—and the ability to gain it—was what Robert saw in the men assembled around his grandmother's hearth that evening.

There was the taciturn Robert Devereux, third Earl of Essex, a peer with a fanatical belief in the cause of Commons. If war did come, it would be Essex who would assume command of the parliamentary army, not because of his military abilities but because he was popular with the people.

To Essex's right sat John Hampden. His strong, compelling face looked to be carved from stone. The lines around his mouth were hard and bitter, and the square set of his jaw never seemed to alter. Hampden, too, was a fanatic for the cause and a cunning one.

John Pym was the acknowledged leader of the Puritan forces. He was a short man, slightly on the stout side, with a wide face made more so by a curled mustache that flowed into a beard. But his eyes were his most arresting feature. Small and shrewd, they never seemed to blink or to miss anything taking place around him. Like Hampden, Pym wore the Puritan uniform of a somber black suit broken only by a wide white collar. With fierce conviction he believed that all the ills of England could be cured by bringing down the king.

The fourth visitor to Stoke that night was an enigma to Robert. He was an unattractive man with a rough-skinned, florid and seemingly swollen face. It was further marred by warts and a large mole conspicuous beneath his lower lip. He also was dressed in black; his suit seemed poorly fitted to his large frame and his linen was soiled. Robert knew little of this cousin of Hampden's other than that he had spoken now and then in Parliament but without much response and that a spiritual revelation was said to have brought him to the cause.

His name was Oliver Cromwell.

The talk had been centered mainly on Pym's various bills before Commons that were intended to take away more of the king's power. When the conversation veered to Ireland, Robert listened intently.

"My informant at court tells me that the king is in constant contact with Lord Ormonde in Ireland these days. He would have Ormonde rearm Wentworth's Irish army and have the men stand ready to sail to England to aid the king in his dispute with the Scots."

Hampden sighed. "But if Charles is able to pacify the Scots *and* mobilize an Irish army, our efforts could well be nipped in the bud."

"I don't trust the Irish Catholics," Cromwell interjected, his voice sharp and grating. "They would as lief turn their guns on Ormonde as march behind him."

"True," Hampden nodded. "But if the king would grant them the right to their lands, these Irish just might fight for him. What says your informant on this, John?"

Pym scratched his beard and narrowed his eyes at the room in general. "If my information is valid, it would seem Charles is up to his old game. He would say yea to the Irish Catholics and the Old English in Ireland now and deal differently with them later—when his throne is more secure."

Essex chuckled, drawing deeply on his pipe. "I would like to know this informant you have at court, Pym. I think at times he is more seer than spy. Perhaps you should just ask him the future and we could stop worrying about the present!''

An ironic smile twisted Pym's thick lips. ''I need not a clairvoyant to see the future, m'Lord Essex. I know it already—an England ruled by Parliament.''

''Gentlemen, I care not about mysterious informers in Charley's court. Indeed, I care little about the court.'' Cromwell stood to his full, imposing height and, his face slightly more flushed than usual, began pacing the study. ''I do care about the threat of an Irish and a Scots army fighting on the side of the king. One is Catholic, the other Presbyterian...and both would dearly love to see an end to Parliament's cause. Methinks we should prepare now by building our own new, model army, dedicated to God.''

''I both agree and disagree with Squire Cromwell.''

All eyes turned to Lady Hatton. It was the first time she had entered the conversation.

''How so, madam?'' Cromwell asked, pausing in his pacing.

''I quite agree that 'tis time Parliament had a strong army of its own to field against the king's Cavaliers. As to the other, I think I know a little of the Irish mind.'' Her eyes flickered momentarily to her grandson before returning to the towering figure of Cromwell.

''And the Irish, madam, how do you see them declare? Not for us, I am sure.''

Lady Hatton lifted her chin. Her deep green eyes stared out from a seamed face bright with intelligence. ''No, Master Cromwell, no Catholic would ever side with a Puritan, that is for sure.''

''Then you think the king will get his Irish army, m'lady?'' Pym asked.

''No, I do not. I think when the time comes, the Irish will declare for themselves.''

BY THE TIME THE EVENING HAD ENDED, Robert had formed a plan in his mind. With a small retinue of horsemen Hampden and Cromwell had returned to London. Lord Essex was staying the night in the great house at Stoke. John Pym was ensconced in a small summer house a hundred yards from Stoke manor, near a grove of tall oaks.

Halfway between the manor and the summer house, Robert had overtaken him.

"Master Pym...a word?"

"Aye, lad."

"This new army—"

"Well?" Pym's eyes urged haste in Robert's speech, as he glanced furtively at the summer house to the heavy gates of Stoke and then back to Robert.

"I would like a commission in the army you plan to raise, sir. You could intercede with Lord Essex."

Pym sighed. "Fifteen, aren't you, lad?"

"Sixteen...this month. I am near a master with a gentleman's blade and well versed with a cavalry sword. I know the pikeman's eighteen postures and the musketeer's thirty-four. I am an accomplished horseman and a crack shot."

Another sigh from Pym. "I'm sure you are, Robert, but at sixteen—"

"At fourteen, Prince Rupert of the Rhine was already engaged in battle. And kings reach their majority at fourteen," Robert continued urgently.

"I do not doubt your bravery, lad—"

Although Pym replied with obvious irritation, Robert would not be deterred. He rushed on, "I stand six foot and two. I gain width of chest and shoulder daily. Grant me a commission, Master Pym, for I see it as the only way to further my expectations."

There had been a tone of flinty steel in Robert's words and no lack of arrogance. The youth's in-

sistence that his request be granted brought a deep
frown to Pym's wide forehead.

"You speak as though you would command me,
Hubbard," he said harshly. "Officers must command their men, lead them. In order to do that, they
must have respect. No man in the common army will
respect a spoiled boy of the peerage."

Robert stiffened at the insult but stood his ground.
"I would be in the army, sir," he repeated, coldly
and evenly.

"Then volunteer as a cadet," Pym retorted, angry
now beyond reason, "and become cannon fodder!"

Then he had stalked away, leaving Robert seething
with anger and indignation. He was the son and
grandson of Irish clan chiefs—a warrior, not the foppish offspring of a weak English aristocrat. But that
truth he could divulge to no one.

When he returned to the great house after his talk
with Pym, Robert took note that the huge main gates
had been left open. The sconced torches near the
summer house had not been lit, and he recalled
Pym's haste to be away from him. These signs told
Robert that more than one meeting was likely to take
place at Stoke Poges that night.

Until long after midnight Robert stood at his bedchamber window, staring at the summer house,
where lights still flickered in the upper rooms. Was
Pym working on his unending bills for Parliament?
Was he reading his Bible or was he on his knees,
"yea, verilying" to his Puritan God of wrath?
Robert thought not.

Then he heard it, the gentle rattle of harness
followed by the sound of horses and carriage wheels
on the cobbled lane. He threw the shutters wider and
leaned far out. It was a coach-and-four. Beyond that
he couldn't see, for heavy clouds drifted across a
moonless sky. He could make out, however, that the
coach drove immediately for the summer house.

Robert hurried from his chambers and, like a cat, silently gained the main floor. From the wide paned doors of the study he dropped into the garden and sprinted toward the summer house.

He was twenty yards away when the coach halted near the cottage's rear door. A footman lit a small *flambeau* and, shielding the light with his hands, ran around to the coach door, where the driver was already helping the passenger alight.

She was bundled in a voluminous hooded cape that was much too warm for the weather. Robert's pulse quickened when she turned full into the light to speak to the footman. She was masked, her face protected by the full, fleece-lined mask usually worn to ward off winter's biting winds from delicate feminine features.

But there were no winds this September night.

The woman had barely entered the cottage when Robert began to work his way around to the opposite side. It was a slow process, for several times he had to cross a wide opening among the trees that was in full view of the footman and driver. Each time he was forced to wait until their attention was diverted.

It was an hour before he was able to scramble over the eaves and across the roof toward the lighted room. He dropped to the ground, then cursed the tightly bolted shutters. He could hear low murmuring voices but couldn't see the speakers. And see them he must, for Robert's devious mind had already told him that the identity of Pym's late-night visitor might well be the leverage he needed to gain the much-prized army commission.

The bolts posed no great problem, however, for Robert had found many means of access to the locked summer house in his youth. Quickly, he slipped a small knife through the narrow wedge where the shutters joined. Seconds later the latch lifted. An opening a scant inch wide gave his eyes access to the whole room, and what he saw made him bite his lip to still a gasp of exhilaration.

The lady's cape, mask, dress, chemise, boots and stockings lay in a trail from the door to the bed. She seemed to be in agony, writhing beneath Master Pym's equally nude body.

Robert watched the couple in fascination, not just because they were engaged in a private act but because here was the most pious and reverend Puritan zealot, Master John Pym, in the act of fornication.

Now and then he felt a stirring of desire, when the couple would roll and he glimpsed the lady's well-turned thigh or lush, full breasts. But essentially he was moved no more than he would have been had they been two animals in the fields.

What he really wanted was to see the woman's face. Calmly, he waited until Pym's groans grew to a crescendo, his body convulsed one last time, and he rolled away.

The woman sat up at once to smooth and rearrange her hair. She was a beautiful woman, with stern aristocratic features and an aging yet still magnificently endowed body.

But her ample feminine attributes interested Robert very little. Her identity did—very much.

IT WAS NEAR EIGHT the following morning when John Pym and his aide were brought up short a mile from Stoke on the London road.

"Master Pym. . . a word—"

"You had my word last night, Hubbard. Now back your mount to the side," Pym ordered.

"I think you would prefer a word with me, sir. . . in private."

As he had the night before, Pym bristled at the lad's arrogance. It was difficult to imagine that this boy had gained so haughty and imperious an air in so

few years of living. His height and build irritated
Pym even more, to say nothing of Robert's dark eyes
and chiseled good looks.

"Your grandmother is a valued friend of Parliament, Hubbard, but our friendship—"

"Means nothing to me," Robert snapped, a line of
white appearing around his tightly controlled mouth.
"The Lady Hatton does not consult me in her dealings, nor do I meddle in hers."

Pym straightened in his saddle, a flush of anger
suffusing his face. "You, sir, are impertinent!"

"And you, sir, are unwise in the security of your
visitors." The words were softly spoken. They came
feather light from Robert's lips, yet they hung in the
air like a poisonous fog.

Pym's shoulders sagged and the color drained
from his face. His narrow eyes closed and remained
so for several minutes before his hand was raised and
a signal given.

Robert waited until the aide was out of earshot
before he spoke. "Lucy Hay, the Countess of Carlisle, was the mistress of Thomas Wentworth, the
Lord Strafford, a very long time. I now see that the
rumors I have heard—that she threw the great man
over on the eve of his demise—were very true."

Pym coughed. When he spoke his voice was raspy,
almost weak. "The countess has provided a service
beyond measure to our cause."

"Aye," Robert replied, with a mirthless chuckle.
"As the chief confidante and handmaiden to the
queen, I'm sure she has. No wonder you amaze your
comrades with intelligence from court."

"If, as you say, you truly believe in what we do,
you will remain silent about the Countess of Carlisle."

"Master Pym, I would not harm your cause one
bit. But not because I truly believe in it. No, I would

not harm it because I believe you will win. And I wish to be on the winning side, to share in the spoils.''

Pym's head jerked upward to meet the steely look of this rash youth, this time as an equal and an enemy. "Sir, if you feel thusly, you are no better than a Cavalier, one of the hot-blooded, proud group who follows Charles, more interested in their own advancement than the success of the king's mission!"

Robert shrugged. "Be that as it may, I would be on the winning side—yours."

"Good day, sir!" Pym was about to spur his horse when Robert seized its bridle.

"Master Pym—"

"I advise you to let go, sir!"

Robert sneered, "When I am ready, you old fool."

The words stung, but the sheer intensity in Robert's dark eyes stilled Pym's tongue.

"It is not the service to the cause that I would feed to the gossip's ears, Master Pym. It is the lady's carnal service to you. What would the mothers of Faith, Prudence and Chastity think of their spiritual leader if they knew he was consorting with a titled whore?"

"How dare you! Lucy—"

"Is a whore who relishes power and would glean it on her feet or on her back. I, too, relish power, Master Pym, and see a way to gain it."

A long sigh escaped the Puritan leader as he massaged his weary eyes. With great effort he answered, "I will speak to Lord Essex tomorrow."

"A senior lieutenancy will do." Robert smiled lazily, releasing the bridle of Pym's horse and backing his own mount.

"I know not what road you have planned for yourself, Robert Hubbard," Pym grated through clenched teeth. "But I predict you will travel it far."

"Aye, Master Pym, that I will. That I will."

Mid-October 1641

CHAPTER FIVE

CLAYMORE MANOR, IRELAND

ELANA CLAYMORE'S GAZE drifted to the mirror as she unfastened the laces of her tourmaline-encrusted stomacher, revealing an underdress of midnight-blue satin heavily weighted with tiers of flounces trimmed with lace and seed pearls. She shrugged her sloping shoulders and the dress fell away. Carelessly she dropped it on a chair and then discarded her chemise. The luxurious garments slid to the floor, but Lady Claymore did not trouble herself to retrieve them; the maids would see to it in the morning.

She donned a cream-colored batiste peignoir and, lightly tying the shell-pink sash beneath her breasts, sat down at her mirrored vanity. Carefully she removed the tortoiseshell combs and a tiny string of seed pearls from her coif. This done, she shook her head, reveling in the feel of her thick hair cascading around her shoulders.

As she stroked a brush methodically through the lustrous strands, Elana thought of the recent supper in Claymore Manor's great room. It had been attended by lords Antrim and Gormanston, along with the latter's nephew, Sir John Redding, who had recently come to Ireland from London.

Elana had instantly been attracted to Redding. He was tall, and thin to the point of emaciation, but she sensed cunning and power in the deep-set eyes and hawklike face. As the introductions had been made, his imperious and brazen look had told Elana that her satin gown did not conceal from him the sensuousness and beauty of her figure. Elana felt that John Redding was the kind of man who knew his way with women. Seducing him would be a challenge, and she was sure that the end result would be more than physical attraction.

Her father, Gormanston and Antrim were all stubbornly resolved in their political views. They favored the king regardless of his shortcomings. During the supper conversation John Redding had echoed their opinions, but Elana had detected many an underlying meaning—and not a few warnings—in his words of agreement.

Without openly admitting it, Redding had intimated that his recent arrival in Ireland, so close on the heels of the new lord lieutenant, William Parsons, was no coincidence. The more he spoke, the more Elana learned and the more she wished her prattling father would hold his tongue.

She was firmly convinced that one should hold back one's allegiance to any cause until the victor began to emerge. John Redding, she felt sure, would agree with her. It was an art she had learned well while at the court of France, where many intrigues were constantly on the boil. To Elana, intrigue was like making love; both were pleasant and exciting passions.

From the moment she had first been introduced, she had sensed that John Redding enjoyed the same pursuits. Parliament needed a man in Ireland to keep them abreast of the mood of the Irish and the Old English, and the last words of the evening had convinced Elana that John Redding was that man.

The three older gentlemen were certain that the Irishmen—O'Neill, O'Hara and the others—would go to the king's aid. "Be not so sure," Redding had warned them. "But in any event I think it wise if all of you keep a foot in both camps."

His nephew's words had brought a flush of anger to Lord Antrim's face. "As a royalist—and a Catholic besides—how can you say such a thing, John?"

Redding had shrugged. Only Elana had seen his lips

curl in a smile and read the words his eyes had spoken: *When the time comes, you will wish you had heeded my warning this night.*

Well, Sir John Redding, she thought, brushing her hair more vigorously, *you have warned me—and I will heed it!*

Her dowry—in fact, all her wealth—was tied up in Claymore House. Elana had no intention of losing it because of her father's silly integrity and allegiance to the king. She, like Redding, would keep one foot in the royalist camp and another in Parliament's. And she would even keep her fingers in a third—that of the Irish. Indeed, she already had.

That thought brought a smile to her lips. How close she had come to taking Redding aside and revealing the conversation she had heard above the stables at Ballylee. What a great debt he and the lord lieutenant would owe her if they knew the Irish rebels planned to strike first!

But not yet, she thought, not until she knew the exact date. What improvidence that she had been flushed from her hiding place by two servants, just as the rebels were setting that date. She hadn't heard it but had since employed her talents to secure the all-important piece of information. Such was her self-confidence that she had no doubt she would soon have it. Perhaps by the end of the next evening. . . .

A sound at the window interrupted her thoughts. Dropping her brush, she came to her feet with a cry as the shutters burst open and a cloaked figure slipped through the opening with the agility of a cat. She opened her mouth to scream, but the sound died in her throat when the figure landed gracefully before her, and the cape's dark cowl fell away from Patrick Talbot's sandy blond hair.

"Good evening, m'lady!" he greeted her happily, and bowed low.

"You fool! My father—"

"Snoring," Patrick finished for her, his teeth flashing in a reckless smile as his hooded eyes appraised her body.

"The servants...?"

"Occupied elsewhere."

Elana noticed his searching look and hastened to fetch a heavier wrap. Her hand was on the door of an armoire beside the vanity when he caught it and took her into his arms.

"I've seen you in less...several times," he reminded her with a grin.

Elana was flustered by his nearness. His sudden arrival gave Patrick an element of surprise and control, something she hated to give to any man. "I agreed to meet you tomorrow night—"

"I couldn't wait," Patrick replied.

"—and God knows not here in the house," she hissed, freeing herself from his arms.

Patrick watched closely as she crossed the room. Every movement was fluid, marked with a deliberate feminine grace. Through the thin gown could be seen the curves of her perfect figure. Three times now he had made love to her since they first met at Maura's wedding, and each time had been more wild and passionate than the last. Young though he was he had had many a woman, but none of them had come close to matching Elana's ability to satisfy him. Indeed, he was beginning to wonder if he would ever enjoy another woman as much.

He stepped toward her and when she turned to face him, gold flecks of anger flashed from her turquoise eyes.

"How dare you to think you can burst into my chamber as if I were one of your tavern strumpets!"

"You've bewitched me," he murmured, with no trace of chagrin. "And while you are the most wanton woman I have ever met, I assure you, lovely Elana, I do not think of you as a common strumpet—"

"Patrick, you must go!"

He reached for the shell-pink ribbons that would loosen the sash of her gown. "And besides, I'm off to Dublin. I couldn't meet you tomorrow night."

Elana put out a hand to stop him, then the meaning of his words registered. "Dublin? You're off to Dublin this night?"

"Aye." He tugged at the sash and her gown fell open. "Dear God, but you are perfection," Patrick moaned, sliding his fingers over the warm flesh of her hips.

Elana suppressed a tiny gasp of pleasure at his touch. She had found Patrick Talbot to be a good lover, experienced in the ways of arousing and satisfying a woman. But this night she wanted more than physical satisfaction.

If you want something from a man in return for your charms, get it before his lust is slaked. For if you wait, he has time to collect his thoughts and reconsider. For men think we're pretty when we're virgins, and afterward, they hardly think of us at all!

Evading his lips, she moved his head to one side. Ignoring the warm breath from his lips at her ear, she ran her fingers beneath his collar to taunt the hair at the nape of his neck.

"What will you find in Dublin more interesting than me, Patrick Talbot?" she asked, her voice low and beguiling.

Refusing to be drawn, he buried his face in her hair. "Such a sheen," he murmured. "And that scent! Methinks 'tis enough to drive a man to distraction."

"Patrick...don't tease!" She ran her fingertips caressingly along his jaw, moving his head until their eyes met.

What dangerous ground do I tread here, Patrick

mused, feeling himself falling into the pools of her faintly slanted eyes. From the strange light in their depths, he sensed she wanted something from him, but had no notion of what it might be.

His fingers traced the by now familiar pattern of her features, the high cheekbones, the aristocratic nose with its slight upward tilt, the mouth with its faintly cruel yet sensual lips.

"You have the eyes of a sorceress, Elana Claymore. Did you know that? Their look and what lies behind them would destroy a man's soul."

"And will your soul be in any less danger in Dublin?"

Patrick threw back his head and a laugh erupted from his throat. "Nay, lass, I think 'twill not be my soul in danger in Dublin town!"

Then suddenly his hand whipped out and the gown fell to the floor with a rustling whisper. He crushed her to him, his mouth coming down hard on hers and his fingers exploring the soft roundness of her body.

"Patrick, no—not now...delay your trip a day...."

"Ah, but I cannot," he murmured, "for I must make market day."

With his superior strength, he moved her to the bed and forced her beneath him. Heaving and twisting from side to side, she cried, "Get off!"

His only answer was a deep laugh as he quickly shed his leather vest and cambric shirt.

The feel of his bare chest against her breasts sent a blaze of desire through Elana, but still she resisted as she heard first one of his boots and then the second hit the floor.

All this time she had been going over his words in her mind, piecing them together. Suddenly they fit, and she ceased her struggle. Today was Tuesday. Three days travel to the Wicklows...Friday. Satur-

day was market day in Dublin. Elana smiled and relaxed. She had the date.

"Better," Patrick whispered, feeling her respond.
"Much better."

He had shed his breeches, and Elana could feel his
naked virility. "Aye, much better," she sighed, parting her knees and letting his leg slip between them.
Slake your lust, Patrick Talbot—and mine as well!
She felt herself open like a wanton flower beneath
him. Yes, she thought, he is a good lover...a wonderful lover!

FOR LONG MOMENTS THEY LAY, basking in the after-
math of completion. Then gently she slid from beneath Patrick. She noted his closed eyes and the smile
of bliss on his lips. Her gaze moved down his lean
body, and just the sight of it renewed her desire.

But no, she thought, *there is much to be done yet
this night!*

She made to slip from the bed, but Patrick's firm
hand grasped her and pulled her to him. He enveloped her in the cocoon of his arms, one breast trembling beneath his trailing fingers.

"You should go," she whispered.

"Soon," he sighed, increasing the pressure on her
breast until the nipple again grew taut.

"Patrick...my maids...."

"They will knock first. Elana...."

"Yes?"

"Have you no...fear...."

Elana smiled. A good lover he was, wise in the
ways of lovemaking, she thought, but still so ignor-
ant of other womanly things.

She held his hand still on her breast and lightly
kissed his brow. "Fear of making a child, Patrick? Is
that what you mean?"

"Aye," he murmured, his tone unexpectedly shy.

"Of course there is that danger," she said, bringing her lips to his, "but there are ways a woman has to avoid it."

The kiss was deep and stirring. Elana could once again feel his arousal and knew there was no other way to be rid of him but to satisfy him. This she accomplished as quickly as possible, using all the feminine arts and wiles at her disposal to hurry him to completion.

Dressed at last, Patrick kissed her, one last time. He walked to the window, then hesitated. "Elana...."

"Yes, yes—what is it?"

"If you did find yourself with child... what would you do?"

"I don't know," she replied, unable to keep the impatience from her voice. "Marry, I suppose. Now, hurry!"

With one leg over the window ledge, Patrick paused again. "Why is it you've not already married?"

"Damme, I don't know," she sputtered. And then with a cry, "Probably because I have never met a man I could not live without!"

His eyes seemed suddenly to gleam more brightly, as though he had made a decision to accept a challenge she had thrown before him. But there was something behind that gleam, an inner glow, that she could not fathom. He opened his mouth as if to speak, but Elana, now in a fever of impatience, hurriedly closed and bolted the shutter before he could question her further. Breathlessly, her heart pounding, she waited until she could no longer hear the creak of vines as he descended to the courtyard below. Then she flew to her dressing table.

From a drawer she took fresh paper and pen. With shaking fingers she dipped the newly cut quill into an elkhorn of ink and then paused, the pen's point directly over the paper.

"Sir John Redding or Sir William Parsons?" she mused aloud.

Parsons, she decided, *for the power is still his. But I will mention Redding, which should put both of them in my debt.*

Minutes later she sanded, folded and sealed the letter. Quickly she pulled on a chemise and donned a heavy velvet cloak to disguise her near nakedness.

Outside, she was struck by the stillness of the evening under glittering stars. *A beautiful night,* she thought, laughing to herself, *and methinks a very profitable one!*

The youthful groom she awakened could barely stutter her instructions back to her. She made him repeat them again and yet again.

"And see that you fly both to Dublin and back, with no tarrying in between," she admonished fiercely.

"Aye, mistress."

"And to Sir William's hand alone do you deliver this! If I hear you haven't, I'll whip you myself, do you hear?"

"Aye, mistress."

Elana watched until the groom was out of sight and then scurried back to her chambers and her bed. To her surprise, as sleep slowly claimed her, Elana found her thoughts dwelling on Patrick Talbot. She shivered as she remembered the magic his hands had worked upon her body. A smile came to her lips when she conjured up his strong features and lithe form. She stretched sensuously, remembering the feel of his chest that tapered into a firm abdomen, slim hips and heavily muscled thighs.

Recalling the last look he had flashed toward her as she had closed the shutters, she suddenly sat bolt upright in bed at the memory of the quiet inner glow she had seen in the depths of his smoke gray eyes. She had thought little of it at the time, but could it have been, she wondered now, a gleam of hope? "Dear God, no!" she gasped aloud. "Surely the fool can't be in love with me!"

October 23, 1641

CHAPTER SIX
DUBLIN, IRELAND

DONAL O'HARA'S EYES WERE NARROWED against the morning mist and chill wind. He rode hunched forward, his chin buried in the fur of his mantle. He was silent, deep in his own turbulent thoughts.

A horse's length behind Donal, Patrick Talbot sat upright in his saddle, and his jaunty smile matched the rakish tilt of his plumed hat.

Donal glanced back at his cousin and smiled to himself. For all the lack of worry on his face, Patrick could have been riding to a ball instead of to the storming of Dublin Castle.

He was neither fooled nor bothered by his cousin's carefree manner, for he knew it belied Patrick's deadly resolve. More than once in his young life, Patrick had exhibited a cool head and a steady nerve when he had needed it. Donal would feel safe this day with the young stallion at his back.

"Donal. . . ."

"Aye."

"Do you see there? The River Liffey."

As they neared the river, the trees thinned out and the misty fog grew thicker. Donal felt a chill go through his bones as it folded around them. It was as though the world had disappeared and there was no one left but the two of them. But the shiver that ran along his spine was only partially due to the cold dampness of the mist. Such physical discomforts meant little to him. Above everything else, it was the fear of losing what he had gained that chilled him to the marrow.

The previous night they had lain in a birch grove near the Bog of Allen. Nearly eighty miles wide, it was one of the most extensive in Ireland. Far better to shelter there than in some miserable wayside inn where they might be recognized. Donal had spread his canvas down and had no sooner wrapped his mantle around him when the last few days and hours with Maura had washed over him like a warm tide.

Never had he dreamed he could love so deeply. When he had left Ballyhara and for months after arriving at Ballylee, he had held only hatred and revenge in his heart. But Maura had replaced that hatred with love, and his lust for revenge with desire for her. During the brief time since their marriage, she had become so much a part of him that he had felt his resolve for armed conflict weakening.

Did that make him a coward?

Aye, in the eyes of some it probably would have done had he revealed his thoughts. But he told no one, for he knew few of his friends would understand that it wasn't death itself he feared, but the thought that, should he be claimed by death, he would lose his beloved Maura.

Donal had spent most of his life waiting for this day: the day when he could strike back at Ireland's oppressors. There was nothing about him that was not hard. His mind and body were as tempered to the task before him as was the sword at his side.

But no matter how hard he tried, he could not erase the image of Maura. He remembered the soft vibrant feel of her body beneath his and the love in her eyes when she looked up to him at the moment of fulfillment.

He lived again those last moments as she had carefully packed his saddlebags and rolled his canvas. He had felt as if his heart had risen to his throat when, finished at last, she had turned and faced him, the candlelight glowing on the golden halo of her hair and the softness of her features.

"How I will miss these wifely ministrations," he had told her with a gentle smile.

"How empty and lifeless Ballylee will be until your return," she had sighed in reply. "How lonely I will be."

As I am now, Donal thought.

"Donal."

The strong male voice shook him from his reverie. "What...?"

"You're asleep in the saddle, man," chuckled Patrick. "Would you go to Ringsend?"

Sheepishly, Donal veered his mount to the right and mumbled something about the fog. Minutes later they came to another fork in the road.

"Here?" Donal asked.

"Aye, 'tis Old Bridge Lane," Patrick replied, and they both turned south.

One thatched-roof cottage became another until, closer to the river, the homesteads were clustered.

"Ahh, the town grows," Patrick sighed. "Not more than a year ago there was naught but a few cottages north of the river."

Suddenly Donal reined up, his head high, his dark eyes staring from beneath his cowl.

"Donal what—" Patrick followed his gaze, then nodded in sudden understanding. Across the river, rising above the shroudlike mantle of fog, were the turrets and towers of Dublin Castle. "Ahh, I forget that you've never been to Dublin.

"The tallest is the Bermingham Tower. There The O'Donnell, Red Hugh, and Rory's father, Shane, spent their days with the rats and damp before the Great O'Neill's uprising. The tower and turret beside it mark the South Wall. We'll go in through the North Wall gate.''

Donal smiled. "Let us hope we won't be spending the night above the courtyard level.''

They were about to move on when a strident voice from a tiny lane to their right called to them. "Be ye for market in Dublin town, lads?''

"Aye," Patrick replied.

"Have a look at my poultry first. The price is better!''

"Nay, old man," Donal replied gruffly. "We've a short time for bargains at the seller's stalls.''

"Ye'd best have a look at *my* poultry first, lads.''

Something in the strident tone of the old man's voice brought them closer. He sat hunched over in an ass-drawn cart. Behind him, chickens and a few wild pheasant cackled and squabbled. Even in a baggy broadcloth greatcoat, he looked to be powerfully built. When he raised his head, they could see a broad face stubbled with a gray-laced beard. His nose was overly large and beaked, as if it had been broken in the past.

But it was the flash of merriment in his dark eyes that made Patrick grin with delight. He had met Connor Macguire no more than a few times, but he recognized him now with ease.

"'Tis a long way down you've come, Connor, from a lord of the manor to poultry seller.''

"Aye, lad, but 'tis God's way for a poor clan chief to make his daily bread." The old man's eyes grew shrewd and penetrating as he glanced from Patrick to Donal. "Ye'll be Donal, son of Cormac of Ballyhara.''

"Aye, but I make my home Ballylee and my fealty to Rory, The O'Hara, now.''

Macguire simply nodded. There was no reason to dredge up the past in this conversation. What they were about to do was more important. "Have ye scarves?"

"Aye," Patrick replied, producing from beneath his mantle a cloth of green edged in scarlet.

"Good," Macguire said. "See that it finds your neck when the time comes. We'll do no good fightin' each other." Then he paused to sort out his thoughts before speaking again.

"Come midday, we'll have about forty lads inside the city walls. Within an hour after that, ye'll all have wandered into the castle yard. We attack at the stroke of two. Should we fail—"

"We'll not fail," Donal whispered.

"Should we fail," Macguire continued, ignoring his words, "and the alarm is sounded, the St. James gatekeeper has been bribed. 'Twill be the only city gate left open for escape. If it must be used, ride south to Naas and then bolt for the Wicklows. There'll be O'Toole and O'Byrne men hiding along the road to interrupt any pursuers."

Both men nodded and turned their mounts.

"And lads, best ye roll your cowls under your mantles in the English way when ye enter the city. An' leave your mantles open as well. Should anyone see ye for Irish gentry, they won't be suspicious of your arms if they can see 'em."

Donal muttered in Irish his understanding of The Macguire's instructions.

"Ah, another thing, lads. Mark ye, trust no one with an idle word. The gaols of Dublin town profit from the English. They're not like country folk and have no allegiance to clans. Speak English."

"I've never learned it," Donal protested.

"Then stay mute," Macguire chuckled, the merriment returning to his eyes. "And you, Patrick, watch how ye spend your time between now and midday. Every street in Dublin sports a tavern, and every tavern a strumpet."

Patrick laughed. "More like five strumpets, and at their head the tavernkeeper himself, who would claim to be a virtuous father figure to them all. But you need not fear my idleness this day, Macguire, for I've a lady, and I'd not want to give her the French pox when I see her again."

"God go with ye, lads."

Leaving Macguire with his chickens and pheasant, they entered Dublin through Dame's Gate and immediately were caught up in the sights, sounds and smells of the crowded town. The streets were narrow and led in all directions. Everywhere there were hucksters, sitting under their bulks or their stalls and peddling their wares. Ragged children darted dangerously close to the horses' flanks, and every few yards a whore would lift her skirts or bare her bosom in enticement.

They rode around the curtain wall of the castle itself and left their horses at a communal stable near St. James Gate.

"This way to Bull Alley," directed Patrick. "I could do with a bit of food before we fight."

Side by side they elbowed their way through the crowds, past the bookstalls along Werburgh Street and the shops of Skinners' Row. Under the sign of The Bear and Ragged Staff, Patrick came to a halt. "As good as any," he said. "Near all of them serve slop, but it'll fill your belly."

Inside, they ordered ale and mutton stew from a huge, slack-jawed, owl-eyed woman who took a great interest in the cut and quality of their clothes. "Are you gentlemen over from London?" she inquired archly.

"Aye, we are that. Wool buyers," Patrick answered, without a trace of an accent.

The woman looked intently at their belts in an attempt to gauge the weight of their purses. Seemingly satisfied, she left and quickly returned with mugs of ale and two wooden bowls of greasy stew.

Before leaving them to their meal, she leaned her bulk over the table until her face was inches from Donal's. "Would ye be lookin' fer a little afternoon sport, sar... with the fairer sex?"

Unable to understand, Donal gazed at her blankly.

"We're not interested," Patrick said.

But the woman assumed Donal's look to be one of interest. "Oh, 'tis not me," she said. "'Tis me daughter, there by the barrels. Twelve she is, and ripe."

"We've business, woman," Patrick retorted, his voice full of distaste. "Get you gone."

"Can't the gentleman speak fer himself?" she spat at Patrick.

"Nay, he's mute. Now be off with you."

With as much haughtiness as her bulk would allow, the woman waddled away.

"What was it?" Donal mumbled, through barely moving lips. When Patrick explained, Donal's face drained of color and his hands began to shake.

Concerned, Patrick leaned over and placed a calming hand on the older man's shoulder. "What is it, Donal?" he asked, his voice tinged with anxiety.

"I was just thinking of my sisters who came to Dublin and...."

"Aye?" Patrick prompted.

"I was also thinking about what would become of Maggie if—"

"Damn him for a fool," Patrick suddenly growled, cutting off his brother-in-law's words.

Puzzled at his cousin's sudden change in tone, Donal asked, "Who?"

"Behind you, near the door— No, don't turn around. 'Tis Hugh MacMahon and two of his lads."

"What about 'em?"

His tone full of disgust, Patrick answered, "They're all three blind drunk."

BALLYLEE, IRELAND

MAURA REPLACED HER NEEDLEWORK in a basket by her chair and stood.

"You fidget, lass," Shanna said, without raising her dark head.

"Aye. I would have some air."

Aileen laid aside the brush she had been using. "I fear I make a sorry painter. I'll join you, Maura."

"They'll be in Dublin town by now," Shanna said, her voice barely a whisper. "'Twill do no good for the both of you to catch your death on the parapets, looking toward the east."

Aileen and Maura exchanged looks but made no reply. With a rustle of skirts they left the chamber. Donning heavy woolen cloaks against the chill air, they climbed a narrow set of stone stairs and emerged on the roof of the inland tower.

Around them soft rain fell from a soggy gray sky. Both women lifted their skirts to avoid the puddles as they moved across the barbican to a round tower.

Abruptly, Maura spoke. "Must all women do needlework, make tapestry and paint portraits when their men are off to war?"

"'Tis our lot," Aileen replied heavily, and then jingled the household keys that hung from a fine chain about her neck. "That, and run the household that the men would fight to keep."

"I've never envied the women of old, the clansmen's wives who spent most of their lives listening to the sounds of their husbands' horses riding away to war." Maura leaned forward, impervious to the cold stone against her bare arms.

"Shanna is right, you know. There's naught we can do."

Maura stood in silence for several moments, listening to the biting wind beat against the bleak tower. It was a lonely, howling sound that echoed her mood and the loneliness in her heart.

When she spoke again her words had the same bite as the wind's howl. "For days we've sat in these silent rooms. We embroider tapestry and talk of preserving jams and churning butter. We are as docile chambermaids chatting of children and the latest fashions.

"Maura..." Aileen began, her tones gentle.

"But none of it takes my mind from him. Without him, each chamber of this castle manor is as lonely as my bed and my heart. The hours are dull and pallid. And if he does not return—"

"He will return, as will Patrick. The king will relent and give us back our lands and the freedom to follow our papal faith. The English Parliament will fail in its bid to deny him of his power to rule, and a measure of Ireland will be ours once and for all."

Maura wrapped her cloak more closely about her. She pressed her chilled hands to the warmth of her body and turned to face Aileen. "You're so sure. You're always so sure of everything. Nothing dims your view, Aileen.... But I haven't your strength."

Suddenly her body was shaking, and tears flowed from her eyes to mingle with the rain on her cheeks.

Aileen stretched her arms toward the younger woman. Tenderly she embraced Maura's quivering body and encased her in her own cloak. "You have strength, my darling," Aileen whispered. "It has only to be tested. Aye, 'tis the men who fight the battles and we women who fight the loneliness. But never forget 'tis Irish we are, all proud Gaels and prouder O'Haras. We have a self-respect and a pride of name that few can claim. That is our strength, and none can take it from us."

Maura's body stopped its shaking and a sudden stiffness came into her spine. "Aye, all you say may be true. But the boredom of being a woman and waiting calmly by a peat fire fairly chokes me. For myself, I would rather be a man and fight the battles!''

Suddenly, above the wind's eerie wail there could be heard the unearthly sound of baying wolves. Both women leaned out over the edge of the parapet as the sound grew louder.

"Odd," Aileen mused, "I've never known them to hunt in the day nor in the rain."

"Hunger drives all wild things from their lairs, no matter the danger."

As if in answer to Maura's toneless words, the hideous baying reached a crescendo. Above it, faintly, could be heard the pitifully shrill bleat of a dying sheep.

DUBLIN CASTLE

IN TWOS AND THREES they passed through the castle gate. Above them in the gate's curved arch the portcullis gleamed like a gaping set of iron teeth.

As Patrick and Donal passed through they heard coarse laughter from the guardrooms to the left and right of the passageway.

"I count twelve," Patrick said in an undertone.

"And nine on my side," Donal replied. "Odd, that many on duty for a market day."

Before Patrick could respond, they found themselves at the entrance to the lower castle green, crowded with carts and the makeshift stalls of vendors. They moved slowly and carelessly, stopping now and then to inspect a bolt of cloth or a cheap trinket. Eventually they came to the upper green and walked toward the Armory Tower. It stood at the adjoining angle of the south and west curtain walls, commanding a view of all the castle's interior yards.

"You can see that once it's taken and the main gate portcullis lowered," Patrick whispered, "five muskets from its tower can hold the whole of it.''

"Aye," Donal agreed, but his gaze was not on the tower. A frown had crept over his face as he looked searchingly at both the upper and lower yards. "Patrick, doesn't something strike you strange?"

"No...what?"

"The lack of wenches and wives. 'Tis market day, and of a hundred here I count not above ten women."

"'Tis the damp," Patrick shrugged. "Even an Irishwoman who's used to it would put off her shopping in this chill. The vendors have to be here, rain or shine."

"I suppose, but still—"

"Ahh, lads, are ye primed and ready? 'Tis near time." Connor Macguire had crept along the tower wall and was now crouched a few feet to their left.

"Aye," Patrick said. "We'll take the two guards at the tower stairs and then make our way to the lord lieutenant's apartments above."

"Good lads," Macguire said. Then he stood and went off to take up his position.

TIME PASSED ON LEADEN FEET. Before long, the clouds opened and the mist became a thin rain. It dampened the old gray stone of the castle's walls to a sheen. Patrick observed the men stationed around the yards anxiously watch Connor Macguire, who would give them the signal to attack. Anticipation drove the chill from his bones and warmed his blood.

Then an abrupt movement on the tower roof above the offices and apartments of the lord lieutenant, Sir William Parsons, drew his attention. A tall gaunt man stood between the parapet's teeth. He wore no cloak and the rain glistened on the mesh of his steel doublet.

Battle dress, Patrick thought, at the same time realizing that the main-gate guards had also been in armor. As he continued to stare up toward the roof, two guardsmen joined the tall figure, who raised the visor of his helmet to give himself a better view of the yards. His face was in shadow but Patrick could just discern the hawklike features and the hollow eyes. It was a devilish face and Patrick was sure he'd seen it before, but failed to remember where.

The oddly familiar face, the guards armored on idle duty, Donal's mention of a lack of women . . . all combined to ring bells of alarm in the young man's quick mind. He was about to say as much to Donal when shouts and a milling crowd made both of them look toward the main gate.

"Damme, 'tis MacMahon," Donal swore.

Even as he spoke, a commanding voice rang out from the tower above them. "Close the portcullis!"

The castle erupted with sudden activity. Musketeers appeared on the walls. The arch of the main gate flooded with guards and on the green below the vendors threw off their cloaks, revealing swords and firearms. And through it all could be heard the loud grating of the iron-toothed portcullis being lowered to block off escape.

"Betrayed, lads!" Connor Macguire roared, drawing his sword. "To the gates!"

The words had barely left his mouth when a musket ball shattered the timbers of a cart nearby him.

Patrick reached beneath his cloak for the scarf, but Donal seized his hand. "Nay, there's no need for it now. 'Twill soon be every man for himself."

Side by side they made their way to the gate, sword in one hand, pistol in the other. Donal slashed a redcoated figure before him, the blade sliding until the sword's hilt locked. With a loud grunt, Donal shoved. The man fell to one knee and levered his blade with both hands toward Donal's legs. The pistol in Patrick's hand roared and the guardsman fell back, clutching his chest.

"My thanks, Patrick!" Donal shouted.

"Keep back to back!" Patrick ordered, throwing the now useless pistol aside and meeting a two-man charge with his sword.

A foot at a time they fought their way toward the main gate, where they joined up with Connor Macguire.

"'Tis no good, lads," Macguire said at last, countering a blow that would have cleaved his head had it connected, and running his blade through its would-be deliverer. "They've planned well. To seize the machinery that controls the portcullis we must get to the winch room, and too many musket and sword now guard the entrance!"

"Aye," Donal panted. "They'll cut us to pieces before we reach the portcullis."

"The wall!" Patrick shouted, turning toward the yard.

Joined by three others, the rebels formed a wedge and again began to fight their way across the lower castle yard. The shouting, the grinding clash of swords and the agonized cries of dying men hung like bedlam all around them.

Near the upper yard their enemies fell back. All too soon they saw why. In the unprotected castle yard, they made easy targets for the musketeers standing on the walls above them.

"Run—run for the steps and your lives!" Macguire roared above the chaos.

Two men fell almost immediately. Seconds later a ball struck Donal, its impact spinning him into Patrick's arms.

Alarm flashed across the young man's features. "You're hit?" he queried sharply.

"Aye, but I can run!" Donal gasped, holding his side.

They managed to get to the base of the steps, where

they were met by more guardsmen. In their midst, roaring and slashing like a hound from hell, was Hugh MacMahon. He was cold sober now, but both Patrick and Donal, convinced that in his drunken stupor Mac-Mahon had somehow alerted the castle guard to their plans, were sorely tempted to run him through. Barely managing to restrain their anger, they both plunged into the melee, with the burly Macguire in the lead.

"Up the stairs, MacMahon!" Macguire urged.

"On with yourself!" MacMahon cried, throwing his body in a lunge behind his blade, forcing the sea of red uniforms to part.

Weary beyond measure now, they staggered up the steps. Halfway up, Donal wavered and Patrick, thrusting a shoulder under him, helped his kinsman to the top. Seconds later, they were joined by Macguire.

Patrick looked down at the dark waters of the moat and then doubtfully at Donal's pain-racked face. It was drained of color, but he managed a faint smile.

"'Tis the only way, Patrick," he said, with a gesture toward the guardsmen now clattering up the steps behind them.

Donal jumped, with Macguire close behind. Thrusting his sword back into its scabbard, Patrick closed his eyes. Seconds later the chill waters of the moat closed over him.

November 1641

CHAPTER SEVEN
BALLYLEE, IRELAND

LIT NEARLY THREE WEEKS BEFORE, the huge bonfires burned from the cliffs in the north across Donegal and Ballylee to Sligo Bay. They served as beacons in the sky to summon the Irish kerns, farmers and gentry alike to battle.

Total surprise had belonged to the Catholics everywhere except Dublin. Under Sir Phelim O'Neill, the rebel forces had taken Charlemont, Derry and Toneragee in the north, while Dungannon and Newry were under siege and expected to fall any day. And already the rebellion was spreading south like a well-fanned fire.

But Rory O'Hara was far from pleased. He had seen the uprising as a means whereby his countrymen could regain lands that had once been theirs. With the king and Parliament in England occupied with their own internal struggle for power, it had seemed an ideal time to strike, and his greatest hope had been that his people could achieve their aims with as little bloodshed as possible. But he knew his countrymen well, and his prediction that rational minds would be unable to prevail upon the masses to exercise restraint was now proving all too true. Reports of massacres of Protestants, both English and Scot, aristocrat and lowly farmer, by Irish officers and peasantry alike, were coming in from all areas. That some of the reports were greatly exaggerated, O'Hara had no doubt, but he also knew it would make little difference in the future. Should Ireland once again be overrun by her enemies, those reports, exaggerated or no, would be remembered, and reprisals would be heavy indeed.

"I leave for Munster tonight," Rory O'More said, without looking up from the maps spread before him. "Already there are outbreaks in the south...here, here and here, near Limerick."

O'Hara only nodded. His jaw was clamped tightly shut and his black eyes burned with rage. Only by dint of great effort did he manage to growl, "Why was Lord Caulfeild murdered when O'Neill took Charlemont Castle?"

"'Twas an overzealous trooper's ire." From across the room came the voice of Heber MacMahon.

" 'Tis no excuse," O'Hara growled, his voice low and ominous as his penetrating stare focused on the priest. "Just as there is no excuse for the wanton slaughter of Protestant farmers."

MacMahon turned his gaze from O'Hara's glare. "Too long we have been under the Protestant thumb. 'Tis time to drive them from our shores."

O'Hara's powerful shoulders hunched forward and there was a ring of steel in his voice when he spoke again. "Heber MacMahon . . . you're a fool."

The black-robed priest whirled, fire in his own eyes now. "They are heretics and as such are not entitled to mercy. One and all they should be put to the sword and driven into the sea. 'Tis a holy mission we serve!" he shouted, his face alive with the passion of a fanatic.

O'Hara's fist came down hard enough on the table to rattle the windows. "Methinks, father, that 'tis precisely your thinking that the English fear. You would have the Pope rule Ireland as a stepping-stone to a Catholic England!"

"We must prove our love and fealty to the Church—"

The fist struck again, cutting off the priest's words. Now O'Hara's voice was a low rumbled that built with each word. "Looking to the Pope or Catholic Spain for aid in this war we've made is as futile and ridiculous as it was in my father's time and that of the Great O'Neill."

At this remark O'More laid a gentling hand on O'Hara's shoulder. "I've sent orders to Phelim to exercise restraint and more discipline. Besides, the reports of Protestant massacres were greatly exaggerated in England."

"Aye," O'Hara sighed, "I'm sure they are and that is what I fear the most. Exaggerated or no, they will be believed, and there will be a cry against us in Westminster such as has never been heard before. Mark me well, O'More, murder will one day become a passion on both sides because of what has passed these weeks!''

There was a rap on the open door, and without bidding, O'Higgin's red-bearded face appeared in the threshold. "M'lord . . . ?"

"Aye, O'Higgin."

"The lad MacGinnis has made it through from Dublin. He's in the kitchen now being cared for."

O'Hara bolted from the room and took the great stone steps four at a time. Servants scattered before his bull-like figure and heavy tread. In minutes he was standing before Ian MacGinnis. There was a wide bandage around the boy's head and his tunic was covered in blood. He looked as if he had had neither food nor sleep for days.

"Sit, lad, sit . . . and tell me all."

In a halting voice the boy told of what he knew. Of the forty-odd men sent to Dublin, ten had been killed. Hugh MacMahon and five others had been captured alive and were being held in Bermingham Tower.

"And of my clan . . . ? Patrick? Donal?" O'Hara failed to hide the concern in his voice.

"They escaped with Connor Macguire. I saw them leap from the tower wall and swim the moat before I myself was captured."

O'Hara sighed with relief. "And you, lad. How did you escape?"

"I didn't. Lord Ormonde, commander of the king's forces, released me with a message for Sir Rory O'More."

O'More moved around O'Hara and knelt beside the lad's chair. "I'm Rory O'More, lad. What is it?"

Ian MacGinnis closed his eyes as if he were dredging up the words from the depths of his weariness. "Lord Ormonde would parlay with you, m'Lord O'Hara, The Macguire and Sir Phelim O'Neill, before all

Ireland is in flames. He has the king's word that all
Irish demands will be met.''

"Is that all, lad?'' O'More asked.

"Aye,'' the boy whispered, his eyes fluttering open
only to close again almost immediately.

O'Hara turned to O'Higgin. "Get him to a bed and
have a woman stay with him.''

Over O'Higgin's shoulder, he saw the white faces of
Aileen and Maura, their eyes wide with alarm. Quickly he crossed the room and embraced them both. "Our
men were betrayed. Lord Lieutenant Parsons knew of
their coming. Some were captured, a few were killed.
Patrick and Donal escaped,'' he told them quickly.

O'Higgin was at his shoulder. "M'lord...?''

O'Hara released the women and turned to his
trusted bailiff. "What news now, O'Higgin?''

"There's something the lad told me that he didn't
speak of in his tale to you. 'Twas spoken among the
men as to the reason for betrayal.''

"What is it?''

"'Twas said that the afternoon of the raid, Hugh
MacMahon was drunk in several Dublin taverns....''

"And?'' O'Hara prompted.

"And he bragged that by nightfall Dublin Castle
would be his.''

O'Hara's face darkened in sudden fury. He looked
up, across the room to where Rory O'More stood beside Heber MacMahon.

"O'More,'' he roared.

"Aye?''

"Get that priest out of here—out of my sight and
off Ballylee, before I would kill him for his brother's
treachery!''

KATHLEEN O'HANLON BLINKED the perspiration from
her lashes and pushed a damp lock of raven-black hair
under the limp material of her *chaperon*. Gingerly she

placed her hands on her hips and rotated the upper part of her body to remove the stiffness brought on by an hour's milking.

Nearby, three cows chewed contentedly on the meager supply of hay she had thrown down for them. The two leather buckets at her feet were barely half full.

"Not near enough even for butter," she groaned aloud, and let her glance travel across the misty plain toward Claymore Castle. The even teeth of the old Norman parapets in dawn's false light looked tiny at such a distance. "But the lord and his flock will have more than oatcakes to fill their bellies this night, like every night. An' they'll have great slabs of butter to spread on their bread and, like as not, meat."

Kathleen's belly growled. Meat!

"Dear God," she said, with a sigh. "When was the last time we had meat on our table?"

She shook her head to dismiss the thought. "Shut you up now, Kathleen O'Hanlon," she told herself severely. "You've taken to talkin' to yourself like an old woman and you just sixteen last spring!"

But Kathleen felt twice her age and had for the past year now, ever since her mother had died. Overnight, Kathleen had assumed that role for her four sisters and brothers and had become caretaker for her father.

Big Kate's death had been the last blow for Hugh O'Hanlon. In the space of a few years he had lost his lands, what little money he had had and then his wife. The day after the burial of Big Kate, Hugh's eyes had taken on a vacant glassiness and his hand had reached for a bottle. Since that time the eyes hadn't changed and the bottle was never empty.

His daughter had stored her silk stockings, sold all her dresses but one and taken over the household. Kathleen had bartered acres from Lord Claymore, and the O'Hanlons had become rent-paying tenants on what had once been their own land.

Up at dawn every day, she saw to the cooking, the milking, the tending to Claymore's sheep, cattle and acres and the tiny plot of land that was allotted for their own garden. It was back-breaking labor that would tire the strongest of men but she did it, and soon it would make an old woman out of her.

Again her eyes drifted to the horizon and Claymore Castle. She thought of the Lady Elana, Lord Claymore's daughter. Two years Kathleen's senior, the most strenuous thing she ever did was a bit of sewing and embroidery or supervising the making of preserves and cordials.

Since returning from Paris, Elana Claymore had often ridden the rocky hills and heathered fields near the O'Hanlon cottage. A few times she had stopped, demanding a noggin of Kate, and once had instructed her to water her spirited mare.

Kathleen smiled when she remembered her retort. "A tenant I might be to your father, m'lady, but I'll not be a slave to you. The stream is yonder."

But Kathleen did envy the fine silks and satins of the Lady Elana's dresses, the way her hair always seemed perfectly in place and clean and the time she had to keep herself beautiful.

"But them that has gets more," Kathleen said aloud. "And them that hasn't just get sweaty." With a sigh, she stooped and grasped the leather thongs of the hide-covered oak buckets and stepped from beneath the lean-to roof. She moved around the side of the one-room thatched cottage that was now the O'Hanlon family mansion and again began to mutter under her breath. "Never done, the damnable work is never done."

She had just stepped into the cottage's murky depths when she heard her name ringing across the fields. Quickly she set the buckets on the rush-strewn dirt floor and hurried to the door.

"Kate! Kate!"

It was her brother, Timothy, streaking across a field of barley about a hundred yards from the cottage. He waved his arms and pointed behind him as he ran.

"Kate. . . Kate—strangers is comin'!"

She looked where he pointed and saw them, two horsemen topping a rise another hundred yards beyond the running boy.

Kathleen wasted no further time. Darting back into the cottage, she snatched a voluminous apron from a wall peg and wrapped it around her waist. A few strides brought her to her pallet where from beneath the straw mattress she drew a pistol.

Two pallets nearer the door, her father lay snoring. She thought of waking him but knew he would be useless even if she did. Poor O'Hanlon, she thought, a simple man who never really realized what had befallen him and now didn't care.

With both hands she grasped the pistol concealed beneath her apron and darted into the clearing in front of the cottage. Timothy had just jumped the nearby muddy creek and slid to a breathless halt in front of her.

"Strangers is comin', Kate!" he panted.

"I can see that," she replied with a nod, gripping the pistol tighter and squinting her eyes.

The day was overcast, the promise of rain in the darkening clouds. Misty fog rose from the creek, partially obscuring the riders. But as they drew closer, she could note some detail. Their dress—or what she could see of it from beneath their mantles—looked to be of quality. The open linen shirts under leather tunics and their tight breeches could mark them as either Irish or English. With the war moving west, they could be rebels or king's men.

The closer they came, the harder she stared.

They wore English-style high cuffed boots instead of brogues, and both wore swords slung from baldrics across their chests. Kathleen could also see a bolstered pistol bobbing on the side of each horse's neck in front of the saddle.

"Think they be reparees, Kate?" Timothy asked anxiously. "Will they be for robbin' us?"

Kathleen's lip curled as she looked down into the boy's fearful face. "Hardly, Tim. What have we left to take?"

The two horses splashed across the creek, circled the nearby barley field and reined up at the edge of the clearing. Both riders were young, one more so than the other, and neither wore beards. But their faces were stubbled as if they hadn't barbered in days. Their shoulder-length hair was cut in the English Cavalier style.

"God save all in this place," said the younger of the two. He was about her own age, Kathleen guessed and spoke Irish Gaelic with a cultured English accent.

Her grip relaxed slightly on the pistol beneath her apron. "And God save ye," she replied, then added sharply, "But state your business!"

"We're but weary travelers, girl, and we've a need for a bit of food and drink."

Again, it was the younger one who spoke. He was the more handsome and full-bodied of the two, although both men were tall and lean. His eyes were hooded, but beneath the lids Kathleen could see smoky-gray irises that seemed to bore into her very soul with their intensity.

Barely had he finished speaking when he made to swing down from his horse. His leg was only half over the horse's rump when she brought the pistol from beneath her apron and leveled it at his chest. "Methinks I didn't invite you down."

"B'gar, would you shoot a man who only wants to fill his belly and would pay for the pleasure?"

"Aye, I would."

"Methinks you take us for men of the road," he observed, eyeing the pistol warily and resettling himself on his horse. "But 'tis not the case."

"Then ye'll be for tellin' me your names," Kathleen said, slowly moving the pistol from one to the other.

It was the older one who spoke this time, and his voice was hoarse with a tiredness she attributed to a long ride. His face was long, with prominent cheekbones and a narrow nose, but only now did she suddenly realize how pale it was. "I'm Donal O'Hara and this is Patrick O'Hara Talbot," he replied wearily: "We've come from Dublin, bound for Ballylee."

"You're of the O'Hara clan?" Kathleen gasped, feeling a flush spread from her neck to her cheeks.

"Aye," Donal said. "An' all we ask of you, lass—"

He never finished speaking. A groan of agony bubbled from his lips and he pitched from his saddle to the ground.

"MY THANKS FOR YOUR HELP, Kate O'Hanlon," Patrick said, extending his hand and helping her up to stand beside him on the rocky crag.

Wearily, Kate shrugged her shoulders and pushed an errant lock of hair back from her forehead. "He's sore wounded, an' you were in no fit shape yourself."

For twenty-four hours she and young Timothy had nursed Donal O'Hara. During most of the time, Patrick had slept fitfully on one of the straw pallets. Every few hours he would awaken, take a slight bit of nourishment and then fall back to bed. Refreshed, that morning he had ridden to Claymore.

"You know m'Lord Byron?" Kate had asked him as he prepared to leave.

"Aye, an' the Lady Elana. Methinks they can provide me with six men and a litter for Donal."

Kate had been oddly happy when he had returned with the news that Lord Claymore and his daughter had gone to Dublin. That had been just after midday. It was eight o'clock and they had just finished a supper of cabbages, oatcakes and potatoes.

All through the afternoon and into the evening she and Patrick had taken turns changing the dressing on Donal's wound and putting cool compresses on his fevered brow. And while they had tended him they had talked companionably. Patrick had told her of the aborted raid on Dublin Castle, and she had related the news she had heard from the north.

When her father had learned that he was hosting two rebels in his cottage—and O'Haras at that—he had come out of his drunken stupor long enough to do the milking and relieve Kate of her other chores so she could continue to nurse Donal.

Now, both she and Patrick had emerged from the cottage for a bit of air and a well-deserved break.

The rain, which had come down for most of the afternoon, had stopped and the stars gleamed cold and distant in the night sky. The moon was just rising, its light flowing like a white sea over the tops of the mountains around them.

"Come dawn," Patrick said, "I'll ride to Ballylee. By the day after we'll be off your hands."

"'Tis no trouble," Kate put in quickly, her pulse unaccountably racing. "An' his fever's still too heavy for travel..." she offered, reluctant to see the end of Patrick's stay.

"Perhaps, but travel I think we must. We'll be safer behind the walls of Ballylee, and you'll be safer without us in your house." As he spoke, Patrick reached over and gently squeezed her arm. It was a friendly almost brotherly gesture, but the warm touch of his hand made an odd ripple on her skin.

During the short time they had spent together, Patrick's abruptness had softened, and a warm friendship had begun to blossom.

Out of the corner of her eye, Kate studied his lithe
form and his lean handsome face. There was an aura
of inner passion and recklessness about him that
stirred her blood. She liked the way his nostrils
quivered when he was deeply moved, and the way his
lips curved with a smile. He had smiled little this day,
it was true, but she had the feeling that Patrick
O'Hara Talbot's mouth was accustomed to smiling.
He turned to face her, and she noticed that his hooded gray eyes grew silvery in the moonlight.

"You do well here, Kate O'Hanlon?" he asked,
gesturing to the garden plot below them.

Kate shrugged. "Aye, as well as we can do, I suppose. We have three acres to call our own, with corn,
oats and peas. We have three cows and a good turf
stack against the cold. And we pay most of our rent
by tending sheep for m'Lord Claymore and helping
with the Claymore harvest in the fall."

"But you're not happy."

"Happy?" Sadness washed over her as she met his
searching look. "Sometimes I think I would be happy if the land were ours again. But then I realize that
even if it were, the work would be the same and I
would be just as tired."

"If your father—"

"Please. . . I don't want to talk of my father."

Suddenly the cry of an owl resounded in the still
night air.

"There!" Kate cried, pointing. "Look how he
glides free in the moonlight!"

"Is that what you would be, lass? Free as an owl in
the night sky?"

Patrick's laugh brought a smile to her own lips just
as his words brought a slight flush to her face. But
there was a touch of mockery in his voice and she
bridled at it. "Aye, for an owl, like the hawk, is as a
man, free before the wind. And like a man, I would

be free with a good horse beneath me, the feel of a sword at my side and the scent of a fight in the air.''

"Damme, but that's the first time I've heard a woman say such things!"

"Ah, but I'll wager there's many a woman in these times who thinks such thoughts!"

Suddenly his hands were at her shoulders, drawing her to him. His eyes gleamed with excitement and his face took on a look of youthful fervor. "As for myself," he told her gaily, "I've dreamed of sailing to foreign shores. Many a time have I seen myself as the captain of a trim three-master with the roll of the deck beneath my feet and the feel of the salt air in my face.''

Kate laughed easily, feeling herself caught up in his mood. "And where would you sail, Patrick Talbot?"

"First I would drive the Algerian pirates from the sea. All English shipping would then be prey for me alone. And when I would tire of the buccaneer's life, 'tis to China I'd be bound.''

"And once there?"

"Why, I'd conquer it, of course!"

Shyly, Kate asked, "Would you never return to Ireland?"

"Aye, for Ireland to an Irishman is like the sea to a sailor. Once 'tis in your soul you can never leave it for good.''

His gray eyes were full of warmth now as he stared down at her. Against the night sky his teeth gleamed in a reckless smile and his profile prompted Kate to think that he was the most handsome man she had ever seen.

It had been a long time since she had talked in such a carefree manner. There was a warmth and companionship in Patrick Talbot's presence she had never experienced before. She felt as though she had known him all her life, and if she read the look in his eyes correctly, he was of a similar mind.

His hands tightened on her shoulders, and her own

fingers longed to curl in his mane of unruly hair and press his lips to hers. But then the smile faded and the lids dropped once again to shield his eyes. His face became hard and dark and the carefree look of youth was gone in an instant.

"I know there'll be no ship and no China," he murmured. "In their place there'll be war, horses and armor—and many a wake before we've finished what we've started."

Kate nodded slowly, feeling the mood slipping away and not wanting it to end. "Aye, an' I'm still a tenant farmer's daughter and you're the son of a lord of Ballylee."

Her voice was bitter, but if Patrick recognized her meaning, he chose not to let it show on his face. "You're a buxom, bonny lass, Kathleen O'Hanlon, so fear not. When the troubles are over, you'll have your land and a fine man to father your babies!"

He tilted her chin up with a finger. Kate was sure he was about to kiss her, and the anticipation made her pulse throb erratically.

He leaned forward, but instead merely pressed his cheek against hers and said gruffly, "We'd best be checking Donal. 'Tis time his bandage is changed again."

THEY RODE IN SINGLE FILE, Patrick at point, then Maura and The O'Hara. O'Higgin and four kerns followed, the makings of a blanket litter strapped to their saddles.

Though it was just past midday the land was gray with a soggy mist. Boulders and rocks were strewn on the path beneath the horses' hooves and gaunt hills loomed around them. A mood of foreboding was in the air, and Maura urged her mount forward in an effort to dispel her fears.

"Easy, lass, easy," O'Hara said, from behind her.

" 'Tis not goats we ride. The footing here is treacherous.''

"Aye. . .aye,". Maura mumbled. She knew The O'Hara's words were wise, but her heart and mind were impatient. Her eyes burned with the need to see her beloved husband.

When Patrick had ridden through the huge arched gate at Ballylee the night before, she had nearly swooned with the shock.

He had been alone.

No sooner had his tale been told than she was in a fever of impatience to be gone.

"Let's let the lad rest a bit, lass," O'Hara had urged.

But Maura had so pleaded with her eyes that Patrick had shrugged off his weariness and called for a fresh horse. Within the hour, they had set off for the O'Hanlon cottage.

"How far yet, Patrick?" she asked now.

"Through the glen and yon forest," he called, pointing the way. "From the hills beyond. . .there, we should be able to see the Claymore lands."

"You're sure this girl tends him well in your absence?"

"Aye, sister, fear not—as sure as Ireland's green. For she's a fine bonny lass, she is, and seems to have a touch with wounds."

Wounds, Maura thought with a shudder. Her Donal was wounded. Patrick had told her that for days after they had failed to rendezvous with either the O'Byrnes or the O'Tooles, he and Donal had hidden in the Wicklows. Even when they had felt it safe to move on, they had ridden only at night to avoid a chance encounter with English patrols.

Now Donal lay with a fever in a damp, wretched tenant's cottage, tended by strangers. Patrick had said he was recovering, but Maura had seen the truth in her brother's eyes. Her husband's condition was far more serious than he would admit.

Her arms aching with the strain, she held her horse in and concentrated on the rhythm of its hooves. The cadence drummed in her mind and she allowed it to numb her as a defense against her fears.

Suddenly the drumming stopped. Leaving the path, they had moved into high grass that muffled the horses' hoofbeats. Thankfully, Patrick spurred his mount to a trot and then a canter. In less than an hour they were through the trees and climbing a brown ridge.

Patrick reined up at the ridge's peak. "There!" he cried.

Maura followed the spiraling smoke of a peat fire to its source, a thatched-roof cottage near a winding creek. Without waiting for the others she kicked her horse into a gallop and flew down the ridge's lee side.

Maura's great cloak billowed behind her and the wind tore the *chaperon* from her head. Before long, combs and pins were also gone and her long golden tresses flowed behind her.

The sound of pounding hooves brought Timothy running from the cottage. By the time the riders reached the creek, Kathleen had joined him.

"Hola, Kate!" Patrick called. "We've come!"

Sharply, Maura reined her mount to a halt near the cottage door and with little thought to dignity, slid from the sidesaddle before Patrick had a chance to dismount and hand her down.

"You're his woman...Maura?" asked Kate.

"Aye," Maura replied, lifting her skirts and running toward the door.

Swiftly Kate moved to block her way. Startled, Maura looked up and into Kate's eyes, and from the expression she saw there, felt a cry of despair in her throat.

"He kissed my hand and bid me tell you that he

loved you as no other man has loved a woman," Kate said slowly.

"No! Dear God, no—" Maura shrieked, swaying on her feet.

"Steady yourself, lass," Kate whispered. "He's gone."

Too shocked to utter a sound, Maura took a faltering step forward and suddenly found Kate O'Hanlon's strong arms around her. Willingly, she went limp, letting her body melt against Kate's as a torrent of tears flooded silently from her eyes.

Behind her, O'Higgin's hoarse voice seemed to fill the air.

"The first O'Hara falls. God grant us victory before the banshee wails again."

March 1642

CHAPTER EIGHT
CLAYMORE CASTLE, IRELAND

INSIDE THE WALLS OF CLAYMORE CASTLE, Scots, English and even a few Irish eyed each other warily. In the huge courtyard of the castle's lower bailey, the soldiers had broken into groups. Shortly after their arrival, kitchen maids and other servants had doled out mutton jerky and barrels of ale. The men ate and drank as their respective leaders sat in one of the castle towers above them, planning their futures.

"Gentlemen, the O'Haras will be here within the hour. A decision must be made." Lord Claymore's round face was wet with perspiration as he gazed across his massive desk at the lords Gormanston and Antrim.

"The three of us represent the backbone of the Old English landowners in Ireland. Where we go, the other English Catholics will follow."

Almost dwarfed by the high-backed chair, Lord

Antrim sat thoughtfully sucking a dry pipe. Then absentmindedly he set down the pipe and asked, "After the last debacle, do we have a choice?"

The other two men shook their heads in unison.

The last debacle had indeed been disastrous. As commander of what little army was left in Ireland, Ormonde had sent six hundred men north to reinforce the key town of Drogheda for the crown. At Julianstown, long before they reached Drogheda, they had been engaged and cut to pieces by rebel Irish forces. Nor was the situation any better in the south. Tipperary and Waterford had fallen, and most of Clare had been captured.

Strangely, Lord Gormanston found humor in Ormonde's setbacks. His tall gaunt body quivered with laughter as he spoke. "Methinks, 'tis a vast irony," he chuckled. "In 1603 the rebels soundly lost their last attempt at independence under The Great O'Neill, and we three gained rich lands because of it. Now, because of civil strife in our own England, the Irish have damn near taken back their own land—and if we don't go along with them, they'll have ours as well!"

Lord Antrim crossed to the fire and put an ember to his pipe. "You know, of course, that if we join them, this rebellion becomes a national movement rather than a simple uprising of malcontent Irishmen."

"Aye," Claymore agreed. "But what can we do? Even the king woos the rebels. He needs their support in his campaign against that damn Puritan Parliament of his."

Gormanston slapped his knee and the grin on his lips turned into a slash of anger. "Pym and Parliament use the Irish rising to discredit the king. And now Parliament has passed that damnable Act of Adventurers—two and a half million Irish acres belonging to the rebels declared forfeit and to be placed on the market for Protestant investors and mercenaries!"

"Aye, m'lords," Claymore said, mopping his face, "some of those acres may be ours if we agree to side with O'Hara and his rebels."

"Aye," Gormanston agreed soberly. "But the rub is this. The king has an unsteady crown. To defeat the rebels, Parliament must raise an army—which we know it will not, because it cannot trust the king with an army. Charles would immediately turn it on Parliament! Without that army to hold them in check, the rebels stand a good chance of retaking all their land—including ours if we *don't* side with them.

"We have no choice," Gormanston continued, as he got to his feet. "We must make a formal alliance with the Irish rebels and hope that in the end, the king is of the same mind."

"'Tis agreed then," Claymore said. Wearily, he added, "Dear God, how this land of Ireland has been fatal to all the kings of England!"

Shouts in the bailey below and the plaintive wail of hunting horns brought the men to the window. The heath before Claymore Castle was rife with spring blossoms. Beyond the heath, up on the hills, the many colors of the wild flowers gave way to one shade, the purple of heather in full bloom. And atop the ridge, like tiny ships in a purple sea, rode three hundred armed O'Hara clansman. Green and gold banners bearing the proud lion of the O'Haras fluttered from pikes and lances. Sunlight danced across the steel mesh of the riders' doublets as they advanced.

"Good God," Antrim thundered, "do they plan on a parlay or a siege of Claymore? I don't have that many cavalry in all of Antrim!"

Lord Byron Claymore smiled at Antrim's words. "Nor I that many foot nor arms for half that number on Claymore lands. 'Tis only because O'Hara has chosen to wait in hopes of a treaty that he hasn't taken Claymore already."

Silently they watched a group of twenty separate from the rest. It was led by The O'Hara, wide and imposing in full battle dress and astride a massive black stallion. Across his barrellike chest the golden stripe emblazoned with the black upright lion seemed like a spear thrusting straight for the heart of Claymore.

Minutes later they passed through the gate and into the courtyard. O'Hara and Patrick Talbot alone dismounted, and side by side followed a groom into the tower.

"Brace yourselves," Lord Claymore said, "for we must not appear too anxious to acquiesce."

Like rolling drumbeats, the heavy cavalry boots seemed to echo ominously on the stone stairs, and when the men entered the room, it seemed suddenly full with their presence.

"M'lords," O'Hara said gravely, "you know my godson."

The three men nodded.

Then, remembering his duties as host, Lord Claymore made to offer a chair or a bit of wine but found that all moisture had dried up in his mouth. So much so that he could swallow only with great difficulty. As he met O'Hara's penetrating stare, he knew that there would be no room for bargaining.

Gone now was the gentle bear of a man with whom Lord Claymore shared many a noggin of wine and tankard of ale. In his place was the reincarnation of Shane, the warrior-prince of Ballylee, who had for years struck terror into the hearts of rival Irish clansmen and English alike. Gone, too, was the ready smile beneath the gray-flecked black beard. The lips were a hard almost cruel line, and the eyes were flinty as black granite.

At last Gormanston summoned the courage to speak. "M'Lord O'Hara, was it necessary to bring an army for a meeting among old friends?"

"Aye, m'Lord Gormanston, it was. One O'Hara has fallen already from treachery. If another dies, I plan that it should be on the field, in open battle."

Lord Claymore sank into the chair behind his desk. "Then let us speak to the point. You've seen Ormonde?"

"Aye," O'Hara answered, loosening the leather straps on his helmet and removing it. "M'Lord Ormonde sees the folly of more killing and wishes peace. Only Kinsale, Cork and Youghal still stand for the crown."

"And the king?" Antrim queried anxiously, averting his eyes from O'Hara.

"Would have us raise an army of ten thousand to come to his aid should Cromwell get his wish for an army of Parliament."

"Do the Irish agree?"

"We do," O'Hara said, returning his gaze to Lord Claymore and letting the bare suggestion of a smile play about his lips, "once King Charles proves to us that his words are not as empty as his coffers."

Claymore nodded. "God grant that for once Charles sees the wisdom of putting actions behind his words."

Lord Gormanston coughed into his kerchief and tapped it against his lips. "Your lands, O'Hara, have been declared forfeit to the crown under Parliament's Act of Adventurers. Would you have ours the same?"

"That will not happen, m'lord," Patrick Talbot said, entering the conversation for the first time, "unless Charley's promises are as hollow as Jamie's were before him."

Of the three English lords only Gormanston took offense at the derogatory use of the kings' names. Instinctively he reached for the hilt of his sword.

"Do not be deceived by past friendships, m'lord,"

O'Hara rumbled, his tones like steel. "I would kill you where you stand."

If nothing else had, these words, coming from a side of O'Hara they had never known, brought home to the Englishmen the truth of their position. Ruled by an English king and Parliament though Ireland might be, to the Irish they were foreigners, and unwelcome ones at that. Without support from England, their presence would be tolerated only so long as it suited Irishmen such as O'Hara.

And to remind them further, Patrick added, "As to your lands, m'lords, they were all at one time owned by the very tenants who now work them."

"Methinks I see the Scot's blood in you, Talbot."

"Aye," Patrick agreed, flashing Lord Antrim a wide smile in reply. " 'Tis indeed a devilish brew when mixed with the Irish."

"Your answer, m'lords," O'Hara said. "Ormonde has agreed to abide by your decision."

Lord Claymore glanced at Antrim and Gormanston, and then back to The O'Hara. He could feel sweat running down the small of his back, and had to force his hands to grip the desk to stop their shaking. For what he and the others were about to do was momentous. By siding with the rebels, they were, to all intents and purposes, committing themselves and their followers to an act of treason that gave much of Ireland back to the Irish.

"I am of an age...a tired and weary old man, O'Hara—I speak for the others. You have our support."

O'Hara bowed slightly, turned on his heel and left the room.

Patrick was the first to break the silence. "M'Lord Claymore, I would ask one small boon of you...."

Claymore listened and then nodded with even more weariness as he reached for quill and paper. "Aye, why not, lad," he sighed.

When Patrick was also gone, the men sat without speaking for several moments, each deep in his own thoughts.

"And so 'tis done," Claymore said finally.

In defeated tones Gormanston replied, "And now we must pray for a settlement in England to undo it."

His remark was answered by Antrim, who suddenly erupted in loud, almost hysterical laughter. "Aye, m'lords, and we'd best further pray that the king wins the settlement—for if he doesn't we are all lost!"

THE PARAPETS OF CLAYMORE were barely visible when Patrick turned his horse toward the stand of thickly leaved oaks. In moments he was making his way through their gloomy darkness.

"Patrick... over here!"

He reined up his horse and dismounted. For a few moments he simply stood there, letting his gaze caress her striking beauty.

Her curls were artfully arranged in cascading ringlets around her provocative face. And though she had been riding, there was not a single strand out of its proper place.

As he did every time he saw her, Patrick marveled at the perfection of her languid eyes and sensuous, slightly mocking lips. The bodice of a rust-colored gown beaded and braided in gold only partially concealed her full bosom. A green pelerine cut for riding was draped carelessly over her shoulders.

"You are a goddess more than mortal woman, Elana," Patrick breathed, stepping close.

Elana accepted the compliment with a flirtatious smile and then raised an eyebrow in mock anger. "'Tis a month since you've found your way to Claymore. I'm vexed, Patrick."

"I think you would agree, there's been a bit of an obstacle—a nasty war—that prevented us from meeting sooner," he admonished her.

"Tell me then, what goes on in the outside world beyond my dreary castle walls?"

Patrick made no reply, but instead reached out and turned her face up to his. As their lips met, his hands moved beneath her cloak to the small of her back. The kiss deepened and he pulled her to him.

For a moment she accepted his kiss and then began to struggle. Pushing hard against his chest, she protested, "Dear God, man, would you take all the breath from my body?"

"I've been too long without the touch of you," he moaned.

"And all this steel and buckles— 'Tis no way to love a woman!"

Undeterred by her cutting remark, Patrick smiled down into her eyes, his arms still encircling her narrow waist. "I've news, and good it is."

"Tell me. . . tell me all! My father confides so little in me I am fair driven to distraction."

"No longer will we be forced into these secret trysts. From now on we can meet in the open. I can call at Claymore again," he related eagerly.

"How so?" Elana asked, a new intensity creeping into her turquoise eyes.

"We are allies now."

"What?"

In his joy, Patrick never sensed the tenseness of her spine against his hands nor saw the sudden narrowing of her eyes. "Your father and the lords Gormanston and Antrim have agreed to an alliance between we native Irish and the Old English."

"Oh, dear God, no!"

Her words cracked like a whip among the silent trees. Patrick dropped his arms from her waist and stepped back as if he had been struck. "Your pardon, m'lady," he said stiffly. "I thought you would be overjoyed that—"

"Oh, I am," she said hurriedly. "I mean as for us. But for my father to desert the king...."

Patrick relaxed. "Ah, but he doesn't. The king has been in secret negotiations with Ormonde and The O'Hara. He prefers peace with us and in return, our help in subduing his randy Parliament."

Her shadowed lashes lowered and her body leaned into his. "Oh, Patrick, thank God! Surely you must understand my outburst. Claymore is all the fortune and dowry I have. If it be lost, *I* would be lost."

"By the terms of such an alliance, the Irish will protect the Old English Catholics—which means I shall protect you!" he offered gallantly.

Her arms slipped around his neck and this time her lips parted, her tongue seeking his in the deep, sensual kiss he remembered so well and for too long had been without. Briefly, puzzlement at the mercurial nature of this woman's moods winged across his mind. At one moment she could be cold, strained and lacking all passion, and in the next she would be a cauldron of desire in his arms. But the thought was quickly swept away as the scent of her hair filled his nostrils and her firm, full body responded sensuously to his touch.

Gently she brought her lips from his and ran them over the strong line of his jaw to his throat. "But be that as it may, this silly war goes on," she whispered.

"Aye, but not for long."

"We can't be sure. I worry for you, Patrick. The king's deceit is well known and there are troops in Ireland who are Parliament sent. They will not lay down their arms."

"True," Patrick replied, his hand moving around to find the supple curve of her waist. "But one day soon the last blow will be struck and our bargain accepted."

His hand had reached the buttons at the back of

her dress, but deftly Elana moved so that they were out of his reach.

"God, what a wench you are," he groaned, giving up the buttons and moving a hand to her breast. "So great is my desire for you that I can hardly stand."

"Then lay my mind at rest."

"How so?" He tensed, knowing she wanted something before she would relent and give in to him.

"Tell me what great miracle is to win the day!" she demanded.

"Owen Roe O'Neill."

"The Spanish general?"

Patrick threw back his head in laughter. "Half the generals around the world are Irish, my sweet. But one and all wait for the day to return to Eire. Owen Roe has raised a force in Flanders. The O'Hara has promises from Richelieu of France that they will be armed."

Elana hid her face in his neck. "And when will this O'Neill land?"

"In four months' time, perhaps sooner." The hand at her breast was urgent now as he lifted her chin to look at her questioningly. "'Tis a month since we've been together. Has your ardor toward me so cooled that you would rather talk of war and politics than make love?"

"Nay, Patrick, nay," she sighed, running her fingers along the sides of his face. "'Tis this place. You know how I feel about such things. Bed your wenches and milkmaids on the bank of a river, but not me."

His eyes narrowed in a familiar look of wariness. "I've had my fill of milkmaids and whores. I would have you . . . for good and all time."

"I've told you—"

"Elana . . . I would make you my wife," he breathed.

Her eyes took on a haunted quality. Then, with a

quick, darting motion she was gone from his arms to her horse. "I'll be no man's wife—yet!" All modesty forgotten, she raised her skirts and with a catlike grace gained the saddle. "Besides, Patrick Talbot, would your family allow such a match?"

"They have nothing to say—" he protested.

"Aye, I suppose they don't—because you're a man!" She reined around and then paused as if another thought had struck her.

"And what of you—of Patrick the man? How many weeks and months—even years—would it take for you to begin to wonder? For you know, Patrick Talbot, that when you've lain with me you've not bounced a virgin."

"Elana—" He leapt forward in an attempt to grasp her bridle, but she had already spurred her horse to a gallop.

As she rode, a sense of loneliness gripped her, a loneliness tinged with fear. Had she chosen the right path to follow? Did Sir John Redding truly have the expectations he claimed? Elana had little doubt now that her father was an aging fool. If he kept to his appeasing ways, she would be a pauper long before she had a chance to be wived. She thought of Sir John Redding and Patrick Talbot, finding it impossible to stop comparing them, both as lovers and as men.

One was slightly cruel, hard, with an almost steel-like quality and fifteen years her senior. The other was alive with wit and full of charm. He was gentle to the point of excess at times and just past her own age. In her eyes this made Patrick little more than a youth.

And besides, he was Irish to the core. Marriage to him would mean a life in Ireland, a country she had come to despise. Marriage to John Redding, on the other hand, would mean London and Paris, attending balls and dressing in the latest fashions, a way of

life much to her liking. But she had grown to fear
John Redding.

And much as she might have forced the thought
from her mind of late, there was a touch of love in
her heart for the carefree ways of Patrick Talbot,
particularly when he shared her bed.

With a determined set to her jaw she pushed her
mount to a dangerous speed in the gathering dusk.
"Think of yourself, girl," she cried aloud to the
wind, "for no one else will do it for you!"

Damme, yes, she thought, *'tis the only way for me.
For I was to the manner born, and by God 'tis in the
manor I'll live—not in this savage land!*

Already in her mind she was composing the letter
relating the latest news she had gleaned from Patrick.

My dearest John. . . it began.

"Now, Kate?"

"Soon, lad, soon. . . just a little longer."

There was barely enough light creeping over the
squat mountains to see the turned furrows, but still
they worked. Kate was determined to get the seeding
done. And the harder she worked, she thought, the
less she felt so young and so alone.

Since midday they had worked side by side in the
fields. The sweat had run down her back, her sides
and felt like a river between her breasts. As they
always did, her skirts had harnessed her every movement until finally she had cursed them—"Damn being a woman!"—and had tied them at her waist. A
breeze had come up, but she had left them tied because the wind felt pleasantly cool on her bare legs.

"Kate. . . Kate, look there!"

The tone in Timothy's voice brought Kate's head
up with a jerk. "Where, lad?"

"There—on the ridge!"

A black-cloaked rider on a massive chestnut horse

stood outlined against the fading sun. As they watched, the animal reared, pawing the air once with its forelegs before coming down in a gallop.

"Tim, the cottage— Get me the gun!"

"Kate, I—I think—"

"What is it?"

"Look you at his chest. 'Tis the O'Hara crest!"

Kate's heart seemed to leap into her throat as she squinted at the galloping horse and rider. "Aye," she gasped, biting her lip to hold back the sudden tears of joy, "'tis him."

Closer and closer he came, a shadowy, towering giant silhouetted against the dusky sky. Before long she could see his tanned features, the set line of his strong chin and the flashing grin that had haunted her dreams so many nights.

"Hola, Kate O'Hanlon!" he cried, as he came near.

"Hola yourself, Patrick Talbot!" she shouted, and sprinted to the edge of the field.

The chestnut snorted to a halt a few feet short of her and sidestepped obediently to her side. When she looked up at his wide shoulders and fierce profile outlined against the darkening sky, his smile warming her blood, it was difficult to keep her resolve and not leap into his arms.

As if he had read her thoughts, Patrick leaned over and slid his hands beneath her arms. Gently but quickly, he lifted her and brushed her lips with his own. Then her feet came back to earth, and in one motion his leg was over the saddle and he stood on the ground before her.

And so, Kate thought, *nothing has changed. He smiles, he laughs, he kisses me.... But always it is done as if he were a brother.* She remembered Donal's death and the all-too-brief time she had had with Patrick before his return to Ballylee.

Kate had been a calming influence, a solace to Maura O'Hara in her grief. She had soon found herself playing the same role for Patrick. Like Maura, Patrick had poured out his love for Donal and had sought Kate's company to assuage his pain. They had grown close, very close, in those few hours.

At the moment of parting, Patrick had taken her in his arms. For a fleeting instant her hopes that there might be more than simple friendship between them had been raised. In the next moment he had dashed those hopes by kissing her like a brother, but still Kate had wondered and dreamed.

Now she knew it was to no avail, for once again she was being treated as a sister.

"B'gar, lass, is that the latest from Paris or have you taken to designing fashion yourself?" Patrick teased.

Kate looked down. Her legs were bare nearly to her hips. Her face flushed hot as she quickly untied the hem of her skirt and let it fall.

"Dear God, Kate, I do believe you blush," he grinned. "Would you forget that I've slept naked in your house in the Irish way and seen you the same?"

"Aye, but—"

Suddenly his mocking smile became a spirited laugh, warm and contagious. It was all Kate could do to keep from laughing herself.

"Ah, I know," he said, throwing an arm around her shoulders and squeezing her to him. "'Tis different in the night by the dimness of a candle than in the day with the sun at set."

Abruptly he dropped his arms and walked up to Timothy, who stood gazing at Patrick with open awe and reverence in his eyes. "Ah, Tim, lad, you grow like a weed. One day I must take you to Ballylee to meet Conor, the future O'Hara." In greeting, Patrick dropped his hands on the boy's shoulders. "What is it, lad— Have you lost your tongue?"

"Nay, I . . . ." Timothy could only swallow as his eyes grew wider.

"Well?"

"I've never seen you in steel and colors. . . . It makes you look as big as a mountain, it does!"

Timothy's awestruck face and his words brought another ring of laughter from Patrick. Moving his long sword to one side, he kneeled so that his eyes were on a level with the boy's.

"There, is that better, lad?"

Suddenly Timothy was embarrassed. He averted his eyes from Patrick's gray, hawklike stare and kicked at a clod of dirt. "I only meant—"

"I know what you meant, lad. But don't be fooled by all these trappings. For 'tis not all these trappings that make the man nor the man a soldier. 'Tis the heart inside him."

With smooth movements, Patrick divested himself of his helmet, the baldric that held his sword and the belt that held his brace of pistols. Quickly, he placed them on Timothy.

The helmet dwarfed the boy's face. The baldric hung so low across his body that the hilt of the great long sword nearly touched the ground and he staggered beneath the weight of the pistols.

"My thanks, general," Patrick said, feigning a sternness in his voice, "for takin' the weight and worries of the war off my mind for a few moments."

"You're funnin' me," Timothy protested, but there was a wide grin on his face and he was valiantly working the helmet's leather straps to make it tighter.

"Aye, lad, but only a bit. Here now." As if the boy were a feather, Patrick swung him into the air and onto the chestnut stallion's back.

"Patrick," Kate gasped, "he's ridden little. . . ."

"Then 'tis time he learned. Right, Timothy, lad?"

"Aye!" the boy whooped, and dug his knees into

the stallion's sides as Patrick slapped the beast's rump.

"Don't worry, lass," he said, turning and taking Kate's hand. "He has only the size and look of a warhorse. He's gentle as a lamb." Turning back toward Timothy, he shouted, "Water him good, lad, and give him a bit of a rub!"

Timothy waved and then disappeared around a stand of trees in the curve of the creek.

"And I could do with a dram myself, Kate, if you've one to spare," added Patrick, grinning down at her.

"On with you," she replied with a smile. "You know I do. Come along!"

As they walked to the cottage, his hand clasping hers radiated a warmth that acted as a balm to her body. Out of the corner of her eye she watched him stride beside her, his movements as lithe as those of a big cat. The darkly tanned face and the powerful wide shoulders seemed to exude strength she found both irresistible and reassuring.

How blissful it would be, she mused, to lie safe and content in his arms. And what would it be like, she wondered, to surrender to desire and follow the instincts of her own passion—a passion she had recognized in herself from the first moment she had seen him. Every nerve ending in her body tingled at the thought.

"How are things?" he asked, giving her hand a squeeze.

"Much the same," she answered with a shrug.

At the door to the cottage, Patrick stopped and turned her to face him. "Mayhap that will soon change."

She stared up into his eyes. They were bright with laughter and Kate was sure she read some new mischief in their depths. "Would you tease me as you do Tim?" she chided.

"Very probably," he replied with a grin. "Now, where's my dram?"

They stepped inside and she moved away to fetch his drink. "You'll sup with us?"

"Nay, Kate, I'd best be back to Ballylee, for things move these days at a dreadful pace." As he spoke, Patrick watched her supple body intently. She was tall and raw-boned but her movements had an earthy, animal grace. Her skirt outlined the curve of her hips and he remembered how she had looked with it tied at her waist. Her breasts, unfettered in the tight blouse, swayed provocatively.

He continued to watch her every move and found himself comparing her to another. This girl would have no moods, no mystery hidden behind her eyes. They were open and clear, and in their depths it seemed a man could see clear into her soul.

I wonder, he thought, *if Kate O'Hanlon would object to making love on the bank of a river beneath the stars.*

As quickly as the thought had risen, he thrust it from his mind, chiding himself. An hour before, he had tried to bed Elana Claymore and had been spurned. Was he so thin-skinned that he would use a sweet lass like Kate O'Hanlon to soothe his injured pride?

"Would you sit!" Kate demanded. "'Tis not as if you've not been invited."

Obediently, he sat down at the table and scanned the bare cottage. "Where are the little ones?"

"Playing. Over by the creek."

"And your father?"

She was turned away from him, but he could see her head come up and her back stiffen. "He's gone off."

"Off? Dear God, girl, off where?"

She set a noggin before him and took the chair opposite. "Off," she replied with a shrug. "He'll be back. He does it now and then...just walks off. He's usually back soon after the jug is empty." A cloud passed over her eyes and she tried to hide her pain by bringing her own cup to her lips.

"Kate...." From beneath his doublet, Patrick withdrew a folded piece of parchment and slid it across the table.

"For me?"

"Aye."

Kate hesitated, then gingerly picked up the document. "It bears the seal of Lord Claymore."

"That it does, lass."

Tears welled in her eyes and her hands trembled with fear. "Dear God," she whispered. "He's evicting us."

"Damme, girl," Patrick cried, snatching the paper from her grasp and breaking the seal. "Must you always play the pessimist?"

What he read so overwhelmed Kate that she could hardly remain still. Her heart began to pound and tears of joy seeped from the corners of her eyes. A tremor passed through her as he neared the end and she jumped to her feet. It was impossible to sit. Almost feverishly, she paced the cottage, tears flowing like twin rivers down her cheeks.

"...and by these hands witnessed," Patrick concluded, his voice trailing off as he came to the end of the document.

She turned to him, her face chalk white. "'Tis hard to believe—"

"But there it is, bonny Kate," he said, turning the paper and holding it before her eyes. "Witnessed by Antrim and Gormanston and signed by Lord Claymore. There's his seal."

"Twenty-five acres...ours...all ours, to do with as we will. And we own it!"

"Aye, lass, you're tenants no more. You're landowners again. 'Tis not a whole estate, but 'tis land and 'tis yours.''

With a cry she rushed to him, throwing herself into his arms. "Oh, Patrick, Patrick, what a friend you are! How can we repay such kindness?"

"By drying up your tears, lass, and doing a meal. I've decided to sup with you after all."

"We'll have us a feast!" she cried, taking his face in both her hands and almost bruising her lips with the fierceness of her kiss.

Patrick's hands began to tighten at her hips when suddenly the kiss was broken.

"Timothy! I must tell Timothy!"

In the next moment, Kate was running toward the barn, her skirts lifted high and her voice shouting her brother's name. Patrick watched her go, a smile on his face and a lump of joy in his throat at the thought that he had been able to bring her such happiness.

As she disappeared from his sight, he looked down at his arms, still thrust forward. It was strange, he mused, how oddly empty they now felt.

June 1642

CHAPTER NINE
BALLYLEE, IRELAND

CAMPFIRES DOTTED THE LANDSCAPE of Ballylee nearly as far as the eye could see. Night and day the boisterous laughter and good-natured arguing of soldiers filled the air. Shanna and Aileen worked from first light until near midnight each day, planning meals, assigning sleeping quarters and in general presiding over the army of servants inside the castle. Around the clock, messengers came and went almost hourly, arriving from all points of Ireland to the small office atop Ballylee's highest tower.

Rarely these days, it seemed, did Rory O'Hara leave that office. Hour after hour he would sit at his desk, poring over letters and writing replies.

O'Higgin was constantly at his side, calmly puffing his pipe and offering advice whenever it was asked of him. But unlike the old days, when the young O'Hara had returned from France, O'Higgin was now less the adviser and more the confidant.

The old man had often wondered what direction O'Hara would take if the call to war ever came. He had always known Rory as a man of peace, something of a philosopher with an occasionally cynical view of his fellow Irishmen. But there could be no doubt now about his leanings. Once he had decided to throw in his hand with the rebels, his body and soul had quickly followed. Total war and total victory was now The O'Hara's creed.

"'Tis said the queen has raised little money in Holland from the crown jewels, O'Higgin. What think you?"

O'Higgin puffed his pipe and studied his lord's bowed head a moment before replying.

"I think the wealth of the king's coffers will make little difference in his decision to make war. This nephew of his—Prince Rupert of the Rhine?"

"Aye," O'Hara replied, his head still bent over his papers.

"He's young, only twenty-three, but a tiger who has already proved himself in battle in Europe. He's bound for fame, and methinks he would try to find it in his Uncle Charley's civil war. These Cavaliers, as the king's men like to call themselves, are a rowdy, self-serving bunch, but a man like Rupert can bring them together."

At this remark O'Hara looked up, lightly chewing the end of a quill. "If Charles and Parliament do go to open war against each other, we've won the day."

O'Higgin's face grew grave. "Mayhap."

O'Hara grinned. "What is your 'mayhap,' old man?"

"I read your dispatches. It seems there's more to this Cromwell than even the king would suspect. Beware of a man who claims he has a personal calling from God, for that man has no fear of death."

O'Hara was about to reply when the door burst open and Aileen's tall figure filled the threshhold. "Methinks 'tis time you took a hand to your son's backside! He's bound—"

Before she could finish, young Conor dashed around her and bolted into the room, not stopping until he was standing defiantly before his father's chair. "M'lord," he cried, his mouth set in a hard line, "I'll not to France!"

O'Hara's voice was like thunder. "You'll not *what*!"

Young Conor trembled and blinked, but he didn't flinch. "I would stay with you in Eire and fight the bloody bastards!"

O'Hara's nerves had already been stretched to breaking. His son's words of defiance only served to fuel his anger and threatened to snap those already taut nerves. Had not O'Higgin restrained him, Rory would have sent Conor sprawling across the room with the back of his hand.

"So you'd not to France with your brother an' Maggie, eh, lad?" O'Higgin said.

"No, sir."

"An' what would ye do then—join the battle?"

"Aye, Dermott, I would," Conor said to the red-bearded bailiff before turning back to The O'Hara. "Father, would you have me to France and learn foppish ways when rebellion is everywhere in my land?"

At the sight of his son's pleading eyes and upright military stance, O'Hara's anger quickly cooled and it was replaced with a tinge of pride. "Lad, you've learned well the use of a sword and the pace of a good horse. I've been to the hunt with you and I know you can shoot. But there's more you must know."

Conor cocked his head of rust-colored curls and narrowed his eyes. "When there's rebellion in the land, what else is there to know?"

"Conor, damme if I won't—" Aileen advanced, one arm raised threateningly, only to be stopped by a look from her husband.

"Enough, my love. Leave us for a moment, for we'd have some man talk, eh, Conor?"

"Aye, m'lord," the lad agreed, giving his mother a smug look.

. Aileen threw her hands in the air and with a muttered curse stalked from the room, slamming the heavy oak door behind her.

"Now, lad," O'Hara said, turning his attention to Conor as O'Higgin returned to his chair and pipe. "Methinks rebellion is a loosely used word these days. What means it to you?"

"It means there'll be no more taxes and tithes paid to a foreign king."

"Good. It does mean that—if we win."

"We're bound to win!" Conor said, puffing out his chest. "We're Irishmen, and O'Higgin says the Irish are the fiercest fighters in the world!"

O'Higgin scratched at his beard to hide his grin. "That we are, lad. So, let us say we win. What then when peace comes to Eire?"

For a moment, Conor's cockiness left him and a puzzled frown creased his impish face. "Why, we'll rule ourselves . . . won't we?"

"We'll try," O'Hara replied. "And that will take statesmen, diplomats, politicians—and thinkers. That's why we're sending you to France, lad. There, you and Brian will get the schooling you'll need to run

Ballylee and Ireland. And your cousin Maggie will
learn to be a great lady.''

Conor thought for a moment and then smiled win-
ningly at his father. "Aye, you're right, father. But
first the war must be won or there'll be no Eire for
the politicians to run. Let Brian do the running after
I've won the war.''

O'Hara shook his head at his son's half-adult,
half-childish reasoning. Then he tried another approach. "I'll agree that you and Brian are destined
for different paths and that a fine politician your
brother might make. But think you not that a while
in France would also make you a better soldier?''

Conor shrugged. "Mayhap," he replied, and then
stepped closer to his father, his face all seriousness.
"But I'm fair scared, sir, that this damnable war will
end before I'm grown into a steel-mesh doublet.
Don't you see, sir? Then I'd miss it all!''

O'Hara's dark eyes rolled upward in exasperation.
Then he looked to O'Higgin for support. The bailiff
rarely smiled, but O'Hara could see that the old man
could now hardly suppress a burst of laughter.

"I know that it will be some time before I can go
into actual battle," Conor continued, clasping his
hands behind his back as he paced before the two
men. "But there's still much that I can do. There's
horses and tack to be seen to, steel mesh to be
repaired. Your boots, sir, will need a daily polish, as
will the rest of your leather. Why, I'm only a boy,
but with my size I can go from army to army with
messages undetected. . . .''

While Conor reiterated the myriad things he could
do for the cause, O'Higgin and O'Hara exchanged another wide-eyed look. It was obvious that the boy had
planned for days the speech he was now delivering.

And as he listened, Rory felt a lump rise in his
throat. Probably Shane O'Hara had felt the same

when, as a boy, Rory had handed up his broadsword
and told the old warrior not to fear. He would protect
the women and Ballylee in Shane's absence. How
could a father not feel pride in such a son?

But education was not the only aspect that prompted O'Hara's decision to send the children and Maura
to France. Above everything else, he had been thinking of their safety, for he knew that this rebellion was
far from won and that the bloody times were just beginning. It would be but a matter of time before the
fighting moved west. Before that happened he wanted
the younger members of the clan well away. Win or
lose, O'Hara wanted his sons to survive.

"So, lad, you'd be a man before your time would
ye? Good. So be it!"

O'Higgin's words caught Rory's attention, rousing
him from his reverie. Conor was grinning at him, his
deep-blue eyes clear with the hope and promise that he
had won the day.

Rory was about to end the parlay with a command
that Conor would do as he was told, when O'Higgin's
eye caught his with a look of mischief.

"Like true Irishmen, let's drink on it." From a
goatskin that O'Higgin kept constantly at his side, he
poured three cups of harsh Irish uisquebaugh. He
handed one to Conor and one to O'Hara, then raised
his own.

"To the men of Ireland!" he toasted.

"Aye!" O'Hara said, and drank, his eye on Conor
over the rim of his cup.

The boy's lips trembled as he eyed the cup's contents. It was a potent brew, and the rising fumes alone
were enough to bring tears to his eyes.

"Well, lad?"

Conor's youthful jaw clenched and his spine stiffened. "To the men of Ireland!" he repeated, then
quickly emptied his cup.

His face immediately drained of color and his eyes
grew round. Both men could see that he was burning
inside, clear to his toes. But to the boy's credit he
stood his ground, determination flashing from his
eyes.

The cup had barely left his lips when it was full
again.

"God save Ireland!" O'Hara cried.

"Aye," Conor said, his voice hoarse. "God save
Ireland." He drank again, and sank to a sitting position on the floor.

"God save Ballylee!"

"Aye." This time Conor's voice was barely audible. He put out a hand to steady himself and couldn't
find the floor.

Two toasts later, O'Higgin gathered the boy in his
arms and delivered him to Aileen.

"The lad will be sick for a few days, but 'twill be a
while before he fancies to do battle again."

July 1642

CHAPTER TEN
LOUGH SWILLY, IRELAND

AGAINST THE PALE SKY the mountains were as sullen as
the misty waters of Lough Swilly were ominous. Few
sounds beyond the crying of swooping curlews and the
jangling of harness could be heard in the still dawn air.

In twos they rode, with Patrick and The O'Hara
taking the lead. In back of them were the O'Hara
sons, Brian and Conor, with Maura, Maggie and forty
heavily armed cavalrymen bringing up the rear.

It had been two hours since the party had left the
main force of the O'Hara clan. Three hundred strong,
they were camped in the hills below Portsalon, there to
wait while The O'Hara welcomed his cousin, Owen

Roe, The O'Neill, back to Eire. By nightfall the
O'Hara force would have merged with Owen Roe's
Flanders army, and on the morrow both forces would
march to join Phelim O'Neill.

"'Twill soon be rain," Patrick said, raising his
head and smelling the air.

"Aye," O'Hara replied, grinning. "'Twill be a fit
homecoming for The O'Neill—a drenching the moment he touches Irish soil after so many years."

The trees thinned as they neared the lough and by
the time their horses' hooves found the sandy shore,
the heavy mist before them was sweeping out to sea.

Try as she might to control it, Maggie could not stop
the panic that made her heart pound violently and
threatened the tears to well from her eyes. Soon she
would be in a strange country, surrounded by strange
people. Could she fashion her ways to those of the
French? She could nearly speak the language, but the
sound of it—even when flawlessly spoken and perfectly accented by Shanna and Aileen—grated on her ears.

Choking down the bile that kept rising in her throat,
she gazed anxiously across the lough, then to the
strong backs of The O'Hara and Patrick and lastly to
Maura, who rode beside her.

The older girl smiled with encouragement at her
cousin. "Think of what we do and where we go as a
new adventure, lass. We'll have a grand time!"

"I know, you've often told me. But still I can only
think of how lonely I will be, how I will miss the walls
of Ballylee."

Maura reached over and clasped the younger girl's
hand. "Neither of us will be lonely, sweet Maggie, as
long as we're together. And mark me, together we will
be."

Maura's touch, her words and the warmth of her
smile did little to comfort Maggie but she managed a
wan smile in return.

The two cousins had grown as close as sisters after Donal's death. They had consoled each other in their mutual grief until now they were inseparable, dependent on one another's comforting words and kinship.

In repose, Maura's eyes still bore a haunted, vacant quality. Maggie could see this, and even though she was ten years and better Maura's junior, she knew how to bring her sister-in-law out of her melancholy mood.

"Perhaps," Maggie said, squeezing Maura's hand, "you will convince me enough that what we do is wise so that I can convince Conor."

This brought an ironic chuckle from Maura. "On that I hope, for the young scalawag will be impossible to handle in France otherwise!"

A few paces in front of the women, Brian rode half standing in his stirrups. His heart thumped in his chest and his eyes peered anxiously through the lough's misty veil, trying to spot the French ships. "I think I see a sail. There, Conor— Aye, 'tis a sail...and there's another!"

Conor kept his eyes well down. Glumly he studied the curve of his horse's neck. His thoughts were not of ships or France, but of Ireland and a means whereby he could remain within its green shores.

OWEN ROE O'NEILL WAS THE FIRST to step from the longboat's narrow bow and splash through shallow water to shore. Reaching the sand, he unlaced his cloak and let it drop from his shoulders to reveal the O'Neill crest emblazoned across his doublet.

"Praise God," he breathed. "The Red Hand of Ulster has returned to Ireland's shores."

He was tall, almost spare, yet his arms and legs were rangy and heavily muscled. His face was craggy and unusually sallow for a soldier who had spent most of his days out of doors. During one of the many battles

his nose had been broken. It was crooked and somewhat off-centered and together with the way in which
his jet black eyebrows met in a straight line over his
dark eyes, his face had a sinister cast.

He approached The O'Hara with solemn dignity,
an almost fierce scowl on his hollow-cheeked face.
"Hola, cousin."

"An' hola to ye, Owen," O'Hara replied, his hand
dropping heavily on the other's shoulder as O'Neill's
dropped on his in greeting.

"Years it's been . . . a lifetime."

"Aye. Welcome back to the land of your clan."

O'Neill nodded solemnly, and then a wide grin
transfigured his face. "You bloody bastard, word has
it that you're one of the richest men in Ireland!"

His words were followed by a roar of laughter that
O'Hara quickly matched in his own rumbling bass.
"Aye, an' a damn good thing I am. How else could I
give you an army to march you to glory!"

"*Merde*, cousin," O'Neill cried, punctuating his
words with another hearty laugh. "You merely sent
for me so I could save your damnable wealth!"

"A lie that is! You've just run out of English to kill
in Flanders, and would seek new blood in Ireland!"

Done with mutual insults, the two came together in
a crushing embrace that would have broken the backs
of ordinary men, and the pounding they gave each
other with gauntleted hands resounded across the
lough.

"And who might this be, this lad whose face scowls
but his eyes laugh?"

As O'Hara introduced Patrick, the frowning scowl
returned to Owen Roe's face. "Talbot, eh? A Scot?"

O'Hara quickly explained Patrick's status, and the
grin returned.

"Good, good!" O'Neill cried, embracing the young
man. "I'm glad our swords are on the same side of this
war, Patrick O'Hara Talbot. With a screaming Scot

on my left and my beefy cousin on my right, I'll have no fear of taking a bloody English dagger in my back!''

He met and advised the boys, Brian and Conor. Spying Maggie, he swept the young girl up to his great height and gave her a hearty kiss. ''Ah, you're a bonny lass, you are. Hurry an' grow, girl, for I've four sons who need a good Irish wife!''

Maura he embraced gently. When he spoke, his voice was as soothing as the coo of a dove. ''Lay your grief to the side, lass, as so many before you have had to do. For grief will not return your O'Hara. But know in your heart that his name will be remembered.''

And then he was gone, shouting his orders to the multitudes of battle-dressed men landing from the boats. It took nearly two hours to unload all the men and equipment, but at last the task was completed and it was time for the younger members of the O'Hara clan to leave.

''You care for Maggie and watch over her, you hear?'' O'Hara demanded sternly of his sons.

''Aye, sir,'' Brian replied.

Conor nodded.

Having received their promise, O'Hara wrapped both boys and Maggie in his powerful arms and kissed each of them in turn.

''Know that I love you, little ones,'' he murmured, ''and will pray for the day when I can hold you like this again.''

A short distance away, Patrick embraced his sister.

''Pray take care, brother,'' Maura said, unable to hold back her tears. ''For to lose you, too, will be my end, I swear.''

Patrick flashed her his raffish smile and kissed her on both cheeks. ''Not to fear, sister of mine, for I do love life too much not to live it all.''

Both Patrick and The O'Hara stood on the sandy

shore until the small boats were hoisted aboard the larger vessels.

"Comes the rain, cousins," O'Neill said at Rory's shoulder. "We'd best be inland."

THE TRUNKS WERE STORED. Maura had gone on deck for a last look at the shore. Maggie was about to join her when Brian burst through the door connecting the two cabins.

"Maggie, Maggie, you must stop him!"

"What? Stop who?"

"Me," Conor said, stepping across the threshhold.

He was bootless and naked to the waist, wearing only a pair of skintight breeches. Two straps ran across his chest and were attached to a canvas sack on his back.

There was a coldness in his blue eyes that Maggie had never seen before and an uncompromising set to his jaw. "What are you going to do, Conor?"

"Leave."

"Aye, we're all leaving," she said, her brow furrowing in puzzlement.

"Nay, Maggie," Brian said, clutching her arm. "He means leave the ship. He would slide down the anchor chain and swim to shore!"

Maggie gasped, her hands flying to her mouth. "Conor . . . what for?"

"To join father," he replied, swaggering to the center of the cabin. "Damme if I'll let this war pass me by!"

Maggie was tempted to laugh, but she bit her lip to hold back her merriment. She had seen Conor in many of these defiant moods and knew they seldom lasted long. In the time she had been growing up with Brian and Conor she had come to love them more as brothers than as distant cousins. She had also come to know them very well and had no doubt that Conor's current declaration was yet another of his many acts of bravado designed to impress both her and his brother.

"I think this much of your swagger, Conor," she declared haughtily. "I'm going on deck now to join Maura." She threw a shawl about her shoulders and made for the door, fully intending to tell Maura about Conor's rashness.

"I'm going, Maggie. I've only waited for Maura to be gone so I could say goodbye."

There was something in his voice, a quality she hadn't heard before, that made her stop and turn to face him. Conor's lip was trembling but there was a flinty gleam in his eyes that spoke more than words.

"You do mean it," she gasped.

"Aye, cousin."

"He does, Maggie!" Brian exclaimed. "An' he threatened to bash me if I told Maura before the ship clears the lough!"

Maggie shifted her gaze back to Conor and suddenly felt her whole body begin to tremble. She didn't want him to go. Not Conor. How would she stand France without him? Who would keep her company when she was lonely or make her laugh at his boyish pranks when her spirits needed lifting? Brian would be with her, it was true, but much as she loved him, he hadn't Conor's ability to cheer her when she was unhappy.

Suddenly the trembling of her lips matched that of her body and she began to weep. "No, no, Conor!" she wailed. "You can't leave us— You can't leave me! I'll not to France without you!"

Conor stepped toward her and folded his strong young arms around her, holding her close. "Don't cry, Maggie. When you return, Ireland will be ours and I'll be a great hero. You'll see. 'Twill be just as before. The three of us will be together. We'll run and ride in the heather; we'll swim in the lough. 'Twill be better than ever, and you'll both be proud of me."

"Nay, Conor . . . please," Brian moaned.

"I must, brother. Take care of our Maggie."

Through the mist that covered her eyes, Maggie could see that Brian, too, was crying. She could see tears welling from Conor's eyes also, but that was the only sign of emotion. The rest of his face was a mask of determination.

"No!" she cried, throwing her arms around his neck and refusing to let go. "I've lost one brother; I'll not lose another!"

Conor's grip was like steel on her wrists. Then he released her arms, bent forward and kissed her on each check. "I love you, Maggie-o," he said, moving away from her to give Brian a bear hug. "I love you, too, brother, an' if you love me in return, you'll not deny me this."

"Damn you for a fool, Conor!" exclaimed Maggie, knowing that there was nothing she could now say to stop him and angered by it. "I hope The O'Hara lashes your backside so hard you can't sit for a week!"

Conor grinned, giving a semblance of the carefree smile she had come to know so well. "I wager he will, but there's naught he can do once the ship has sailed. Do I have your word— Not a sign to Maura 'til the ship clears the lough and is to sea? Maggie?"

She swallowed and averted her eyes. "Aye," she whispered.

"Brian?"

"Don't I always do what you say?"

"Good lad." Conor made for the door and then turned back one last time. "God grant you good wind going and an even better one when you return."

"God save you, Conor," Brian managed to gasp.

Maggie's heart was in her throat. She couldn't speak.

And then he was gone, padding quietly along the

narrow passageway. Moments later he slid down the anchor chain and into the lough's chilly water.

THE OUTRIDERS CHEERED when they saw the Red Hand of Ulster emblazoned across Owen Roe's doublet. With a wave O'Neill acknowledged them and rode on, his ear attentive to O'Hara's voice beside him.

By the time they reached a break in the heavy firs and birches that opened to the main camp, Owen Roe knew the position of every friendly and enemy force on Irish soil. He also knew the state of unrest in England and which Irishmen were in disagreement with other Irishmen.

The rain was coming down in heavy sheets now, pounding the purple heather and making the rocky crags rising around them glisten with wet. A large tent had been erected in the center of the camp. Together, O'Hara and O'Neill made their way through cheering men. All around them, faces glowed with determination and eyes were fierce and bright with desire for battle.

"By God, I do believe the spirit of my uncle, Hugh O'Neill, does live on," Owen Roe muttered, his eyes growing watery as he accepted the idolatry shown him.

"Aye," O'Hara replied, "believe that it does, for it lives on in you, cousin."

At last they reached the tent and passed their horses on to waiting grooms.

"And now we'll talk and eat and drink, cousin," O'Neill said, clamping his great hands together. "Damme, 'tis been an age since I've whetted my thirst with good Irish whisky!"

They entered the tent, filling it with their commanding presence. Aides took their great cloaks, baldrics and steel-mesh doublets. By the time they seated themselves at a long rough-hewn plank table, noggins of wine and uisquebaugh awaited them.

"I saw no women in the camp, cousin."

"Aye, for the time being I've forbidden them," O'Hara said. "We'll pick up enough on the march east."

O'Neill nodded, wiping his lips and beard with the back of his hand. "Before battle, men need wenches as much as they need this—" he raised his cup "—or food. In Flanders I saw men die happily with the pox."

Food was served, and O'Neill set to it with a vengeance. He ate heartily, stuffing his mouth with hunks of partridge meat and oatcakes. When he could hold no more, he washed the whole down with great gulps of wine.

Several moments went by before he noticed O'Hara watching him in silent amazement. He roared with laugher, "I fear I've been too long in the field, cousin— My manners lack a courtly turn!"

O'Hara shrugged. "And myself, I've probably been too long in the manor. My sword arm will be as rusty as your manners. 'Tis no matter."

"Aye, none at all, for we are The O'Hara and The O'Neill, and a month hence all Ireland will ring with our names!"

O'Hara frowned. "Methinks, cousin, you've not changed from the time we were lads together."

"Nay, not a whit," O'Neill roared, pounding his noggin on the table for more wine. "I've sought trouble and unrest since the time you and I sailed with the earls during the great flight in 1607. I was but seventeen then and three years later a captain with my own regiment."

O'Hara nodded, chewing his lip in thought as he studied the mercurial features before him, features that could become so animated in one second and cruel in the next. His cousin's face was mostly in shadow, but there was illumination enough for

O'Hara to ascertain the arrogance it held. It was a trait the man did not try to hide.

O'Hara was sure that when the time came, Owen Roe would laugh in the face of the devil himself.

"You love it, don't you, Owen—war, I mean?"

"Aye, cousin, I revel in it."

"And you love the glory it brings."

"That, too," O'Neill nodded, again lifting his noggin for more wine. "To war, cousin— For God, glory and ourselves!"

"And our beloved Ireland."

"Aye, for isn't that the greatest prize of all? Why else risk our neck to a stretching? I've always thought 'tis a foolish man who would be hanged for only a slice and be forgotten when he could have reached for the whole pie and made history."

"Your pardon, m'lords...."

"Ah, Talbot," O'Neill roared. "Sit, fill your gullet with us!"

Patrick made no reply nor did he move. His gray eyes were filled with alarm, his gaze fixed directly on O'Hara.

"What is it, lad?"

The young man snapped his fingers and gestured toward the entrance to the tent. Through it stepped two soldiers, holding between them a struggling Conor O'Hara.

"We found him hiding in one of the food wagons," Patrick explained.

The sight of his young son made O'Hara flush deeply with anger. "Damme!" he thundered, raising a massive arm as he went for Conor.

Before the blow could land O'Neill caught his wrist. "Hold a moment, O'Hara," he said, and turned to the trembling Conor. "You've jumped ship then, lad."

"Aye, sir."

"And you've a reason for it?"

"I'd join the army."

"B'gar!" O'Neill cried, turning to a red-faced, furious O'Hara. "He'd join the army, he would!"

"He'll to Ballylee," O'Hara growled, "until there's another ship for France."

"And what do you say to that, lad?" Owen Roe asked.

Conor moved closer to his father. Tentatively, he placed a hand on each of the huge man's knees.

"Father, I do love you; I think you know that," he pleaded. "And I don't mean disrespect. But I can't bear to be shuttled off with the women when I know there's others here not much older than me. If you love me, father, you'll let me be with you and Patrick."

Wrath and frustration tore at O'Hara as tears came to his eyes. From the determined look on Conor's youthful face he could see there would be no denying his son's request. If the boy were sent to Ballylee, he would only run and turn up again.

"Sad are the times that make young men so stern before they've reached their prime. Patrick, find the lad some proper clothes. And, Conor...."

"Aye?"

"An army's punishment for disobeying an order is twenty stripes across your back. See that you never do it again."

"Aye, sir," Conor replied, the barest suggestion of an impish grin curving his lips. "I'll not have to."

October 1642

CHAPTER ELEVEN
EDGEHILL, ENGLAND

LIEUTENANT ROBERT HUBBARD had learned to play his part well. Outwardly, in both speech and manners, he had exhibited the Puritans' contempt for the Cavaliers' frills and laces. In time, he knew, he would have his own fine trappings, but in the months prior to the August declaration of war between king and Parliament, it had behooved the young man to ingratiate himself with his fellow officers.

He had cut his hair short in the fashion of the Roundheads, as the Puritans and Parliamentary supporters were called. He had worn black at all times, relieved only by a plain white collar. Often he had gone so far as to wear the ridiculous stiff-crowned cylindrical hat of the Puritans.

On the streets of London, he had entered into the fashionable game of insulting the king's Cavaliers, whose flowing shoulder-length hair and gaily colored plumes set jauntily in rakish, wide-brimmed hats made them easy targets for scorn. In skirmishes with the king's men, Robert had become as fierce as his older brethren.

Even Pym had admitted on two occasions that, in Robert's case, the end had justified the means. By deeds and actions, and the considerable charm Robert could summon when he chose, enmity between the ambitious young officer and the Parliamentary leader had been erased.

At last the day they had all been so anxiously awaiting had come. On the twenty-second of August, 1642, King Charles I had raised his standard at Nottingham and declared war on his Parliament.

Among the Puritan ranks it had been said that it had taken twenty sturdy men to raise the huge royal banner while Charles made the declaration. And it was considered an omen that so fierce had been the wind that day and so unsteady the pole's purchase in the ground that the banner had blown down that same evening.

For more than a month both sides had furiously armed and trained for the day of the first battle.

And now that day had come.

Robert waited on the plain below Edgehill. The snorting horses, the waving banners and the steel-jacketed men around him made his blood run cold and knots tighten in the pit of his belly. He had looked forward to his first opportunity to prove himself in battle, but nothing had prepared him for the tension of the situation in which he now found himself.

His fear and uncertainty must have been apparent on his face, for the one friend he had made since joining Lord Essex's Roundhead army, Thurgood Walker, sidewalked his horse toward Robert's and clamped a gauntleted hand on the young man's shoulder.

"'Tis only the first few moments that are bad, Robert," he assured the young officer. "Once you feel your steel bite the first time, you forget and it all comes natural."

"So I've been told," Robert replied, managing a faint smile.

Born the son of a cobbler, Thurgood Walker had seen a way to better himself by joining the army of Parliament. Like Robert, publicly he professed a keen belief in the Puritan faith. But like so many others of his station he longed to emulate the customs, manners and dress of those born higher than himself—the very aristocrats and Cavaliers he was about to kill.

This desire for better speech and manners had drawn Walker to Robert Hubbard despite the fact that he was eight years Robert's senior. And Robert had abided the man's company, as he did others of his ilk, not because he desired their friendship for its own sake, but because that friendship might one day well prove useful. He had no doubt that Walker's low birth and fighting nature would put the older man in line for rapid promotion and, should that be the case, Robert had every intention of using that promotion to gain one for himself.

"An' there they be!"

Walker's cry brought Robert's gaze up through the sun's slanting rays toward the ridge above them. "Dear God!"

"Aye, a sight, ain't it?"

For as far as the eye could see, the ridge was a seething mass of color. Banners waved in the breeze, and the sky was nearly blotted out by a sea of men and horses.

"'Tis a sight," Walker repeated, "but our numbers match theirs. Believe me, Robert, they're lookin' down here seein' the same thing we're seein'."

"Look there!" Robert cried, pointing with his sword.

A Cavalier all in black sat a full head taller than the others. His helmet was adorned with huge white plumes and his body seemed to merge with the magnificent black animal he rode.

"Aye, 'tis him," Walker hissed. "The devil Rupert himself."

The words had barely been spoken when Prince Rupert of the Rhine, Charles's nephew and appointed General of Horse, turned to face them. Slowly, he raised his right arm and sunlight seemed to form a halo around the gleaming blade of his sword.

From along the massed line of riders, trumpets blared the charge. A cry from five thousand throats quickly drowned out their sound.

"For God, England and the King!" And forward they came like an ocean's cresting wave.

An answering cry sounded from the plain. "For God, Country and Parliament!"

Without realizing he had touched spurs to his mount, Robert found himself hurtling toward the oncoming wall of riders. The two sides met in a thundering head-on charge. The cries of shouted curses and the furious clanging of steel were deafening.

Stilling the knot of fear in his belly, Robert struck

blindly at the nearest rider bearing the king's colors. Neatly he parried the first thrust of the Cavalier's blade and reined his mount around for a second encounter. The man surprised him by coming up under his blade. Managing a quick block, Robert barely avoided being run through. He thrust again, and the hilts of the two swords came together.

Robert found his own sweaty face inches from the prim, mustachioed features of the Cavalier.

"Od's blood, they've mounted an army of boys!" cried the king's man. "Back off, lad, and come over to our side. I've need of a stout lad for a groom!"

The man's sarcasm was all Robert needed. As fear gave way to sudden anger, the wrenching tightness in his belly eased. The eyes that had looked in awe at the mounted cavalry on the ridge only minutes earlier narrowed to dark slits.

Dropping his reins, Robert slid his dirk from its leather sheath. With a grunt he shoved away from his opponent and kneed his mount forward, driving the other back. His blade slashed and thrust mercilessly. Twice he struck his adversary a telling blow, nearly unseating the man.

The look on the Cavalier's aristocratic face changed from one of sardonic humor to that of open fear. Robert's continual rain of blows soon made his opponent careless, and the young man quickly took the advantage by thrusting from below. Sword hilts met once more, but this time Robert held fast and with his left hand struck with the dirk.

The point went true and found its mark just below the Cavalier's chin strap. Without a sound the man fell back, only to be replaced by two others. They, too, met their comrade's fate, and Robert became like a man on fire, killing without thought or emotion.

Time and again the king's men came at him and fell away washed in blood.

And then there were none. Coated with grime and

sweat, Robert reined in his horse and surveyed the carnage around him. A mere ten yards away was Thurgood Walker, in much the same position. There were no more Cavaliers at their end of the field. "We've won our day, Hubbard," Walker gasped, "but I fear the main line doesn't fare as well."

Robert followed the other's gaze. All too quickly he understood. Prince Rupert's well-disciplined horsemen had broken through Parliament's main line, leaving slaughter and unhorsed cavalrymen in their wake.

Rupert's forces were readying for a second charge, of which the outcome was sure to be the same as the first. And when that was done, Rupert would turn his attention to the flanks, where Hubbard and Walker would be directly in his path.

"To the trees, Robert!" urged Walker. "We're near the rear of their lines, but 'tis better to go around a rearguard than to meet the main force head on!"

"Lead on!" Robert roared.

In single file they rode madly from the unprotected plain toward the woods. With the confusion of battle behind him, Robert once again found himself able to think clearly. If he and Walker continued in the direction they were headed, they would skirt far behind the Cavaliers' lines—a dangerous move, for they were sure to meet rearguard troops somewhere in their path.

He looked ahead, to see that the trees were thinning no more than fifty yards before them. "Walker," he called, overtaking the other man. "Hold up!"

"Are you daft, man? Someone was bound to see our retreat."

"All the more reason not to charge across that clearing together. If there's horse or pikeman there, one of us will make it better than two."

"You're sayin' we should split up, then?"

Hubbard nodded solemnly. "You to the left. . . . I'll to the right."

The other man waved. "God be with you, friend."
Walker guided his mount to the left and thundered
off.

"And with you," Robert replied, a faint smile curling his lips. He walked his horse a few steps to the
right, then stopped and listened intently. When the
sound of Walker's mount had subsided to his satisfaction, he turned back and followed Walker, carefully skirting the clearing. He had gone no more than a
few yards when the woods ahead of him erupted with
shouting and the clash of swords. The sound brought
another smile to Robert's lips.

He reined in, still in the shadow of the trees, and
waited. He had no doubt that Walker had run into
several Cavaliers. Minutes later, much to his satisfaction, came the sound of pounding hooves and more
shouting. Five of the king's cavalry emerged from the
right and galloped across the clearing to join the fray.

It was just as he had thought. Charles had set men at
intervals throughout the woods to block any retreat by
Parliamentary troops.

"Better you than me, friend," Robert said, under
his breath, as he turned and skirted the clearing under
cover of the trees. In minutes he was through the gap
left by the second group of soldiers and galloping
along a worn path.

Without warning he burst from the trees into a
clearing. Directly in his path stood a shepherd's hut
with a poorly thatched roof. An old man and two
pikemen stared up at him, evidently too astonished to
move. Robert never gave the pikemen a chance. Lifting his blade, he slashed at the first man, then wheeled
his horse and ran down the second.

Galvanized into action, the old man rushed to the
cottage door, his voice high-pitched from fright.
"Run, Your Highness! Run!"

A dark-faced youth appeared in the doorway.

"Your Highness, you must flee!" the old man babbled.

"Nay, Harvey," the youth replied calmly, brandishing a pistol from his belt. "I fear him not."

He aimed and fired, the ball whistling past Robert's helmet and missing him by no more than an inch. Startled, his mount reared, forelegs pawing the air, and then came down in a charge. Robert raised his sword and sighted along its blade at the boy's chest.

In the brief moment before he would run the lad through, there was sudden recognition. The boy's oddly dark features, his heavy-lidded eyes, the rounded cheeks and the mop of curly black hair. . . .

Hubbard was about to run through the Prince of Wales. Abruptly he reined his mount aside.

"'Tis a pity Dr. Harvey marred my vision, villain," the youth said, thrusting his firm young chin forward. "Kill me now and have done with it."

But Robert simply touched his blade to the front of his helmet and then sheathed it. "Nay, Your Highness. I'm not in this war to kill kings or their heirs."

"I would have killed you."

"Indeed," Robert said, "and I admire your grit for it. How is it the king allows the future Charles II to wander unguarded on the field of battle?"

If it was possible for so swarthy a face to flush, the prince's did so now. "We were separated from our guard."

At that moment, a face appeared behind the prince's shoulder. This time, recognition was instant.

Dear God, Robert thought, *what a coup this would be—Charles, heir to the throne, and his younger brother, James, Duke of York!*

Grasping his brother's hand, Charles stepped from the cottage, his chin still tilted defiantly upward. "I suppose you'll take us prisoners."

"I suppose," Robert replied, "that is what I should

do. But I fear that trying to make my way back to my own lines with so much baggage would be foolhardy."

Amazement spread across the young prince's face. "Good God, man, if you'll not kill us or take us prisoner, what do you propose to do?"

"I'll be bidding you good day, Your Highness," Robert replied, wheeling his horse around.

"Wait! I would know your name!"

"Hubbard, Your Highness, son of—" He stopped. He had almost said, "son of Viscount Poole." But there was no Viscount Poole, and never would be again. "Robert Hubbard."

"Here, Robert Hubbard," Charles said, pulling the crested gauntlet from his right hand and handing it up. "One day you may need a like favor to the one you've shown me."

"Aye, Your Highness," Robert grinned. "I might at that."

Shoving the glove beneath his armor, Robert turned his horse and galloped into the trees.

AROUND THE COMMANDERS' TABLE and the officers' table beside it, tempers flared and arguments raged, but not one man had yet raised his voice to speak the truth. Almost to a man they were calling the day's battle a stalemate. Robert Hubbard knew better.

As the youngest officer and the lowest senior lieutenant, he sat near the end of the lower table. But his position didn't deprive him of even the most hushed conversations, for it also afforded him a full view of each man's face as he spoke.

"Rupert is surely of the devil born. The man should have fallen at least three times. I myself struck him a blow that would have felled a tree."

The speaker was a captain named Henshaw. Hubbard knew him to be a braggart and a coward. Had he come within a sword's length of Rupert, it was more than likely he would be dead.

" 'Tis God who will weld our army together for victory come the next battle."

This from John Hampden, who sat near the head of the commanders' table. Robert could sense that Hampden was far more at home on the floor of Parliament or at a Puritan meeting than on the fringes of battle. Beside him, at the head table, sat the commander of the army, Robert Devereux, Lord Essex. He said little, simply puffing on his pipe and nodding to all that was said, while around him his officers, both senior and junior, lauded the merits of their men in the day's foray.

There was only one exception. Opposite John Hampden sat his cousin, Oliver Cromwell, who said not a word and whose usually florid features darkened more and more with rage the longer the idle and futile talk wore on.

Robert eyed him with interest, remembering the tales told of this man when, two months earlier, war had suddenly become a reality. Of all of Parliament's supporters, Cromwell had been the first to take action. He had moved like a man possessed—as indeed some claimed he was—riding from Westminster to Cambridge and recruiting along the way. Once in Cambridge he had intervened with an armed force to prevent the university from following the example of Oxford University and melting down their precious plate to supply King Charles with money for arms and men. If further proof of his faith in the cause had been needed, he had supplied it by the donation of his own funds to pay and equip a troop of horsemen.

He alone had refused to deceive either himself or his men on the reasons for his country's looming civil war.

Parliament had tried to legitimize its cause by declaring that, in truth, it fought *for* the king, not against him. All its supporters wanted, they claimed, was to save Charles from his foolish advisers.

But Cromwell had told his men the truth. "We fight not for the preservation of the throne, but for the good of the country and the right of free worship. If the king should appear before my pistol in battle, I would shoot him as I would any other man."

As Robert recalled Cromwell's statement, he looked at the officers around him and chuckled to himself. What would the good Master Cromwell say, he thought, if he knew that this very day Robert had spared the two heirs to the Crown of England? Indeed, had not only spared them but had failed to capture them—a deed that might have ended the war before it had really even started.

But ending the war was the last thing Hubbard wanted. Quite the opposite, in fact. He wanted it to last for many months to come.

As he continued to watch, Robert could see Cromwell's rage grow. The muscles of his neck swelled until Robert thought the man's collar would surely burst from the strain. But it was Cromwell's eyes that truly held his attention. Darkly hollow, they emanated a visible gloom that seemed to hang over the men around him. Yet, with the exception of Hubbard, none of them appeared to notice it.

Suddenly Cromwell jumped to his feet and twice crashed the tankard in his hand down on the table.

"Gentlemen!" he called out in his harsh Midlands accent.

No one paid him the slightest attention. Again the tankard rose and fell, with the same result. His face was bright red now and his mouth quivered with fury. "Laggards!" the man thundered and wrested his sword from its scabbard. The flat of the blade came across the table like a crack of thunder, its point narrowly missing John Hampden's shoulder on its descent.

Startled, Hampden jumped in his seat and stared at

the officer in shock. "Oliver!" he cried. "What—"

"I have something to say about this petty talk that threatens to curl my ears!"

All eyes were now on Cromwell, and not a rustle of a sound disturbed the sudden silence.

"I hear you all puff your chests with pride and words—hollow, empty words. I hear you wrangle, bicker and argue over this day's deeds. 'Tis air, all hot air, winded through the seat of your breeches rather than your lips. Never have I seen quarreling dogs win the piece of meat. And, gentlemen, we did not win today. Nay, it was not even a stalemate. It was defeat."

A general murmur of unrest sounded around the table. Cromwell ignored it. Pulling himself up to his full height, he continued in a voice more thunderous than ever.

"There is not one of us—myself included—who is above fault...above sin. But let us not repeat the faults we were guilty of today and commit the gravest sin of all—losing this war!"

"Oliver, I beseech you—" John Hampden stood up, arms outstretched.

"Sit down, John! You are my kin, but you are a bigger fool than the rest of them!"

Mouths opened in shock as Hampden regained his seat, and the silence around the table was like the deathly stillness before a storm.

"Aye, we are right in this war," Cromwell went on. "On that we are all agreed. Our enemies fear us because we are the weapon of the Lord. But I say to you, gentlemen, that their fear will fade when they fathom how blunt is our sword!"

He was sweating now, drops of moisture dripping from his face and chin. "This army we fielded today was indeed a blunt sword." He looked directly at Essex and John Hampden, fire in his eyes. "These, your troops, are most of them old and decayed, serving-men, tapsters and the like. The enemy's troops, on the other hand are gentlemen's sons, young and persons of quality. Do you think that the spirits of base and mean fellows such as ours will ever be able to battle successfully gentlemen that have honor and courage and resolution in them? You must get men of a spirit—and take it not ill what I say—of a spirit and courage that can take them as far as gentlemen can go. Otherwise, I am sure you will be beaten still!''

He was breathing heavily now but was not done. ''We need a new kind of army... an army of men of faith, who fear nothing but God. An army of men who march to the dreams of God! And, gentlemen, one day I will build that army. Mark you, I will!''

A hush followed Cromwell's last words as he turned and stalked away, leaving his sword on the table. Robert Hubbard found himself sitting bolt upright, astounded at Cromwell's speech. Outwardly, little had changed in the man since the last time Robert had seen him. But inwardly, there was a difference. In his tirade against his leaders and fellow officers, his voice had been strident, full of command. He was a man imbued with confidence and lacking in fear, and Robert knew that those two qualities alone could win the day.

Men who fear nothing but God....

It was obvious to Robert that Cromwell intended to go about the conquering of England with single-minded devotion while speaking to his troops with the rhetoric of his God, the wrathful Jehovah. And it was equally obvious, now, where Robert's own path to the future lay.

When others finally came round to Oliver Cromwell's way of thinking, when he was given the permission and funds to recruit and train his new army, Robert Hubbard planned to be one of its first officers.

December 1642

IN THE BAILEY OF CLAYMORE CASTLE, small fires for both cooking and warmth turned night into day. Looking down from the comfort of her room, Elana could see soldiers stamping the courtyard stones and pounding their hands together to ward off the chill. They had arrived two days earlier, with Patrick Talbot at their head. His face had been lined with dust and his hair lay damp on his forehead.

Having barely alighted from his horse, Patrick had whisked her to the privacy of an antechamber and took her roughly into his arms. The smell of leather and horse had assaulted her nostrils, and with a moue of distaste, she had avoided his punishing kiss, turning her face to the side and pushing with all her might against his chest.

"Patrick," she had protested, "let me go!"

"And what will you do if I don't?" he had laughed. "Summon my troops?"

"I might."

"Then shout away so that the whole castle will know my lust for you— Oh, Elana, I need you as I need food and drink," he had declared.

"And for the same reasons, most likely!" she had retorted, tossing her hair. "I have not heard from you. I have seen you twice, briefly, in the past four months...and suddenly you appear and make demands?" she bristled.

His gray eyes had darkened at her reply and he had stepped back. "Pardon, m'lady, I was too much on the move, warring and killing, to write," he had apologized coldly. "But from your letters to me I assumed that I was the man whom you...."

"Well?"

"The one you could not live without!" With that, Patrick had turned on his heel and marched into Claymore's great room, demanding to see the lord of the manor at once.

Elana had followed, hoping she had not gone too far in holding him at bay. In truth, much of her anger had been feigned, for if she were to continue to glean information from Patrick she needed to maintain a hold over him. His lust for her was the one trump card she had. Although she had every intention of using it to its fullest, she had to admit she was finding it more and more difficult to judge when to give and when to deny. And as much as she might try to dismiss the thought, she feared that much of her uncertainty was because her desire for him was almost as great as his for her.

Upon entering the room Patrick had rounded on Lord Claymore immediately.

"M'lord, your defenses for Claymore Castle are in a sorry state of naught!"

Her father had bridled and grown red in the face, but in the end he had agreed with Patrick and blamed the disrepair on a lack of funds. The reason for his shortage of gold he had kept to himself, but Elana knew it only too well. Despite her entreaties for caution, the old fool had been sending regular donations to King Charles.

"M'lord, we go into winter retreat," Patrick had said. "O'Hara returns to Ballylee, O'Neill remains in Tyrone, and I have been assigned to reinforce Claymore."

As his words registered, Elana's heart had skipped several beats. *Dear God,* she had thought, *a whole winter under the same roof with him! Am I not confused enough as it is?*

From Patrick they had learned that in April of that year, Major-General Robert Monro had brought a force of 2,500 Scots Presbyterians to support the

Ulster Protestants against O'Neill's Irish Catholics and on the side of Parliament. To complicate matters further, when Charles had declared war in Nottingham in August, he had appointed Lord Ormonde commander of his forces in Ireland; under Ormonde a second Protestant, but this time royalist, army had been formed. Seesaw battles had been waged throughout the fall with large losses on all sides.

Patrick had also had the latest news from England. Prince Rupert and his Cavaliers were defeating the Parliament forces under Essex at every turn.

When Patrick had finished, Elana had barely been able to hold her tongue or her composure. Had she been backing the wrong horse?

All the hours she had spent listening to Sir John Redding's smooth and slippery tongue had convinced her that in the end Parliament would win England's civil war. But now she wasn't so sure.

John Redding, she knew, played a dangerous game. As nephew to both Lord Gormanston and General Thomas Preston, who was commander of the Old English Catholic forces in Leinster, Redding had constant access to Catholic troop strength and movement. What information he couldn't glean from his kin, he had been able to obtain from Elana and pass on to Parliament supporters.

The tide seemed to have turned against Parliament. Should its forces eventually be defeated, Redding might well be exposed as a spy and executed. Even if he were not found out, he would certainly find himself on the losing side. Either way, Elana greatly feared he would drag her down with him if Charles triumphed over Parliament.

Such were the thoughts that tormented her this night as she continued to peer down at the bailey, searching the faces of each of the heavily cloaked figures for Patrick Talbot.

Since his arrival he had declined every invitation to

sup with her and her father in the comfort of Claymore's dining hall. And she knew from the servants that he had also spurned the chamber given to him beneath the castle roof, choosing instead to sleep in the open bailey with his men. She would have liked to have been able to believe that his rejection of their hospitality was due to a fit of pique at her; that as a lover he had been hurt by her rejection of his initial effort at reconciliation. But of this she couldn't be sure.

Was she losing her control over him, she wondered. She had seen him only briefly during the past two days, but even in those few moments she had found him changed. He seemed harder, with a cynical flash in his eyes and a sternness in his voice.

Was it only the fighting that had made him so? Or was it because he was beginning to suspect that part of O'Neill's lack of immediate success against the Protestants was some of her doing?

For the first time since the game had begun, Elana Claymore felt a tinge of guilt at what she was doing.

Closing the shutters, she cast a nervous glance at the gold clock near her bed. *Near eleven o'clock,* she thought. It appeared as if Patrick intended to decline the summons she had sent earlier that evening.

One by one she snuffed the wall-sconced candles and moved toward the fire. The bedchamber was warm and cozy, lighted softly only by the dancing flames of the fire and by two tapers that burned on her dressing table. Outside, she could hear the wind blowing fiercely down from the north. It made her wrap her fur-lined velvet robe tighter around her legs.

The fool, she thought, scenting a brush with musk and bringing it to her hair. It was insanity to sleep in the cold wind beneath chill skies when a warm bed and chamber awaited.

She loosened her chignon and felt the satin softness of her hair fall across her shoulders and down her back. She had just begun to pull the brush through the luxurious thickness of her tresses when a light tap sounded at the door.

'Tis he, she thought, elation filling her breast. She struggled from the heavy robe and, in passing the bed, reached for her light overgown. She had barely touched the delicate fabric when a languid smile crossed her lips.

Her sheer nightdress was of a filmy midnight-blue silk. Its false sky-blue stomacher gathered beneath her breasts, making their rounded fullness swell above the lace of her bodice. Elana hesitated, then left the overgown where it was and stepped to the door. Carefully she opened it a crack and was about to speak Patrick's name when she realized there was no one there.

"Good evening, m'lady," came a voice from below.

Startled, she looked down. A stocky lad of ten or so with a mop of rust-colored curls grinned impishly at her.

"Who are you?" she demanded.

"Conor," replied the young man matter-of-factly.

"Conor *who*?" she asked, tapping her foot impatiently.

"Conor O'Hara, m'lady. A message for you."

Elana took the folded piece of paper and let the door swing wide as she backed into the room to read it.

My dear Lady, This is to acknowledge your most kind invitation tendered earlier this evening. These past two nights of dicing have sorely depleted my purse, and I hope this night to make amends.

Mayhap another evening.

Your obedient servant, Patrick Talbot

"Damn him!" she cried aloud. "Dicing! He would rather spend the evening dicing than with me!"

"My cousin said I should wait for your answer."

In her sudden anger Elana had completely forgotten the lad. At the sound of his voice, however, she looked up to find that he had taken a few steps into the room. Abruptly she realized that the boy's blue eyes were calmly appraising her.

"What are you looking at?" she demanded.

"You, m'lady," the boy replied calmly. "You are very beautiful and a fine figure of a woman."

"Get out of here!" she ordered, her anger rapidly approaching epic proportions.

The boy shrugged and went to the door. Then he paused and turned back, boldness once more shining in his youthful eyes. "I take it there's no answer?"

"Aye, there is!" Elana cried, feeling a blush suffuse her cheeks. "Tell the bloody bastard to go to hell!"

"I'll do that, m'lady," Conor said, grinning widely. "But he'll be devilish mad at me cursin'. He says 'tis not gentlemanly, Patrick does."

Elana could stand no more. With a shriek of blind fury, she sprang for the door reaching it in a single bound. With all her might she slammed it shut behind him, then fell heavily against it.

"Damn him, damn him, damn him!"

She folded her arms and cursed again when she felt their tender ache. For it was only then she realized how much her body had been yearning for Patrick Talbot that night.

THE NEXT MORNING Elana's ire had cooled enough to let her common sense prevail. Seated on a damask stool before her mirror, she painstakingly rouged her cheeks and applied color to her lips and eyes.

Her hair took longer than expected. The oafish

Irish maid had to be directed practically strand by strand. With clenched teeth, Elana endured the girl's awkward tugging and pulling until at last her head was a dark brown splendor of cascading ringlets with puffs at her temples and an underswept chignon at the nape of her neck.

From her wardrobe she chose a narrow-sleeved green velvet gown that made jewels of her eyes. The cut emphasized her tiny waist as well as the womanly swell of her hips. By the time she had draped a fur-lined pelisse of crushed velvet about her shoulders and descended to the bailey, she was in high spirits. Not a trace of the previous night's anger remained on her beautiful face.

The first two men she tried to engage in conversation spoke nothing but infernal Gaelic. It was some time before she finally spotted a man in the O'Hara colors who looked more like an officer and soldier. She approached him with her seemingly idle inquiry.

"Nay, m'lady," he answered in heavily accented English. "Talbot went off early this morning to Ballylee to deliver the young O'Hara."

That would be last night's messenger, Elana thought, a slight flush darkening her already blushed cheeks at the memory of the boy's brazen appraisal of her, as though he had considered her little more than some Irish camp follower. "And when that is done?"

The soldier shrugged. "He'll return."

"And when will that be?" she demanded, her anger beginning to rise again at the man's offhand manner.

"A fortnight, if the weather be good."

Elana barely managed to contain her rage. He had planned as much, she thought furiously. *The bastard planned to humiliate me, planned to have me come searching him out, when all the time he would be gone!*

She needed something other than an ill-spoken

O'Hara kern on which to vent her anger. "Have a horse saddled," she commanded abruptly. "I will change and ride."

"Aye, m'lady, I'll ready an escort."

"Escort?"

"'Tis The Talbot's orders. No one is to leave the castle without an escort."

"Damn The Talbot's orders!" she cried. "This is Claymore Castle, these are Claymore lands. I am a Claymore. I will ride where I please, when I please and with whom I please. And this day I please to ride alone!"

"I have my orders, m'lady," insisted the man.

"Damn your orders— Saddle my horse!" Lifting her skirts and cloak, she marched back into the castle with as much dignity as she could muster.

A half hour later she returned to the bailey. The same cloak was draped about her shoulders, but now she wore a matching green dress cut and gathered for riding and knee-length boots instead of slippers.

With the hood of the pelisse up and her head bent against the chill wind, she stalked across the bailey to the postern gate. There she found her mare, saddled and standing amid six riders, all bearing the O'Hara crest. Holding the bridle of her horse was the officer she had spoken to a half hour earlier.

"What is the meaning of this?" she cried.

"I have my orders, m'lady."

Elana took a deep breath in an effort to control her ire. "As I said before, damn your orders!"

"There are English patrols about."

"*I* am English!" she hissed from between clenched teeth.

"I know, m'lady." He made no effort to disguise the sarcasm and distaste in his voice.

Elana's fury was such that had she held a knife in her hand, she would have thrust it at his throat; if a gun, she would have shot him in the heart.

"What is your name?" she demanded.

"MacQuinlan, m'lady. . . Captain MacQuinlan."

"Well, Captain MacQuinlan, you'll be a sergeant come the fortnight."

He raised his head, and Elana suddenly realized that his downward-directed gaze had had nothing to do with respect for her station. Indeed, far from it, for to her humiliation, she saw that it had merely hidden the smile plastered across his broad features.

For the second time that day she marched back through the great room of Claymore and up the wide stone stairs. But this time she did not turn toward her own quarters. Circling the wide balcony, instead she entered her father's study without bothering to knock.

"Are we to be prisoners in our own house?" she queried abruptly.

Her father looked up from his desk and took in his daughter's agitation with bored, tired eyes.

"Prisoners. . .?"

Elana hastened to fill him in on every humiliating detail.

With an audible sigh, Lord Claymore dropped the papers he had been perusing and leaned back in his chair.

"My dear Elana, we are not prisoners," he began, in conciliatory tones. "Though I do not at all times condone Patrick Talbot's manner, I do recognize his intelligence. The security of Claymore is vital to both Ulster and Ballylee. At the same time as O'Hara and Talbot protect themselves, they offer us protection as well. Under the circumstances, I think we should respect the young man's orders and do the best we can."

Elana paced, throwing her proud head in such a way that the curls of her hair seemed to dance with a life of their own. "Then have we come to such straits that it is we, the conquerors, who must abide by the rules of the conquered?"

Exasperation crept into Claymore's weary eyes. "I

would think, Elana, that by now you would consider yourself a part of this land, a part of Claymore—which is, as you well know, a part of Ireland.''

"Yes,'' she replied, in a biting tone, "I do consider Claymore mine. For it was through my mother's wealth and her good station with Queen Anne that you acquired it.''

Lord Claymore's face darkened and his jaw began to quiver with anger. "Were you only slightly younger, I would thrash you for your insolence.''

Elana continued as if he had never spoken. "And as an Englishwoman, I resent being ordered about and virtually imprisoned by an Irish peasant. *I* have some pride left, dear father, even if you do not. Loss of pride is too high a price to pay, even for what you call security!''

Claymore came to his feet like a shot. "Madam!'' he thundered, and pounded the desk in front of him. "I think you know the price of everything and the value of nothing. And as for taking orders from an Irish peasant, I notice that when he visits you at night you accept a great deal more than his orders!''

Elana gasped. Her hands smoothed at her skirt to cover her sudden nervousness. *Servants,* she thought. *Those damnable, nosy, gossipy, Irish servants!*

Before she had a chance to reply, Claymore continued, "I think 'tis long past time we saw to wedding you, Elana.''

"I beg your pardon, father,'' she interjected coolly, "but I must remind you of the agreement we made when you saw fit to order me back from France. I obey you in all things but that. When I marry, 'twill be a man of my choosing. You agreed.''

He nodded, "I did. And your part of the agreement was that you would bring no more scandal upon my name.''

"I don't know what you mean," she cried in a strangled voice as she backed toward the door.

"I think you do, Elana. They are both dangerous men."

His words seemed to clutch at her throat. *Redding,* she thought in dismay. *Dear God, he couldn't know! We've been too careful, too discreet....*

But a nervous glance at her father's face told her that he did, indeed, know about John Redding. Did he also know, she wondered, that their relationship was more than an affair?

"If you mean John Redding," she said carefully, "he has been merely a friend. I do need *some* friends of quality in this godforsaken place. And after all, he is Gormanston's nephew."

Claymore sighed and dropped back into his chair. "That he is.... My dear Elana, early on I realized that you were your mother's daughter...both a reward and a torment. Even when you were a child I think I saw that one day your great beauty would be a curse. But a word of wisdom to you, daughter. Do not play these two men against each other. For in the end, you will be the sufferer."

With an inner sigh of relief, Elana closed her eyes and felt the tension leave her body. So her father didn't know. He considered John Redding merely a lover.

There was a moment of silence before she was suddenly struck by another, more alarming prospect. *Patrick,* she thought, *if he should ever suspect....*

"Father?"

"Aye."

"You won't mention...to Patrick, I mean... about Sir John?" Glancing quickly at her father, she saw the pain that crossed his face before he dropped his head in his hands. But she cared little for his torment. It was his answer she was concerned with, and she awaited it eagerly.

"Nay," he said at last, sighing heavily. "I won't reveal your amorous adventures to Talbot. But I tell you this, girl: you must choose. If it is to be one of them, decide—and do it quickly, for I fear your rashness could one day bring them together. If it does, a wedge could be driven into this thin alliance we have with the Irish that would ruin us all."

Smiling, Elana left the room. She was still safe. And now, commanding herself to ignore her unruly heart and return her actions to the cold, hard logic of her mind, she had every intention of regaining Patrick's devotion once and for all.

ELANA SWALLOWED THE BITTER PILL of being escorted on her rides. But even with the battle-dressed men following at a discreet distance, she had to admit she enjoyed the outings. The winter winds were invigorating as they tugged at her *chaperon* and filled her lungs with fresh, clean air. Somehow, her mind seemed to clear the instant she reached the freedom of the heath.

Daily she rode, extending the distance a little farther each time, always in the same direction, planning to lull her damned escort into boredom as they traversed the same terrain over and over again.

On the day scheduled for Patrick's return from Ballylee, she headed in the usual direction. Alternately she cantered and trotted her mare, putting more and more distance between herself and The O'Hara's soldiers. When she judged she was barely in their sight, she spurred her mount up and over a series of ridges. Now hidden from them completely, she broke the horse into a gallop. Without slowing her pace, she entered a long stand of birch and wove her way toward an even larger stand of oaks.

In the distance she could hear confusion and then pounding hooves. She laughed aloud, and the bell-like tones joined the keening of the wind in the trees.

Near a stream she found an unusually dense stand of trees. So close together had they grown that day was like night beneath the arbor of their branches. It was here that she sat, calmly patting the mare's neck and listening as her erstwhile guards crashed through the trees all around her. They were closer now, and it was all she could do to refrain from revealing her presence by laughing once more at their curses and bumbling attempts to find her.

She knew well the road Patrick and his entourage would take from Ballylee. If she had judged correctly, she would meet him shortly after midday. She relished the look she imagined would appear on his face when suddenly she emerged, *sans* his wretched escort, to meet him sweetly on his return.

She hoped her actions would make two things abundantly clear to him. First and foremost, she was neither to be trifled with nor ordered about. But she also hoped that by riding out to meet him on a cold December day, she would show him she cared about him and sincerely wanted to dispel the ill will that had grown between them.

She waited nearly an hour. When she was sure all six of her pursuers had ridden off in various directions, she forded the small stream and followed it toward its source in the distant mountains.

She had no need to travel the full distance. Less than an hour later, she spotted horses and men grouped in a meadow across the stream from a small, thatched cottage.

She was about to ride into their midst when a horse tethered near the cottage caught her attention. Cautiously she urged the mare along a rim of rocks that would shield her progress from the larger group of men. When she was directly behind and above the cottage, she halted and slipped to the ground. Gathering her cloak in front of her to ward off the damp chill of the rocks, she stretched across a ledge and looked out.

No doubt remained in her mind. The large chestnut stallion was Patrick's own mount.

But why, she wondered, had they stopped here in the open for a midday meal when Claymore was such a short ride away? More to the point, why had Patrick left his men?

Vaguely, Elana remembered the grouse-faced old man reeking of whisky, the raw-boned girl and the clutch of brats that lived in the cottage. She had ridden this way several times but couldn't recall their names. But then, she thought, why would she? She was hardly in the habit of inquiring after the names of her father's peasants. They were chattels who did the lower forms of work on the land, caring for the smelly sheep and the endlessly bawling cows.

What on earth, she wondered, *could interest Patrick in this place?*

Losing interest in the scene below her, Elana was about to get up when her body seemed suddenly turned to stone.

Around the side of the cottage came Patrick, arm in arm with a tall, raven-haired girl. She turned and spoke to him, and as Patrick's handsome head rolled back, the crisp air was filled with the sound of his robust laughter. Elana gasped as he picked the girl up by the waist and gaily whirled her in a circle. When he returned her to the ground, he leaned forward and brushed the tip of her nose with his lips.

Elana waited to see no more. Rising to her feet and using a low rock as a mounting block, she gained the saddle and galloped the mare into a froth as she rode for Claymore.

The stinging wind brought tears of anger and frustration to her eyes. Never had it occurred to her that Patrick's sudden independence from her charms might be caused by another woman. But surely not, she thought. Not by that peasant, anyway, who dressed in dun-colored ragged clothes and whose hair was a wild tangled mane that hadn't seen a brush in weeks. Not by an unkempt field laborer who looked more like a rangy horse than a woman!

But as she galloped furiously toward Claymore, Elana recalled how Patrick had taken her in his arms and kissed her. Suddenly she wasn't so sure that the girl wasn't her rival for Patrick's devotion after all.

But she vowed that in the days ahead, she would see to it.

THE BATH WATER WAS wonderfully warm. It caressed her skin like liquid silk and eased at least a portion of the worry on her mind. For by the time she had reached Claymore, Elana had been truly alarmed.

The last thing she could afford now was a loss of control over Patrick Talbot. Her value to Dublin and John Redding still needed bolstering by the information she could glean about the Irish forces. And as much as she hated to have to admit it, she had missed the animallike power of his body in her bed. But above all, her pride had been wounded. Elana Claymore was not in the habit of losing lovers to other women, least of all to peasant wenches. If there was any losing to be done, she would be the one to cast aside the man, never the other way about.

As she had lowered her body into the water, she had spied its nude perfection in her dressing-table mirror. Her skin was creamy peach, and the sight of her lush hips and long tapered legs had helped to ease her worry further. "Nay," she had said aloud, her sensuous lips curving in a satisfied smile, "no gangling horse of a girl can match me!"

Now as she worked the lather in her hair into a creamy richness, she remembered her father's words.

"...your great beauty will one day be a curse."

Nay, father, she thought, *my great beauty will one day be my fortune!*

The lilac-scented lather turned her thick tresses a foamy white and cascaded down across her face and over her shoulders. Giving up on her maid, who had disappeared to fetch more clean towels, she was about to dip her head in the water for a rinse, when she heard the click of the latch on the door.

"'Tis about time you were back, you lazy girl!" she cried. "Be quick with the bucket and rinse this. 'Tis beginning to burn my eyes!"

She heard footsteps and then the creak of leather as the bucket was picked from the stand beside the tub.

"Damn you!" she shrieked, when the water was poured over her in one great torrent. Barely had she caught her breath when yet another bucketful was unceremoniously dumped over her head. "Girl, would you drown me with your stupidity?" she raged. "Quickly, a towel!"

Using the sides of the tub, Elana pulled herself to her feet. Vigorously she rubbed the towel over the front of her head and then dabbed the water from her eyes.

"Well, girl, do my back before— *You!*"

Across the room, leaning negligently against the wall, was Patrick Talbot. Casually, he filled a goblet with brandy from a crystal decanter on a nearby table and turned to gaze lazily at Elana's nude body.

Almost crimson with embarrassment, she fumbled with the towel and cursed when it fell from her hands. In an effort to maintain some semblance of dignity, she tried to cover her nakedness with her arms.

"What are you doing in my—" she began.

"Rinsing you," he interrupted calmly, giving her no chance to finish her question. With catlike grace, he moved toward her, his stride easy and controlled.

For a moment she thought he was reaching for her, but instead he bent and retrieved the towel. As he pressed it into her fumbling hand, he saluted her with the goblet.

"Congratulations on your little escapade today."

Elana swore under her breath. Again he had taken her unawares, naked and vulnerable. It was not, she recalled in exasperation, the first time his brazen conduct had given him the upper hand.

Her vexation increased considerably when she discovered that the towel was too small to cover her completely. If it hid her breasts, the dark triangle between her thighs was visible. When she lowered it, her nipples protruded above its edge.

Deciding that the latter was the lesser of two evils, she looked up at him defiantly. "My robe," she demanded imperiously. "There, on the bed!"

His gaze drifted idly to the garment and then back to her. The smile on his lips was pure arrogance, but she saw something more dangerous in the cold glare of his eyes. Patrick, she sensed, was in a black mood, and it would take little to set him off.

"There's no need," he said, gesturing at the robe. "I won't be long. I came up here the moment I arrived and was told of your foolish actions."

"'Tis not such a weighty thing that you could not wait until I had finished my bath!" She was outraged, but the dark warning in Patrick's eyes made her voice wary.

"I beg to differ, madam," he returned coldly. "'Tis a very weighty thing. There are Scottish patrols all over Donegal. You would be a prize catch, bringing a great ransom—a ransom, my dear Elana, that your father has not the funds to pay."

Embarrassment at Patrick's insolent gaze began to give way to mirth at his words. If only he knew, she thought, struggling to contain her laughter. How dearly she would have loved to have wiped that smug, arrogant smile from his face by telling him how little she had to fear from the Scots. They were, after all, hardly likely to remove one of their prime sources of information.

"You find my train of thought amusing?" he queried.

"Somewhat," she replied, stepping from the tub with as much grace as she could muster and moving toward the bed.

"How so?"

"'Twas easy enough to elude your men," she replied pointedly. "I'm sure the Scots would be twice as simple to deceive."

The ghost of a grin curved the corners of Patrick's mouth. "*Touché,* madam," he acknowledged, then paused to drain the contents of the goblet in one swallow. "Nevertheless," he continued, setting the cup aside, "from now on you will not attempt to do again what you did today."

Elana was turned from him. She slipped into her robe, then dropped the towel from beneath it. She heard him move and sensed his nearness. Against her will, she felt waves of sensuous desire flow through her when he lightly touched her arm.

"Do you understand, Elana?" he asked. His voice was soft, but with a faintly menacing quality she found disturbing.

"I understand that you make a prisoner of me in my own house!" she retorted. But her voice lacked its usual bite. She had meant to be angry with him, to demand that he allow her her freedom, but she sensed in him a newfound authority that was beyond her control, and uncertainty prevented her from giving full rein to her anger.

"Not yet," he replied. "But I will, if you disobey my orders again."

"Get out!" she ordered, then quickly bit her lip, wishing she had said something else. An angry command for him to leave was hardly the way to regain his complete devotion.

For once, she was thankful that Patrick ignored her demand and remained where he was.

" 'Tis only your safety I worry about, Elana, believe me," he assured her earnestly. "And if making you a prisoner will keep you safe, then a prisoner you shall be."

Sensing a sudden softening of his attitude, Elana saw her opportunity and seized it. She had been about to belt the robe but now dropped her hands and turned to him. The garment parted as she moved and his gaze lowered at once to linger on the lusty sensuality of her pose.

"Perhaps 'twould be easier to play the prisoner's role if my chambers weren't so lonely through the night," she purred, her voice seductively low and husky.

Almost tentatively, he raised his hand and reached toward her. His fingertips caressed her skin, then traced a line downward between the deep valley of her breasts.

Elana shivered. His touch was like a cool flame slowly branding her, inch by delicious inch.

" 'Tis a pity," he murmured, a sudden weariness in his voice. "This damnable fog that seems to forever lie between us of late. If it would ever recede, mayhap then we could see the truth in each other."

"Perhaps it has receded..." she suggested quietly, as she made to move into his arms.

But Patrick suddenly withdrew his hand and stepped back. "I think not," he said softly. "I sense a war within you, girl. For the life of me I cannot understand it or its cause. You taunt me with your body, you draw me like a moth to the flame with your eyes, but beyond the beauty of your body I know you reject me with your heart."

The slight sound of defeat in his voice, oddly tinged with menace, triggered alarms in Elana's mind. She hastened to reassure him.

"Nay, Patrick..." she declared earnestly. She was about to prove her devotion further by throwing herself into his arms when the door burst open and her maid ran into the room.

"Pardon, m'lady, I'm late—" She stopped abruptly with a gasp of shock at the sight of Patrick. Elana seized her robe and belted it. "Out! Get out!" she cried.

"I'm sorry, m'lady," the girl stammered fearfully. "I didn't know. I—"

"Go!"

The maid needed no further urging. Quickly, thankfully, she fled from the room. In her haste to obey her mistress's command, she left the door ajar and Patrick moved to close it. He paused on the threshold and turned back to face Elana.

Out of the corner of her eye, she could see the turmoil of indecision in his face.

"Patrick...?" she queried tentatively.

"Aye."

"I'll leave my door unlatched tonight."

As Patrick disappeared behind the closing door, his face gave her no hint of an answer.

THE MOON'S SILVERY BEAMS SLANTED through the shutters, joining with the light from the room's single taper to create cool, dancing shadows on the walls. The fire had burned down until it was now only a saffron-hued ember glowing in the hearth.

Elana lay trembling in her bed, clenching and unclenching her fists spasmodically beneath the downfilled satin coverlet. Now and then she would run her palms across her belly and over her naked hips and thighs.

How wanton I am, she thought, with only the slightest tinge of guilt. *Not a shred of an underdress, nothing . . . naked beneath a single coverlet. Naked, waiting and hoping.*

She was sure he would come. His desire for her had shone from his eyes that afternoon when he had devoured the golden splendor of her body in the tub. But, she reminded herself, there had been nothing in his eyes to indicate his feelings when he had departed without a word. His look had been coldly vacant, as if his mind had been far away and occupied with other, more pressing problems.

Twelve o'clock came and passed. "He will come, he will come," she kept repeating to herself.

By one o'clock she was fighting sleep and losing the battle. But even in her drowsy state she was conscious of the ache that had now spread throughout her body.

Dear God, I do want him, she thought, letting her eyelids remain closed at last. *But do I love him?*

How could I, she asked herself with a tinge of bitterness. *I'm not at all sure I know what love is. All I know is that I want him, tonight, here in my bed.* And how could that be love, she wondered, *for I don't know if I will want him tomorrow or the day after or the day after that. I'll need him to be sure, and I'll use him for as long as he fulfills my needs, but the day will surely come when I will want more than Patrick Talbot, more than he can or will offer.*

What a mass of confusion I am, she thought as the drug of sleep pulled her deeper and deeper into its vortex. In her half-sleep she began to toss. She was faintly conscious of a light sheen of perspiration over her body even though the room had grown slightly cool.

The sound of the latch being lifted wafted to her

ears. She heard the door ease open and close gently, but such was the state of her drowsiness, she could not immediately bring herself to query the import of what she was hearing. She sensed rather than heard someone crossing the room, and then the rustle of clothing being removed and discarded reached her ears.

She parted her lips in a smile as the meaning of all the sounds finally combined to pull her back from sleep. As she felt the coverlet being drawn from her naked body, she came fully awake. Opening her eyes, she saw his lean, tall form above her, silhouetted in the candlelight. She was fascinated by the way the muscles of his shoulders and back rippled as he moved closer to her. The red glow from the dying fire and the candlelight lent a coppery sheen to his smooth skin.

Dear God, she thought, *the mere sight of him is heating my blood.*

"Elana...."

Her name spoken so suddenly in the stillness disturbed her, for it was as though she had been gazing at him with another's eyes. "You came," she murmured, absurdly she knew, but just at that moment there seemed little else she could say.

"Aye," he replied, his voice hoarse with the unmistakable huskiness of desire. His gaze roamed over the blush of her body, sweeping downward to the smooth indentation of her waist and over the rounded curve of her hips. "How could I help but be drawn back to you... for no matter the turmoil you cause in me, I cannot deny my need for the vision that is you."

Elana raised her arms as he leaned forward and slowly eased himself into the bed. She took his head in her hands, running her fingers through the unruly mane of his hair. Tenderly she guided his lips to a breast and groaned when she felt his response. Patrick caressed the gentle swell of her belly, then moved his hand upward to cup the fullness of her other breast.

He's mine, she thought, exultantly, her mind thrilling to her victory as her body did to his touch.

Moving his head upward, Patrick sought her lips with his own. She felt her body come alive beneath his touch, drawing her into a whirlpool of sensuousness. Wrapping his powerful arms around her, he crushed her to him almost ruthlessly, until his maleness burned against her thigh and she could feel the pounding of his heart against her breast.

He raised his head to gaze down at her in the dim light. "I would give all the acres that I fight for in Eire if you would be my wife," he whispered huskily.

For one moment in time, Elana almost forgot who and where she was. Never before had she concerned herself with the feelings of the men she had used and then cast aside like so many pieces of worn-out clothing. But such had been the naked appeal in Patrick's voice that she had to struggle to prevent the tears that formed in her eyes from rolling down her cheeks. For the first time in her life she had felt her heart touched by a man, and the knowledge that she was using him simply to satisfy her own selfish desires filled her with a feeling of guilt that was almost more than she could bear.

She was tempted to assuage that guilt by agreeing to his proposal. Nor was she entirely persuaded that it was such a bad notion. Certainly, he was more than experienced enough to satisfy her physical demands. But even as she thought this, she realized he would never be able to please her in any other way. His view of Ireland was heaven on earth, yet if he had all of it, it wouldn't be enough to buy her. How shocked he would be if she were to tell him that if Claymore were hers at that very moment, she would sell every inch of it to the highest bidder and be off this dreadful island an hour later. Nay, she thought, almost sorrowfully, marriage to Patrick O'Hara Talbot would never give her everything she wanted.

Nevertheless she had to struggle to keep her voice

even as she replied, "I don't need your Ireland, Patrick, I need your love...now."

She hid her face in the hollow of his neck and moved against him with all the yearning in her body. Again the muscular hardness of his thighs pressed against her and his breathing quickened. She allowed her own breath to grow heavy in his ear, accompanying it with teasing flicks of her tongue.

"You are a witch," he rumbled.

"Aye, that I am," she agreed, satisfied now that he sensed nothing amiss. "And you daren't break my spell. Love me, Patrick Talbot. Love me now!"

Her body was stretched taut with desire, every pore in her flesh aching for him. They came together in one instant like two soaring spirits and Elana, willing the moment never to end, reveled in each new rise of passion and mellowed with each new peak of pleasure. And as Patrick continued to love her with a slow, teasing intimacy, she forgot about her victory and her ambition. Indeed, she forgot about everything and responded only to being a woman loved by a man.

March 1643

CHAPTER THIRTEEN
CAMBRIDGE, ENGLAND

DEFEAT HAD FOLLOWED DEFEAT until, wisely, the men of Parliament had begun to listen to the outspoken but seemingly tireless Oliver Cromwell. Though he had not seen an army until beyond his fortieth year, the former squire had quickly proved himself a born military leader. Quietly he was raised in rank to colonel and sought to recruit more and more men to train along the lines of his Puritan ethic. In the coming months the command of Lord Essex's army would shift increasingly to this large, dour-faced man who invoked the word of God as a reason for his thoughts and actions.

Robert Hubbard had remained under Lord Essex's command but had managed to maneuver himself into the position of liaison officer between the two camps. The longer he stayed at Cambridge, where Cromwell had his headquarters, the more he noted the difference between the two leaders of Parliament's army. And to him, at least, the reasons for Cromwell's rapid rise in power were all too apparent.

The men recruited by Cromwell were of a different mold than the gentlemen who rode under Lord Essex. Sons of tradesmen, laborers and men of the land, they had stern, hard-bitten faces and wills of iron. Like their leader, they believed in Jehovah, the God of wrath. Original sin was their reward for being born and if they were to escape hell and damnation in the hereafter, their lives were meant to be spent eradicating that sin.

To these men, Oliver Cromwell became an instrument of grace. They were willing to obey his rules without question and to follow him blindly into the very jaws of death. Such men, Robert surmised, might well lose a few battles, but ultimately they would surely win the war.

He began to find reasons to stay in Cambridge for longer and longer periods. He watched men train and drill in the cold, wintry winds of January, February and March with high morale and no argument. Among Cromwell's troops he heard little swearing and saw no overindulgence in wine or hard spirits. Only occasionally did he notice a camp follower circulating among them of an evening, and rarely would she make a wage before dawn.

But above all, Robert witnessed discipline, an almost natural regimen of discipline inherent in men born to a way of life that left them with little choice but to toil unceasingly if they were to survive in a world that cared little whether they lived or died. At a time when war was frequently considered a sport, to be pursued by those of quality who would seek glory in physical rather than mental exercise, Robert found the stolid determination of Cromwell's men almost uncanny.

By the end of March, Hubbard considered that he had ingratiated himself enough with Cromwell and his junior officers and so requested a change in his commission.

His heavy brows drawn together in a frown, Cromwell regarded Robert sternly from behind his desk. The tips of his thin fingers drummed against the oaken surface as his agile mind contemplated the young man's request.

Robert felt as if he could read Cromwell's thoughts. "Because of your hesitation, it seems you are in doubt of my loyalty and my faith," he observed quietly.

"You are the grandson of title... the son of a viscount," Cromwell pointed out. "Born to the manor as you are, 'tis difficult to think you don't harbor just a slight bit of the Royalist in you."

"I have publicly foresworn any and all claims to an English title," Hubbard rejoined. "My parents left me with nothing. My only claim to fortune is what little bequest I may receive from my grandmother, the Lady Hatton, when she passes on. If the king should continue to rule, I would lose that also."

Cromwell stood up. Placing his hands against a knot in the small of his back, he began to pace the small Spartan office. "Then 'tis gain you would fight for."

Cromwell's astute observation brought a faint smile to the corners of Robert's mouth. Quickly he erased it as the man spun around to face him.

"I want only those men around me who are convinced that they fight for the true God and the true religion,'' declared the commander, with all the authority of a man convinced of his infallibility.

Robert was not to be deterred. He had studied this man carefully and had come fully prepared to defend his request. "Men who lead must be ready not to doubt God's word but to interpret it correctly to those who follow them,'' he said.

Cromwell arched his right eyebrow while the corners of his mouth turned slightly downward. It was, Robert knew, the man's particular version of a smile and he took it as a sign to continue. "When men fight to win, they must be prepared to give their all. What more is there for a man to give than that which he holds most dear—his life? 'Tis not a thing a man gives lightly, but he goes to his death more willingly if convinced that he fights as one with his God. And it is the duty of the officer who leads him to convince him that that is indeed the case.''

Cromwell narrowed his eyes and steadied his gaze more fully on this tall, swarthy-skinned youth whose body had already filled out to that of a man. "How old are you, Hubbard?'' he queried abruptly.

"Near seventeen, sir,'' Robert replied. He paused, then added pointedly, "Four years older than Prince Rupert of the Rhine was when he entered his first battle.''

His remark drew a loud laugh from Cromwell. "You have as sharp a memory as you do a tongue,'' commented the commander approvingly. "My officers would do well to weigh my words, as you have obviously done. 'Tis true, lad, men draw a fierce strength from their faith.... Always remember that!''

"I plan to,'' promised Hubbard. "But I shall also remember that there are demands made upon us by expediency just as there are by faith.''

Once again, he drew a laugh from Cromwell, and

this time tears threatened to form in the man's eyes. "Methinks" he spluttered, when he could once more draw a breath, "I should send you down to Parliament. You speak to the point, whereas those arguing jackals merely slide around with their constant bickering."

Inwardly elated at the apparent success of his mission, Robert remained outwardly calm. "They would appease with words; you would defeat with the sword," he replied, with a shrug.

"Aye, they argue while we fight their battles!" Cromwell began to pace again and as he continued to speak his voice rose to oratorical heights. "Mark me, lad, one day the army will be forced to take command. Most of Parliament are fools. John Pym is a man of cunning and foresight, but he is old now and near death. The others talk of conciliation with the king, of appeasement. They would restore him to the throne with limited powers. Bah, Charles will never accept such an agreement. Witness Ireland...."

Instantly, Robert became more alert. "'Tis rumored in London that they near a cease-fire agreement in Ireland," he remarked. "'Tis said that Sir John Winter, the secretary of Charles's queen, Henrietta Maria, communicates with Owen Roe O'Neill, the rebel leader in Ulster."

"Aye," Cromwell agreed with a chuckle. "He probably does."

"'Tis also said that a Catholic army stands ready on the ports of southern Ireland to sail for Lancashire on the side of the king."

"Don't believe that, lad," Cromwell returned quickly.

"But they dearly fear a Puritan victory—"

"They do. But they fear the king also, for they know full well that no matter his promises, Charles will bend no more for the Irish rebels than he will for us. 'Tis true they appear to rebel against Parliament and for the king, but do not believe it, lad. They fight only for themselves and against England as a whole."

"But this alliance—"

"Is between the Irish and the Old English Catholics. But 'tis only their battle cry that is for king and church!"

There was silence for a moment. Robert knew the situation in Ireland as well as did Cromwell. Having a personal interest in the fortunes of the island, he had made certain to find out as much about it as possible. But he sensed it would be unwise for a junior officer to profess as great a knowledge on the subject of war as his commander. And, he thought, by furthering the present conversation, it was possible he might learn something that would aid him in the future.

"I have to admit," Robert sighed carefully, "I find the situation in Ireland confusing."

Cromwell moved to his side and dropped a heavy hand on the younger man's shoulder. "You shouldn't, for you yourself have already given the answer."

Deliberately Robert said nothing but looked up at the older man with a puzzled frown.

"'Tis the same in Ireland as 'tis in England," Cromwell explained. "What do you think it is in the common man that will move him to rebel against his king? Do you think it is because he sees his liberties violated or is taxed to strangulation? Is it because he has no love for his king?"

"Those are the reasons I've been given."

"And sound ones they are—but not enough to topple a throne. Our good Tudor queen, Elizabeth, made her subjects prosper but gave them few liberties. Since the dawn of man's rule over his fellow man, taxes have been too heavy but paid if profit were high enough. As for love.... Ask any Englishman if he ever felt love for Charles's father, King James, who ruled like a buffoon and chased little boys with as much energy as he did stags.''

Robert's puzzled frown was replaced with a smile of understanding. ''But under James they prospered and were at peace,'' he noted.

''Now you're listening. So what is it that makes a common man fight?''

''His faith.''

''You're learning quickly, lad,'' Cromwell chuckled. ''Tamper with a man's faith and he will go to war. He will even topple a king. This war we fight—just as it is in Ireland—is fought over religion. In our case, it is fought out of fear of Popish practices, out of fear that England will once again be dictated to by a senile and greedy man in Rome who would create an empire in God's name for the benefit of bishops and cardinals.''

''But surely that is what the Irish want,'' put in Robert, feigning puzzlement once more. ''They are all Catholics, so why do they fight?''

A broad smile spread across Cromwell's heavy features. ''Ah, now you begin to understand what separates a leader from his fellow man,'' he observed approvingly. ''While the common man fights for religion, his leader fights for power. And make no mistake, lad—land is a necessity for power. Before this uprising in Ireland, much of the best land was held by Protestants. Catholic leaders had little trouble convincing their followers to make war against such men on the basis of religion and in so doing, they regained possession of their lands, and hence power. Mark you this well: no ruler can rule without power, and if he would have power, then he must have land as well.''

Aye, thought Robert, well-pleased by the outcome of his mission. *I'll mark you well, Oliver Cromwell. I will listen to you and follow you, for I sense that you*

*are as cunning as you would seem to be devout, and
those two qualities will one day make you ruler of
England. . .and Ireland.*

June 1643

CHAPTER FOURTEEN
DONEGAL, IRELAND

Framed against the pale sky, Rory O'Hara in battle
dress still presented a powerful appearance. But closer
inspection revealed that he felt the weight of the heavy
sword at his side more keenly now than he had in the
past. The streaks of gray in his otherwise black beard
and hair were more obvious and the weathered lines in
his face had deepened, especially around his eyes
where he seemed to hold a perpetual frown.

"Dear God," he sighed at last, breaking a silence
that had seemed eternal, "but I feel old and tired. 'Tis
as if every new bit of news that reaches me serves to
ebb my strength."

Rory O'More and Patrick Talbot exchanged worried glances and then returned their gaze to O'Hara.

The early Catholic victories had soured. The forces
of both O'Hara and O'Neill had been pushed from Ulster by the marauding Scots, who seemed to have advance warning of every move the Catholics made. But
much of their trouble had been caused by division
among the leaders of the rebellion. In October of
1642, a Confederacy of Catholics, both Irish and Old
English, had been formed and had set up its own Parliament at Kilkenny. It had, under its ultimate military
command, two major armies: one led by Owen Roe
O'Neill with O'Hara as his second-in-command,
which represented the Irish, and one under General
Thomas Preston representing the Old English.

But while the formation of the Confederacy might

have been expected to ease the problems of communication between Irish and Old English, it had, in fact, done nothing of the sort. Fired by their early victories, the Irish were all for pushing ahead with the rebellion while they still had the chance. The Old English, on the other hand, were seriously considering pressing for a truce until the outcome of the see-saw battle between king and Parliament in their homeland became more obvious.

"'Tis foul air I breathe," O'More sighed, "when I must stand up in the Confederacy and speak to no one who will listen."

"Aye," O'Hara replied, leveling his gaze on O'More. "'Tis a wonder we breathe at all in a place where men change their allegiances as they do their underclothes."

"Damme," Patrick spat, emptying the remnants of the contents of his tankard onto the ground. "Cessation, ceasefire, a truce! Even a partial truce is suicide now!"

"Aye," O'Hara agreed. "We have more of Ireland under our control now than the Great O'Neill did at the height of his power."

O'More nodded. "And we would have it all if we could but agree on a common aim. 'Tis an Irishman's curse in war—always to depend on each other but never to agree with each other!"

Wearily, O'Hara placed the cool palms of his hands against his burning eyes. "Men, horses, supplies... everything we need to fight this bloody war comes from the Confederacy," he sighed. Dropping his hands, he leveled his gaze accusingly at O'More. "And the Confederacy doles them out to the generals who shout the loudest."

"Which are Preston and his comrade-in-arms, Barry, our English allies," Patrick remarked disgustedly.

"And both military idiots," O'More said. "Good

God, don't you think I know that? I'll do what I can," he promised.

"You'd best," O'Hara nodded. "And also go back and tell them that if we go to truce now, we'll lose all the advantage we have!" With that, he turned on his heel and strode down the ridge toward the tents and fires below.

Patrick gazed for a moment at O'Hara's broad back and then turned to O'More. "Did you do what I asked?" he queried.

"Aye," O'More nodded. "I've spies in Lord Gormanston's household as well as on the staff of both Barry and Preston."

"And?"

"Gormanston quakes with each new victory in England by Parliament's new man, Cromwell. And well he should. If the Puritans win, their retaliation will surely be swift in Ireland. Gormanston stands to lose all, but there is little doubt he stands full behind the alliance he originally signed with us."

"And Barry and Preston?"

"'Tis no doubt they are both asses, but not traitors. They give Parliament no information, I'm sure of it."

"Damme," Patrick growled. "Somewhere there is a spy. There has to be! The damned Scots and Parliament troops know every advance we make and await us on every line of retreat!"

O'More grasped Patrick's shoulders. "A little more time, Patrick," he urged. "We'll find him out. No one can operate this long and this successfully without leaving a trace somewhere. Have you talked to Lord Claymore?"

"Aye. Like Gormanston, he is committed. His fate is too tied to ours to betray us."

"AND THEN PATRICK CAME DOWN the ridge at the head of a hundred horses! Oh, mother, you should have seen him! He was the very devil, he was! I couldn't count the men that fell, his sword cut such a swath between them!''

Aileen gasped in horror, her heart beating wildly beneath her breast. "Conor..." she managed in a choking voice.

"Aye?"

"You mean you were close enough to the battle to see it all?"

"I was," the boy replied proudly, his face animated and his eyes wide with excitement. "Reloading for the foot, not a hundred yards away!"

"Oh, dear God!"

"Don't cry, mother. There's nothing to fear from the English or the Scots," he assured her quickly. "We're O'Haras!"

Aileen felt the bile of fear rising to her throat but she forced herself to speak sternly. "And because you are an O'Hara, my son, do you think God will protect you from harm?"

"I'm sure of it," Conor replied matter-of-factly. His blue eyes twinkled and his full lips creased in a smile that Aileen felt could light up the whole world. "God and a good right arm. Oh, mother, you must...."

The rest of his words were lost as Aileen watched him pace the tent's rush-strewn dirt floor. With his hands clasped behind his back and his stocky shoulders thrust slightly forward, she could be seeing a miniature of The O'Hara.

How like his father he is, she thought. *And will be in everything but color. The rusty curls and the fair complexion he got from me. We made you, little warrior,* she added to herself. *Together from our love, we made you. And now, dear one, what will happen to you?*

"Conor, come here, quickly...hug me. Put your arms around my neck and hug me!"

Having reached an age when he was torn between a

childish love for his mother and a need to prove his manhood by showing independence from her, Conor felt a flush of embarrassment at her desire for a display of affection. But seeing her distress at his hesitancy, he swallowed his pride and rushed to throw his arms around her neck.

How big he has grown, she thought. *Soon he will be a man. But 'tis no matter, for I've already lost my little boy.*

"You'll see, mother," Conor assured her. "One day this war will be over, and father, Patrick and I will ride home to Ballylee flush with victory!"

And then he was gone from her trembling arms, pacing again and recounting yet another tale of battlefield heroics. He was still narrating when the tent flap lifted and Rory O'Hara entered. "Here now, lad," he chided. "Would you frighten your mother half out of her wits with your war stories?"

"I was just telling her how Patrick saved your life, papa!"

O'Hara gritted his teeth as his eye caught the look of pain that contorted Aileen's lovely features. "Out with you, lad," he commanded, "and see to the horses. We move forward at dawn."

Conor scampered from the tent. The flap had barely dropped when Aileen threw herself into her husband's arms. "Is it true?" she asked fearfully. "Were you nearly killed?"

"Nay," O'Hara replied soothingly, running his fingers through the silky sheen of her blond hair and inhaling its sweet scent. "The lad elaborates like a poet."

"But he speaks of it so vividly. As I listened and watched his face when he spoke, I could hardly think of him as still a child. I could hardly believe that he was once small and tender enough to come from my womb!"

O'Hara sighed. "Boys become men very quickly when they wade in gore."

Aileen stiffened at her husband's words and stepped away from him in panic. "He was near to the battle, then, wasn't he?" she demanded, now truly frightened for her son's safety. "He was as close as he said."

O'Hara hesitated. "Aye," he sighed reluctantly, "he was. But there's naught for it, lass. There's no safe place on a battlefield. At least I've been able to keep a sword out of his hand and his body off a horse."

"Dear God, can you speak so casually of it?" Aileen exclaimed. "He's your son, Rory! Would you have him killed?"

"Hold your tongue, woman!" O'Hara cried, grasping her shoulders with his powerful hands.

Aileen gave a gasp of shock and stared up at him in disbelief. In all the years of their marriage and their love this was the first time her husband had ever raised his voice at her in anger. She was about to retort in kind but checked herself as she saw the pain and sadness that filled his eyes. Instead of lashing out at him, she slid her arms about his neck and pulled him to her.

"I shouldn't have come," she whispered. "But you were only three days' ride from Ballylee. I wanted to see you, touch you, so much. And now, I fear, you'll see me as a flighty woman, prone to vapors and fainting spells."

"Nay, lass." Gently he embraced her and ran his hands lovingly along the delicate arch of her back. "I'm glad you came. The camp followers we picked up in the past few months were beginning to look uncommonly good."

He had hoped his teasing would change her mood, but she gave him no answering laugh and he felt no relief to the tension in her body.

"Will there be a truce as O'More says?" she asked, hope in her voice.

"I don't know. But even if there is, 'twill be only a respite. In a month—or a year—we will have to take to the field and do it all over again. And in the end, I find myself asking what difference will it all make?"

"Shanna would say that in the end it will mean the difference between freedom and bondage," observed Aileen with a smile.

"Indeed she would," O'Hara laughed, with more weariness in his voice than humor. "But then she always did. 'Tis a pity she's woman. Like her husband, David, and now her son, Patrick, she would take to war if she were a man."

"As Conor does now," whispered Aileen, unable to suppress the sob that escaped her.

Rory's heart went out to her and there was little he could say or do that would still her fears. His beautiful, loving wife was in the halcyon of her life. It should be a time away from wars and warriors, a time to relax and enjoy the years of hard work she had put in to raising children and making a home.

"'Tis a hard world here, lass," he said softly. "I would have you back safe at Ballylee."

"Aye, back on Ballylee, to suffer quietly...."

"Aileen—"

"...while you follow that harsh master that shouts in all men's ears—responsibility!"

She glided away from him and lifted the tent flap. She wore nothing but a night smock and a velvet robe and O'Hara could see the lithe movements of her graceful curves outlined by the garment. He felt a stirring of desire, but it quickly faded when she spoke again.

"I don't like it," she told him, her voice little more than a choked whisper. "And there are days when I think that I will not be able to stand another hour of it."

"Of war?" he queried.

"Aye, of war and of wondering. Will a rider come one day to tell me that all my O'Hara men have gone to glory? And if that day comes, what will I do?"

Rory moved in close behind her. He slid his hands around her body and beneath her robe until they found the softness of her breasts. It was the way they had stood often at their chamber window at Ballylee, watching the great orange ball of the sun dip into the ocean. From habit, Aileen crossed her arms and covered her husband's hands with her own.

"He is so young, my Conor."

"Aye, he's young," agreed O'Hara. "And rash on the surface, but underneath I can see the steel tempering."

Aileen sighed and lifted her head to gaze up and beyond the starry heavens above them. "A young lad," she murmured, "tempered like a fine sword inside a sheath of tender skin.... Ireland will have need of him one day, as she does of Patrick now."

"'Tis not Ireland's fault, lass, what men do in her name, no more than what we do in God's name."

His words were followed by a long silence. Her body seemed to settle more heavily against his, but when she spoke again O'Hara knew that the dark mood had not left her.

"Even now," she said, "somewhere in England, a spindly-legged little man sits, his crowned head in his hands, wondering what fools are his fellow men. And on the morrow, a man—Cromwell I think is his name—I care not—Cromwell will charge into battle with the shout, 'For God and Country.' And against him will be this Rhinish prince.... What's his name?"

"Rupert," supplied O'Hara.

"Aye, Rupert," she went on. "He will meet this Cromwell's charge with the cry, 'For God, King and

Country.' And whoever rides off alive will be sure that it was because God was on his side!"

" 'Tis as I've told you before, lass. 'Tis a time all England is drunk on the Bible and all Ireland in flames over what can be wrested from her drunkenness."

"Oh," Aileen suddenly cried, and twisted around to face him. "Hold me, Rory, my husband," she pleaded. "Hold me tightly!"

"I'll hold you all this night, my love."

" 'Tis so hard. . .so very hard," she sobbed.

"What?"

She looked up and felt as if she were drowning in the dark pools of his eyes. "To imagine what life would be like without you," she whispered.

August 1643

CHAPTER FIFTEEN
CLAYMORE CASTLE, IRELAND

HORSES CLATTERED in the courtyard below. Elana searched the riders' faces until she was sure her father's was among them. A chill blast of air threw cold and dampness into her face through cracks around the panes. "Cold and rain, mists and damp," she exclaimed in exasperation. "How I hate this place!"

Angrily, she slammed the shutters closed and latched them. Still shivering, she drew her shawl tighter around her shoulders and cursed as the fire hissed in the hearth behind her. *Rain,* she thought in disgust. *It is even drawn down through chimneys to mock me.*

Elana was not only angry but also frightened. No longer was she finding the game of intrigue and manipulation exciting. Now it was becoming dangerous, both in England and Ireland, and she longed to be free of it. She thought wistfully of France, where there would be little of this constant rain and where she would be able to turn her face up to the sun.

For weeks she had heard from neither Sir John Redding nor Patrick Talbot. What little news she had been able to obtain had come by way of her father, and none of it had set her mind at rest.

The tide of the civil war in England was favoring the royalist side more each day. Parliament's defeats were now too numerous to count, including a devastating loss of the important port of Bristol to Prince Rupert. Warships in the port had declared for the king, who now had every reason to believe he could command the Bristol Channel. Certainly, he seemed to have secured the west of England.

Elana was now more fearful than ever that she was backing the losing side. In a letter to Sir John she had admitted as much. His reply had failed to stem her fears: "The tide will change, my dear Elana, and even if it does not, we have nothing to fear. Have we not openly declared for the king? Trust me. No matter who loses, *we* will win!"

His postscript to the same reply had unnerved her further, for Redding had told her it was no longer safe to send letters openly by courier. She was instructed to use instead two of her most trusted young grooms to send messages secretly. These would be relayed to him by others he trusted, and his replies to Elana would be handled in the same fashion.

Although worried, Elana had complied with his request. But of four messages she had sent in the past three weeks not one had been answered.

Her alarm at Redding's silence had grown until fright had begun to consume each moment of her day. Seven days ago, she had gone to her father and begged to be sent to France.

"I confer with Gormanston," he had replied. "I will return in a week's time. We shall talk then of your leaving."

Now he was back. Should she rush to him at once and risk seeming too anxious, she wondered. Or should she wait for his summons and appear unworried? Parting her shawl, Elana inspected her appearance in the dresser mirror.

Her gown was of a cream moiré striped in soft peach. The bodice was long-waisted and boned, with a low square-cut neckline. Her skirts flowed like a shimmering waterfall to the floor and were darted on the sides to display taupe-hued satin petticoats.

She turned in a full circle before the mirror, and suddenly noticed how the light danced over her peach-colored skin and highlighted the curves of her breasts. *That will never do,* she thought, rummaging in a drawer for a whisk. *Too daring, too much décolletage for father's delicate sensibilities.*

"The man should be a Puritan, he would have me so demure!" she grumbled aloud as she carefully adjusted the whisk to cover even the barest suggestion of feminine flesh. For good measure, she pulled the shawl tighter around her shoulders and in front of her.

"There, perfect...and dull," she whispered, then whirled at the sound of a tap at her door. "Aye?" she queried of the maid standing on the threshold.

"M'lord would see you, m'lady...in the library."

"Tell my father I will be there in a few minutes," she ordered. "I—er—must dress."

"Very well, m'lady."

Elana listened as the maid padded away down the hall. Nervously she paced until she felt a proper time had elapsed and then left her room. With her back straight and her head held high, she walked around the curved balcony that overlooked Claymore's great hall. The pungent smell of steaming clothes rose from below, where the men, damp from riding, stood before the fires. They had been laughing over mugs of ale but now fell silent as they saw Elana pass.

Arrogant Irishmen, she thought, stealing a glance

at their smiling faces. Half wore the Claymore crest, while the other wore the uniform of Patrick's O'Hara guard.

Left behind, she mused, *to keep an eye on my father...or me?* A slight chill ran up her spine at the thought. Almost tentatively, she knocked on the door of the library.

"Come in."

Lord Claymore stood before the hearth, a delicate crystal goblet of brandy in his hand. Behind him burned a huge log fire. He had thrown his cloak aside but still wore a heavy leather buff jacket. His shoulders were stooped, and he barely lifted his head to greet his daughter when she entered.

Dismay filled Elana. He was obviously in no mood to listen to her whims objectively. If she were to gain his permission to leave for France, she would somehow have to lift his spirits first. Fixing a smile of pleasure at his return on her face, she walked demurely across the room to stand in front of him. "I do hope, papa," she said in dutiful tones, "that the ride was not too harsh."

She realized as soon as her lips brushed her father's cheek that the somber quality she had sensed in him was anger. She could see now that his face was drained of color, and when he looked down at her, she noted that one eye seemed to twitch uncontrollably.

"Pray you, Elana," he rasped, "play not the little girl nor the innocent any longer."

"If I do," she retorted, "it is because it seems the only way you will listen to me."

"Granted, I should have listened better—to my own common sense. And watched you closer, also, for I should have known well the trouble you could cause."

Elana dropped her gaze and clutched more tightly at the handkerchief she held in her hands. She sensed danger—and was certain of it when she looked up from the floor to her father's face once more. A white line now ran along the line of his clenched jaw, and she could see the throbbing beat of his pulse in the raised veins of his neck.

"Elana, you are a selfish, self-willed, empty-headed little fool," he went on, barely pausing for breath. "No, don't speak—don't gush any of your innocent mouthings and tear at my heart further." He pulled a thin packet of letters from beneath his jacket and dropped them onto the table between them. "Not until you've perused those."

The packet was tied with a narrow leather strap. Elana's fingers trembled so much it took her a minute or more to untie it. When at last she did so and the letters fell apart, there was no need for her to glance beyond the first one. On the table before her, their seals broken, lay the last four messages she had sent Sir John Redding.

Keeping her head bent, Elana pretended to read while planning her next move. Restlessly, her father moved his goblet back and forth beside the letters. Its crystal and the amber liquid it contained seemed to burst into flames from the fire's reflection.

When she finally did look up, her father's eyes were narrowed and the vein in his neck seemed to pulse at a pace more wild than ever.

"I see no harm..." she began.

"No harm?" he cried. "I'll admit, my dear Elana, that you see very little beyond the tip of your nose and the size of your wardrobe, but I am positive that you are not stupid enough to believe you have not caused irreparable harm!"

"I cannot see how," Elana answered calmly, her eyes wide saucers of innocence. "After all, Sir John is Lord Gormanston's nephew. Surely he must be spying on Parliament for the king—"

Suddenly her father flung his hand backward. It struck the goblet sending the glass hurtling toward the stone hearth, where it shattered into a myriad of crystal fragments.

"Damme, how you can lie!" he stormed. "How, in so few years of life, has your beauty turned so far inward and curdled to make of you such a devious, cold woman?"

His voice thundered with anger and his eyes burned fiercely, seeming to leave a searing brand on her flesh wherever his gaze alighted. Moving with a vigor and speed she hadn't thought he possessed, he grabbed her arm with a grip of steel. With his free hand, he grasped one of the letters. Then, letting go her arm, he forced the letter open.

"You didn't know?" he sneered. "I beg to differ, Elana. You knew exactly what you were doing!"

He began to read aloud, and with the utterance of each word his voice rose reaching at last a crescendo of unbridled fury.

" 'My father is as obtuse as ever. I have little word to send this time, my dearest. Pray, send word soon on the treaty of which you spoke, between this silly Irish Confederacy they call a government and the king. I fear the war does not go well in England. Would it not be wise, for the time being at least, to leave off our Parliament leanings until we see which way the wind blows in England?' "

Lord Claymore crumpled the parchment and flung it from him viciously, then leveled his rage-filled eyes on Elana. "Gormanston's own nephew is the funnel of information O'Neill and O'Hara have been trying to stop," he declared bluntly. "And much of that information has come from myself and Patrick Talbot through you, my own daughter. I feel shame for myself and pity for Talbot. How you have deceived him. At first I thought you were merely wanton, not content until you had satisfied every man in Ireland!''

Until now, Elana had let her father's anger run its course. She had no doubt she could appease him later and somewhat, guiltily, she had to admit he had a certain right to be angry. But the unfairness of his last words and the sarcastic tone in which he had uttered them stung her to sudden fury. Dropping her shawl from her shoulders, she raised her head defiantly to meet his gaze, her eyes blazing.

"You would not have needed to worry on that score if you had not commanded me back from France," she retorted. "For at least there I could consort with gentlemen and not squander my charms on peasants! And if John Redding and Patrick Talbot can be counted as 'every man in Ireland' then this accursed island is in an even sorrier state than I thought!"

Lord Claymore's face was now a burnished red, as if the fire from the hearth had suffused his features with its heat and flame. "John Redding has but one object in Ireland," he stated. "To keep it in turmoil, with every faction fighting the other. In this way no Irish troops can come to the king's aid. And you have aided him in his task. In so doing you have ruined me—and yourself as well."

"You old fool," Elana cried. "Have you told the Irish of this? They will run over Claymore like locusts!"

"Not yet," he replied, advancing on her. "As yet only Lord Gormanston and myself know of your and his nephew's perfidy. We are agreed that if both of you are sent away to a proper exile, we may mend this break still."

Elana's spirits lifted. *Sent away.* The thought brought a smile to her face. She would win after all.

"I'll gladly return to France," she told him.

"Nay. . .not France."

"Then where?"

"Gormanston has property elsewhere. This he will deed to Redding, on the condition that he never speak of his betrayal and that he leave England, Ireland and Scotland for all time. I have arranged a dowry—"

"Dowry?" she queried sharply.

"Aye," replied her father. "For you shall accompany your treacherous lover into exile. If once there, you wed, it makes little difference to me."

The smugness in his tone, the slight sneer at the corner of his lips, the finality of his words...all combined to reawaken Elana's alarm.

"Exile.... Where?" she breathed.

"An island in the West Indies—Barbados."

Elana gasped in horror. Her hands flew to her ears as if by shutting out his words she could ignore their existence. "Exchange one savage island for another?" she shrieked. "No! I won't do it.... I won't go!"

"You will go, daughter," he declared firmly. "For I would wash my hands of you, now and forever."

"No...*no*!"

He stood directly before her now, his face more florid than ever, his lips trembling. "You will. 'Tis a fit place for you, a place where I will have to hear no more about your trysts, a place where you will bring no more shame upon my honor or my name."

"Honor? How dare you speak of honor!" she flung at him. "You who squandered my mother's dowry on your rakehell escapades! How dare you have the nerve to denounce what I do, decry my ambition, look down your nose at my beauty and my wit—the only things I have that will lift me from the mire you made of our affairs?"

"Aye, that I truly admit. You were indeed born a courtesan."

"As you made my mother!" she retorted furiously. "I know, for she told me how, almost daily, you used her in James's dissolute court to further your own designs. And that brings us to your precious name. She told me about that, as well."

Sensing a faintly triumphant ring in her voice, Claymore glanced at her uncertainly. "What do you mean?" he queried sharply.

"I do bear your name, but that is all you've given me," she replied equally sharply. "Can you honestly look at me and see yourself? Are you so naive as to think this face and figure came from you?"

"If you think to shift the blame..." Claymore began.

"Look closely, dear father, and tell me what you see. No, I shall tell you!" Elana hissed coldly. "Who was the most striking man in James's court?"

"Dear God—Buckingham...."

Elana's eyes glittered as she watched the pain of realization pass over Claymore's face. "Aye, father," she gloated. "George Villiers, Duke of Buckingham. I bear everything but his name."

His daughter's latest revelation was too much for Claymore. Raising his arm, he swept it in a wide arc and struck her across the face. The sound, as his hand met her cheek, was like a clap of thunder and Elana staggered backward from the blow, striking her head heavily against the wall behind her. The salty tang of blood from a cut on her inner lip filled her mouth. As she shook her head to clear it, she saw her father raise his arm to strike her again.

But the blow never landed. Instead, Claymore gave a cry of agony as his face suddenly contorted in pain. His eyes widened in shock and he clutched at his chest with a gasp.

"What is it—what's the matter?" she cried.

His only answer was a rattling gasp as he sank to the floor.

Elana ran to him and kneeling beside him, leaned over and placed her ear to his mouth. She neither

heard nor felt a breath. She pressed her ear to his
chest, but could detect no heartbeat, nor a pulse
when she placed the tips of her fingers at his temples.

For several minutes she remained kneeling at his
side, watching the color slowly drain from his face.
Then, rising to her feet she dabbed the spots of blood
from her lip and her chin with a kerchief, carefully
smoothed her dress and straightened her coif.

Satisfied at last that her appearance would not be
cause for unwarranted comment, she opened the
door, stepped into the hallway and screamed.

CLAYMORE MANOR WAS HERS, what little was left of
it. In going over the accounts of the house and lands,
she had quickly discovered just how much money her
father had been sending to England.

How ironic, she thought wryly. *I aid Parliament's
cause to save my fortune, while my father squandered it on the royalists!*

Immediately after Lord Claymore's burial, she had
reestablished communication with John Redding. He
had assured her that he held a sword of reason and the
threat of scandal over his uncle's head and had since
begun to urge her to make more frequent contact with
Patrick Talbot. Rumors flew that, during the coming
truce, troops and arms might be forthcoming from the
Dutch, to whose country King Charles's wife, Queen
Henrietta Maria, had fled for safety at the start of
England's civil war. It was further rumored that arms
might also come from France. Henrietta Maria had returned to England in February, but while she was on
the Continent she had requested aid from Cardinal
Mazarin and her sister-in-law, Queen Anne of France,
who was ruling as regent for her five-year-old son
Louis XIV since the death of her husband, Louis XIII,
earlier that year. Should the rumors be true, many of
the arms might go to Irish troops to fight in England

for Charles. This was information of vital importance to Sir John's superiors.

He also informed Elana that Pym, as leader of Parliament, was considering the signing of a Solemn League and Covenant with the Scots Presbyterians. His words shouted at her from the paper. "Should such an agreement be signed, my dear Elana, it will mean that the Scots will not interfere in England's war. That—and the ascendancy of Oliver Cromwell as military commander for Parliament forces—will surely swing the tide of this war our way."

Elana was not so sure. She was also not sure that her way was still that of Sir John's.

As the days wore on, her decision drifted more and more toward fleeing. She could, she reasoned, sell everything that couldn't be packed and moved and run to France until the war was over. When it finally did end, she could then return to dispose of Claymore once and for all. With this in mind, she answered Redding's messages with little more than ramblings and committing herself to nothing.

The sudden and unexpected arrival of Patrick Talbot convinced her once and for all she should leave.

"M'lady...."

Elana looked up at the red-liveried servant in the doorway in time to see Patrick brush by him and step into the room without waiting to be announced.

"Elana, I'm sorry to hear of your father's death. I had hoped to come to you sooner but it was impossible," he explained apologetically.

For some unknown reason, she felt a sense of shock at seeing Patrick standing beside her. During the stress and strain of the past two weeks she had almost forgotten he existed. It was as if he had gone completely from her life and now, suddenly and unexpectedly, had come back into it. It caught her unawares and she found herself in the unusual position of being unable to speak.

"Patrick...I..." she began hesitantly, then subsided into silence.

It became an awkward moment as they stood staring at each other, neither of them uttering a sound. Then Patrick swept his gaze upward to rest on her face, and Elana was surprised at the sudden feeling of warmth it brought her. When his darkly tanned face broke into an open smile of sheer pleasure at the sight of her, her knees threatened to give way under her and send her spinning to the floor.

Unable to resist his smile, she answered it in kind and at last found her voice. "You look as though you've ridden far," she observed. "I'll call for wine."

She had nearly reached the velvet bell-pull near the door when he caught her in his arms. "The only wine I want or need at this moment is the taste of your lips on mine," he declared fervently.

Tightly he pulled her against him and caressed her hair softly with his free hand. Then, cupping his hand under her chin, he tilted her face upward. She tried to turn her head to one side but his hold was too firm and in the next moment he had bent his dark head over and covered her mouth with his own.

For a moment she reveled in the sense of comfort and security she felt in his arms. But as the kiss deepened, became more demanding, it brought with it a turmoil between the resolution of her mind and the passion in her body.

No, she thought, *no more. I will to France and be done with it all!*

It took all the will she possessed for her to resist the sweetness of his lips, the urgent demand of his kiss and the feel of his lithe body pressed against her.

Sensing her sudden coldness Patrick lifted his head and searched the depths of her turquoise eyes for some answer to the riddle of this woman. Her eyes seemed to stare through and beyond him, toward nothing. "From your coldness, 'tis obvious you've not missed me," he remarked, bitterness in his tone.

But I have, she thought, her heart sinking as the sudden truth of it struck her like a blow. *But I cannot, will not, admit it.... To France, dear God, to France!*

She let a languid smile cross her lips and lifted one eyebrow in a mocking gesture of surprise that he should have hoped for anything different. "You should know by now, Patrick, that I miss no man," she replied evenly. But even as she spoke she felt a painful lump rise in her throat. Patrick stepped away, tugging at the tie of his riding cloak. The garment fell from his shoulders and he dropped it carelessly on a nearby chair as he began to pace. Beneath the cloak he wore a light cambric shirt unlaced at the neck and a leather vest.

"Claymore is yours now," he remarked suddenly.

"Aye," she agreed, pushing a stubborn curl from her forehead. "What there is left of it."

At Patrick's questioning look, she went on to explain how her father had been bleeding the land to help Charles finance his war for his throne.

"We can bring Claymore back," he assured her, "when these troubles are over."

"We?" she queried.

"Elana—"

Again he moved to embrace her but stopped when her palms came up to press against his chest. He watched as her eyes narrowed to scan the smooth skin over his cheekbones and the slight curl at the corners of his lips that gave his mouth a look of perpetual sardonic humor. He sensed a sudden relaxation in her, and a faint look of relief crossed her beautiful features as she unexpectedly smiled up at him.

"You have the Irish look, Patrick Talbot," she declared candidly.

"Oh?" he queried, somewhat taken aback by the apparent change of subject. "Oh? And what is that?"

" 'Tis a look, if I were a man, that I would hate to face in battle. You face danger with contempt, Patrick Talbot. You have no respect for it. I've heard the tales of you in the field, even from my young serving girls. You are a legend among them already. They tell me that on the battlefield you kill with insolence. You should love the same way, Patrick. In fact, I thought you did when first we met."

A quizzical smile creased the corners of his lips and he gazed down at her with a puzzled frown. "You are the most unfathomable creature, Elana," he sighed. "You do twist thought and meaning like you twist men around your finger."

Her smile was enigmatic as she moved to him and placed her slender hands on his cheeks. She had made her final decision. She knew now that she could never love Patrick enough to give up her dreams for him. But she also knew that she could no longer hurt him or use him as a means to her own ends. For her, such a decision was enough to allow her to leave Ireland with a clear conscience.

"Patrick, you must know by now that a marriage between us is impossible," she said, forcing a decisive firmness into her voice.

He stepped away from her, his eyes searching her face for some break in that icy coolness. He found none.

"Have I been such a fool then to believe that, beneath your flippancy, beyond your coldness outside the bedchamber, you felt love for me?"

"Ah Patrick," she replied, managing a gay laugh, "all men are fools when it comes to women!"

He looked at her for a long moment, then abruptly turned away and retrieved his cloak from the chair. To her surprise and relief, when he faced her again there was no trace of anger or sorrow on his face. Instead his eyes were alive with mischief, and the smile of sardonic arrogance she had come to know so well played once more around his lips.

"'Tis not over yet, Elana," he promised. "You shall see!"

Swiftly he moved toward her and crushed her to him. His mouth came down on hers in a punishing kiss, and then releasing her, he swept from the room without a backward glance. She heard the sound of his booted feet thunder down the stone stairs and rushed to the window to see him mount his horse in the courtyard below.

She watched him ride beneath the arched gate and appear again beyond the castle wall. When he reached the heath, he broke into an easy canter. "Ah, but it is, Patrick," she whispered. "It is over now and forever."

But for Patrick, reveling in the feel of his horse beneath him and the wind in his face, it was far from over. That Elana could not return the abiding love he felt for her, he never doubted for a moment. But that made little difference to his decision. Quite the opposite, in fact, for in the conquest of Elana he saw challenge, and Patrick was a man who enjoyed a challenge above all things. There was no doubt that Elana desired him, and the knowledge of that was enough to convince him that persistence on his part would one day break through her emotional aloofness. Then and only then would he at last fathom the enigma that was the woman he loved.

Elana took no joy in her bath that night. Indeed, she rushed through the usually hour-long ritual in a matter of minutes. As her maid dried her body with soft towels, her mind spun with plans for the morrow.

She would, she decided, separate and catalog the jewelry by the value of each piece. They would be sewn into the linings of gowns and cloaks. The plate and other silver would be secreted in the false bottoms of her father's large trunks.

"M'lady...."

"What?" she queried absentmindedly. "Oh, yes."

The maid slipped a lace-trimmed green batiste undergown over her head. It slid sensuously down over her naked body.

"You may go," she told the maid. "I shall do my own hair."

She had just begun to stroke an ivory-handled brush through her hair when she heard shouts from the bailey and then the clatter of horses.

Rushing to the window, she opened the shutters just enough to peer out. "The fool!" she gasped, as she recognized the cause of the commotion and hurried toward the bed.

She was still struggling into a fur-trimmed robe as she burst into the hall and made for the wide stone stairs. By the time she reached the top step, Sir John Redding was already halfway up, effortlessly taking the stairs three at a time.

"Ah, Elana," he purred. "I am so happy I'm not disturbing your rest."

He paused not an instant when he saw her and took her firmly by the elbow. It was all she could do not to run to keep up with his pace as he guided her back down the hall to her chamber door.

"John, you do indeed border on madness coming here like this." Elana kept her voice low but her anger was obvious.

"How so?" he asked, and then in equally hushed tones answered his own question. "I think not, my dear. You forget I still roam Ireland as the nephew of Preston and Gormanston. Who would question a devoted subject in pursuit of the king's work?"

"But coming here, at night...and to my bed-chamber!" she exclaimed. "What of the servants?"

Deftly he maneuvered her into the room, then closed the door and fastened the latch. "I hardly think your reputation will be any the worse for it," he observed mildly.

At this piece of insolence she whirled to face him, her fists clenched, her eyes blazing. "Get out!" she hissed. "Leave me!"

"I'm afraid not, you little wench," Redding replied calmly, sloughing off his riding cloak and pouring himself a glass of claret.

Furious at his arrogance, Elana marched purposefully to the door and reached for the latch.

"I wouldn't, m'lady," he warned. "You would do well to sit and listen to what I have to say."

There was an ominous tone in his voice that arrested the movement of her hand. Slowly, she turned to face him, and a shiver went through her when her gaze met the two black stones that were his eyes.

His deceptively thin figure towered above her. The candlelight played eerily over the hollows of his cheeks and his glittering deep-set eyes. His face, set under thick raven black hair touched with gray at the temples, seemed more cruel than she remembered. His look, as usual, was inscrutable, but she sensed in him a seething anger.

"Why haven't you answered my messages?" he queried abruptly.

"I have—"

"With silly female chattering," he acknowledged with a look of disgust. "Not with answers to the questions I asked."

Elana shrugged, gliding on slippered feet toward the bottle of claret. "Would you have me trump up an answer when I have none?"

As she poured a goblet of wine, Redding raised his hand and entwined the silken mass of her hair in his fingers. "You wouldn't be thinking of leaving dear

Ireland, would you, Elana?'' he asked softly, dangerously.

He pulled her hair to one side, making it impossible for her to hide her reaction. ''Of course not,'' she
replied, with a calmness she was far from feeling.

''You are indeed a wonderful liar, Elana,'' he observed mockingly, his mouth twisted in a cruel smile.
''Very adept. I have little doubt that I would have believed you...had I not been informed that your servants have brought out both your trunks and those of
your father. And that even now, in your stables, your
carriages are being rewheeled. Is it possible, my dear
Elana, that that is being done in preparation for a
journey?''

''How—'' she gasped, catching at the sob in her
throat.

''Damme, girl, do you think I have no one but you
behind these walls to tell me what goes on?'' Redding
growled.

She tried to escape him but found herself held
firmly and painfully by his fingers still entwined in
her hair.

''Stop, you're hurting me!'' she cried, but quickly
ceased struggling when her demand was met only by
a harder and yet more painful grip.

With ease he turned her to face him. His gaze
swept over her, noting with mocking interest the
curves of her body beneath the thin batiste fabric
of her gown. And under his arrogant scrutiny, she
suddenly realized that she had given no thought
to modesty since he had so rashly intruded on her.
Accustomed as she was to being admired by a man,
she nevertheless suddenly felt her cheeks blaze
with embarrassment. *Damme,* she thought angrily,
*I will not let myself feel like a giddy fool before
him!*

''Of course I'm leaving...for France,'' she told

him, raising her chin to glare at him defiantly. "I have nothing to keep me here now."

"Come now, Elana," Redding chided, a derisive edge to his voice. "What of all our plans together?"

"Little plans we can make if we are both hanged," she hissed.

Redding was silent for a moment then gave a slight chuckle. "True enough," he acknowledged. Then, satisfied that she was now ready to talk rather than flee, he loosened his purchase on her hair and placed the goblet he had been holding in his other hand down on the table before him. "And that," he added, "is why one more deed must be done. Then we can both flee."

He poured more wine into both their glasses, and turned to face her, his smile turning wicked as he noted her quizzical look.

"Let me bring you up to date, my beautiful Elana," he said. "This damned Irish Confederacy has come to terms with Lord Ormonde and King Charles. There has been much talk of a truce of late, and I had hoped that was all it would be—talk. But it seems not. The treaty has been signed and the fools have even agreed to send money to Charles. It seems likely that troops will be next. Even now O'Hara's regiments are retreating from Tyrone back to Ballylee." Here Redding paused for a moment, then added, "But you probably already know that, since your lovestruck young fool visited you this afternoon."

Underneath the contempt in his voice, Elana detected a tinge of sardonic humor that filled her with anger. "If your spies are so adept," she retorted, "surely they told you that Patrick told me nothing but how much he still adores me."

"No matter." Redding dismissed her answer with a wave of his hand. "I already know their line of march."

Suspiciously, she surveyed his face through narrowed eyes. She still had no idea where this talk was leading and what part in it he expected her to play. "If the truce has been signed, what more can be done now?" she asked.

"I have decided to play both sides of the game no longer," he informed her. "I am in both name and actions, declaring openly for Parliament."

"Good God, you'll be dead in a day!" she exclaimed, both shocked and frightened by the import of his words. Where did his decision leave her?

Redding paid no attention to her obvious dismay. Indeed, there was nothing in his hawklike eyes to indicate he had even heard her. "I have also decided," he continued, "that the Scots Covenanters here in Ireland will pay no attention to the truce."

"I still don't see what I have to do—"

"'Tis very simple, Elana," he said, his voice lowering to a conspiratorial murmur. "A week from tonight you will lower rope ladders—which I will provide—over the south wall of Claymore. Over those ladders will come Scots troops under my command. 'Twill be so much easier than a siege."

"But how will you march through O'Hara's army? It is encamped between the Scots and here."

"I won't. We will be landing by sea . . . behind Claymore. At the same time, General Monro's Scots regiments will be to the south and the north, with a smaller force covering the one remaining small area through which O'Hara's men could retreat." Redding laughed, then added, "If there are any left alive to retreat after they find themselves trapped on all sides."

The color drained from Elana's face and she suddenly felt nauseated. "No, no, John—such a thing I cannot do!" she protested urgently.

"Why? Because you have no stomach to stand on the parapets and watch the slaughter?" he taunted. "You fool, you have caused nearly as many deaths already! What means a few more? In the meantime, you must continue to oversee Claymore's affairs as if nothing were afoot.''

Suddenly the truth of all her actions these past few months washed over Elana like a tide. She had never seen the killing, only heard of it in vague terms, and as far as she was concerned, it had had nothing to do with her.

Now, however, the thought of an O'Hara massacre filled her with both horror and shame. Was this to be the result of all her intrigue, all the shrewd planning she had done simply to save the fortune she considered rightfully hers?

''No, 'tis impossible! I cannot do such a thing!'' she gasped.

''Come, come, dear girl. . .don't tell me you've fallen in love with our youthful Romeo?'' sneered Redding, his eyes boring into her like two bits of black steel.

''No, that's not it at all—''

''Isn't it?'' he said sharply.

''No, I swear it!'' she cried, turning so that the curtain of her hair would conceal her features. ''I. . .I just don't want to be the cause of his death.''

''You have no choice in the matter, and neither do I,'' he said. ''You will do this last thing, Elana. . .or you will never reach France.''

Elana stared at him, her eyes wide. ''You would—''

''Not I,'' he shrugged. ''The Scots. Even now they are massing. Do this, Elana, and my work here is finished. It will smash this treaty once and for all. We can both leave then, return to England, even, if that would be your desire.'' He paused, a cold smile curving his mouth. ''Or has your mind changed about our beautiful plans together?''

''I—I'm not sure any longer,'' she stammered. ''I'm confused.''

"Oh? Then let us cease your confusion!"

He reached for her. Elana cringed and spun from his grasp. "Don't touch me!" she cried. She felt her whole body tremble as she looked up at him. Before her frightened gaze, the gray at his temples seemed somehow to change, to grow and become horns on his head. "You're—you're a devil!" she gasped.

"Aye," he thundered. "And you're a witch!"

He gave her no warning as he reached forward and snatched her practically from her feet into his embrace. He held her poised for a moment and stared down at her. And as she gazed up into his glittering eyes, her heart began to pound more wildly than ever. For in those two bits of gleaming black steel, she could see not a shred of tenderness or love, but only wildness and frightening evil. Suddenly, she realized that this man, to whom she had given her body and soul and for whom she had risked her life, only wanted the one thing she refused to grant any man—complete and utter control over her.

She struggled to free herself from his grasp, but he simply tightened his grip. She could feel the heat of his body through the thin fabric of her nightgown.

In addition to her sudden fear of him and her loathing of what he had demanded she do, Elana felt a gnawing distaste toward herself. She had surrendered so easily in the past, had carelessly given herself to him so many times. Now she felt nothing for him but loathing. She hated his arrogant self-assurance, his certainty that she would deny neither his demands nor his desire.

His lips found the soft hollow of her throat and traced a searing path upward to her mouth. No matter how much she struggled, she could not escape him. Cool air bathed her flesh, and she knew that he had somehow undressed her. She heard the unmistakable sounds of his own clothing being discarded. He forced her down onto the bed. Seconds later, she felt the heat of his naked flesh beside her and his hands, stroking, probing.

"No," she gasped.

But he would not be stayed nor, to her shame, would the passion he built in her be denied.

"You are a very sensuous woman, Elana," he observed coolly. "Your body, no matter how much you would deny it, cries out for a man's touch. You crave excess and satisfaction in all things. That is why, my dear, we make a matched pair in this harness we have made for ourselves."

Her eyes flew open in horror at the thought.

Redding hovered above her, his cruel lips curved into an evil grin. In his burning eyes she detected a look of triumph.

With a cry of anguish, she made one last attempt to free herself, but to no avail. His mouth came down hard on hers, his tongue probing.

And then he took her, demandingly. Powerless, she arched to meet him.

Damn you, she thought in despair. *Damn you!*

September 1643

CHAPTER SIXTEEN
CLAYMORE, IRELAND

KATE O'HANLON BIT HER LIP to keep from weeping as she closed the door of Elana Claymore's office. Down the wide stone stairs and across the courtyard she walked, her head high, her back straight. Beneath her threadbare cloak she clutched the sealed parchment the grand lady of Claymore Castle had just given her.

"There is no need to read it now, girl," Elana had said, her voice becoming more and more imperious with each word she spoke. "I'll tell you what it says.

'Tis an eviction notice. Nay, don't bother to tell me about this silly deed you have, purportedly signed by my father. 'Tis a forgery, I'm sure, and if need be I'll prove it in the English courts of Dublin.''

She had paused, standing regally and leaning toward Kate across the massive desk. Kate shivered as she remembered those catlike eyes full of mocking laughter that bored into her own.

"And if that should happen, girl, I think you already know the outcome."

Then Elana had walked in front of the desk and stood beside Kate like some beautifully plumed bird. Her sea-green velvet gown and petticoats of silver-and-olive stripes had emphasized the lines of her exquisite bust and tiny waist. Kate was sure she had moved to stand in front of her simply to stress the vast difference between them.

"I realize what little belongings you have must be moved," the young woman had continued. "I'm sure you have a cart—most Irish peasants do. I've instructed a horse be lent you. 'Tis waiting now at the postern gate. I'll expect its return—*soon*."

Then, with what had almost seemed a gentle, reassuring squeeze, she had dropped one of her slender hands on Kate's shoulder. But when she spoke again her tone had been harsh.

"You may go now, girl, be quick about it!"

In the courtyard Kate passed lounging soldiers, who with open lust eyed her tall figure in the homespun cotton cloak and dress. A few commented loudly on the nearness of the stables and the softness of the straw in the stalls. Looking neither to right nor left, Kate ignored them all.

True to Lady Claymore's word, a horse was waiting. There was no saddle, so she had no choice but to ride astride. Her face blushed crimson when the soldier's hand slid beneath her dress while giving her a leg up. How dearly she would have liked to have kicked his leering face, but she checked the impulse and turned the horse away as if nothing had happened.

Once through the gate, she urged the animal into a trot. A hazy rain had begun to fall from the gray sky, its drops mingling with the tears coursing silently down her cheek. Land, she thought in despair. Their own land. How short their happiness, and how foolish she had been to have believed it might be theirs forever on that day when Patrick Talbot had brought the document from Lord Claymore.

She had been paying little attention to the horse underneath her and without a steady hand to guide it, the creature stumbled slightly over the rough ground. Instinctively, she grabbed the mane with both hands, letting the parchment slip from her fingers.

"Damn," she cursed, bringing the animal to a halt and sliding from its back.

She retrieved the hated document and looked around until she spotted a stump from which she could remount. As she led the horse toward it, she wondered what words were used to rob someone of their life, their dreams. She reached the stump and, before mounting, broke the seal to find out.

"My dear Kate O'Hanlon," she read. "I have seen you with Patrick Talbot. Therefore, I assume you and the gentleman are at least friends. Miss O'Hanlon, I ask you now to ride like the wind, for you can do Patrick a great service if only you will...."

As Kate continued to read, her tears dried and the lump disappeared from her throat. Unable to believe her eyes, she read the document through once more, and by the time she had finished her heart was beating wildly. Turning, she gazed back toward the towers and parapets of Claymore, now barely visible through the misty rain.

Slowly, she began to recall incidents that had

seemed out of place during her conversation at the castle but to which she had paid little attention at the time. She remembered the soldiers with the O'Hara lion emblazoned on their chests, who spoke Gaelic with a decided Scottish burr; the Claymore Castle guards, who spoke with the same accent; the strangely reassuring squeeze of Lady Claymore's hand on her shoulder; and, above all, the two stern-faced guards who had hovered near the lady during the whole of her interview. And as she finally pieced it all together, she realized with sudden and horrifying clarity what must have happened. Somehow Claymore Castle had been infiltrated by the Scots. Lady Claymore herself was being watched like a hawk and, wanting to warn Patrick, had chosen the only way she could think of to be sure he received the news. She had summoned Kate and given her the message under the guise of an eviction notice.

Wasting no further time, Kate hurled herself onto the horse's back and urged the animal into a gallop.

CONOR LIMPED INTO THE TENT and set a fresh leather-jack of beer on a low table between his father and Patrick.

"Hola, my son!" O'Hara shouted heartily. "How goes our warrior's wound today?"

Embarrassed, Conor blushed and averted his eyes from his father's stare. "Better," he replied in a low tone. "The stiffness is nearly gone. May I sit?"

"Aye, son...sit. Eat!"

Conor dropped on a stool and helped himself to meat and oaten bread. As he ate he stared steadfastly down at the table, until Patrick finally clapped a hand on his shoulder.

"Think nothing of it, lad," he advised with a reassuring grin. "'Tis better you got in the way of a nervous horse than a Scottish musket ball. We'll have a turn together with short swords later. That will ease the soreness.''

The color eased in Conor's face at once. With the hearty appetite of an active and still growing adolescent, he continued to eat; but now gazed eagerly back and forth between his two heroes as he did so.

''Tell me about the charge,'' he demanded with youthful enthusiasm. ''The one you made side by side! Duncan says between you, you must have killed a hundred!''

''How many?'' Patrick chuckled.

''Well, twenty, then. Tell me!''

''Dear God, son,'' O'Hara exclaimed with a grin, ''you've heard it ten times already.''

''I know,'' replied Conor, beaming up at his father's broad, bearded face. ''But I want to remember every bit of it so I can tell everyone at Ballylee when we arrive!''

His explanation drew a rumble of laughter from his father. Lovingly, O'Hara ran his fingers through his son's rusty curls. ''Methinks Patrick and I should make you our harper, lad,'' he declared. ''Od's blood, you would write ballads that would make us better known than even O'Donnell or the Great O'Neill!''

''Mayhap,'' Conor replied, grinning, ''one day I will.''

The tent flap lifted and a helmeted head appeared in the opening. ''Patrick, there's a lad just rode in to see you.''

''Me?''

''Aye, an' only you. Says he has some dire word that he'll tell only to your person.''

Patrick draped his baldric, complete with sword, over his shoulder and strode from the tent.

''There. . . by the fire,'' indicated the soldier.

The young man nodded, then stopped short in surprise. The lad who had demanded to see him was astride Elana Claymore's favorite mount. He would have recognized the horse anywhere.

"Ho there," he exclaimed. "Where did you—Kate!"

"Aye," she replied, pulling the quilted cap from her head and sliding to the ground. "An' if 'tis the horse you mean, Lady Claymore gave it to me herself."

"Your clothes—"

"Timothy's," she replied. "I thought the ride would be safer dressed as a lad."

"Perhaps while you are riding, lass," he acknowledged with a grin. "But on the ground I fear those clothes hide nothing."

"Aye, Patrick," agreed a soldier standing nearby who had overheard the conversation. " 'Tis a bonny pair of breeches indeed!"

Kate quickly surveyed herself, front and rear, and then looked back up at Patrick with a shrug. "No matter. 'Twas easier riding without bulky skirts and petticoats anyway."

"Good for you, lass," Patrick laughed, giving her a quick hug. "Now, what brings you?"

Kate's dark eyes narrowed and he sensed immediately that her wild ride from Claymore had had some definite and unpleasant purpose behind it.

"What is it?" he queried, his tone wary.

Wordlessly she handed him the parchment. He read it through carefully and then looked up, his face dark with anger. "Dear God!" he exclaimed. "What else do you know of this?"

Kate explained the ruse of eviction Lady Claymore had used to bring her to Claymore Castle. She also told him of the Scotsmen in O'Hara garb and the other oddities she had pieced together.

As she spoke, Patrick's face darkened more and more with anger. "My men," he growled harshly when she had finished. "I'll see the Lowland bastards damned in hell for betraying me! Come!"

He spun on his heel and Kate had practically to run to keep up with him.

"O'Hara!" he bellowed, bursting into the tent. "Read this!"

The silence was tomblike as O'Hara did as he was bid. Conor wanted to throw his arms around Kate in greeting and ask about Timothy, but he sensed that keeping his seat would be wiser. Patrick had retreated to the far side of the tent and now paced back and forth, rubbing his temples furiously.

Kate's eyes drifted from O'Hara's stolid build to Patrick's lithe but powerful form. Simply being near him gave her a feeling of security. In his black battle dress with the gold and green O'Hara crest, he had never looked more irresistible. Somehow, the colors seemed to emphasize the steel flint of his eyes and the strong, lean line of his jaw.

"Damn...damn, damn, damn!"

O'Hara's thundering voice made them all whirl to face him.

"The bloody Scots Covenanters would break the truce we've signed and take Ireland for Parliament while the issue is still undecided in England and the king still holds the throne. We have no choice but to attack them first!"

"Attack Claymore?" Kate asked, wide-eyed. "But from Lady Claymore's message 'tis obvious she thinks you march straight for Ballylee."

"Aye, Kate," Patrick said, moving to her side. "And so we were. But Elana sought only to warn us of the trap. She wouldn't know that if the Scots plan to break the truce, we daren't let that strong a force of Covenanters stay on our flank above Ballylee." He turned to Rory. "O'Hara?"

"Aye?"

"I ask but one thing. Grant me permission to remove Lady Claymore from the castle first."

Kate gasped but no one seemed to hear her, and as Patrick continued speaking, the truth suddenly became clear to her. It was obvious from the way his gray eyes danced when he spoke her name, the way pain creased his face when he spoke of her imprisonment amid the Scots. It was in the anxious tone of his voice as he insisted that Elana Claymore be safely beyond Claymore's walls before the beginning of the siege.

No wonder he had never looked upon her as anything other than a close friend or a lovable sister, Kate thought, her heart sinking. *For there is no doubt, he is in love with Lady Elana Claymore.*

Tears sprang unbidden to her eyes. Slowly she began to back from the tent lest she start to weep openly and reveal her feelings.

"Aye, lad, it might work at that," O'Hara said, nodding in agreement.

"It will work," Patrick insisted, "with Conor and Kate's help. Kate!"

Suddenly he was before her, his hands grasping her shoulders. There was an uncharacteristic expression of pleading in his eyes as he looked beseechingly at her. "Say you'll help, Kate," he urged.

And then he noticed the tears in her eyes but misinterpreted the reason for them. "Your family," he exclaimed. "Damme, I forgot. What of them, Kate?"

"They're safe," she said, a choke in her voice. "My father took Timothy and the children to a cave in the mountain. 'Tis very hidden. The children play there often."

"Good." He paused and searched her face once again. "Say you'll help. . .please!"

Blinking the stinging tears from her eyes, she swallowed hard, took a deep breath and nodded. "Aye, Patrick, I'll help save her for you."

"Good lass, Kate!" he cried, and turned back to where O'Hara was already spreading maps and charts on the table.

"I can give you twenty-four hours, lad, no more...."

Kate reached the tent flap and lifting it, began to run. When she reached the woods she continued on, oblivious to the sharp twigs that tore at her clothes and flesh.

Not until she was sure she was hidden from view did she stop by a tree and slide slowly to the ground. Then, with her elbows resting on her knees, she dropped her head in her hands and began to weep.

"Kate," came a sudden small voice.

Startled, she looked up and bent her head again quickly to hide her tear-filled eyes. "Go away, Conor!" she mumbled.

"I'm sorry, Kate," he said softly, ignoring her request.

"For what?" she asked, almost viciously angry that this young lad should have caught her at her most vulnerable. "You have no idea—"

"Aye, I do, Kate."

Something in his tone caught her attention, and lifting her head once more, she gazed up at him. Slowly the watery mist before her eyes cleared and she could see his youthful handsome face. It lacked its usual impish grin and the flashing mischief she had always seen in his deep-blue eyes. Now, it seemed, she was staring up at a wise-eyed little man instead of a lad of near twelve years old.

"I do know, Kate," he said, in a low voice filled with gentleness. "I saw it in the tent just now in the way you looked at Patrick. I've seen that look nearly every day of my life. 'Tis the way my mother looks at The O'Hara.''

THEY STOPPED THE CART halfway up the rise leading to Claymore Castle's looming gray walls. Patrick kept the hood of his cloak pulled low over his forehead as he looked up.

"Hola!" he cried in a loud but cracking voice. Softly he added, "Keep your head low, Kate. Surely one of them will remember and recognize you if you show your face."

A helmeted figure appeared between the parapets. The face was unfamiliar, but Patrick gritted his teeth when he saw the O'Hara crest.

"What's your business?" called down the sentry.

"Scots," Patrick muttered to Kate.

"I told you.... I think all of them are," she whispered.

"Sweeps...sweeps, we are," he called up, broadening his accent. "Would ye have your chimneys swept? My lad 'ere's a monkey goin' down a chimney 'e is. Would ye have us sweep?"

"Nay, we've no need. On wi' you!"

"Would the lord be of a mind to let us camp the night in yon woods...an' be Christian enough to grant us a bit of leavin's from the evenin' table?"

From the high wall above them, Patrick could see the sentry's already surly countenance become more sullen than ever at his request. "'Tis not much we're askin', sar," he added, in whining tones.

"A minute," the man called down, and disappeared. Returning a short time later, he called down to Patrick. "Aye, the lord says you can spend the night in the woods...but, mark you, just the night. I dinna want to see your scurvy selves come dawn's light!"

"Aye, sar, thank ye, sar. And the leavin's?"

"Knock on the postern gate after supper hour," came the reply, with a wave for them to be off.

Patrick urged the horse into motion back down the rise. As they bounced and swayed over the heath, he looked to the sky and inhaled deeply. "There's a cool breeze from the north," he observed. "There'll be no fog this night but no moon, either. Let us hope for a bit of Irish mist come nightfall!"

A short way into the trees they found a clearing. Conor was dispatched on foot to the far side of the wood to retrieve a second horse they had left behind. Patrick and Kate set about preparing a makeshift camp including a fire that they made sure could be seen from the ramparts of Claymore.

When Conor returned with the second horse, he and Patrick carefully wrapped cloth around the animals' bits, bridles, stirrups and any other part of the tack that could conceivably make a noise and give them away. Then Patrick cleared a space in the dirt. With a stick he schooled Conor thoroughly on the layout of Claymore's interior. This done, the three of them stretched out near the fire to wait until evening.

All afternoon they watched horsemen stream in and out of the castle's main gate. From the pouches some of them carried, Patrick concluded they were messengers from General Monro's Scots army.

At last darkness came and with it, as Patrick had hoped, a gentle misting rain.

"'Tis time," he said, getting up and donning a heavy black cloak over his shirt and breeches.

Together they moved to the edge of the wood and parted without speaking. Patrick moved swiftly to the right and was quickly lost among the gently moving shadows of the night. Kate and Conor walked side by side across the open heath.

"Are you all right, Kate?" the boy asked softly.

"Aye," she replied with a smile, placing an arm around his shoulders. "I'm fine...truly."

She looked down at his grinning face and his sturdy young body. He wore one of Patrick's leather vests. It was far too large for him but at least served to disguise the thick coil of rope around his middle and the dagger belt slung at his hip.

If he has to, can he use that dagger, Kate wondered. She thought back over the past few hours, and recalling how much she had learned about this boy who was so quickly becoming a man, she was suddenly sure that not only could he use the dagger but would do so should the need arise. The thought made her shudder.

They were halfway up the rise toward the castle wall before he spoke again. "If it does any good, Kate, I think you're prettier than she is."

Kate couldn't refrain from giggling. "Thank you, sir," she replied gravely. "Mayhap I shall stop aging and wait for a fine gentleman like you to catch up with me!"

Conor was saved from replying by their arrival at the castle gate. As Kate rapped on the heavy oak, he moved into the shadows on one side and flattened himself against the rough gray stones of the wall.

"Aye?" came a muffled voice from beyond the door.

"'Tis the sweeps," Kate called in low tones. "'Twas granted us some leavin's from the supper table."

The night was chill, but Conor could nevertheless feel sweat rise on his back and trickle down between his shoulder blades. On the wall high above him he could hear swords clank on stone and booted feet treading monotonously back and forth.

What if he should be discovered by a sentry he thought, suddenly afraid. He took a deep breath to steady himself and squared his sturdy shoulders. He was a soldier now...on a mission he reminded himself firmly. If necessary, he would just have to kill the sentry.

At last the door's talk-hole opened and a shaft of light slanted through it. Carefully, Kate made sure most of her face was hidden in the shadow of her hood.

"Who be ye?" demanded the gatekeeper.

"Sweeps," she replied. "We're camped in your woods. The lord said we might have some leavin's."

The sentry growled under his breath. "I dinna know if there's any slops for the likes o' ye, but I'll see."

"I've a bucket," she told him, raising it into the light.

There was a moment's hesitation during which Conor thought his lungs would burst from pent-up air. Then the slide over the talk-hole closed and he could hear the chain being removed and the heavy iron bar being lifted.

Slowly, one half of the huge, arched double doors slid open. Torchlight flooded Kate's robed figure and the ground around her. To the still-nervous Conor, it seemed as though night had suddenly been turned into day. With the opening of the gate came the smells of cooking from the scullery and the equally strong but more unpleasant stench of garbage from the offal carts nearby.

"Let's have it," the sentry ordered.

Kate thrust the leather bucket through the opening and Conor tensed. He waited, his breath like fire in his lungs, until he saw Kate turn toward him. Almost imperceptibly, she nodded, and he scurried to her side and bolted through the opening. Darting into a passage behind the kitchen, he pulled a bridle from beneath his cloak and in plain sight slung it over his shoulder.

The wait seemed like an eternity but it was, in fact, only a few minutes until the guard returned. With a curse he thrust the bucket to Kate through the opening and then closed the door. Once the chains and the iron bar had been put back in place, he returned to his post.

Conor waited, counting to himself as Patrick had

told him. Then, assuming an air of confidence he was far from feeling, he stepped into the light. As he rounded the corner and passed the scullery, he started to whistle.

"Here, lad, what are ye up to?" demanded the sentry.

"A bit to eat while I was mendin' this," Conor replied, forcing his voice to remain calm and holding the bridle aloft. "I'm for returnin' it to the stables now."

The man scowled but questioned him no further.

Assuming the best swagger he could manage, Conor began the long walk across the bailey. Out of the corner of his eye he could see sentries on both the inner and outer walls, but no one stopped him. Inside the stable he discarded the bridle and went up the ladder to the loft. Once there, it was an easy matter to get through the roof-trap and from thence onto the battlements.

Patrick's words rang in his ears as he doubled over in a crouch and moved along as fast as he dared. "'Twill be dark, and your size will allow you to slip into the empty cannon mounts as you work your way by the sentries."

He moved silently and stealthily, using his hand on the outer wall to guide him. A chill ran up his back at the sound of the sudden approach of booted feet. Quickly he worked his way back until his hand found the nearest space. Doubling over, he crawled into the hole and waited. Seconds later he saw a pair of shiny knee-high boots move past only inches from his face.

Twice more Conor had to hide in a cannon well, until at last he ran up the steps and found himself facing the old wooden timbers of the tower door. Gently he lifted the latch and pulled, only to cringe at the loud scraping sound of rusty iron against rusty iron.

"The round tower isn't used," Patrick had told him. "'Twas once a dungeon. Be careful the old hinges don't squeak when you open the door. If they do...."

Quickly he popped two stones from his pockets into his mouth. Sucking on the stones, he worked up mouthful after mouthful of spittle, which he deposited on the hinges. At last he felt secure enough to try again. There was still a grating noise as the door swung open, but he hoped it was not loud enough to raise an alarm.

Guided by the faint grayness coming from the outside, Conor quickly located the privy chute. The next five minutes he spent in feeling frantically along the walls for a fetters ring. He was nearly halfway around the room and fearful that they had all been removed when he finally found one. Hastily he removed the coiled rope from around his waist and looped and tied it through the iron ring. Then he played the rope out to the privy chute.

"Here now, what are ye up to, lad?"

For an instant, Conor froze at the sudden harshness of the voice in the stillness of the night. Then he whirled and the color drained from his face. A sentry stood on the threshold one foot on the outside step and the other in the room. Mentally, Conor cursed himself for forgetting to close the door behind him when he had first entered the room.

With a trembling hand, he slid the dagger from his belt and held the hilt in both hands beneath his cloak. "I..." he began, then stopped, his voice choked in his throat.

"Well, out with it, lad!" demanded the sentry. "What brings ye up on the battlements this time o' night?"

"I—I've to use the privy chute," Conor managed finally.

"Damme," the guard laughed, "be ye more lass than lad? Hang yourself over the wall! Here... what's this?"

He had entered the room far enough to collide with the rope. Now he took a step back to investigate it.

Again Patrick's words hummed in Conor's ears: "...there's nothing for it, lad. If you're found out, there'll be no good excuse for you to be on the walls."

"Here now, lad. You'd best come with me!"

The sentry was standing directly over Conor where he crouched at the mouth of the privy chute. Leaning forward, he clutched at the lad's shoulder. He had pushed his helmet up to ease the irritation of the two leather straps beneath his chin.

That was where Conor aimed his dagger, at a point directly between the two leather straps.

The man's eyes suddenly shot wide open and his tongue burst forth from between his lips. For a second Conor was afraid he would cry out, but there was only a gentle gurgling sound as the man pitched forward across him, propelling him to the floor and driving the breath from his body.

Too shocked to move immediately Conor remained immobile beneath the man's weight. Then, grunting with the effort, he rolled the corpse from him and retrieved the coiled rope.

Once, quickly, he looked down at the white face on the floor. With a shudder, he then crawled into the entrance of the chute, drawing the rope after him. Holding the rope's weighted end before him, he looked out and down into the misty grayness below him. "Damn," he gasped.

Though he couldn't see the ground, he knew it was a long way down. He played out the rope until there was no more. Then, with his heart in his mouth, he began to descend.

THE SOUND OF A STEALTHY TREAD made Patrick reach for his dagger.

" 'Tis me."

1. How do you rate _____ ?
   (Please print book TITLE)

   1.6 ☐ excellent   .4 ☐ good   .2 ☐ not so good

   .5 ☐ very good   .3 ☐ fair   .1 ☐ poor

   E 1 2 3 4 5 6 7

2. How likely are you to purchase another book in this series?

   2.1 ☐ definitely would purchase   .3 ☐ probably would not purchase

   .2 ☐ probably would purchase   .4 ☐ definitely would not purchase

3. How do you compare this title with similar books you usually read?

   3.1 ☐ far better than others   .4 ☐ not as good

   .2 ☐ better than others   .5 ☐ definitely not as good

   .3 ☐ about the same

4. Have you any additional comments about this book?

   _____ (4)

   _____ (6)

5. How did you first become aware of this book?

   8. ☐ in-store display   11. ☐ talk show

   9. ☐ radio   12. ☐ read other titles

   10. ☐ magazine _____   13. ☐ other _____
                 (name)   (please specify)

6. What most prompted you to buy this book?

   14. ☐ title   17. ☐ picture on cover   20. ☐ back-cover story outline

   15. ☐ price   18. ☐ friend's recommendation   21. ☐ read a few pages

   16. ☐ author   19. ☐ product advertising   22. ☐ other _____
                                                  (please specify)

7. How do you usually obtain your books?

   23. ☐ bookstore   26. ☐ department/discount store   29. ☐ borrow

   24. ☐ drugstore   27. ☐ convenience store   30. ☐ other

   25. ☐ supermarket   28. ☐ subscription
                                                  (please specify)

8. What type(s) of paperback fiction have you purchased in the past 3 months? Approximately how many?

	No. purchased		No. purchased
☐ contemporary romance	(31) _____	☐ espionage	(45) _____
☐ historical romance	(33) _____	☐ western	(47) _____
☐ gothic romance	(35) _____	☐ contemporary novels	(49) _____
☐ romantic suspence	(37) _____	☐ historical novels	(51) _____
☐ mystery	(39) _____	☐ science fiction/fantasy	(53) _____
☐ private eye	(41) _____	☐ occult	(55) _____
☐ action/adventure	(43) _____	☐ other	(57) _____

9. On which date was this book purchased? (59) _____

10. Please indicate your age group and sex.

   61.1 ☐ Male   62.1 ☐ under 15   .3 ☐ 25-34   .5 ☐ 50-64

   .2 ☐ Female   .2 ☐ 15-24   .4 ☐ 35-49   .6 ☐ 65 or older

Thank you for completing and returning this questionnaire.

NAME _____

ADDRESS _____
(Please Print)

CITY _____

ZIP CODE _____

He breathed a deep sigh of relief when he saw Kate's white face emerge from the gloom.

"Not yet?" she asked in dismay, scanning the wall above them.

"Nay," he replied, sheathing the dagger. "But not to worry. 'Twill take time. The lad must go round nearly half the castle." He paused. Then, hoping to keep her mind occupied and free from worry, he added, "'Twas just as I expected. The vinery beneath her window has lost its sap. 'Twould be far too brittle to hold the weight of one, let alone of two."

"It...sounds as though you've used that vinery before," Kate observed in a hollow whisper.

"Aye," Patrick admitted, not noticing the tone of her voice. "I have...many a night."

Kate felt her heart give a lurch at his words. *How well he must know the location of Elana Claymore's bedchamber,* she thought miserably. She was about to turn away when a sound made them both look up.

"Ah, 'tis the rope!" Patrick murmured excitedly. "Good lad, good lad!"

Quickly, he wrapped it around him and relaxed his weight. The rope went taut and somewhere far above them they could hear the faint sound of scraping as Conor began his descent.

"Go slow now, lad.... Take your time," Patrick whispered as loudly as he dared.

Kate's fists were clenched so tightly she was sure her nails had cut into the flesh of her palms. Fearful for Conor's safety, she gazed upward into the mist, and it seemed like an eternity until she finally saw him coming down the knotted rope hand over hand, guiding himself with his boots against the stone.

Moments later Patrick plucked him from the rope and set him on the ground. He turned to face them, and it took all Kate's willpower to choke back a scream. The lad's eyes were wide with shock, his usually pink-cheeked face was now chalk white and the whole front of his shirt was damply crimson.

"Oh, dear God . . ." she whispered.

"Are you wounded, lad?" Patrick asked, kneeling before him.

"I've been blooded," Conor replied in a thin voice.

"Patrick—" Kate cried.

"Nay, lass, 'tis all right," Patrick assured her. "He means he's had to kill someone. Was it a sentry, lad?"

"Aye. He's in the tower . . . on the floor."

"Conor, are you sure he's dead?"

The lad made no reply but simply stared blankly at Patrick. Almost roughly, Patrick shook him "Conor— Listen!" he commanded. "Are you sure he's dead?"

"Aye," the boy replied dully as life slowly ebbed back into his eyes. "He's dead."

"Don't think about it, lad," Patrick advised gently. "Remember what The O'Hara told you: if you would fight the war, 'tis better you than the enemy who rides away from the field with the breath still in your body."

Getting to his feet, Patrick slid his baldric, with its sword, from his shoulder and handed it to Kate.

"'Twill be dangerous without a blade," she gasped.

He shook his head. "Its clanking sound will prove more dangerous if it should alert someone to my presence. I have a dagger and pistol; 'twill be enough."

"God go with you, Patrick," she said in a choking voice.

"Aye, let's hope He does," he murmured, turning and grasping the rope. "Now get you and the lad gone, Kate. You know where to wait."

Hand over hand, he began to pull himself up, his feet scraping on the wet stone as he ascended. With his powerful shoulders and arms, he went up the rope as quickly as Conor had come down. Entering the tower room, he made sure the sentry was dead before pulling the rope up behind him. Quickly, he coiled it around his waist and scrambled onto the roof.

The rain was coming down harder now, making the leaded slate horribly slippery underfoot. Twice he lost his footing and slid wildly down the roof's sharp incline. Each time he barely managed to save himself from hurtling into space by digging his toes and fingers into faulty cracks where the slabs of slate had been poorly set.

The second time he slipped, his pistol fell from his belt. "Damn," he hissed, as the weapon clattered once on the slate and then was lost.

At last he reached the rounded dome over Claymore's great room. Foot by painstaking foot he worked himself around the catwalk, mentally ticking off the third-story rooms as he passed over them: chapel, Lord Claymore's former chambers, library, office, balcony hall. . .Elana's bedchamber.

With the wind driving stinging pellets of rain into his face and eyes, Patrick unwrapped the coiled rope from around him. Looping one end around the smoking chimney, he tied it off, and threw the remainder as far out into the darkness as his precarious position would allow. Cautiously, he leaned over the edge of the catwalk, grasped the rope firmly and swung himself out into the darkness. As he walked backward down the sheer wall, he could see slivers of light escaping through the shutter slats of Elana's window below him.

Long before reaching his goal Patrick had decided on his method of entry. Between the eerie keening of the wind and the steady drumming sound of the rain, he knew Elana would never hear rapping on the window or shutters. Precious time would be lost trying to attract her attention in that fashion. Using his legs,

Patrick pushed himself as far from the wall as possible as he descended. On the fourth swing he stiffened his legs and crashed through window and shutter, landing solidly on his feet inside the chamber.

He froze in sudden shock and anger as his sweeping gaze took in the intimate scene before him.

Elana was lying in her high-backed tub, a tall figure in a wide-sleeved linen shirt and black breeches standing beside it. His hands covering her breasts, he had been leaning over her and kissing her when Patrick had crashed unceremoniously into the room. Now the man spun around to face the intruder, his dark eyes flicking from Patrick to a baldric slung across the back of a chair.

Instantly the whole truth washed over Patrick like a sickening tide. He knew not this tall, dark-haired man's name, but he would forever remember his face. He could still see his black helmet and recalled how the rain had glistened on the man's steel-mesh doublet as he stood on the parapet of Dublin Castle that day Donal had received his mortal wound.

With a supreme effort of will, Patrick calmed the erratic beating of his heart and banished the sinking feeling from the pit of his stomach. His self-control once more intact, he tilted his head slightly in a bow toward the unknown man.

"Since you are here, sir," he remarked coldly, "with the Scots Covenanters—and you were with the English at our raid on Dublin Castle—I would assume we have found our spy." He paused and swept his gaze from the man to the white-faced figure in the tub. His gray eyes flamed with ruthless violence and unbridled hate as he stared at the cowering Elana. Her eyes were opened wide in an expression of pleading mingled with pain and guilt. Tears streamed from their turquoise depths, but they moved him not. "Or I should say," he added grimly, "our two spies."

Redding's control of his emotions was fully equal to

that of Patrick's. "Sir John Redding at your service, sir," he said, sweeping a low bow. "And I assume from m'lady's pained expression that you are Patrick Talbot."

"I am," the young man acknowledged quietly. "Patrick O'Hara Talbot."

" 'Tis a pity that your lust has stirred you through the storm this night," Redding observed arrogantly.

"Nay," Patrick replied, the glint in his hooded gray eyes like a saber slashing at Elana's flesh. "It was not lust that moved me this night."

Elana trembled under the bone-chilling iciness of his gaze. He looked dispassionate, but there was a savage tenseness in his taut stance. *This,* she thought almost fearfully, *is what he must look like just before a battle.*

"Nay, not lust, Sir John," he repeated quietly. "But forgive me, I seem to have interrupted yours."

The man moved swiftly. From the chair he retrieved his sword before Patrick had a chance to turn. With a strength surprising for one so thin, he picked up the chair in his free hand and hurled it at Patrick.

The young man shouldered it aside and drew his dagger. Truly frightened now, Elana cried out and leaped from the tub.

Redding faced Patrick, short sword in hand. "Not an even match, I fear," he remarked, glancing pointedly at Patrick's dagger. "But then, 'tis not a gentleman's game we play."

"I doubt either of us have been overly strong in gentlemen's pursuits," observed Patrick sarcastically. Then he leaped aside, barely avoiding Redding's first pass.

A few long strides took him to the bed where, earlier in the evening, a heavy gown of silk brocade had obviously been carelessly discarded by Elana. Hurriedly he wrapped the gown around his left arm, mentally cursing his lack of sword and the loss of his pistol, then spun around barely in time to deflect a second pass of Redding's sword. Both men backed away now, gauging the other's strength.

" 'Twould be wiser, Talbot," sneered Redding, "if you would lay down the dagger and become my prisoner."

"How so?" queried Patrick, feinting with the dagger and, moving swiftly forward, slamming his bound left harm heavily across the other man's chest.

Redding staggered slightly and fell back a pace but quickly regained his balance to come on again. "You would make a fine hostage," he replied. "And perhaps would end this fray before it begins."

"I think you overvalue my worth, Redding," declared Patrick. "And besides, I would rather be gone from here to shout the perfidy of you and your slut to all of Eire."

Cautiously, the two men circled around the room, filling it now and then with the harsh sound of steel meeting steel as one or the other lunged forward. Patrick's face held an expression of total concentration, while Redding's confident smile did not waver.

"Stop—now! Both of you!"

The command rang out sharply. Both men halted in surprise and turned to Elana. Still naked, dripping wet and trembling from her matted hair to her toes, she looked ridiculous standing with her back against a wall. But her hands were remarkably steady as she swung a pistol back and forth between the two men.

"How charming—the lady wants to practice her aim," Redding sneered. "I wonder which of us she would choose."

Even as Redding spoke, Patrick saw the sudden movement. He jumped away from the slashing blade but had no chance to avoid it entirely. The sharp point cut its way from his right shoulder down across his back to his hip.

With a cry of agony Patrick twisted and fell to the floor only to cry out once more as he hit the stone. The dagger fell from his hand and spun noisily away across the floor.

Elana screamed, too shocked to fire the pistol even had she wanted to.

Redding moved swiftly to stand directly over him. He held the sword in both hands, turned downward like a dagger. But, as he leaned forward and thrust the blade downward, Patrick deflected its already bloody tip with his bound arm. With a strength born of sheer desperation, he then pushed himself from the floor and thrust upward with his elbow, smashing it viciously into Redding's face.

Through the maze of pain partially blinding him, Patrick saw his opponent fall to his knees. Blood oozed from between the fingers of his hands covering his face.

Gasping in agony, Patrick struggled to regain his feet and swayed unsteadily for a moment before catching sight of Redding's dropped sword. Groping for it, he managed to retrieve it and holding it in both hands, raised it high above his head over the moaning figure of John Redding.

Without warning, Elana suddenly thrust herself between the two men. Her skin glowed in the light from the fire and candles, and her lustrous hair flowed over her shoulders to caress her dancing breasts. But still she held the pistol, now aimed directly at Patrick's heart.

"Step aside, wench," he commanded harshly.

"I'll not," she declared.

"Then fire!"

A flood of emotions swept across her lovely face and her eyes clouded with indecision. Then, slowly, she lowered the pistol.

Repaying her in kind, Patrick lowered the sword,

and dropped it. "Very well," he said quietly. "A life for a life."

He moved to the window. Gritting his teeth at the awakened pain, he found the rope and struggled to the ledge.

"Dear God, Patrick, your back!" she exclaimed. "You'll never—"

"I will," he growled at her. "For if I'm to bleed to death, I'm damned if 'twill be on Claymore land!"

She moved toward him and then suddenly stopped, the compassion that had been in her eyes suddenly draining away.

"'Twas you who played the fool, Patrick," she insisted defiantly. "I sought to warn you, to save you. I told you and The O'Hara to turn back, not come forward—and least of all to Claymore."

"Aye, you did," he agreed coldly. "And a fool I was. A fool, it seems, I've always been. And for it I was the cause of Donal's death in Dublin. That I'll have to live with always. I'll have but one consolation, and that is the thought of what you will have to live with, Elana."

She gazed at him with a puzzled frown.

"Him, Elana," snarled Patrick, gesturing toward John Redding. "I hope to God you'll have to live with him forever."

And then he was gone into the mist and the grayness of the night.

—

January 1644

CHAPTER SEVENTEEN
DONEGAL, IRELAND

IT HAD BEEN A PARTICULARLY cold December, with chilling winds and constant rain out of the north, nor was January much better. The day The O'Hara,

Conor and two guards rode into the clearing in front of the O'Hanlon cottage was particularly bad.

Warm greetings were exchanged between the O'Hanlons and their visitors, then they all moved inside. The fire was dying and the wind beat against the thatch with as lonely a sound as it had over the meadows and heaths it had crossed.

"The stock is low," Kate murmured in apology. "We didn't cut enough in the summer."

O'Hara took in the situation at a glance. "Cut fresh peat," he instructed Conor and the two guards, "no matter the hardness of the ground."

"Tim," Kate directed her brother, "go with them!"

The guards and two boys left as ordered. O'Hara moved to the fire and seated himself wearily, smiling at Kate's look of concern.

"My bones," he explained with a chuckle. "'Tis too many Irish winters, I fear. Come sit, lass."

While Kate did as he asked, O'Hara glanced at her two wide-eyed young sisters cuddled together in their bunk for warmth. When he spoke again it was in a low voice. "You have been well?" he asked.

"Aye."

"And the children?"

"A cough or two. . . nothing serious."

"A harper told me of your father. May he rest in peace."

Kate crossed herself and nodded. "'Twas bound to happen one day," she observed sadly.

"You're still welcome, all of you, on Ballylee."

"I thank you, but we'll make do here. 'Tis our home," Kate replied softly.

O'Hara nodded, appreciating both her stubborn acceptance of her hard life and her decision. He stared for many moments into the dying fire before speaking again. "And how's himself?" he queried finally and without much hope.

"I see him twice, mayhap three times a week, the weather allowing," replied Kate. "He's still got the wild look in his eyes but he seems fit. If you're wonderin' if he'll leave his booley retreat. . .he will not."

" 'Tis the guilt," O'Hara rumbled.

"Aye, he lives it still," she agreed sadly.

"And well he should, for 'twas reckless and foolish the way he let the wench use him. But what's done is done and once 'tis over we've naught to do but to get on with livin'."

"I can talk little to him," Kate said, brushing a stray tear from her cheek. "He'll not listen."

They both lapsed into silence, wrapped in their private thoughts.

Vividly, Kate remembered that night months ago when, heartsick with fear, she had felt Patrick let go of the rope and stagger toward her and Conor. He had fallen before reaching them, and she had become paralyzed with fear at the sight of his gaping wound.

Young Conor had proved his mettle then. Although he, too, had been crying, the lad had shaken Kate from her hysteria and together they had been able to tie Patrick to a horse. Conor had mounted behind him, and through the cold damp night they had flown to the cave the O'Hanlon family had moved to for safety during the fighting.

Several times during the ride Patrick had awakened with a cry of agony. Even now, in the security of the little cottage, the memory of it brought a sharp stab of anguish to Kate's heart.

At the cave her father, Timothy and Conor had managed to carry Patrick inside and clean the wound. It was then that he had awakened long enough to pour out in feverish gasps the tale of Lady Claymore's duplicity and beg Kate to mount once more and ride to O'Hara with the news.

It had taken The O'Hara's army a week to rout the

Scots Covenanters and another week of siege before Claymore Castle fell. It was after that that O'Hara had come to take Patrick to Ballylee. Because of the children, Kate had been unable to go with him but almost daily O'Hara had sent a rider with news of his recovery. And then just after Yuletide, Patrick had appeared.

There had been no greeting, no warmth, hardly a sign of recognition, in fact. There had been only a request.

"I'd much appreciate it if I could have the use of your booley house, Kate," he had asked of her in empty tones.

She had simply nodded and into the mountains he had gone. He had been there ever since.

" 'Tis you, Kate."

With a start Kate realized O'Hara was speaking to her, dragging her back from the painful memory of the past few months.

"What?"

"You love him, Kate.... We all know of it at Ballylee," Rory said softly.

Kate held her breath, then released it in a long sigh. "Aye, I do love him," she acknowledged quietly. "I think all of Eire knows it except Patrick."

" 'Tis you who can make him join the world of the living again," O'Hara said, leaning toward her intently. "All men need the love of a good woman."

Kate's jaw tightened and she met the pleading in O'Hara's eyes with a determined stare. "I can do naught for him if he's not a mind to let me," she declared firmly. "When he looks at me, I swear he's blind in one eye and cannot see out of the other."

O'Hara sighed and with an effort, rose slowly to his feet. "I'll be for seein' him. Will he be in the booley house?"

"Nay most probably among the crags," replied

Kate. "He walks there almost daily now, good weather or bad."

"It'll repair his strength at least," observed O'Hara.

"An' 'tis a proper place for him to do his brooding," Kate added, failing to hide the sadness in her eyes. "Come along, I'll show you the way. I know well the paths he takes."

THEY FOUND HIM perched among the jutting gray rocks of a craggy peak. Chin in hand he sat staring out into nothing, oblivious to the way the wind billowed his cloak open around him.

"I'll wait here," Kate said, moving her horse to the leeward side of a large boulder and dismounting.

O'Hara rode as far as his horse could take him. He painfully continued the rest of the way on foot. At last, gasping for breath, he stepped out onto a rock near Patrick.

"'Tis a hateful nephew who makes a man my age play the billygoat to share his company," he declared breathlessly.

Patrick turned at the sound of his voice and O'Hara's blood ran cold. The young man's eyes, usually so full of life, gazed at him with a vacant stare. He had obviously allowed his beard to grow, for it was bushy and unkempt, matted with food residue as well as from the rain that beat down on his bare head. His clothes had become those of a vagabond, tattered and filthy.

"You shouldn't have come," Patrick said dully.

"I had to," replied O'Hara. "Your mother insisted. And you know my willful sister—when she commands, all Ballylee trembles!" The older man chuckled, but Patrick simply returned his gaze to the far heath.

Repressing a sigh, O'Hara sought to interest him in the latest news on England's civil war. "The Covenanters have crossed the Scots border into England and have declared for Parliament," he said. "'Tis too early to tell what good it will do them against the king."

Patrick made no response.

"The news is that Cromwell has begun matching Prince Rupert victory for victory."

O'Hara waited a few moments. Rapidly becoming desperate he changed the topic to news of his family. "We've had a letter from Maura," he told his nephew. "She and Brian sound happy enough but sweet Maggie longs to return to Eire."

He saw a slight movement of Patrick's shoulders, but still the young man remained silent.

"Gormanston came to me at last with the full tale," O'Hara went on doggedly. "He takes the blame for not telling what he knew when Claymore first told him of Redding. To keep the peace and not let Sir John become a wedge in the treaty negotiations, I agreed to let Gormanston handle the matter quietly himself."

Rory paused, then continued, "He's deeded his Barbados property to 'em. They sailed a week ago, to be wed on the ship. She asked of you."

"And did you tell her?" asked Patrick suddenly.

"Aye," O'Hara replied, breathing a sigh of relief that his nephew had spoken at last. "Just as you said. I told her you died."

"Thank you."

"Lad, your mother wants you at Ballylee, near her. She sent this."

Without turning his head, Patrick felt for the note O'Hara thrust toward him and grasped it.

O'Hara pulled his cloak tighter around him and crouched lower on the rock as he waited for Patrick to read.

My dearest son, Age is a terrible thing when it is fraught with loneliness. I have a daughter in a foreign land and a son who assumes that he has lived so much that he can die. You think your heart is so full of pain and guilt that you will never recover. Such youthful conceit!

I have had a seizure of paralysis in my legs that has spread through my whole body. I sometimes think all my weight lies in my bowels and my belly. And in my heart. And when I think of you, I feel as though it were suffocating me. At those times I can scarcely stir and am doubled up in pain. Yet tonight as I have done every night I will walk the battlements of Ballylee and look out across my land.

I will miss you tonight, my son.

Finishing the letter, Patrick gazed down at the parchment for long moments. Then, lifting his head he looked at O'Hara. "I'll come," he whispered, folding the letter. "But I cannot stay—not yet."

O'Hara nodded in satisfaction. Patrick's answer wasn't perfect, but for the moment, it was enough. He straightened and turned back down to the stony path. After a few steps he paused and looked back.

"Patrick, the truce here in Ireland holds...for now," he said. "But methinks the time will come again. When it does, will you fight?"

Patrick turned and faced him squarely. "Aye," he replied. "I'll fight."

For the second time that afternoon, O'Hara's blood suddenly ran cold. It seemed as though a hundred years had passed since he had last seen a smile such as the one Patrick wore now. O'Hara had been but a youth at the time, witnessing a duel to the death.

The name of the man who had worn it had been James Blake. And he had smiled in the same fashion just as death had claimed him.

CHAPTER EIGHTEEN
PARIS, FRANCE

"I THINK I am not destined for feminine pastimes!" Maggie declared, casting her needlework aside and gingerly running the tip of her tongue over her wounded thumb.

Maura smiled and bent her blond head back over her own work. "Methinks 'tis not the needlework that bores you as much as an old widow's constant company," she observed.

Maggie jumped to her feet with a tinkling laugh and brushed her lips across the top of Maura's golden head. "Aye, I'm sure that must be it. Why just the other day while walking with Brian by the stalls of Pont Neuf I was thinking along the same lines!"

"Along what lines?" Maura asked, taking the girl's bait as always.

"We were passing a cane shop," explained Maggie with a grin, "and I thought perhaps I should buy you one. Poor, dear old Maura. At twenty-two, 'tis near time for your joints to lock up, isn't it?"

"Get on with you!" Maura chided the girl with a light laugh. "Oww!"

"What is it?"

Maura glanced up with a slight flush in her cheeks, then immediately bent her head again. "You've made me prick *my* finger!" she exclaimed reproachfully.

Maggie laughed gaily and moved to the high arched windows, the hem of her heavy skirt rustling over the carpet as she walked. She looked down the hill from Montparnasse, across the fields to the houses and then to the larger buildings of central Paris. From there her gaze traveled across the red roofs to the Seine. She was glad they had chosen the Hôtel de Montparnasse. It was near the city yet far enough on the outskirts so that the stench of the crowded streets did not reach them. Idly, she wondered how much the city had changed since Rory O'Hara and his sister, Shanna, had left it to return to Ireland. Certainly, the monarchy had changed, for in 1643, Louis XIII had died, leaving the crown of France to his five-year-old son, now Louis XIV. Cardinal Richelieu, the power behind the throne of Louis XIII had also died, and the young Louis XIV's Spanish mother, Queen Anne, now ruled as regent with the assistance of the much-disliked Italian, Cardinal Mazarin.

It was a bright, clear summer day, with the sky tinted a deep blue. It was the kind of sun and sky she had rarely seen in Ireland...warm and cloudless. Yet despite its beauty she longed for the fog and the mists. She missed the sweet untainted taste of Irish rain on her lips. And somehow when the Irish mists lifted, the sun seemed to shine so much brighter.

In fact, there were many things she missed about Ireland: the huge rooms and eerie splendor of Ballylee, its parapets rising mysteriously through the mist of a summer day; the raucous and gay laughter of the whole family gathered around the long table at the evening meal. But above all, she missed Conor with his impish, laughing face, his bright, mischievous eyes and his warm companionship. Would she ever chase him wildly through the heather again or ride like the wind over the green hills with him, she wondered. And when again would they be able to discard their clothes and scream with abandoned joy as the lough's chill waters caressed their naked bodies?

She almost laughed when she remembered how she, Conor and Brian had frolicked naked in the water. Then she thought of her budding breasts and realized rather wistfully that those days were gone forever.

How long must they remain in Paris, she wondered. Beautiful though it was, it would never be home, and she sighed with longing at the thought of her green Ireland.

"Dear me," Maura chuckled, "it sounds as though the weight of the world is on your shoulders."

"Nay," Maggie replied, sighing again. " 'Tis the weight of Paris. Nearly more than I can bear."

Maura looked up from her needlework to gaze at her cousin. *How beautiful she is,* thought the young widow, with the sun slanting off her red gold hair, turning it to fire. *Sweet Maggie with the turned-up nose, the dimpled cheeks and the smile that no one can resist.*

And, thought Maura, it would not be long before she became still more lovely. Like all the O'Hara women, she was blossoming early. She was not quite twelve, yet her small, lithe body was already taking on a decidedly feminine shape. The thought made Maura both glad and fearful.

Willful and to the point in thought and speech, Maggie had the soul and spirit of an Irish lass. In Ireland, such a nature would pass without comment, but in Paris, the jaded young gallants might well be inclined to interpret it as an excuse to work their ways. The girl had mastered the manners and speech of the French but not their subtlety of deed and thought. She was the beauty and innocent soul of Ireland but in France she was but another rose to be plucked.

"Maura. . . ." came her clear voice from across the room.

"Aye?"

Maggie turned her attention back to her older companion. As she leaned against the window ledge, the sun cast a radiant copper glow over her hair. "How long must you wear your widow's weeds?" she asked.

"I've told you before, darling," replied Maura patiently. "I don't have to wear them at all. I still wear them because I want to."

Swiftly, Maggie crossed the room and knelt before her. Placing her hands on Maura's knees, she glanced upward with a look the young widow knew only too well.

"Will you never marry again?"

A look of pain crossed Maura's features. "I don't know," she replied sadly. "No one knows what is in their future. That is supposed to be the joy of living—looking toward tomorrow."

Maggie would not be deterred. "I've seen the way men look at you on the street, even in those drab weeds," she declared, with childish innocence.

Maura couldn't suppress a smile. "Methinks most of those men don't have marriage in mind, lass!"

"Would you marry a Frenchman, Maura?"

Maura shook her head and clucked her tongue. "How wild you talk today, young lady!" she reproved.

"Well, would you?" Maggie persisted.

Maura shrugged. "I don't know."

"I wouldn't!" Maggie cried, jumping to her feet and running back to the window. "I want no foppish, bewigged, hand-kissing Frenchman for a husband. When the time comes, I want a bold Irishman!"

It was seldom these days that Maura found much to amuse her greatly, but Maggie's words now drew a peal of laughter from her. "One day, little one, you'll find that beneath their thin coat of manners, all men are bold!" she assured the girl.

Maggie's eyes gleamed wickedly as her lips curved in a mischievous grin. "Not as lusty as our Irishmen, I'll wager," she returned promptly.

Before Maura could reply Brian rushed into the room, a news sheet in his hand.

"Rupert was defeated by Cromwell at Marston Moor in the north of England!" he cried, waving the single sheet before him. "And the new papal nuncio to Ireland, Rinuccini, Bishop of Fermo, has arrived here in Paris to announce the Pope's support of the war. 'Tis said he brings arms and money for our cause in Eire!''

"Is there no light news?" Maura asked.

"Aye, Queen Henrietta Maria gave birth to a daughter while running and hiding from Parliament troops! Methinks she should have remained in safety in Holland instead of returning to her husband's side in England."

"The poor woman," Maura sighed, crossing herself.

"Wonderful, Brian...so marvelous," Maggie groaned, daily becoming more and more bored with political news. "And what does your news sheet say of lusty Irishmen?"

"What?" queried the youth, gazing at her blankly.

"Nothing," she giggled, running up to him and kissing him lightly on the cheek before gliding from the room.

"What the devil has gotten into her?" exclaimed Brian, staring after her with a puzzled frown.

"Spring," Maura replied.

"'Tis summer, and hot as blazes!''

"'Tis still spring to Maggie!''

November 1644

CHAPTER NINETEEN
HATTON HOUSE, LONDON

TALL AND SPLENDIDLY ATTIRED in black from head to toe, Captain Robert Hubbard dismounted and carelessly tossed the reins of the big white stallion to the groom.

"'Tis a grand animal, sir," noted the man with approval.

"Aye," Robert said. "A gift from General Cromwell. It is my personal sign of purity for our cause."

Not noticing the smirking smile or the flash of caustic humor in his master's black eyes, the groom nodded and led the magnificent animal away.

His helmet under his arm and his sword jangling at his side, Robert mounted the courtyard steps to the huge rear facade of Hatton House. The tall glass-paneled doors opened before him and he stepped into the muteness of the mansion's regal great room.

"Good day to you, Master Robert," greeted Christopher, who had opened the door for him.

"Captain Hubbard," corrected the young man coldly. "Lady Hatton sent for me."

Like his father before him, Christopher had been Elizabeth Hatton's man for years. He had taken care of Robert Hubbard even before the lad could walk. Now Robert was captain in Cromwell's army, and the icy stare in his eyes and the imperious tone in his voice made the old man step back in shock.

"Where is she?" Hubbard asked curtly.

"In her chambers, sir," the old servant replied, the hurt clearly evident in his eyes. "I think you know the way."

"I do."

Christopher could only shake his head in disbelief as he watched this stranger ascend the grand staircase.

With purposeful strides Robert made his way through the maze of hallways to the chamber wing of the house, stopping before the heavy oak door that led into his grandmother's private rooms. He squared his powerful shoulders, took a deep breath and rapped sharply on the heavy door. The voice bidding him enter was faint but recognizable.

Robert went in and closed the door behind him, then paused to let his eyes adjust to the dimness. The draperies were closed, blotting out even the waning rays of the setting sun. The only illumination came from a tiny ornate lamp on a delicately carved small table. It cast an eerie, almost ghostly light on the silver-haired head lying back, against a mound of pillows.

Robert moved to the foot of the four-poster bed. The room was neat and clean but displayed all the signs of tiredness and old age. The damask canopy and matching draperies that hung down the four hand-hewn, heavily scrolled columns were musty. Time had frayed the threads and the linings were badly in need of repair. Even the rug was now more a show of poverty than the symbol of style and wealth it once had been. In many places it had worn so thin that the gray tiles of the floor showed through the silk fabrics.

He was close enough now to see that the seemingly ageless beauty of his grandmother's face had at last succumbed to time and had deteriorated into a network of sagging lines. The delicate forearms and wrists that had once waved imperious commands to husbands and servants were bony and shaking slightly.

"Robert?" she queried.

"Aye."

"Come closer." Obediently, he moved forward. "Dear God, how ominous you look, like something from hell," she breathed.

Robert grinned. "General Cromwell would not appreciate that, madam. Black is the color of the godly."

"And are you godly, Robert?" she asked.

"I've learned to exude piety," he replied evenly.

"Of that I've no doubt," she acknowledged dryly, turning her head in his direction so that a shaft of light fell across her face.

And as Robert gazed down into her unblinking eyes, he saw why she had summoned him. The eyes that had once glowed with a lust for life, their beacon-like radiance missing nothing, were now like fading embers looking at a dying world.

"The war goes well?"

Robert nodded. "The king has little hope now."

"There must be a great deal of killing. . . you reek of death."

"I'm sure I do."

"You never write," she commented, her voice faintly accusing.

"There is little time in the course of killing," he observed.

Elizabeth Hatton's eyes seemed to come to life as her gaze raked up and down his tall, black-clad form. When she looked again at the swarthy, chiseled features of his face, a tremor seemed to ripple through her.

"I never dreamed that defying the king would come to this," she murmured.

"Few people did," he pointed out with a shrug. "But it has, and there can be but one end to it."

"And you, Robert. What of you?" she asked. "I've heard the many threads they weave to make the fabric of your legend. On your white horse, they call you the Puritan answer to the black-horsed devil, Prince Rupert."

Robert said nothing. He merely stood gazing down at her, his pose militarily erect.

"I'm dying, you know," she said abruptly.

" 'Tis sadly evident, madam," he replied, his voice containing no hint of emotion.

For the first time since he had entered the room, a smile crossed the old woman's lips. His answer was so like him that it amused her.

"All that I have is yours," she told him. "I have already talked with my solicitors. Do you have plans when this horrid business is over?"

Robert's jaw stiffened. He hesitated for a moment and then decided to tell her. "Come spring, General Cromwell has decided to send another troop to Ireland. I'm to command it."

The light in her eyes faded and she shook her white head slowly. "'Twas your plan all along, wasn't it?" she sighed, in a tone that stated a fact rather than posed a question.

He nodded. "Officers and men will be granted vast acres—whole plantations as pay—once the Irish are beaten."

"And you will have Ballylee. All will come full circle," she murmured. She coughed slightly and her diminutive hands clenched the edge of her quilt. "I cannot dissuade you, convince you that this form of revenge is not sweet but useless?"

"I think 'tis only natural and, perhaps, fated," Robert said, with a sardonic smile.

"By God, I suppose," Lady Hatton contemptuously replied.

"Doesn't God preordain all things?"

Robert hadn't expected an answer, nor did his grandmother supply one. Instead, she changed the topic.

"I never loved you as I should have, and now I am sorry for it."

"'Tis no matter," he replied with another shrug, uneasy at his grandmother's rare expression of sentimentality.

"It is," she insisted, "and I fear one day you will realize it—too late. I look back over the years and I see now that the brief time of love I had was all that mattered." She paused for a moment, then added, "Leave me now, Robert.... I'm weary."

"As you wish, madam." Bowing slightly, he left the room and retired to his own chambers in Hatton House.

Shortly after dawn the following morning, Christopher rapped on his door and entered the room. "She's gone," he said simply.

His face devoid of all emotion, Robert nodded. "Have my horse made ready," he ordered. "And there is a leather-bound volume beside her bed. 'Tis all I'll be taking with me."

"You'll not be staying for the interment?" Christopher asked, his eyes wide with shock.

"Nay," replied Robert. "Her life was a whole era and now 'tis ended. Mine is just beginning."

July 1645

CHAPTER TWENTY
DONEGAL BAY, IRELAND

A LIGHT WIND FILLED THE CURRAGH'S SAIL, moving the small boat at a steady pace around the headland. Kate stood atop the cliff, where the breeze was stronger. It flattened her muslin skirt and light blouse against her body and riffled through her raven hair. With an unwavering eye she watched the bearded man at the tiller guide the boat skillfully over the breakers and between the rocks. When it was out of sight she found a rock and sat down to wait.

All along the top of the cliff lay a pink carpet of sea thrift, and on the cliff face itself newly blossoming burnet rose wove an intricate tapestry of white and yellow. Their scent filled her nostrils, giving her a heady feeling of ease.

It was gone as quickly as it had come when she heard Patrick's step on the cliff path below.

How often they had been together in the past year and a half, she thought. And how little had changed. Before he had taken long lonely walks but he now preferred to sail, and the weather was of little consequence. How many times had she stood on this cliff, with the thunder rolling and the rain soaking her, staring down at the tiny white sail bobbing in the mountainous waves, she wondered.

"Why, Patrick?" she had asked, over and over again. "Why must you dare the sea in such weather?"

Stony silence had been his only answer.

Nor had anything changed in their relationship. He was neither distant nor warm. Twice a week he would come down from his mountain to help with the heavier farm chores. Kate would feed him in the evening, and after a single pipe he would leave.

When at last she had accepted Rory O'Hara's offer of fosterage for the two younger children, Patrick had delivered them to Ballylee. He had made only one comment. "'Twas a wise move, Kate. They'll be well cared for at Ballylee. You're too young to take full responsibility for such a brood."

I am, she had thought then, and still did. *And I'm getting older each day waiting for you to come to life, Patrick Talbot. Waiting for you to open your eyes and see in mine the love I have for you.*

But so far both his eyes and his mind had remained closed, and the greatest fear in Kate O'Hanlon's life was that they would remain that way forever.

"Kate...."

He appeared at the top of the cliff path. Rising to her feet, she went to meet him. As she stood on tiptoe, he turned his head so that her lips found only the matted growth of beard over his cheek.

"The sheep are fatting well in the booley this summer and the spring calves grow like weeds," he said.

"Aye, Tim has told me," she replied. He moved along the inland path and she followed. "Patrick, Conor was here yesterday noon... with news."

He stopped and turned to her. Since the day he had discovered Redding in Elana's bedchamber, his gray eyes had been vacant, Now, however, she could see in them a tiny glow of life, and it brought a chill to her body that no amount of warm sun could dispel.

"Aye?" he queried.

"There was a battle in England at a place called Naseby," she went on. "The king's men were routed and several royalist officers were captured."

Kate paused for a moment, searching her memory for the right words.

"Aye, lass?" he said, insistence in his voice.

"I'm trying to remember just the way Conor told me," she explained. Patrick waited impatiently, digging in the path with the heel of his brogue until she began again. "All the correspondence between the Irish Confederacy and the king was also captured. Among the papers was the king's letter giving Irish Catholics full religious toleration and all their lands back in return for arms and troops numbering ten thousand. Parliament published the letter."

"And the king lost what little support he had," concluded Patrick. There was a smile on his face now—the first she had seen in years—and the light in his eyes had grown to a silvery glow. For some reason Kate found it difficult to face him. She averted her gaze and rushed on.

"'Tis said Parliament can't lose now. So sure are they that they've sent a regiment of five troops to Ireland captained by a Robert Hubbard. The Scots have landed a fresh force at Carrickfergus."

Patrick now seemed positively overjoyed by her news. "There'll be no Irish troops to England now," he observed happily. "We've our own war again."

"Aye," she replied, a great deal more soberly. "Conor brought you a horse and trappings as well as arms and proper clothes. They're at the cottage now."

"I'll stay the night, if you don't mind," he said decisively, "and leave with the first light."

As they walked down the mountain, everything

suddenly became crystal clear to her. Patrick was alive again. He had only been dormant, waiting for the war to begin anew.

FROM THE WINDOW Kate watched him bathing in the creek. So perfect was the symmetry of Patrick's naked body in the light of the setting sun that she felt herself tense with longing and desire. She longed to go to him and touch the sinewy muscles of his thighs to see if they were as hard as they looked.

Her eyes drank in the wildness of his hair. He had shaved and she could see how he had changed. The lines of his face had become more hollow and rugged. His jaw looked as if it had been set in granite.

Patrick turned around and bent forward to wash the lather from his face. The muscles in his legs and taut buttocks rippled with every move he made. When he stood straight again, Kate gave a gasp of shock. So loud was her cry that he heard it and turned toward her.

Biting her lip in dismay, Kate waved to him and called, "Supper's near ready."

He nodded and turned away again.

The scar was an ugly ragged line nearly two inches wide, running from his shoulder to his opposite hip. The flesh had turned purple and in places it had furled, giving the impression of a dark mountain range running over a tanned plain. It was the first time Kate had seen the wound since it had healed and now she crossed herself with thanks that he had lived.

Minutes later Patrick entered the cottage, dressed again in shirt, trews and brogues. "I'll be obliged if you'd cut this mop up a bit," he said. "At least to my shoulders."

"We'll eat first," she replied. "'Tis ready."

Considering the reason behind the sudden change in him, Kate was saddened to see him so animated. He spoke constantly during the meal and in less than an hour talked more than he had in the past year. His gray eyes danced with life when he looked at her. But still he didn't see what was in her eyes, failed to notice the way in which she was memorizing the texture of his bronzed skin, or the width of his shoulders and the breadth of his chest.

When the meal ended they cleared the table together and Kate directed him to sit on a stool near the fire. "Take off your shirt," she demanded.

"No."

"I've seen the damnable thing already," she suddenly flared. "I—"

Without another word, he drew the shirt over his head and dropped it carelessly beside the stool. "'Tis not a pretty sight up close," he warned her.

Indeed, it wasn't. In fact, it seemed more ugly than ever from such a short distance. Nevertheless, there was something akin to raw power in the look of it. Kate couldn't resist reaching forward and running the tips of her fingers over it.

"Must you?" he asked sharply.

"I'm sorry." Her voice was low and apologetic. She found a muslin remnant from a castoff and draped it over his shoulders.

"Kate, I. . . ." He paused, staring at the brown char of a long-dead fire. "A little above the shoulders, if you would, and the front as well. It finds its way into my eyes."

Damn you, she thought as she began snipping with a vengeance. *Can you never speak what you really mean?*

It took her nearly an hour to make him look somewhat akin to his former self. When she was finished cutting she took a brush and tried to give the unruly dark curls some direction.

"'Tis no use," she laughed, moving her hands down each side of his face and tilting his chin to

— gauge her success. "They have a mind of their own, they do!"

Her fingers grew warm where they touched his jaw. When she applied more pressure, she could feel the muscles of his cheekbones tighten. Slowly she moved her hands back, combing her fingers through his hair until they met and entwined at the back of his head. Her breath caught in her throat at the nearness of him; even this slightest of contacts with his powerful body made every pore in her body come alive with the wanting of him.

"Patrick..." she began, then stopped, unsure of what it was she wanted to say.

He stood up, lifting her arms as he did. For the briefest of instants she thought he would kiss her. Instead he loosened her hands from around his neck and shook the hair from his shoulders. "'Tis fine, Kate, I thank you," he said briskly. "I'd best to bed now; 'tis a long ride come morning."

She swept the hair from the floor while Patrick extinguished the candles. They undressed by the light of the single shaft of moonlight coming through the cottage window. As Kate slipped her chemise from her body she turned, naked and expectant, toward him.

Patrick was already asleep in the cot near the door. Sadly she donned a nightdress and slid beneath the coverlet on her own cot.

As she lay awake, the minutes seemed to pass like hours. Now and then she turned her head to look at him. The moon had risen full now, its light streaming through the window to make a pale-blue path from where she lay to his cot.

She loved him. There was no doubt of it now; surely only love could cause the ache, the nearly paralyzing pain she felt whenever she was near him.

What value pride, she thought bitterly, *when love rules your mind as well as your heart.* The tears on her cheeks burned like tiny rivulets of flowing fire. *I love him. And I must know.*

Silently Kate arose from her cot and crossed the short distance between them, letting the nightdress trail to the floor behind her. Once she reached him, she didn't hesitate for fear the beating of her heart would halt her resolve. In one fluid motion she lifted the coverlet and slid beneath it. Barely was she able to suppress a gasp of pleasure when she felt the warmth of his lean, hard body pressed against her. It was like a heady wine, and the joy of it brought the words to her lips.

"Patrick," she murmured hesitantly.

"Aye," he mumbled, obviously awakened by her arrival.

"Patrick, I love you," she said, more firmly now.

"I know, Kate," he replied evenly.

"I think that I've always loved you since that first day when you rode up with Donal."

She could feel a stiffness run through his body, and then slowly he relaxed. "I know that, too, Kate," he admitted softly.

"Do you think you will ever love me, Patrick?" she asked.

There was an instant of silence before he replied. "I don't know."

She took his hand and placed it on her breast. Patrick didn't remove it but neither did he caress her.

"'Tis no matter if you don't," she said, silent tears running from her eyes. "For damn you, I shall wait for you to love me if it takes forever!"

Tenderly he rolled her to her side, facing away from him. Then he moved in close behind her and returned his hand to her breast.

"Good night, Kate," he whispered.

August 1645

CHAPTER TWENTY-ONE

PARIS, FRANCE

THEY MADE A STRIKING YOUNG COUPLE as they walked arm in arm through the Tuileries gardens. Brian wore a slashed doublet of blue crushed velvet lined in white. At his side hung a short sword in a matching velvet scabbard. The plumed and wide-brimmed cavalier's hat perched rakishly on his dark head contrasted sharply with his scholarly and intense expression.

Her arm linked through his, Maggie looked a great deal gayer than she felt. Her cream silk gown was striped in sea green a shade darker than her emerald eyes. The neckline of the lace-trimmed bodice dipped to reveal the curve of her blossoming breasts.

They had walked the full circle of the gardens twice, inhaling the rose and lilac scents of late summer. And each time they passed the low narrow door in the rear wall of the Palais des Tuileries, their conversation had ceased and their eyes had filled with anticipation.

"Again?" Brian said, gesturing toward the path.

"Nay," Maggie sighed. "Let us sit. I do believe I have more gravel in my slippers than is left on the paths."

They found a stone bench near a fountain ornately adorned with gargoyles and cupids. Maggie folded her parasol and removed the bonnet from her head. The sun felt warm on her head and the light breeze riffled her red gold ringlets until their ends tickled her bare shoulders.

"You'll freckle," warned Brian.

"Good," she said, giggling. "'Twill be another thing that will set me apart from my pale-skinned French sisters."

He laughed and kneeled beside her. Gently he removed her satin slippers and shook tiny stones from them.

"I told you," she reminded him with a grin. "Had I known we were going to walk the Tuileries' gravel paths for two hours, I would have worn boots."

"Aye," Brian said, replacing her slippers and again casting a glance toward the double doors that led directly toward the privacy of the royal chambers.

At that moment, somewhere behind those doors, Maura was in audience with Charles's queen, Henrietta Maria, who had fled from England to France in late July 1644. The queen's messenger had arrived at the Hôtel Montparnasse in a plain coach just after dawn that morning.

"Why, do you suppose?" Maggie mused, as Brian seated himself beside her on the bench.

"'Twill have something to do with the renewed fighting in Eire, we can be sure of that."

They again fell silent and sat watching the door. At last Maggie leaned back. She rested her head against the stone and, eyes closed, let the sun's rays bathe her face.

"Brian," she queried, "do you ever miss Ballylee?"

"Of course I do," he replied, a slight note of pique in his voice. "Not as much as you, I fear, but I do miss it."

"But you've come to love Paris?" she persisted.

"Not only Paris, Maggie. I love what I get here. I love the excitement of learning. . . the books, the conversation."

Maggie smiled. "In a few years' time you'll be the darling of all the salons," she observed. "You amaze me already with the way you discourse on things I can't even comprehend."

At Brian's laughter Maggie sat up.

"What are you laughing at?" she demanded.

"A fie on your musings, Maggie," he said. "Ad-

mit it—you're comparing Conor and me again... and
'tis not fair.''

"I don't mean to, Brian, honestly I don't," she
replied earnestly. "But I miss him. It seems as though
we're not whole without him, our third part. Don't
you miss him, too?"

Brian turned his gaze from her penetrating stare to a
flock of birds soaring above them.

"Aye, I miss him," he admitted, "and fear for him,
too. But I don't envy him, Maggie. The thought of
war, blood, battle.... It makes my blood run cold. I
don't think I'm a coward, but I think I can fight
another way one day—a better way. And something
deep in my heart tells me that Paris will be the place I
will do it.''

"Will you marry a French girl, Brian?" she asked.

As always, he found her bluntness disturbing. It
even brought a slight flush of embarrassment to his
pale cheeks. "Silly girl," he reproached her. "How
should I know? We're both too young to think of such
things.''

"I'm not," she declared emphatically.

Not for long, anyway, he admitted silently, surveying her figure and beautiful dimpled face. *How we
have changed,* he mused, *since coming to Paris.*

At near thirteen, Maggie was quickly blossoming
into a full-figured woman and he was sprouting into a
tall, reed-thin man. Often he had stood naked before
his mirror and wondered if he would ever stop growing and start growing out. He wondered if Maggie ever
thought about boys as he did about girls. In particular, he wondered if she, as he did with her, ever looked
on him as anything more than a childhood friend.

Guiltily he tore his gaze from her bodice and
searched the sky for the circling birds. They were
gone.

"What is it, Brian?" she asked.

"Uh...nothing," he replied evasively.

" 'Tis so," she argued. "I can tell when you—"

"There she is—Maura!" he cried suddenly, relieved at having escaped Maggie's inquisition.

Maura had emerged between the two scarlet-coated musketeers in front of the door and was now hurrying toward her two charges as fast as her billowing skirts would allow.

"Quickly," she breathed. "To the coach!"

"What is it?"

"Did the queen—"

"Shh, I'll tell you soon enough!"

Maggie and Brian were both hard-pressed to match Maura's pace. In minutes they had reached the coach and were clattering over the cobbles toward the city's outer wall. With hardly a pause they passed through the gate and climbed the hill to Montparnasse. Not once during the entire ride did Maura speak. She sat, tense, her reticule clutched in both hands.

Once at the hotel, she moved through its ornate lobby with the same hurried pace she had used to gain the carriage. No sooner had they reached their quarters when she dismissed the servants and then stood between the suites of rooms to make sure they left. With the door bolted and locked, she turned at last to face Maggie and Brian.

"I was summoned by the queen because we three are not spied upon as most other Irishmen in France are during these troubles," she began, rather breathlessly. "The situation in both England and Ireland is dire—much worse than the news sheets would lead us to believe."

Brian and Maggie stood as though transfixed by Maura's news. Open-mouthed, they hung on every word.

"The king's position is lost," continued the young widow. "He has no army that can withstand—much less defeat—this New Model Army of Oliver Cromwell. The only hope left now to the royalist cause is from outside England.''

"Ireland," Brian whispered.

"Aye," agreed Maura in a low voice. "Without Irish Catholic troops, the Puritans will run England.''

"Why should we help King Charley?" Maggie cried, throwing her arms into the air. "I thought we wanted to get rid of him!''

" 'Tis what I've been trying to tell you," Brian interjected, a hint of impatience in his voice. "Things are bad enough in Ireland under the king, but if Irish affairs were to be taken from his hands and put under the control of Parliament, we can expect no leniency at all.''

"We'll not need leniency," Maggie retorted, lifting her chin. "O'Neill will drive the bastards into the sea!''

"That is what the papal envoy, good Cardinal Rinuccini, recently arrived in France from Rome, would have Owen Roe do," Maura replied dryly. "But saner minds in Ireland are not so sure he can succeed. All the leaders in Eire are pulled in different directions. Some think—and O'Hara is one of them— that if the Puritan army wins in England and their full force is loosed in Ireland, the Irish cause will fail. Even now the Irish forces in Munster are getting a taste of Puritan strength under a man named Hubbard.''

"Coming from the queen, how do we know all this is true?" Brian asked, his brows furrowed. "And even if it is, why does Henrietta Maria summon you?''

"The king's Irish correspondence was captured," replied Maura. "To save face in England he was forced to deny publicly that he intended calling on Irish Catholics for aid.''

Here she paused and withdrew a packet from her reticule. Brian and Maggie gasped. Even from where they stood they could see that the packet was stamped with the royal seal of King Charles.

"In fact," continued Maura, "the king has agreed to all Irish demands in return for our aid. These are his signed agreements." She laid the packet on the table between them. For several moments the three of them stood in tense silence, staring at it.

Then Maura spoke again, her voice low and even. "No regular courier could get this into Ireland. They are all known and suspect. The queen thinks that one of us could succeed."

With growing excitement, Maggie stared at the packet. Her entire body seemed on fire, every nerve ending alive and vibrant. Suddenly she darted forward and snatched the packet from the table.

"I'll go!" she exclaimed.

November 1645

CHAPTER TWENTY-TWO
BALLYLEE, IRELAND

THEY RODE THROUGH THE BOG three abreast, the mist rising to settle around them like a foggy blanket. In each man's mind was the anticipation of the winter's respite from war. But in each man's memory was defeat. Time after time through the fall campaign the Scots and Parliament forces had driven huge wedges between the armies of O'Hara and O'Neill. As a result, the Catholics had been unable to mount a single concentrated attack or score a victory for months.

Now they were retiring for the winter with still no end in sight. Even young Conor O'Hara, who tended to see everything in terms of black and white, could feel the gray mood of the men around him.

For the past four years they and their families had been living with the sword of war over their heads.

The quick victory that had been predicted by Sir Phelim O'Neill, Rory O'More and, later, Owen Roe O'Neill had not happened. And as they rode wearily toward Ballylee to lick their wounds for another winter, many wondered if there ever would be a victory. Indeed, many wondered if it would ever end at all.

Even Conor was beginning to doubt the ability of the Catholics to succeed. Since he had been blooded that night at Claymore Castle, he had been tried in more skirmishes in the past two months than he could remember. The first had come without warning, when he had become separated from the main force. He and two O'Hara kerns had ridden directly into a group of six Scots Covenanters. Before he had even realized it, Conor had been in the thick of battle, with the harsh cries of dying men and the whinnying of frightened horses all around him.

His only emotion had been fear and his only thought survival. It had not been until it was over, when he had sat his horse, gasping for breath in the midst of dead and dying men, that he had thought about what had happened.

All too soon had he left behind the childish games of marching to imaginary martial drums and crossing wooden swords with an aging warrior in the peaceful fields of Ballylee. Now the beat of those drums was real, the swords were made of steel and how well he crossed his with that of his opponent was a matter of life or death.

How had he fared, he had wondered after that first skirmish. How had the sudden experience of violence, the sight of blood and death, the smells and sounds of battle affected him? It hadn't taken him long to discover that it had invigorated him. He had thrown off for all time any claim he had left to childhood and, in the very next skirmish, had ridden directly into the midst of battle at his father's side.

"Hola!"

O'Hara's upraised hand halted the long column. Far below them, rising through the fog and mists, was Ballylee. "Praise God, who has seen fit to see us safely home again!"

"Praise God!" rippled along the line and then led by O'Hara they moved forward again. Gradually the line diminished as one by one the riders returned to their own homes and families. Outriders met the remaining troops on the heath and escorted them over the drawbridge and into the huge lower bailey of Ballylee.

Her once magnificent tall figure now bent with age and her raven-black hair tinged with gray, Shanna hobbled forward on two canes and tearfully embraced her only son.

Aileen kissed Rory with a murmured, "Thank God," and found herself swept into the air by a son who was nearly as tall as the father. "Conor, how you've grown!" she cried, as he put her down again. "How could you grow so much in so short a time?"

"'Tis the battle dress," Conor explained, with a grin. "It adds pounds that make the enemy fear me. I wear it like a cat puffs his fur!"

And then over his mother's shoulder he saw her standing in the arched door leading to the great room.

"Maggie!" he shouted, and sprinted toward her. Two steps before her, he stopped, suddenly overcome.

In the misty light she appeared more like a vision than the Maggie he remembered. Her hair was done up in some new fashion, the curls gently framing her face. He didn't remember her eyes being such a striking green or her skin such a golden color.

"You've changed," he blurted out.

"As have you, Conor," she acknowledged with a shy smile.

"Od's blood, girl, you've grown as well. You're a woman!" he declared.

"Thank you, sir," she replied primly, giving him a curtsy that revealed the swell of her bosom.

"You've got breasts!"

"Conor!" she hissed, her face turning crimson.

He roared with laughter and picked her up from the floor as if she were no more than a feather. Around and around he whirled her, until they were in the center of the great room.

"Damme, I'd forgotten until now how much I've missed you, Maggie-o," he exclaimed.

"Oh, Conor," she cried, throwing her arms around his neck and hugging him with all her strength. "I've missed you, too!"

DURING THE LONG WINTER MONTHS, Maggie and Conor were together constantly. More often than not, they would ride madly across the heath to investigate the little corners of Ballylee they had known as children. On particularly nice days they would sail with Patrick.

These times were not easy for Maggie. Although Patrick had not returned to the O'Hanlons' booley house or reverted completely to his hermitlike existence, he still held himself responsible for her brother's death and remained distant and reserved. When she had learned the reason for the change in his personality, she had taken it upon herself to lecture him.

"It could as well have been you, Patrick—or both of you—who fell at Dublin," she had pointed out reasonably. "I thank God that at least one of my brothers was saved. For I look upon you as much my brother as was Donal. I beg of you, Patrick, cast aside your guilt and gladden the hearts of all of us who love you!"

He had brushed his lips across the tip of her upturned nose and promised, "One day, little Maggie. When Donal has been completely revenged."

She had found it an unsatisfactory reply but the only one he would give.

In the evenings Maggie and Conor frequently played cards in front of the huge fire in Ballylee's great room. And they talked, endlessly. Conor of the war, Maggie of the wonders of Paris and both of a peaceful tomorrow.

The results of Maggie's mission in bringing the king's signed treaty to Ireland were still inconclusive. The papal envoy, Cardinal Rinuccini, proved to be the main stumbling block. With papal money in support of the Catholic cause he had arrived in Ireland in October of 1645, foolishly believing that once Parliament and then royalist forces were expelled from Ireland, the country would stand united under the leadership of Rome. As such, the Irish would be entitled to papal assistance to repel any future invasion from England.

When this news was brought from the Confederacy in Kilkenny by Rory O'More, The O'Hara's anger could be heard throughout Ballylee.

"Damn the fool!" he stormed. "His fine Eminence would have us wage an endless struggle against England just so we could be vassals of Rome! And what of this great amount of aid Rome sends us? Do the Pope and Rinuccini think to buy Ireland with twelve thousand pounds, five hundred muskets and a little powder?"

And so the political battle raged on, with couriers flying daily between the Confederacy in Kilkenny to O'Hara in the west and Owen Roe O'Neill in the north. Hopes of peace hinted at on one day would be dashed the next by warnings of renewed war.

SPRING CAME with warm rains and an occasional sunny day. Maggie and Conor were oblivious to the political maneuverings in both Ireland and England. They had become totally immersed in each other and their attachment for one another had blossomed into something more than a simple childhood friendship.

"Bah, it's not love," O'Hara countered when Aileen enlightened him. "They're barely out of the cradle!"

"Oh?" Aileen commented knowingly. "You yourself have said Conor has become a man. He's near your match in size and strength and more a tiger in the field than any three others. And as old and tired as your eyes are, O'Hara, methinks they've not missed the fact that our sweet Maggie has ripened."

O'Hara flushed. "That she has," he said softly. "An' I've a mind to give Conor a word in the counsel. But, still—"

"What a memory you have," Aileen laughed. "I was two years Maggie's junior when I set my cap for you."

"Well, now," said O'Hara with a grin. "Then the lad hasn't a chance!"

MAY TURNED THE LAND into an unending blanket of purple. Through the heather Maggie galloped with wild abandon. Her light pelerine billowed as she rode and her red gold mane danced in the wind.

"Veer toward the lough!" Conor cried, swerving his own mount and coming up beside her.

They wove their way through a stand of oaks and then slowed to a walk through tall slender birch trees. Before long, they emerged on a wide sandy stretch leading down to the water.

"Remember when we would swim here—you and I and Brian?" said Conor.

"Aye, and how you always lost the water games we played," she reminded him with a grin.

"'Twas two on one!" Conor protested, sliding from his saddle.

He moved around Maggie's horse and took her by

the waist. When she was halfway to the ground, he stiffened his arms to hold her aloft.

"Look here," he exclaimed. "My hands are nearly large enough to span your waist!"

"What conceit," Maggie groaned with mock haughtiness. "Nay, my waist is small enough for your hands to span!"

He set her down on the soft sand then took her chin between his thumb and forefinger. She could see the mischief creep into his eyes as he flashed her a taunting smile.

"Want to swim today?" he asked teasingly.

He was daring her and she knew it. To say no outright would be admitting that she would now be embarrassed to undress in front of him. But then why shouldn't she be embarrassed, she thought. They weren't exactly children anymore. On the other hand they weren't really adults, either....

"Well?" he prompted, as the silence between them lengthened.

The brazen look in his crystal blue eyes made her want to slap him. It also brought an unwanted flush to her cheeks. Even as a child, Conor had shown supreme confidence in himself, but she had always been able to keep him in his place. His self-assurance had by no means lessened over the years, but for some strange reason she found it more difficult to counter now than she had in the past. Somehow, the easy camaraderie she had shared with him as a child had been lost, replaced by a deeper feeling she didn't understand. She now felt uncomfortable in his presence.

"I—I'll think on it," she muttered finally.

"Oh?" he queried disbelievingly. "Good!"

"Oh, damn you!" she exclaimed crossly. "'Tis too cold, anyway. Come, let's skip some rocks!"

Forgetting her disquiet, she lifted her skirts and with a gay laugh ran toward the water. He made no attempt to follow her immediately, and the thought that he was probably sulking at her rejection brought a smile of satisfaction to her lips. She knelt on the sand and began to search for suitably flat rocks.

"'Tis a child's game, the skipping of rocks," he observed suddenly from behind her.

"Aye, 'tis," she agreed, nevertheless standing and arching her arm to throw.

Just as the rock left her hand, there was a flash of white beside her and then a huge splash in the water. Seconds later Conor's coppery head surfaced. Maggie turned her gaze up the beach to a neat pile of clothes and then back to where he swam in a wide circle.

"Ahh," he sputtered and laughed, "'tis so refreshing!"

"'Tis freezing," she chided, having noticed the cold bumps that had spread across his back. "You'll catch your death!"

"'Tis a pity Paris has robbed you of your spirit for adventure," he said, shaking his head solemnly. "But then, mayhap women grow older and more conservative faster than men." And with that scathing observation he struck out across the lake.

She watched him move through the water with powerful strokes and marveled at the change in his body. His back and shoulders were broad and muscular. Now and then he would lunge forward with a stronger stroke and for an instant his whole body would break the surface of the water. The sight of him caused a strange ache deep within her. It was an invasion of her senses stronger and more probing than any she had ever experienced.

Once back near the shore he stood in waist-deep water, shaking the droplets from his hair like a large shaggy dog. "I've never felt so alive!" he cried, his teeth chattering.

"Nor so cold, you fool," added Maggie, unable to suppress a bubbling laugh.

"Aye," he admitted. "Damme, I'm like to freeze to death! Hand me my clothes."

She made a move toward the pile of clothes, then stopped. "Nay," she said, turning back to him with her arms folded in front of her. "Get them yourself!"

His blue eyes were bright with laughter and mischief as he stared up at her. "Very well," he agreed with a shrug, and started to move toward the beach.

"No, wait—*Wait*!" she cried, her resolve suddenly breaking. "Damn you, I'll get them!" Quickly she retrieved the clothes and brought them to him.

"Many thanks, my lady," he gasped, his teeth chattering audibly now.

"Dear God, Conor, you *will* catch your death," she declared anxiously. "Wait a moment."

She turned away and lifted her skirts. Quickly she removed one of her petticoats and, keeping her gaze averted, passed it back to him.

"Here, dry off before you dress," she directed. "If you ride back wet, you'll be abed by nightfall."

She heard him dress and then felt his hands on her shoulders as he turned her to him.

"You don't mind my funnin', do you, Maggie?" he asked seriously.

Without warning, he wrapped his powerful arms around her and rocked her slightly. His mouth came down over hers in a kiss that was warm and vibrant, making a tremor run through her.

And then they both lost their balance and tumbled to the ground. Maggie landed atop Conor, and for a moment she remained lying against his chest, catching her breath. As she pushed herself away from him, her gaze met Conor's and they both burst into laughter.

"Damme for a blundering oaf," Conor wheezed.

"First I make a fool of myself freezing, and then I can't even decently steal a kiss!"

Maggie, too, was laughing but inwardly she was glowing. Her first kiss might not have been exactly as she had imagined it in her dreams but it had been with Conor, and for some reason that had made it even better.

June 1646

CHAPTER TWENTY-THREE
BENBURB, IRELAND

FROM OUTSIDE THE TENT came the normal evening sounds of an encamped army. Rations of oatmeal, mutton, cheese and beer had been distributed, and those men who had already finished eating were settling in for the night. An early start was planned for the morrow.

Inside the tent, Rory O'Hara stretched his aching limbs and leaned closer to the candle to give himself a better view of what he had written on the parchment before him.

4 June 1646
Benburb, Ireland

My dearest Aileen, Can it be only a month since we said our last sad goodbyes? Like this damnable madness we call war, it seems our times apart are unending.

Today we met the full force of Monro's dogged Scots for the first time. They ranged like armed locusts across a place called Thistle Hill and swept toward us like the tides of the sea. Our brave lads held their charge time and time again, though the Scots' pipes and war cries alone were enough to chill a man's blood and make him quake in fear.

By day's end the field was ours. There will be another battle come morning, but I doubt there will be any difference in the outcome. Our strength is superior, and although I still consider Owen Roe a political fool, there is little doubt of his military genius.

Your loved ones are well and bring honor to our house. Conor is seasoned now. He has become such a wily and ferocious warrior that I no longer fear for him. But like you, I do fear that he learns naught of living and life beyond the power of the sword.

As for Patrick? My darling, I don't know. I'm sure my couriers have relayed to you the tales of his deeds. His bravery has become legend, but there are times when I shudder and am sure that 'tis suicide he intends. He leads every charge that would seem to be without hope. If the battle lulls on his part of the field, he will ride to where it rages. If he is unhorsed, he stands his ground and fights with dirk and sword rather than retreat.

Pray as I do that peace is declared before he has used up all the many lives that seem to be his.

Lastly, I can set your mind at ease about the matter we both feared so much. Captain Robert Hubbard is occupied in the south, and I've been told there is little chance he will move out of the Pale. I thank God for this, for I dread to think what I would do if I were forced to meet my own son in the field.

God bless you. I remain,

your loving husband, O'Hara

Carefully he sanded the letter, folded it and sealed it, and called for his orderly. "How soon does the courier leave?" he asked, as the man entered the tent. "Within the hour, sir."

O'Hara nodded and handed him the letter. "See that this gets into his pouch," he directed.

When the orderly had left, O'Hara extinguished the candle and, fully clothed, rolled into his blankets.

As he drifted toward sleep he suddenly wished that he had said more in the letter—more about how happy had been their years together.

TWO HOURS BEFORE DAWN they were astir. By first light they were mounted and had advanced to within eight hundred paces of the Scots.

The sound of swords being unsheathed echoed down the line while, from the opposite hill, came the eerie wail of the Scottish pipes. On that signal the enemy cavalry began its approach, with musketeers, foot soldiers and pikemen preceding them.

"Damme," O'Hara growled. "Look at 'em. You would think they had lost only two yesterday instead of two thousand."

"'Twill be four thousand today," Conor grinned. "I can feel it in my bones."

The front lines of each side engaged fiercely. The sound of heavy musket fire quickly filled the air and their nostrils soon were assaulted with the acrid smell of gunpowder smoke. Before long the Scots' front line broke and the cavalry moved forward to take its place.

"The carnage begins," O'Hara muttered, spurring his mount forward to the charge.

He was engaged almost immediately and from then on swung his heavy blade at anything that moved before him. Screams and curses and the clashing of swords resounded through the air, drowning out the wail of the Scots' pipes. All around him O'Hara could see grim faces already blackened by the smoke of battle. He gripped his sword more tightly, finding comfort in the hardness of its hilt against his palm.

The conflict raged on with unceasing ferocity. On

the field opposite, O'Hara could see the Scots break ranks. Men had cast aside their weapons and were scurrying in retreat, trampling their own dead and dying. Many of the wounded and limping fell to their knees and begged for mercy. He heard the cry "No quarter!" ring out and turned away from the slaughter to wield his sword and create more.

From the corner of his eye he saw Conor fending off the blows of one Scot with his shield while matching swords with another of the enemy. When yet a third approached the lad from his blind side, O'Hara forgot everything but the need to save his son from certain death.

Swiftly, he kneed his mount around and, raising his sword, struck the third Scotsman from his horse with ease. Almost immediately he felt his mount jostled by another. He tried to turn but was too late. The blow struck the side of his helmet and he felt himself sway slightly in his saddle. Blinded by a sudden explosion of pain in his head he tried to raise his shield, only to have it struck from his arm. The sound of battle suddenly receded as a strange ringing set up in his ears; he barely felt the second and third blows as the pain was replaced by a numbness that spread throughout his body.

He knew he was falling and, vaguely remembering that he was mounted, reached out for his horse's neck with both hands. They found only air, and with a dull thud that he heard rather than felt, he struck the ground. As the blue sky above him turned gray and then black, he was engulfed by an all-consuming silence.

IT WAS A GLOOMY DAY that seemed reluctant to dawn. Around the tents torches still burned, filling the air with their acrid smoke. The camp stirred to life but with an uneasy, tentative sound much like the restless wind that had keened through the trees during the night.

The usually ebullient grooms saddled horses with hushed words of morning greeting to one another. Men on sentry duty stamped their feet quietly to ward off the chill of the dawn's clammy mists. Even the sound of harness or the clanking of a metal bit seemed subdued when a rider chanced near the big tent's open flap.

Inside the tapers burned, throwing their flickering light in oddly moving patterns over the inert white-robed figure on the narrow cot. Tension filled the air as the surgeon finished packing O'Hara's head wound with peat moss and, groaning, stood to wipe with a bloody hand the sweat from his own brow. He turned toward the foot of the cot, where Patrick and Conor stood. The gesture he made was one of futility. Of the two of them, only Conor was moved to speak.

"Nay," he whispered chokingly, biting his lower lip until blood stained it. "Nay, he'll not die!"

At his words O'Hara's eyes fluttered open and a smile creased his leathery face. "Aye, lad, you're right...for no man dies as long as he has a living son," he said hoarsely. "Come nearer...'tis hard to see."

Conor moved around the surgeon and knelt beside the cot. "I killed the bloody bastard, father," he declared fervently. "The one who struck you. I took his damnable head from his body."

O'Hara winced noticeably and then cast his fading eyes upward. Over his son's shoulder his gaze met that of the surgeon. Satisfied, he let his gaze flicker to Patrick, whose steadfast look in return told him much the same as had the surgeon's.

A faint expression of sorrow flitted across his face; then slowly he relaxed in acceptance. He looked up once more at Conor's contorted features, and as he

did so, an intense stab of pain that left him gasping
for breath exploded in his head. He closed his eyes to
try to block it out, and when he opened them again,
everything seemed hidden behind a dark misty veil.

"Conor?" he murmured hesitantly.

"Aye, father?"

"I—I can't see you."

"I'm here, right here beside you," the lad assured
him.

"Patrick...."

"I'm still here."

"Patrick," O'Hara began, his voice barely audible. "My life was Ballylee and my family. See to
them both when I'm gone."

"Aye, O'Hara," promised the young man quietly.

"You'll not die!" Conor cried, the tears spilling
from his eyes as he clutched his father's arm. "You'll
not!"

"Conor, my sweet lad," sighed the old man.
"Mark well what I say to you now. There is no honor
in this killing we do. For all your days, lad, work to
stop it; for war is not the measure of a man's mettle
nor the solace for his heart. 'Tis the land—and the
working of it—that gives a man happiness. My wife,
my children and my land have been my pleasures in
life. Indeed, I would have you and all your sons after
you remember me not as a killer of men but as a
planter...a tiller of the land.

"I beg that you, my son, will find the same joy I
have found in the soil. Love Ballylee as I have loved
it. For there Ireland is greener, the birds sing longer
in the summer, the flowers have more scent, and the
lasses' cheeks bloom with a darker blush."

O'Hara's voice alternated between a passionate
whisper his son could barely hear and a hoarse shout
that filled the tent. At times, his words were slurred,
as if his failing mind were creating them faster than
his lips could form them.

Conor looked at the surgeon and Patrick with pleading in his eyes, but they were powerless to help him. "Father, lie quiet...please," begged the lad.

But O'Hara seemed not to hear him, for he went on as though his son had never spoken. "Conor, you must never let a man who lives upon your land taste poverty," he insisted. "For in that way you will know no enemies. Worry not if your purse grows thin in the lean season, for it will fatten again if you've put the coin back into the land and your people."

"Father—"

"When I close my eyes I can see the parapets of Ballylee....I can see...Aileen—"

"No!" Conor's voice was an anguished sob as he reached out to cradle his father's head in his arms. For many moments the only sound was the lad's labored breathing as he held the lifeless, graying head and rocked gently back and forth.

At last Patrick leaned forward and touched Conor's shoulder. "Conor, lad.... He's gone," he said quietly.

"I know."

Slowly Conor relaxed his hold. Then he raised his head and looked down into The O'Hara's vacant eyes. The sight made him shudder. Then gently he lowered the lids and stood.

"We'll not follow The O'Neill south," he said, quietly and decisively. "We'll to Ballylee."

"Aye," Patrick nodded. "I've the same mind. For finally I'm tired of killing. O'Hara was right. Methinks 'tis time we all go a'boolying again."

THE WAKE WAS QUIET AND SOLEMN, for no ordinary man had died.

Five hundred people—men, women and children—stood on the heathered knoll in front of the tiny chapel. Hats in hand, men stood looking steadfastly at the ground. Women openly wept, and every now and then a keening wail rent the air, severing the hushed stillness that surrounded the occasion. Children gaped in awe at the ornate bier draped in black.

The O'Hara family stood near the bier and the chapel. Their faces bore expressions of stoic majesty, and their kerns and tenants, who had come to know them well over the years, expected no less. Even though the English queens and kings had stripped them of their titles of glory, to their fellow Irishmen they were still lords of the manor and were there to mourn and bury their prince.

A deep silence settled over the gathering as Patrick, his black-clad figure tall and imposing, stepped forward and raised his arms. A low rumble of thunder greeted his gesture and light drops of rain cooled the upturned faces.

" 'Tis fitting that the heavens speak on this day in memory of a great and honest man," he proclaimed in strong, clear tones. "The O'Hara was a man who knew happiness without bounds as well as great misery. He knew the love of a good and noble woman. He had the heritage of birth and name and in his lifetime added glory to his father's crest."

Then, he paused to gaze at the throng. It seemed to everyone present that those gray eyes looked directly into their own.

"Like us and all Irish before us," he went on, "he was exposed to the outrages of fortune. In O'Hara, God gives us the lesson of the worthlessness of pomp and grandeur and shows us a simple man who wanted only his woman and his land. 'Twas for that he died."

A murmur of sorrow rippled through the crowd and somewhere in the rear women again began their mournful keening.

"God bless Rory O'Hara as we bless you now. . . ."

And as Patrick continued to speak, five hundred

solemn voices joined with his to give O'Hara his final blessing.

"A blessing on you, Lord of Ballylee, wherever you may be. May the road rise to meet you, may the wind be always at your back. May the sun shine warm upon your face and the rains fall soft upon your fields. May your sons live without the strife that you shouldered in your life. And until we meet again, may God hold you in the palm of His hand."

August 1646

CHAPTER TWENTY-FOUR
DONEGAL, IRELAND

HE FOUND HER in the hills near the mouth of the sparkling stream that eventually wound its way down onto the plain and flowed beside the O'Hanlon cottage. She was perched on a rock with her skirts pulled high to bare her long legs.

Head tilted back, she sat facing the sun's warming rays. The dress she wore was a working frock of cream muslin. She had lowered it off her shoulders and pulled the neckline low to give as much of her body to the welcome sun as possible. Her arms were clasped about her knees, bent in such a way that the firm line of her thighs was clearly visible in the shadows beneath her skirt. Her long, thick hair was undone and it shimmered like a shiny raven's wing down the arch of her back.

For many moments he stood in silence, drinking in the picture of tranquillity she made with the green hills and the sparkling stream as a backdrop.

Then, as if she sensed a presence other than her own, her head rolled lazily to the side and her eyes flickered open. She looked directly at him and an expression of pleasure and surprise crossed her fea-

tures. But she didn't move. It was as if she had been
sitting there for months simply waiting for him, knowing he would come.

"Hello, Patrick," she murmured.

"Hello, bonny Kate," he said, his voice low.

She stood up but held her ground, gazing at him
steadily. All was silent between them except the gentle
ripple of the meandering stream.

Then he closed the distance between them and drew
her gently into his arms. Holding her, feeling the softness of her, the pliable smoothness of her body as she
leaned willingly against him, Patrick bent his head until their lips met. They kissed leisurely, until the fire of
uninhibited desire engulfed them both.

The sun warmed her hair and shoulders as his lips
warmed her soul. At last she knew that the waiting, the
weeks and months of loneliness, were over. She returned his kiss with all the pent-up longing and love
she now knew he welcomed.

Too soon his mouth left hers. When she opened her
eyes, she found him smiling softly down at her. Suddenly he gave the raffish grin that had first touched
her heart so long ago, and in his eyes she saw the
renewed gleam of life she had awaited with such longing.

It brought a laugh of uninhibited joy to her lips.
"Welcome back to the living, Patrick O'Hara Talbot," she said happily.

"I love you, Kate O'Hanlon," he returned.

"I know," she replied with a warm smile. "And
there's no need for me to say how much I love you."

Unexpectedly, he lifted her, and a moment later she
found herself sitting upon a boulder. His loving eyes
were level with hers as he curved his tanned hands
around her face and drew it toward him.

The depth of his kiss and his physical nearness
brought a pain so sweet it was more than she could

bear. This time when his lips left hers she felt cheated and told him so with her eyes.

Patrick's chest ached with the pounding of his heart as he looked deeply into the dark depths of those eyes. Her independence and strength of will were evident in the tilt of her head and firm line of her perfect jaw. He slid his fingers into the thickness of her raven-black hair and gloried in its silkiness.

Now it all seemed so simple, and he wondered what had taken him so long. How clear had been her image each time he had thought of her on the eve of battle.

Gently he lifted her and, before setting her on the ground, held her high above his head against the sun.

"How lovely you are," he breathed, "with your black hair so soft against your face."

"God grant you will always think so," she murmured, feeling the breath catch in her throat as she ran her slender fingers along the powerful line of his jaw.

Arm in arm they walked down the stony path and across the purple-heathered plain to the cottage.

"Would you eat?" she asked.

"Aye," he replied, "for I do believe I'll need my strength comes the night."

The obvious meaning of his words brought a faint flush to her cheeks, but his grin had a measure of the old devilment she remembered and it drew her even closer to him.

They ate as the stillness of evening descended. By the time the moon had risen and the dark sky twinkled with stars, they had both borne all they could of the sweet agony of anticipation. Draping a large down quilt over his shoulder, Patrick took her hand and led her outside.

"Out here?" she queried in surprise.

"Aye," he replied gravely. "Before God and the land, beneath the stars and the moon."

Suddenly Kate stopped, bringing Patrick up short as well.

"What is it, lass?" he asked. "Are you afraid?"

"I..." she began hesitantly, then stopped and started walking again. "What is wrong with me!" she exclaimed with a laugh. "No, I'm not afraid. I've waited too long to be afraid!"

Patrick spread the quilt on the stream's grassy bank and then turned to her.

"A quilted bier for the death of my maidenhood?" she teased, her gaze noting how white was the quilt against the dark earth.

"Nay, darling Kate," he said, running the tips of his fingers up the sides of her neck. " 'Tis an altar for our love."

He moved to her with a confident step. Kate turned her face to his, and as their lips met, all her fears melted away, to be replaced by reawakened desire and need. Aching for the feel of his body against hers, she slid her arms around his neck and together they sank to the quilt. Deftly his fingers worked the laces of her bodice and then his hand found her breast.

His touch suspended her in time and space. She sensed rather than felt her dress and chemise being removed. The cool night air kissed her bare flesh as his mouth again found hers. His kiss was firm, demanding that her lips yield to his. Kate moaned as the touch deepened, and even when he raised his head and broke the contact, she felt faint and limp.

His gray eyes, dark now with desire and intensity, devoured her silken curves in the silvery blue light of the moon. Her stomach was flat and smooth, her hips seductively rounded and her legs long and slender. In the pale moonlight her body seemed radiantly alive.

"You are so beautiful," he murmured. "There is not a flaw in your loveliness."

Her eyes flickered open. He stood naked above her, outlined like a god against the moon.

"Oh, Patrick," she whispered, "how long I have waited for you to want me!"

Still he continued to look at her, his gaze warm and intent. It was, she thought, as if he were content merely to drink in her naked beauty with his eyes, memorizing it for all time.

But to her, his body had now become a powerful magnet, drawing her closer to him. She took his head in her hands and guided his lips to her neck. They remained there for a moment, and then his burning, hungry mouth moved to her shoulders and finally to her breasts.

Her hands caressing his powerful shoulders, Kate clung to him, fiercely reveling in the feel of the hard muscle that rippled beneath her fingertips.

"Patrick," she pleaded, thrusting her body toward him, "love me now. Love me as I have dreamed for so long you would!"

Obediently, he moved over her, encircling her with a gentleness and tenderness she had never dreamed possible. The heat of his body enveloped her as his caress became more urgent, more demanding, and made her gasp with pleasure. He whispered her name again and again, until his lips possessed hers in a searing kiss of passionate longing.

Her senses reeled as a rending pain tore through her body, only to be followed by a flowing sweetness that melted the core of her being.

For a moment they were still, their hearts seeming to beat as one. Then he moved, filling her whole being with radiating waves of warm pleasure. Quickly, she joined him and her own burning passion built with his until her nails dug at his shoulders and her voice cried out in joy. What had begun as a soothing warmth built to a white heat that engulfed and consumed her. Within moments he had joined her, hurtling them both to the peak of fulfillment.

Then slowly, like a gently ebbing tide, she retreated to a warm quietness filled with love.

LIKE HE HAD THE FATHER, old O'Higgin schooled Conor the son in the overseeing of Ballylee. And Conor applied the same grit and determination to the role of planter as he had to the role of warrior.

August was a month of uneasy peace. In the south, the armies of Parliament sat back to await the king's fate in England. After his decisive defeat at Naseby, King Charles had surrendered to the Scots Presbyterians in the hope that, with the growing rift he saw between them and the English Puritans, he might yet raise another force to fight for him once more. So far, he remained their prisoner.

In the meantime the alliance was proving difficult to establish. The papal envoy to Ireland, Rinuccini, together with a number of the more hard-headed Catholic leaders rejected it completely. Others were inclined to accept it. And so the arguments continued.

Nevertheless, Charles managed to keep his pulse on Irish affairs and instructed his lord lieutenant, Ormonde, to make an alliance with the Catholics, guaranteeing them freedom from religious persecution and promising the return of their lands and titles. Peace was proclaimed while the alliance was being sought but it was a troubled lull, for the Scots Covenanters in the north disdained to give up their gains and allow the Irish time to heal their wounds.

When the news of the wrangling reached Ballylee, O'Higgin tugged at his red beard with one hand and rubbed at his watery eyes with the knuckles of his other.

"Naught will ever change. Damn their eyes!" he

growled. "Put one Irishman in a room and he'll drink to God's health. Put two in a room and they'll drink to each other's health. Join them with a third and they'll destroy the room!"

But if Irishmen still fought each other and Englishmen remained at odds in England, in the west all was peaceful at Ballylee. The fall crop was meager but it was harvested. Weddings took place and births were reported. Catholic services were held openly and Protestants were denounced.

Each morning Conor assumed his most businesslike expression and, with O'Higgin at his side, oversaw the running of Ballylee. But in the afternoon he threw off his mantle of solemnity and searched out Maggie.

"Come along, Maggie-o," he would demand. "For I've a mind to have the wind in my face to blow away the musty smell of O'Higgin's office!"

They rode along the cliffs and sprawled on the grassy slopes to sit quietly and listen to the pounding waves and the cries of the curlew.

"Maggie?" he queried one day.

"Aye," she replied idly, feeling lazy in the warmth of the sun.

"Do you think of me as a brother?" he asked.

A tiny smile played about Maggie's lips as she chanced a quick look at him, sprawled on the grass beside her. Conor seemed to grow taller and wider each day. The muscles of his thighs were tautly outlined in his tight breeches and she could see golden hair blossoming on his chest where his cambric shirt had fallen open.

"Nay, I don't, Conor," she told him truthfully. "Why do you ask?"

"Because I don't think of you as a sister," he mumbled.

Her smile grew wider and she turned away to hide

her mirth. "Then how do you think of me, Conor?" she asked demurely.

He made no reply, and the silence lasted so long that she could bear it no longer. She turned back to him, only to find him lying full length on his belly, his chin cupped in his hands as he stared impishly up at her. From the twinkle in his eyes she could have guessed his reply.

"I think of you as the pretty little copper-haired wench who dearly loves to tease me," he told her with a grin.

"Oh? How do I tease you?" she queried coyly.

He rolled over onto his back and suddenly became very interested in the clouds rolling lazily across the sky.

"Look there—how that cloud appears like a ship," he said, raising his arm and pointing. "And that one like the towers of Ballylee . . . and there, that one—"

"Conor O'Hara," she interrupted in severe tones.

"Aye, Maggie O'Hara?"

" 'Tis you who teases me!" she protested.

"I?" he queried, feigning a comical look of surprise that she could suggest such a thing. "Nay, 'tis not I, but you. Look at you now in that brazen French dress!"

"Brazen?"

"Aye," he said, covering his eyes in a mock gesture of shock. "Old O'Higgin says if 'tis French it must be brazen."

"Old O'Higgin hasn't given me more than a passing glance since I returned from Paris," she countered. "Besides, he's long since lost his eye for a woman!"

Conor uncovered his eyes and let his gaze roam unabashedly over her. She wore a riding costume of opal crushed velvet trimmed in green. Her bonnet was modish and braided with ribbon and dyed plumes that matched the fawn tones of her petticoats.

"He probably has at that," he admitted, his brows pinched in a seriousness that did nothing to hide the devilment she saw in his eyes. "But me? I do believe, Maggie, that I've just *found* my eye for a woman!"

Raising his arm, he pulled at the ties of her bonnet and lifted it from her head. Released from the bonnet's constraint, her flowing hair billowed out into the sunlight to cascade down around her shoulders like a coppery waterfall.

Without warning he pulled her to him. His mouth found hers in ruthless exploration as his strong young arms crushed her to him. Her hair fell forward to form a curtain around their faces and she felt the fullness of her breasts pillowed against his chest.

For a moment she stiffened and fought him but as his kiss gentled and deepened, she relaxed and responded in kind. When his fingers slid beneath her hair and lifted her face, she made no effort to draw away from him.

"You are a beauty, you know, Maggie," he assured her earnestly. "Methinks God sent you from Ballyhara just for me."

"Did he now?" she exclaimed, straightening her arms and lifting herself above him.

"Aye, now I'm sure he did," said Conor approvingly. "Don't move, Maggie-o, stay just like that."

There was a strange gleam in his eyes that made her drop her gaze to follow his. She gave a gasp of dismay. Above the lace edging of her bodice her breasts swelled dangerously.

"Damn you!" she cried, rolling off him and springing to her feet.

Conor lay convulsed with laughter as she straightened her dress and retied her bonnet. "Don't be angry, Maggie-o," he entreated her. "'Tis as The O'Hara used to say about Patrick. I'm just a lusty lad!"

"Not at my expense!" she retorted indignantly. "Hie you to the stables and be a lusty lad with a scullery maid!"

She turned to flounce away toward her horse, but Conor jumped swiftly to his feet and caught her shoulders before she had taken two paces.

"I've already done that," he admitted with a chuckle, "more times than I can remember."

She gasped, "You have?"

"But that's only being a lad, remember?" he replied. "Methinks soon I'll be man enough to marry."

"Will you now!" she cried, foolishly letting her anger at his arrogance overshadow the control she usually held when with him.

"Aye," he assured her. "An' I've decided that when that time comes, 'tis you, Maggie, I will wive."

"Conor O'Hara," she gasped, the flush in her face blossoming clear up to her hair, "you are the most arrogant, conceited—"

"Eligibly handsome lad you know," he finished for her, roaring with laughter and again pinioning her to his chest with a hold that threatened to squeeze the breath from her body.

For a moment, she melted against him as he kissed her. Parting her lips beneath his she gave a sigh of pleasure, as though powerless to refuse him. Then she clamped her teeth down over his lower lip.

Conor yelped in pain and released her. Gingerly, he put his hand to his lip and it came away with a few drops of blood on his fingertips.

"Damme, but you've wounded me, you little wench!" he cried.

"Aye," she laughed over her shoulder as she ran to her horse. "You yourself have bravely stated that when you enter the fray you have to expect to get bloodied!"

He started after her, but she had already mounted

and was galloping across the heath. Suddenly the ties gave way on her bonnet. It flew off and her thick tresses billowed behind her. Paying no attention to the loss, she bent lower over the horse's neck.

The sight of her made Conor smile. "Ah, Maggie-o," he murmured. "You ride like a man, and you've got the tongue and stubbornness of a man. But you're every bit of you a woman. An' you know it yourself, Maggie—one day you'll be my woman."

THEIR DAYS WERE BOTH FULL and tranquil. Patrick cast aside his ominous black clothing in favor of a coarse woolen shirt and faded trews. He took up a hoe and, alongside Kate, attacked the soil as fiercely as he had attacked his enemies with dirk and sword.

"You work, Patrick, as you must have fought," Kate observed with a laugh. "With more zeal than finesse!"

"Aye," he chuckled, "for it makes the day go faster."

"Faster?"

"So night comes quicker. . . with you."

The leaves began to fall and soon after the chill winds from the north began to blow. Patrick went to the mountain booley and helped Timothy drive the livestock down to the winter shed near the cottage.

Once a month he rode to Ballylee, always returning within four days. If he had news of the world outside their little corner of Ireland he never volunteered it, and neither Kate nor Tim asked. They simply were not interested. Tim was a born farmer and cared about little else. Kate had Patrick and, for the time being, at least wanted nothing and no one to interfere with the tranquil life they led.

Only once during the long winter months did anything intrude on their peace.

"Patrick," said Tim one day.

"Aye, Tim?"

"There," he indicated. "On the far hill."

There were six riders, shaggy and bearded, about a half mile away. Patrick dropped the shovel he had been using and walked to the cottage. When he returned he was carrying his sword in its jeweled leather scabbard, a brace of pistols and a carbine.

"Reparees," he explained, hanging the weapons on a nearby tree. "Poor sods of soldiers who had no land to return to when there was no war to fight anymore."

A few minutes later the men reined around and rode off.

Patrick and Timothy continued their work in silence. And then the boy asked quietly, "There's still fighting, isn't there?"

Patrick nodded. "In the Pale and the south—Munster."

"Will you ever fight again?" queried Tim.

"Aye," Patrick replied without hesitation. "For you, your sister, this land . . . and Ballylee. But only if they come west."

"And will they, Patrick?" persisted the lad.

Patrick leaned on his shovel and looked east, in the direction of Dublin and the Pale. It seemed a long time before he replied.

"Aye, lad, one day they'll come," he sighed finally. "For they always have."

Yuletide they spent at Ballylee. It was a joyous time; war and intrigue were forgotten as young and old alike immersed themselves in celebrating the occasion to its fullest.

The only sad note was provided by Aileen, whose spirit and will had both been broken by the death of O'Hara. The loss of her beloved husband seemed to have affected her mind, as well, for her talk at table often rambled.

There was one particularly embarrassing incident

for Maggie and Conor when Aileen walked the full length of the table and laid her hands on their heads.

"Marry!" she cried out, startling everyone. "Marry and have sons before the troubles begin again. Marry, soon!"

Abruptly, she broke into tears, and rising quickly from the table, Maggie and Kate embraced her and gently took her off to bed.

When they were gone, Shanna turned first to her son, Patrick, and then to Conor. "You should," she said. "Both of you. For in times of troubles, the young ones must always live faster."

On the long ride back to the O'Hanlon cottage, Patrick thought about his mother's words. He thought also about his pledge to O'Hara to look after the family and Ballylee.

"Kate," he said suddenly, "do you think we live in sin?"

She paused only briefly before answering. "Love and loving doesn't make a sin," she declared firmly. "And even if it did, a few words over us wouldn't do away with it."

That night, with her cradled in his arms, their bodies pressed against each other, Patrick whispered, "Would you marry me if I asked you?"

"Aye," she replied without hesitation.

"Would you leave this place—go with me to Ballylee if I asked?" he persisted.

"I would go with you to hell if you asked, Patrick," she avowed.

WITH THE ABLE ASSISTANCE OF TIM, Kate and Patrick worked night and day to harvest the spring crops. Side by side they helped birth the calves and lambs. When finally it was all over, there was a lull of only a few weeks before booley time.

Patrick was awakened just after dawn one morning by the sound of jangling harness. Over Kate's shoulder he could see that Timothy's bed was empty. He leaped from his own bed and, tugging his breeches up over his long legs, scrambled outside. He found Timothy strapping his horse's bridle into place.

"Hola, Tim. A knapsack and all?" queried Patrick. "'Tis a month yet 'til booley time."

"I know," replied the lad.

"You're not leavin' us!" exclaimed Patrick in surprise.

"Nay, not for good," Tim assured him, swinging himself into the hide-covered wooden saddle. His handsome young face broke into a wide grin. "I'm goin' courtin'," he declared proudly.

Dumbfounded, Patrick stood and watched him ride across the stream and over the hill to disappear from sight.

"He's grown," came Kate's voice from the doorway. "I was expecting it."

It was two weeks before Timothy returned, a beaming smile on his fresh, young face. "Her name's Cathy Dougherty," he announced. "She's a lovely lass. You'll come?"

"Aye, lad," Patrick said, slipping his arm around Kate's waist. "We'll be honored."

The Dougherty family was poor, and with seven more daughters to marry after Cathy, the wedding was small.

Timothy's bride was a tiny blond girl with enormous blue eyes that saw nothing but her husband-to-be. She was two years older than he, but both Patrick and Kate knew the lad would have to search a long time to find a girl who would love him more.

Immediately after the ceremony, the younger Dougherty children gathered around Patrick in awe, for he had worn the golden velvet and crest of the O'Haras. Like all the children of Eire, they had heard from traveling balladeers the tales of Patrick

Talbot. They asked endless questions about Ballylee and about Conor as well, for the younger O'Hara had gleaned almost as much fame as Patrick during the recent troubles.

The elder Dougherty, a hard-bitten leathery-faced man of the land, took Patrick's hand almost with reverence. "This land is sad and there's little of it," he said. "I've a large family. Would ye talk to The O'Hara?"

With a nod of understanding, Patrick replied, "I'll speak of it. Ballylee is large—there's room enough."

Dougherty turned away, tears rolling down his brown cheeks. "Bless ye, Patrick Talbot," he thanked the younger man fervently. "And best ye be thinkin' of sons an' daughters of your own."

Two weeks later the newlywed couple set off with the herds for the summer booley.

That night Patrick and Kate made love with a savage tenderness. Later, as they lay in one another's arms, Patrick gently kissed a strand of her hair and whispered in her ear. "When the booley's over this year, we'll be off for Ballylee."

"Aye," she agreed.

"And once there," he added, "we'll wed."

Kate rolled over and buried her head against the wiry mat of hair on his chest. "Aye," she sighed happily.

August 1647

CHAPTER TWENTY-FIVE
DUBLIN, IRELAND

ROBERT HUBBARD REVOLVED the crystal goblet of claret slowly as a thin smile creased his lips. His gaze flicked from the crested gauntlet that had been given him by the Prince of Wales during the battle of Edgehill in 1642 to a letter of commendation received less than an hour earlier from Cromwell in England.

"A job well done," Cromwell had written.

And indeed it was, Robert thought.

Ormonde had despaired of bringing the king and the Irish rebels together. Although many Catholics had wanted to accept Charles's offer of an alliance, in February Owen Roe O'Neill and the Catholic Confederacy at Kilkenny had upheld Rinuccini's verdict to reject it. In the same month, the king had been sold by his Scots' captors back to the Puritans in England. At that point, Ormonde had given up the struggle and had surrendered Dublin to the Parliamentary forces. Since then, Robert had made successful forays into both Munster and Leinster. He had cut Preston's Old English Catholic army to ribbons at Dungan Hill and had made a shrewd bargain with Theobald Toaffe, the new rebel commander in Munster.

Toaffe was an Irish intriguer given to lining his own pockets with monies given him to pay his army. Wisely, Hubbard chose to let the man continue to destroy his own force rather than waste Parliament men defeating him in the field.

Robert's smile broadened as he leaned comfortably back in his chair. Yes, he thought, thus far he had done well in Ireland—and he would do better yet.

Ruthlessly, he had threaded a thin line between control and excess. As a result, he was feared and probably hated by friend and foe alike, but that mattered little beside success. And there was no doubt he had been successful.

On the eve of the Dungal Hill battle against Preston's men, a fortnight before, he had followed Cromwell's example in whipping up his men's fervor for battle.

"We will ask no quarter and we will give none," he had vowed. "And God will smile upon our deeds. For this is a holy war we fight—to avenge your Protestant brothers murdered by the Catholic rebels in 1641 when this bloody rebellion began!

"Remember," he had continued in oratorical tones, "that your Parliament is behind you. Feel no guilt for the death of these popish savages. Did not Parliament reward our good Captain Swanley with a chain of gold worth two hundred pounds? And for what good service? He sieged a transport carrying one hundred and fifty Irish. How did he keep them in line? By the simple method of selecting half of them and throwing them overboard!"

Between fear and faith, Robert mused, the battle had been won in hours.

"Sir?"

The entrance of a sentry brought Robert back to the present.

"Aye," he replied.

"The Irish harper, Maggus, is here, sir."

"Send him in!"

Seconds later a stoop-shouldered little man with a balding head and narrow, furtive eyes entered the room. He stood before the desk, worrying his cap between his hands and rocking back and forth on his heels.

"I've been in the west, cap'n... around Ballylee country," he announced timidly.

"And?" queried Robert.

"They buried The O'Hara, sar," the man replied.

"That I know, you old fool," said Robert impatiently. "Tell me something I don't know!"

"Patrick Talbot is back on the land, with a wench.... They've wed."

"Damn you, Maggus! 'Tis O'More I care about," declared Robert, his impatience beginning to give way to anger. Getting information from Maggus was, he reflected briefly, a little like pulling a tooth: one had to draw it out of him bit by bit. "Did you see O'More!"

"Aye," the little man answered. "He's there with an Englishman."

There was silence for a moment before Robert weighed this piece of news: O'More with an Englishman at Ballylee. Robert's other spies had reported Englishmen in the camps of both Phelim and Owen Roe O'Neill, too. There could be only one explanation. Ormonde was making a last effort to convince the Irish leaders to forget their religious differences with him and rally round his royalist banner to drive Parliament and the Scots from Ireland.

Having reached this conclusion, Robert turned his attention back to his spy. "What else, Maggus?" he asked brusquely.

"'Tis all, sar," the man replied.

From a drawer in the desk, Hubbard withdrew a small purse and threw it to the old man.

"I thank ye, sar, I thank ye," Maggus cackled, backing toward the door.

"One moment, old man," called Robert abruptly.

Obediently, Maggus halted. "Aye, sar?" he queried.

"Tell me of Ballylee," Robert said, leaning back in his chair and closing his eyes. "Tell me of the fields and herds. Are they keeping the castle itself in good repair during this respite from war?"

Maggus frowned and shook his head at this odd English captain. The man had laid waste to a third of Ireland since his coming but each time Maggus appeared before him, Hubbard inquired about the well-being of Ballylee.

The old man didn't understand it, but as always he recited what he had seen of prosperity on Ballylee. And as he spoke, the cruel smile on Robert Hubbard's face grew wider and his expression became one of deep satisfaction.

July 1648

CHAPTER TWENTY-SIX

BALLYLEE, IRELAND

THE CURRAGH SLIPPED QUIETLY among the rocks. In the bow crouched a short, thick-bodied man in a dark blue doublet and long black cloak. His face was stern and his watery eyes looked weary.

When the small boat grounded on the shingle, Conor and Patrick offered their hands to its passenger as he stepped onto the rocks.

"You've the look of your father," observed the man to the younger O'Hara. "You must be Conor O'Hara."

"Aye. Welcome to Ballylee, m'Lord Ormonde," replied Conor formally.

"Patrick Talbot, m'lord," said Patrick, introducing himself as the man turned toward him.

"My thanks to both of you for allowing me the use of Ballylee for this meeting," returned their visitor.

"The others are waiting, m'lord," Patrick said. "If you'll follow us."

Conor and Patrick led the way, with James Butler, Earl of Ormonde, directly behind them and Dermott O'Higgin bringing up the rear. They entered Ballylee through the little-used prisoner's gate and climbed a set of narrow stairs to the high round tower and O'Higgin's office. There several men awaited them anxiously.

"Gentlemen," Conor announced to the gathering, "James Butler, Earl of Ormonde."

One by one the men stepped forward, mumbling greetings. Sir Phelim O'Neill seemed uncomfortable. Rory O'More, whom Ormonde already knew was perhaps the most relaxed of the group, while Connor Macguire introduced himself in tones that failed to hide his distaste of the whole proceedings.

"Gentlemen," began Ormonde, ignoring the undercurrent of tension, "I thank you one and all for coming to hear me out." Then he paused and peered into the darkness beyond the candlelight. "Owen Roe?" he queried abruptly, his voice tinged with concern.

His audience exchanged quick glances before Patrick, choosing to act as spokesman, replied, "The O'Neill refused to come, m'lord. He claims this meeting to be but another bit of English perfidy to use Irish steel for the crown's salvation."

For the first time since he had entered the room, James Butler allowed himself a slight smile. "For my part, I believe we have given General O'Neill every reason to think as he does," he acknowledged. "But I fear, gentlemen, that the king now has little chance left for perfidy. Shall we be seated?"

They arranged themselves around the room while O'Higgin silently moved among them with claret. Conor felt uncomfortable in the company of the older warriors, but a reassuring look from both Patrick and Rory O'More gave him confidence.

"For years now," Ormonde began, "we have fought each other and fought alongside each other. I am Protestant, you are Catholic. I am a royalist, you are Irish patriots. But I say to you now, gentlemen—nay, I warn you—we must put aside our differences."

He pulled a handkerchief from his sleeve and gently mopped his brow before continuing.

"The king's cause is lost. Even now Parliament moves the court from Carisbrooke Castle, where Charles has been prisoner for nigh on a year, to Hurst Castle. There are rumors that the next step will be Windsor and a trial. Gentlemen, I believe those rumors."

The general mutterings of disbelief were stopped by Rory O'More's calm voice. "M'lord, 'tis well known I care little for King Charles and even less for his rule. But I can hardly believe Parliament would go so far as to place a king on trial."

Ormonde smiled again, a sad smile. "Parliament won't," he admitted readily. "But others will. True, Parliament has won its war, but it has now discovered that it has no power to rule. The power rests with the army."

"Cromwell," Patrick muttered.

"Aye, Oliver Cromwell," agreed Ormonde with a quick nod. "He is a canny man. I do believe that he is now convinced that only the king's death can prevent anarchy. The English are a strangely law-abiding people. They have defeated their king, yet still look to him as their arbiter of law. They would leave him on the throne, but with limited power. Should that be the case, then under the terms of the Constitution, Parliament can rule only by his consent. With Charles's death the army would have little trouble stepping in and ruling by force."

Ormonde stood and in turn looked directly into each man's eyes. "Once the Puritan army rules England, it will move on to Ireland and Scotland," he said solemnly. "Cromwell will have no choice. As long as there is rebellion in Ireland there is a chance for the monarchy to return to England. That he cannot allow.

"I leave it up to you, gentlemen. None of us can stop Cromwell if we act alone. But if we join together, we may be able to once and for all."

February 1649

CHAPTER TWENTY-SEVEN
BALLYLEE, IRELAND

ONLY THE RUSTLE OF HER SKIRTS announced Maggie's entrance. Quietly she closed the door and leaned against it.

Conor sat on a window seat, his chin resting on one knee. His face was masklike, the blue eyes staring unseeingly across the mist-shrouded heath. In his hand was the recently arrived letter from Brian in Holland.

Maggie knew its contents. As soon as it had arrived Conor had called the entire household together and read it aloud.

The first part dealt with news of the O'Hara family. Maura had joined Queen Henrietta Maria's meager court in France. Brian had insinuated himself into the court of the young Prince of Wales at The Hague, in Holland, to where the heir to the throne of England had fled for safety.

The second part of Brian's letter concerned itself with more important matters. And Brian's answers to his brother's questions had been emphatic. In the event that Cromwell invaded Ireland, yes, the family should flee to safety in France. As to joining Ormonde's English force, Brian left to Conor and Patrick the decision of whether or not to commit the people of Ballylee to such an alliance.

As Maggie stood silently watching the young O'Hara, she could see that the responsibility for such a decision weighed heavily on him.

Sensing a presence in the room, Conor turned from his contemplation of the heath. "Maggie," he said softly.

She moved closer to him and stood looking down at him with an expression of expectation and concern. "Have you made your decision?" she asked, almost fearfully.

"Aye," he sighed heavily. "I've talked with Patrick. We're of the same mind. Ormonde's way is the only way. If Cromwell does come to Ireland, 'tis better to fight him in the east."

"And the others?" Maggie queried, choking back

a sob in her throat. "What have they decided?"

Conor's face darkened slightly with anger. "Phelim and Owen Roe stay at odds," he replied in tones of deep disgust. "Macguire will defend his own lands only. And O'More has no army and cannot help us even if he would."

"Then why must it fall on you and Patrick—"

"Because," he interrupted firmly, "we can still hear my father's warning. If Cromwell comes to Ireland, he will hold all Catholics responsible for the excesses of some during the early troubles in 1641."

She studied his profile against the gray of the February sky. He seemed to be aging almost daily and the realization of it brought tears to her eyes. It wasn't fair, she thought wistfully. They were both so young and already they had gone through so much. They had had no chance to grow up, to fall in love slowly and experience the joys of anticipation.

Rising to his feet, Conor fumbled in the front of his shirt and removed the gold chain from around his neck. On it was a tiny cross. He removed the O'Hara ring from his finger and added it to the cross on the chain. When he turned his attention back to her, his face held an expression of deep resolve.

"Maggie-o," he said quietly, "there's no more time for funnin' and teasin'. I love you. Do you love me?"

Impulsively Maggie slid her arms around his neck. Suddenly she wanted him, wanted to give him the one thing a woman could give a man that would tell him that she was his.

"Aye, O'Hara," she replied softly and sincerely. "I do truly love you."

She held her breath as Conor slipped the chain over the coppery cloud of her hair and watched as the ring and the cross slipped into the valley between her breasts. Placing his hands at her sides, he drew her toward him. His touch seemed to burn right through the fabric of her gown to sear her soft flesh. Her knees threatened to give way and she swayed against him.

"I do believe that we are now betrothed," he observed solemnly.

"Aye, we are," she agreed softly, lifting her face to him and gazing deeply into his eyes. "Now seal it with a kiss."

Their lips met more with tenderness than with passion. It was the kiss of young lovers who were unsure of what lay beyond it—a kiss that bespoke a love they had always known but only now admitted to each other.

"Conor," interrupted a voice from the doorway.

Conor lifted his lips from Maggie's and, still holding her in his arms, stared over her shoulder at Patrick standing on the threshold of the room. His heart sank at the expression of bleak solemnity on the older man's face.

"Aye?" he replied heavily.

"It's come—word from Ormonde," said Patrick without preamble. "The king was beheaded a fortnight ago, on the thirtieth of January. Already Cromwell readies troops for Ireland."

MARCH WINDS TORE AT THE CLOAK covering Shanna's frail body. Her blue-veined hands holding the canes at her sides trembled. Wisps of gray hair escaped the *chaperon* she wore and, dampened by the heavy mist, matted against her forehead and temple.

Dermott O'Higgin scowled down at her. "M'lady, 'tis a bone-chilling wind," he reminded her succinctly. " 'Twould please me if you'd go inside by a warm hearth."

Shanna's weathered lips curved in a smile. "After all I've lived through O'Higgin, do you think a little

wind will shorten my days?" And then to mollify
him, she added, "Soon, Dermott, soon. I would see
the last of the line disappear."

In the distance the long line of cavalry, pikemen
and wagons was slowly fading into the mist. Somewhere at their head, already out of sight, rode the
O'Hara family and the younger O'Hanlon children.
In a fortnight they would be in Drogheda and within
a month after that they would be at sea, bound for
France. Only Shanna had refused to go.

"Damme then, mother, I'll force you!" Patrick
had ranted. "I'll roll your beautiful bones in a
blanket, hoist you into a wagon and remove you by
force!"

Shanna had only smiled and stubbornly shaken her
head until his ranting had subsided.

"No, you won't, my son," she had replied firmly.
"For you know that I am as right in what I do as you
and Conor are in what you have decided. 'Tis good
that Kate's child be born in France, beyond the
sound of booming guns, and that her younger kin
will have a chance to live and grow old in safety.
Conor will fight better when he knows Maggie is
safe. Poor Aileen knows not what she does or where
she is most of the time. She would be more of a hindrance than a help here if a siege comes. But me? Nay,
Patrick, I am too old and my bones would quickly
fail me if I couldn't look out each morning and see
Ballylee. One O'Hara must stay on the land with
O'Higgin, my son. I've been exiled once. I spent my
spring in France, I'll not spend my autumn there, as
well. I'll stay."

And stay she had, to watch until the last rider disappeared from sight.

"O'Higgin?" she queried, as she turned at last to
go inside.

"M'lady."

"How many men have we?" she asked.

"Near a hundred and fifty," he replied.

"Take as many of them as you need and transfer the O'Hara and the Talbot bones to the lower crypt beneath the chapel," she commanded. "When that is done, set powder on all four corners and the foundation of the chapel."

"Powder, m'lady?" inquired the old man, surprised by her request.

"Aye," she replied firmly. "If there's a siege, you know as well as I that we will never withstand it. I want your word that before Ballylee falls you'll blow up the chapel and cover the crypt."

O'Higgin gave a sigh of deep sorrow. "You know I will, m'lady," he promised, his voice heavy with regret. "But why?"

Her eyes still sharp despite her age, Shanna turned her gaze on her old and trusted friend. "Because," she declared, "if Ballylee falls into someone else's hands, I'll not have that someone gloating over the bones of my mother and father, my brother and my dear husband. I would have them hidden in the earth so that no one will ever be able to remove them from the land they loved."

Part II

August 1649

CAPTAIN ROBERT HUBBARD WAS THE FIRST to greet General Oliver Cromwell when he stepped from the ship's gangway onto Dublin Quay.

"Welcome to Ireland, sir," said the young man formally and carefully.

"Verily, lad, 'tis the glory of God's calling that brings us here," declared Cromwell with satisfaction. "Congratulations on your work here, lad. Your leadership has given rise to decisive victories."

Robert studied the big man's face for any sign that Cromwell had reservations about the compliment. He found none and decided that that very evening he would make the request that had been his goal for the past seven years.

"Ormonde's royalist army is quartered around Trim," he advised the general. "On behalf of Ireland, he has declared the Prince of Wales King Charles II and tries to rally the Irish."

"And?" queried Cromwell.

Robert's smile told the story, but he added the words in a tone of contempt. "There are some who follow him," he admitted. "But for the most part, the Irish still can't agree on whom to fight."

Cromwell laughed heartily. "By the time they do, they'll be on their way to hell!" he observed, evidently highly amused by the thought. "What of Drogheda?"

"Ormonde has it defended by a garrison of

twenty-five hundred and some soldier-civilians under the command of its governor, Sir Arthur Ashton,'' replied Robert. "We've had the mouth of the harbor blockaded for weeks, so no reinforcements have been able to come in by sea."

"Good," Cromwell mused. "We'll strike at Drogheda first."

For the next four hours, Cromwell himself saw to the landing of his force of six thousand cavalry and four thousand foot soldiers.

"Not nearly as large as the combined armies of the royalists and the Irish Catholics," he pointed out. "But then, those two aren't combined, are they, Hubbard." The general was in a mood of gaiety almost unheard of for him. "And even if they were," he added, "methinks we would still win; our men have come to fight for a purpose. Mark me, captain, in two years from now—perhaps less—the men you see before you will be the new citizens of Ireland. For that will be their reward."

The Black Staff Inn near St. Patrick's Cathedral had been commandeered as Cromwell's headquarters. When the landing was near completion, he and his officers retired there for the evening meal.

The fare was plain, served on wooden dishes, with beer in pewter mugs the only drink. Throughout the meal Cromwell held forth on the reasons for their presence in Ireland and on the merits of their cause.

"Make no mistake," he advised his men. "We will give no quarter if our terms are not met. We are the instrument of God's hand and He is a God of wrath. What we do in the months to come will secure our English Commonwealth for all time. Ireland is the key, and Englishmen have known it for years. This cursed island is the back door of England, and a Catholic Ireland would bedevil us for years. Verily we will win, for men of God cannot be defeated.

And the men I have brought with me fight for God!''

Robert sat stony-faced, watching with inward mirth the adulation on the faces of the men around him. As Cromwell spoke, he remembered the man's words at Edgehill.''

''...This war is right, I say, for we fight for the right of free worship!''

Robert cared little how any man worshipped, but it was amusing to think that in Ireland the Catholics were fighting for exactly the same right.

By the end of the meal, Cromwell had worked himself up to an almost feverish pitch of fervor. '' 'Tis a religious war, this Irish campaign,'' he thundered, thumping the table with his fist. ''We fight for God!''

Bah, Robert thought. *We are all fighting for the one thing that means anything—land.* Nevertheless, at this point he considered it judicious to nod his head and murmur in agreement with the rest of Cromwell's officers.

An hour after the meal was finished he knocked on the door of the general's room and entered.

''Aye, lad. What is it?'' queried Cromwell when Robert requested an audience.

For seven long years, Robert had waited and fought for this moment. Now that it had arrived, he found himself unusually nervous and he made his request in what were for him almost humble tones. To his great relief Cromwell listened without interruption, then nodded in solid agreement.

''Fair enough, captain, considering your service,'' he said. ''Fair enough.''

Robert could hardly contain the swelling of victory that burst in his chest when he stepped from the room and closed the door behind him. With a single stroke of a quill pen, Oliver Cromwell had made Ballylee his. The acquiring of it would come with conquest.

The holding of it would come with the assumption of the name. Conquest worried Robert Hubbard not at all. That was a foregone conclusion.

The name he would worry about later.

September 1649

CHAPTER TWENTY-NINE
DROGHEDA, IRELAND

THROUGH THE NARROW RECTANGULAR SLITS in St. Peter's belfry, Maggie looked with fearful eyes across the rooftops of Drogheda town. Beyond the Boyne River was South Quay and the narrow lanes leading to St. Mary's Church and the Duleek Gate.

Somewhere on Duleek's battlements or in the tall steeple of St. Mary's, Conor and Patrick waited. Better than she, they could see beyond the city's walls, where the fires of Cromwell's troops glowed in the damp evening air.

For five days they had been massing in the hills south of Drogheda. How many thousands there were no one knew, but it seemed that the arrivals would never end. Each evening the fires appeared to stretch farther along the plain. And still they had not attacked nor had they sent a summons of surrender into the garrison.

Vividly, Maggie recalled Patrick's words.

"He's a wily devil, this Cromwell. He would wait in hopes that Ormonde would attack his flank. For if Ormonde were beaten, we would have no hope of reinforcements or diversion."

A familiar groan came from behind her and Maggie turned her attention back to the little room in which she was standing. It looked dim and unreal in the flickering light provided by the solitary candle.

Maggie knew the groan had come from Kate, lying

on a cot against the belfry's inner wall. She took a step toward the woman and then halted when Aileen left her own cot to go to Kate's side.

Maggie sighed and turned back to the window to inhale more of the chill but fresh night air. The babe had come three days earlier—stillborn—and since then Maggie and Aileen had nursed Kate's every movement.

Patrick had ranted and raved. Each of them had tried to calm him, pointing out reasonably that no one, least of all he, was to blame for the fact that the French ship Brian had hired to take all of them except Conor and Patrick to France had been unable to leave its home port.

Taking its cue from England's civil war, in August 1648 the Parliament of Paris had finally rebelled against the tyrannical measures of Cardinal Mazarin, the power behind the throne of Louis XIV. All France was in an uproar over this so-called Fronde Rebellion, and Paris as well as the French seaports was still blockaded.

And now, even if a ship could have gotten through, Cromwell's navy had blockaded the mouth of the Boyne River at Drogheda.

Thinking of it made Maggie's breath come in quick, sharp snatches and her heart pound furiously. The calming words of Drogheda's governor, Sir Arthur Ashton, had done nothing to assuage her fears.

"The wall of Drogheda is nearly twenty feet high and six feet thick," he had pointed out. "'Tis impenetrable and made more so by the shooting holes of St. Mary's and the Duleek Gate. He who could take Drogheda could take hell."

As she stood in the damp belfry, the cries of the younger O'Hanlon children behind her, the groans of her beloved Kate echoing in her ears and the fires of

Cromwell's soldiers on the far hills, Maggie felt as if she were already in hell.

Earlier in the day, she had crossed the Boyne and had made the trek down Duleek Street to the gate. The effects of the siege had begun to show. Offal was piling up on the cobbles outside the houses. Between shuttered slats she could see children's faces wide-eyed with fear. And in the streets knots of people muttered in hushed tones.

She had climbed the wall and walked the battlements in search of Conor. It had been a frightening sight, watching the mists whirl and twist as the morning winds blew their vapors among the enemy tents. Even then she had thought, *how long will they wait and be forced to lie on the cold ground while the warm roofs of Drogheda beckon them?*

When she at last found Conor, their time together, as it had been since their arrival, had been all too brief. Barely had they embraced, their lips touching in frustration and need, before he had been called away to see to one of the unending tasks that had been assigned him.

Dressed in slate-colored breeches and black cavalry boots, with the yellow and green O'Hara crest emblazoned across his doublet, Conor had acquired a masculine elegance that was both awesome and frightening to Maggie. Reluctantly, her heart pounding with longing and desire, she had watched him go.

Now it was night. The city had withdrawn behind locks and shutters. The only sounds on the streets were the occasional challenging call of a sentry or the steady marching of troops.

THE MORNING DAWNED even wetter than the night before had been. High in the steeple of St. Mary's, Sir Arthur Ashton stamped his wooden leg against the stone floor in frustration as he conferred with

Lieutenant-Colonel Boyle and Sir Robert Hartle-poole, his seconds-in-command. Junior officers, among them Conor O'Hara and Patrick Talbot, stood by the fire-holes watching the enemy movements. The cold rain gusted against their faces and even though it was fresh from the heavens, it carried the salty tang of the sea.

"How many do you count?" Conor asked in a hushed voice.

"From here I see eleven siege guns and at least twelve field pieces," Patrick replied, his lips barely moving as he spoke.

"And men?"

Patrick's smile was thin-lipped and cold. "Too damn many to count."

"Look there!" came a voice from the far side of the belfry. 'A white flag!"

As one, the men rushed to the slits, narrowing their eyes into the gloom.

A group of three riders had detached themselves from the main tents and were riding under a white flag up the hill toward Duleek Gate.

"Gentlemen," Ashton said solemnly, "I think our summons has come. Colonel Boyle?"

"Aye, sir?"

"You'll meet them at the gate."

All eyes watched the approaching horsemen as the sound of Boyle's heavy tread on the stone stairs echoed through the steeple.

"Hola the wall!" cried the black-clad leader.

"Aye!" replied a sentry.

"I be Captain Robert Hubbard, of Parliament's force in Ireland, come from Lieutenant-General Oliver Cromwell with a summons of surrender for the garrison of Drogheda!"

Then they saw Boyle step forward, salute and take the parchment from the Parliament captain's hands.

The captain's gaze raked the battlements and the towering steeple.

In a loud booming bass voice he shouted, "We are ten thousand and more, with heavy siege guns. We know your force to be under three thousand. You have less than two hours. If no reply is forthcoming in that time, let the siege begin!"

Boyle disappeared back into the shadows of Duleek Gate, and after dipping the flag toward the battlements and steeple, the three riders turned and cantered back down the hill.

Moments later, Ashton broke the seal on the parchment and began to read.

Sir, By your rebellion, and the slaughter of innocent Protestant souls, you have caused the army belonging to the Parliament of England to be brought before this place. As commander of this army and a soldier of God, I deem it my duty to reduce this place to obedience.

I have had the patience to peruse your dispositions and I look upon them with disdain. To be short, I shall give the soldiers and non-commissioned officers quarter for life and leave to go to their several habitations, carrying only the clothes they wear. There they shall engage themselves to live quietly and take up arms no more against the Parliament of England. As to the commissioned officers, I give quarter for their lives but do render them prisoners. As for the inhabitants, I shall engage myself that no violence shall be offered to their goods and that I shall protect the town from plunder.

I shall expect your positive answer instantly, and if you will upon these terms surrender and within two hours shall send forth to me four officers of field quality for the signing of this surrender, I shall thereupon forebear all acts of hostility.

However, if these terms be not met, so the effusion of blood may be prevented, mark you that the rules of war and siege are clear. If these terms I hereby give you be refused, know you that no quarter shall be given. And further know, in the sight of God, you will have no cause to blame me.

Your servant, O. Cromwell

The silence in the room was tomblike, as if the bells of death had already tolled. In each man's mind the thought was the same: refusal to agree to such a summons of surrender meant but one thing if the town were eventually won by force. Not only would the garrison be put to the sword, but civilians as well.

Sir Arthur's face was white when he looked up from the parchment, but his jaw was clenched fiercely and his eyes were bright with resolve.

"You all know my decision in this matter," he said, heavily, "but 'tis not mine wholly to make. Go you to your billets and poll your junior officers. Return here in one hour."

AT HIGH NOON, the heavy siege guns began to bombard the walls of Drogheda. The gunners concentrated on the corner below the steeple of St. Mary's and the wall on each side of Duleek Gate. Almost at once, the stone began to crumble.

For nearly five hours the sound of the thundering guns filled the air. Almost before the defenders' eyes, the breaches in the walls widened.

And then came silence—awful, lonely silence—until the men crouched tensely near the breaches thought to scream to end it. Across the void of dirt and rubble, Conor and Patrick exchanged solemn glances. One thought was uppermost in the minds of both of them: under no circumstances must the invaders be allowed to cross the Boyne into the northern end of the town. If Cromwell could be held long enough at Drogheda's south defenses, surely Ormonde would arrive with reinforcements.

"What is that?" exclaimed Conor, as a mournful chanting sounded from beyond Drogheda's walls.

"Hymns," said Patrick firmly. "They chant their songs as they march."

"Damme, 'tis worse than the Scottish pipes!"

And then they saw them. Three thousand strong, they marched as one, their armor gleaming with damp as they emerged from the mist. The first charge was held and repulsed. It was evening before a second could be mounted, and both sides retreated.

In the Parliament camp, Cromwell received a tally of the day's dead and wounded with fury in his heart but calm in his voice.

"Today the breaches were not wide enough for horse to enter," he declared. "Let the guns begin at dawn. Tomorrow we will make them wide enough to storm, and with God's help the town is ours."

"And once the walls are breached? Still no quarter, sir?" asked one of his officers tentatively.

"You know how I do hate the heathen Irish. And even if I pity the Englishmen who are in there with them, 'tis their fault the lot they have chosen," replied Cromwell mercilessly. "Nay, no quarter."

On the other side of the town walls, battle-weary men slept standing up, their heads propped against their muskets for support. In the belfry of St. Peter's, Aileen, Maggie and Kate sat staring silently at one another. The younger O'Hanlon children had cried themselves to sleep and now lay quietly, their heads in the women's laps.

Before that day, war had never been closer for

Kate and Aileen than the ballads of traveling harpers. Neither of them had seen the flow of blood in battle nor heard the terrible thunder of guns and harsh metallic ringing of clashing steel. Of the three women, only Maggie had gone through a siege and that had been when she was very young. Nevertheless, what she had seen this day had brought back all the terror of Ballyhara when the Scots had come over the walls.

Now all three of them sat stunned by what they had seen through the belfry windows. Even more terrifying was the thought of what the next day would bring. But not one of them dared to voice her greatest fear: that in the carnage they had witnessed, Patrick or Conor—or both—might have fallen.

The sound of heavy footsteps on the stairs brought Maggie instantly alert. She seized a musket from the stone floor and turned toward the door, ready to defend herself and her companions from the all-too common looters who would steal whatever they could before the town fell.

A rap came and then a voice. " 'Tis me—Conor."

"Conor!" she exclaimed joyfully and, casting the musket aside, ran to unlatch the door.

They were in each other's arms at once. Maggie wept, unable to hold back the tears of relief. "Thank God! Oh, thank God, Conor," she murmured fervently.

"Conor?" came a quavering voice. "Patrick . . . ?" It was Kate, struggling to her feet with Aileen's help.

"He's fit, Kate. We've both survived the day," Conor replied, slipping unwillingly from Maggie's grasp. "And there's much to do this night."

He was out the door and back in seconds with a large bundle. "There's blankets and canvas in here to wrap the little ones and men's clothing for the three of you."

"Men's clothing!" Maggie exclaimed.

"Aye, Maggie-o." Then Conor looked solemnly at each of them in turn. "Patrick has found a way to get all of you out of the city."

THE LANTERNS HANGING ON THE WALLS sputtered and threatened to go out with each tiny gust of wind. They were hung yards apart, with nothing between them but stark darkness, and for this reason Conor had strung a line between them.

With Conor in the lead and Maggie bringing up the rear, the O'Hara women and O'Hanlon children made their way more by feel than by sight. They stayed clear of Ship and St. Peter's streets. Instead, Conor led them in a twisting and turning route down narrow alleys and between houses using the smell of the river as his guide.

"Here," Conor whispered, coming to a sudden halt.

Above them a chandler's sign swung to and fro in the wind, its rusty hinges making a grating sound. In the blackness, Conor somehow found the shop door and rapped three times. Three answering raps sounded from the other side and then the door was opened to reveal even more blackness beyond.

"Patrick?" Kate whispered, in the darkness.

"Aye, sweet Kate. 'Tis me," he replied, in a hushed voice. "Hie you in, all of you—and watch your footing, there's three steps."

One by one they stumbled through the opening and down the steps. They found themselves in a large room with a high beamed ceiling. Scattered all around them were molds, vats of tallow and other of the chandler's trade.

"Is this the lot of them, lad?"

The speaker was a large, gruff-voiced man whose florid complexion nearly matched the red of his hair.

"Aye, 'tis," Patrick replied, and turned to his flock. "This is Colin Dougherty."

Kate gasped with pleasure and embraced the big man immediately.

"Aye, lass," Dougherty wheezed. "'Tis myself, the uncle of your brother Tim's wife, little Cathy!"

"He's agreed to help us get you out of Drogheda," Patrick explained.

"Ah, 'tis the least I could do for what you've done for my brother and his brood—givin' 'em a home on Ballylee," declared the man modestly. He gave a throaty chuckle. "Besides," he added, "when the lads here found me, I was about to be off myself!"

"This way," directed Patrick in answer to the puzzled looks from Kate, Aileen and Maggie. Lighting a second torch from the one already flaming on the wall, he moved through a low alcove into an adjoining room.

"Get along with you," Dougherty said, herding them all before him.

The room was obviously the man's living quarters. Silently, he pushed aside a rough-hewn oak table and two chairs. An old threadbare carpet was quickly rolled away, revealing an iron ring set into the floor. Grasping it, Dougherty gave one powerful pull and a trap door creaked open.

"Leads to the river, it does," he said, disappearing into the blackness. "And watch your step on the ladder. 'Tis narrow and ripe with the river's dampness."

With one torch below and one above, each of the women descended the ladder. The two O'Hanlon youngsters were then handed down, and Patrick and Conor quickly followed.

Dougherty led them along a narrow passageway that seemed to lead deeper into the bowels of the earth. When the sound of the rushing river was strong in their ears, he halted and turned to them.

"We'll have to snuff the torches here," he said, in hushed tones. "They can be seen around the next turn."

Once the torches were extinguished, they continued on into the blackness. Before long, they emerged onto the rocky shore of the Boyne River. Across the water they could see the lights from the back of shops and houses along the South Quay.

"Over here, lads," Dougherty said.

From beneath an overhang of rock the three men pulled a narrow timber raft. Grunting with the effort, they managed to pull it over the wet rocks until it was half submerged in the stream.

Patrick straightened and flashed a smile at the red-headed giant. "If I didn't know better, Dougherty, I'd say you've done a bit of smuggling!" he observed knowingly.

"Aye, that I have, lad," replied the man with a chuckle. "But never with a cargo as valuable as tonight's. Now let's get 'em aboard!"

The children were placed on the raft, told to lie down and given leather straps to hang on to. Kate was instructed to lie between them and was given the responsibility of directing Dougherty, who would be using his body in the water behind the raft as a rudder.

"No," she said suddenly, stepping back from the water's edge.

"What ails you, Kate?" Patrick cried.

"I don't want to go," she replied decisively.

"Nor do I," Maggie declared.

"Are you daft, both of you?" Patrick asked, his voice full of exasperation.

Kate threw her arms about him and buried her head against his chest. "I waited too long to be with you," she sobbed. "I cannot bear to leave you now."

"You must, Kate. Think of the little ones." In a

whisper he added, "Go, Kate—for Aileen's sake as well. Dougherty can't look after her and the children, too, when you get downriver."

As Maggie embraced Conor the tears streamed down her cheeks.

"Maggie-o, please," Conor whispered, his head swimming with the scent of her hair.

"We've not had one night together," she reminded him, her voice low and choking. "I would stay, for I would have us that at least."

He tilted her chin upward so that she could see his smiling features in the pale light of the moon. "You have no faith, Maggie-o," he declared. "I'm no coward, but I'm too damned young to die. Now get you gone so when the time comes we can make babies."

"No!" she cried, gripping her hands together behind his back, unwilling to release him.

"Get to the raft—both of you!"

The voice, sharp and commanding, had come unexpectedly from behind them. Maggie and Kate both turned as one from their men and gave a gasp of surprise. Aileen stood thigh-deep in the water, her hands on her hips, her chin lifted defiantly. For the first time in months, they saw life in her eyes and determination in the set of her jaw.

"Damme, did you not hear me?" she demanded. "I said to the raft! If 'tis a war they must fight, they cannot fight it behind our skirts. And if they die, we can't wail them if we're dead ourselves."

Her tone was like steel and her eyes glinted icily. The old Aileen had somehow returned, and in the absence of Shanna, she was the family matriarch. If for no other reason than that, Maggie and Kate at last succumbed to the hands that urged them toward the water. Kate took her position between the two children while Maggie and Aileen slipped into the water beside Dougherty behind the raft.

"A lass on each side," directed the old man. "And paddle like a frog. Once we've hit the midstream the current's strong, so do just as I tell ye."

Patrick and Conor helped guide the vessel into the current until the water reached chest level. At that point, they let go and stood watching until they were lost in the vapory fog.

"God go with you," Conor whispered.

"And God go with us as well, lad," Patrick sighed, sliding his arm around Conor's shoulders and pulling him close. "For methinks this may well be the last dawn we see."

THE WATER WAS COLD but sheer will to survive kept them at least partially warm. More than once, when the raft lurched crazily to one side or the other, Kate had to quiet the whimpers of the fearful children.

When they reached midstream they found that the current had a tremendous pull. It was all Maggie and Aileen could do to kick their feet in rhythm to keep the raft pointed downstream.

Dougherty warned them, in no uncertain terms, what would happen if they lost that rhythm. "Listen close to me, the both of ye," he said. "We must stay on an even keel, for if we get turned sideways the current will spin us like a top and there's no tellin' where we'll end up."

But it was hard and demanding on both the mind and body. Maggie's legs became so numb she found it difficult to tell if they were moving or not.

Forest debris from upstream added a further hindrance to their progress. Now and then a whole tree would loom near them, only to sweep by as Dougherty deftly maneuvered their course with his body.

"Quiet now," he suddenly hissed. "We're goin' by the spot where the city wall meets the river. There'll be troops just beyond the wall."

It was too much for the women to try to understand how on earth he could possibly know where
they were in the vapory mists. And by now they were
too tired to care. It was enough just to hear his
whispered commands and somehow make their aching bodies carry them out.

A deep groan came from Aileen's side of the raft
and then her spluttering voice. "I—I don't think I
can hold on much longer.... My arms—"

"You can, Aileen, you can!" Kate insisted in a
loud whisper, alarmed as Aileen's head disappeared
into the water for longer and longer periods of time.

Reaching across one of the children, she entwined
her fingers in Aileen's hair. With all her strength she
pulled, bringing the woman's face from the water
and her body closer to the raft.

Choking back a cry of pain, Aileen looked up at
Kate with an expression of gratitude as she somehow
forced her legs to resume their kicking.

"I hear something!" Maggie warned suddenly in
hushed tones.

"Aye," came Dougherty's gruff whisper. "We're
nearing the bend now. 'Tis probably where they've
posted sentries. The current will carry us wide around
the bent. 'Tis here—"

Dougherty never finished his sentence. With the
bend in the river came a shift in the current and a gust
of wind that blew away the mists that had concealed
them. Suddenly, besieging Parliament troops came
into full view. Flaming torches set on tall poles
turned night into day.

"There, a raft!" came a sentry's voice from their
right. It was quickly answered from the Boyne's opposite bank with a volley of musket fire.

"Kick! Kick for all you're worth now!" Dougherty yelled.

Fifty yards around the river's bend was another

cloud of fog like the one they had just left. It meant safety if only they could reach it.

Kate gave a cry of horror as one of the children suddenly screamed; then fell abruptly silent. Through the water cascading into her eyes, Maggie could see a splotch of dull crimson spread across the child's back.

In the next moment, Kate called to Maggie for help. They had let the raft slip sideways and now it was passing right over Aileen.

"Maggie. . .Maggie, I couldn't hold her," gasped Kate desperately. "She's slipped under the raft!"

Wildly Maggie searched for Aileen's blond head. It was nowhere to be seen. At that moment, a sudden surge in the current tore the raft from her grasp. "Maggie!" Kate cried again, as the raft spun crazily for a moment, then disappeared into the fog.

Frantically, Maggie pawed the water around her. From somewhere she could hear a voice screaming Aileen's name and it was several seconds before she realized it was her own.

The current was weakening now, its pull against her legs lessening. But where was Aileen, Maggie wondered frantically.

"Aileen. . .*Aileen*!" she screamed, but there was no answer.

Aileen is gone, she thought sadly. *They are all gone. And I'm so tired. Legs like lead. Can't move my arms any more. Body's heavy. . .so heavy. Odd, everything's suddenly so warm. . . .*

She felt a sudden relaxation, a blissful peace, as the water closed over her. There was no sound, only a serene void of blackness swallowing her as she began to pray. *Blessed Mother, I come to you—*

Suddenly her body was wrenched from its peaceful slumber. Cool air bathed her face and stung her body.

" 'Tis a lass,'' exclaimed a man's voice in surprise.

"Dead?'' asked another voice, almost indifferently.

She felt a rough hand press against her breast.

"Nay, she lives.''

Blinking, Maggie opened her eyes, and through the watery film that covered them saw the round black helmets of Cromwell's New Model Army troops.

"BREACH. . . *breach*!'' Robert Hubbard cried, slashing with his blade at anything that moved before him. Vigorously, he urged the big white stallion over the rubble that had once been Sir Arthur Ashton's impenetrable wall of Drogheda. Before him, pikemen moved like a steel-pointed wedge, driving the defenders back. When one fell another quickly took his place.

The breaches on either side of Duleek Gate had been doubled in width during the morning's bombardment. Now, eight abreast, horsemen poured through the wall behind Hubbard.

The steeple of St. Mary's was but a stone scar. From that corner of the wall, Hubbard could hear the voice of Oliver Cromwell urging his troops onward.

All was chaos and confusion. The moment one voice was raised with the cry, "We hold!'', another voice nearer Hubbard would cry out, "They flee!'' Besieger and defender alike were caught up in milling troops and frightened, rearing horses.

Those in the forefront of the defenders were held at bay by the Parliament pikemen and slashed to ribbons by the cavalry. "Retreat!'' they cried before dying. Those in the rear, not realizing the momentum of the opposing charge, still screamed "Advance!''

Before long the breach in the wall was a surging tide of rust-red doublets. They rolled like a bloody wave into the courtyards and filled the streets beyond. Sheer numbers alone pushed the Irish and royalist defenders back from the walls. In as orderly a fashion as possible they retreated up Duleek Street to the secondary fortification of Mill Mount. Barely had they established themselves there to face Captain Hubbard's charge, when from their flank came Cromwell with a thousand men behind him.

"Colonel Ewer...Captain Tomlins!" the general roared.

"Aye, sir!" the men replied.

"Divert your troops to the South Quay and the drawbridge," directed Cromwell. "Cut off all retreat possible across the Boyne. Captain Hubbard!"

"Sir," saluted the young man crisply.

"The situation here, captain?" asked Cromwell in brisk tones.

"Boyle defends the south wall, with Ashton to the north, general," replied Hubbard, the information at his fingertips. "I have ordered Boyle's surrender and he asks for terms."

Beneath his black helmet, Cromwell flushed bright red. "*Terms*, captain?" he queried sharply. "Verily, they were unanimous in their resolution to perish rather than deliver up this place. So perish they shall!"

"Aye, sir," replied Robert, unmoved by the harsh command. It was a matter of complete indifference to him whether the enemy lived or died once it was defeated.

At the head of a thousand foot and horse, Cromwell charged the huge fortification of Mill Mount. To the south, Captain Robert Hubbard led the same number over the walls. Over half of Ashton's and Boyle's eight hundred men fell dead or wounded in the first charge. Ringing loud above the attackers' sing-song chant came the constant cry of "No quarter!"

Captain Robert Hubbard wounded Lieutenant-Colonel Boyle and was the first to break through the ring of defenders to Sir Arthur Ashton. Just as he spurred his horse toward the defending commander, three of Cromwell's soldiers swarmed past him. By the time he reached Ashton, the soldiers had ripped off the man's wooden leg and used it to bludgeon him to death.

WITH TWO HUNDRED MEN Patrick and Conor held the bridge across the Boyne for as long as possible. Eventually they were overwhelmed by sheer numbers and were left with no chance to draw the bridge.

Yard by hard-found yard they were forced up Ship Street. And with the passage of each yard their numbers diminished. Between the two opposing lines, wounded men raised themselves to their knees and, casting their weapons aside, cried out for mercy. Ruthlessly, they were run through and the wave of red rolled inexorably on.

At the corner of Horse Lane and St. Peter's Square, an old man and a young girl blundered between the lines. Too late the man saw his mistake. With a scream he turned and threw his body protectively over the little girl. A single sword thrust killed them both.

"Dear God!" Conor cried, his stomach churning at the sight.

Beside him Patrick growled, "'Tis truly no quarter. There'll be no stopping them; they have the blood lust. Ho, lads, to St. Peter's!"

Left with only thirty men, they made the church and barricaded the door. Outside there was a momentary lull while the Roundhead soldiers massed.

And then they charged. Wild-eyed, drunk with the fury of battle, they stormed the door with no thought of personal safety. Wave after wave of them fell before the deadly Irish musket fire from inside St. Peter's.

But still they came, until the steps and the square in front of the church doors were piled high with bodies.

"Fall back to the edge of the square!" came an officer's cry from the rear of the charging men.

Beyond the square, Captain Edward Tomlins and Captain Robert Hubbard reined in their horses and surveyed the scene before them.

"They can hold from that belfry for hours," Tomlins mused.

"Aye," Hubbard nodded, and turned in his saddle. "Sergeant!"

"Sir?" the man replied.

"Turn out all the houses on both sides of this block!" commanded Robert.

"Aye, sir."

"A human shield?" Tomlins asked.

Hubbard nodded. "Do you not read your Bible, Tomlins?" he queried. "'Tis the 137th Psalm. 'Happy shall he be that taketh and dasheth thy children against the storm.' The slaughter of women and children must be allowed in the right of war."

His orders were carried out in minutes and the sergeant returned to announce that all was in readiness. The two captains exchanged an unguarded look, then gave a shrug of indifference.

"Sergeant," Hubbard intoned, "storm the church."

Inside the church, Patrick, Conor and their comrades-in-arms, reloaded and then examined themselves for wounds. They all knew only too well that in the fury of battle, they could have been wounded and felt no pain. Satisfied that none of them was injured, they once again looked to their defenses.

Patrick, turning to Conor, was the first to speak. "Lad, keep half the men here at the doors and windows," he ordered. "I'll to the belfry with the other half."

Before leaving Conor, he addressed the men in general.

"'Tis no doubt the day is lost," he told them despondently. "We'll hold here 'til nightfall if possible. Discard your tunics and make for the river. 'Twill be your only chance."

They had barely reached the belfry when a soldier turned from one of the windows with a horrified gasp. "Lieutenant—look here!" he cried in disbelief.

Patrick looked out and then gasped when he saw the approaching line.

"Dear God in Heaven," he whispered.

BY THE TIME Conor reached the east wall his lungs were near to bursting. His eyes were red-rimmed and his face blackened with smoke. Two hundred yards to the west he could see the flames from St. Peter's belfry leaping to meet the slow-coming dawn.

It was all over. Not only had they been soundly defeated, they had been slaughtered as well. Tears of anguish squeezed from his eyes when he closed them in an attempt to blot out the memory.

But it was still there, as clear and as bright as if it were happening once more before his eyes: the leering devil on the white horse, riding behind the wide line of musketeers and pikemen. And in front of them the old men, the women and the children.

Conor had found himself totally incapable of giving the order to fire and even if he had been able to, he had doubted that his men would have obeyed it. He assumed Patrick had felt the same way, since there had been no fire from the belfry, either.

Only when the Parliament muskets had begun to fire over their shoulders did the civilians break their ranks and flee. Answering fire had come from the church as soon as they were clear, but it had been too late. The lower floor had been overrun in minutes. Conor and the men with him had drawn dagger and sword, but their gallant efforts to defend themselves had been futile.

The last thing he remembered seeing was the butt of a musket coming at him. After that there had been only blackness. He had awakened beneath a pile of bodies. The back of his head had hurt like fire, and he had felt blood dripping from a gash across his skull. But he had been alive, which was more than could be said of the bodies piled around and over him like so much cordwood.

Hearing shouts from the belfry above and becoming aware of smoke filling the room, cautiously he had moved a grotesquely twisted leg from in front of his eyes. Immediately he had seen the New Model Army's plan.

Wooden pews from the chapel had been jammed into the narrow stairwell leading to the belfry tower. To these had been set a torch and already the flames were licking upward toward the belfry.

No quarter.

When the smoke had grown so heavy that he had been barely able to see, or breathe, Conor had crawled from beneath the carnage the length of the chapel and out through the priests' door.

Had he been the only one to survive, he wondered now as he leaned back against the tower wall to catch his breath. It was, without doubt, a very real possibility and tears began to flow down his cheeks at the thought.

Patrick, he thought in anguish. Was his older childhood friend and comrade buried somewhere in the middle of that flaming pyre?

'Tis every man for himself, lads. Discard your tunics and make for the river.

Patrick's words of advice came back to him now and with startling clarity. Every muscle and joint aching with fatigue, Conor dragged himself to his feet. He pulled off the remnants of his tunic and then the heavy leather jacket beneath it. His cambric undershirt he left on. It was as tattered as the clothes he had removed, but it wouldn't mark him as a soldier and might at least provide him with some protection from the damp chill of dawn.

Keeping in the shadow of the wall, he started south toward the river, moving past St. Lawrence Street and its gate without a backward glance. At Batchelor's Lane he came to a sudden halt and was forced to hide in a ditch until a number of New Model pikemen herding a group of women and children had passed.

At last he reached the quay, only to find it lined with soldiers on guard. Backtracking to an alley, he was about to enter its mouth when a voice greeted him.

"'Ere, laddie, would ye be wantin' out of the city?"

Conor's hand closed over the dagger at his belt. "Come out where I can see you!" he called.

A stooped, balding old man groped his way into the dim light. "No need for fear, lad. You're Irish, ain't ye, same as me?"

"Aye," admitted Conor.

"Well, is it outta the city ye'd go?" persisted the stranger.

"Do you know a way, old man?" queried Conor, his voice tinged with hope.

"Aye, I do," the man replied. "Uh...do ye have any coin, lad?"

Conor's heart fell. He had not even a purse. "Nay, not one," he answered sadly.

The old man shrugged. "'Tis no matter, lad—you're Irish. Come along!"

Conor followed the old man through a maze of
doors and alleys until he quickly lost all sense of
direction. At long last, he heard something familiar,
the sound of the river.

"Down here, lad," directed his guide. "Watch the
steps. They're steep, they are, and damp."

Conor could see nothing. He stepped toward the
old man's voice in the darkness and found air beneath his boot. With a cry of surprise he fell, spinning once in the air before striking the ground with a
bone-jarring thud.

Almost at once a torch was lit and he found himself staring up at a circle of soldiers, all with drawn
swords.

"Here's another one, sergeant," the old man
cackled above him. "Now if ye'll pay me quick, I'll
be off an' huntin' another one who'd run."

"WHAT IS IT, CAPTAIN?" Cromwell inquired, continuing to massage his temples with his fingertips.

"We have an early count, general," replied Hubbard.

"And?"

Robert unrolled the parchment he held and began
to read in an unemotional monotone. "Field officers
slain: Sir Arthur Ashton, Sir Robert Hartlepoole,
lords Garson, Harrison and McLean, as well as
seventeen Irish clan lords, four colonels, forty-two
captains, forty-four lieutenant-colonels and majors.
Junior officers include forty-four lieutenants, two
hundred and twenty reformadoes and the entire com-
plement of forty-four companies, with the current
count of dead at two thousand, three hundred and
thirty-two."

Hubbard finished reading and, lowering the paper,
remained standing at attention until Cromwell finally
looked up.

"Do you want a count of the civilian dead, sir?" asked the young captain.

"No," replied the general flatly. "Are there any survivors of the garrison?"

"Aye, sir," Hubbard answered, and again lifted the parchment. "Two junior officers—a Lieutenant Moore, English, and a Lieutenant Patrick Talbot, Irish. Talbot is wounded—a broken leg he received in leaping from St. Peter's belfry after we fired the church."

Cromwell's brows furrowed in a frown of disbelief. "He leaped from the *belfry*?"

"Aye, sir," confirmed Robert impassively, "with his clothes in flames."

Cromwell shook his head in wonder at a man's will to survive at any cost. "Are they the only survivors?" he asked after a moment's silence.

"No, sir," replied Hubbard. "One field officer, Lieutenant-Colonel Boyle also lives. I wounded him myself at Mill Mount. He is currently under house arrest in the company of Lord Garson's widow."

Cromwell leaned far back in his chair and let escape a long sigh as he rubbed his eyes. "The two junior officers?"

"Moore and Talbot?"

"Aye. Chain them as prisoners," the general directed. "We'll use them to spread the word of God's will here today so no other foolish garrison commanders will doubt my sincerity when I say no quarter will be given."

"And the field officer, Boyle?" asked Hubbard.

Cromwell replied eloquently by swiveling in his chair to gaze silently out the window at Drogheda's smoldering fires.

A half an hour later Captain Hubbard entered the dining room of Lord Garson's Drogheda house. Lieutenant-Colonel Boyle, his left arm in a sling, and

Lady Jane Garson were just sitting down to the evening meal.

"Your pardon, sir," Hubbard said, stepping forward and leaning down to whisper in Boyle's ear.

"Very well, captain. Thank you," Boyle replied.

He waited until Hubbard had exited the room and then lifted a glass of wine to the lady across the table.

"My compliments on the meal, Lady Jane," he said, "but I fear there will be little time to enjoy it."

He stood and, adjusting the sling on his left arm, used his right to sweep the wide-brimmed plumed cavalier's hat to his head.

"But colonel," the lady asked in surprise, "whither do you go at such an hour?"

"I go, madam, to die," he replied stiffly.

THEY SAW EACH OTHER AT ONCE across the mass of milling bodies. Crying out his name, Maggie ran into Conor's arms, with tears of joy rolling down her cheeks. Conor buried his face in her tangled copper curls and ran his hands up and down the softness of her back, as if he had to touch her again and again to make sure she was real.

"Oh, Conor, Conor," she moaned, kissing his ear, his neck, a shoulder and then his ear again. "They said that the entire garrison had perished!"

A sudden painful lump filled Conor's throat. The entire garrison. That meant neither Patrick nor anyone else had survived the fire in St. Peter's. Silent tears began to run down his cheeks as he closed his arms tight around Maggie.

"Conor, my darling, 'tis as if I were dead and the sight of you has brought me to life again," she told him, almost breathless with joy.

For many moments they stood in each other's arms, each fearful to relax lest the other disappear.

Then, oblivious of the sad-eyed souls around them, Conor guided her away from the crowds, and still entwined, they dropped wearily to the ground.

In a halting voice often broken by a choking sob, Maggie told him what had happened on the river. By the end of her tale, Conor sat as though in a trance, his glassy-eyed gaze fixed at a point somewhere far in the distance.

"Mother..." he whispered.

"Aye, Conor, 'tis almost a certainty," she said, her voice full of sorrow and her expression one of deep sympathy. "The others—" she paused and bent forward to nestle her head against his chest "—I don't know."

"Maggie...are we all alone?"

His voice was no more than a whisper, yet his words came as a cry from a despairing heart, sending a chill through her feverish body. At that moment it seemed as though all the agony and sorrow of Maggie's entire life joined as one to flood her heart and soul with grief. It began as a quiver deep in her stomach and built, finally exploding in uncontrollable, racking sobs.

"Maggie, Maggie-o," Conor whispered in her ear in a futile effort to comfort her.

"What did we do to deserve all this, Conor?" she gasped between sobs. "What can we have done to have brought such wrath down upon us?"

"I know not," Conor replied helplessly, wrapping his arms tighter around her and rocking gently back and forth. "Truly, I know not."

It seemed to him as though he rocked her for hours, but eventually exhaustion overcame their need for mutual comfort and they both fell into a fitful sleep. Sometime during the night an old woman gently shook Conor's shoulder.

"Here, lad," she said, tucking a ragged blanket

around Maggie's shivering form, " 'twill help the lass dry out a little.''

"Thank you, mother," Conor replied gratefully, and finished the job of wrapping the blanket around her as the old woman moved away. In her sleep Maggie moaned and nestled closer to him.

Conor smiled. *Sweet Maggie with the copper hair, the full-lipped, flashing smile, the upturned nose and the laughing eyes that no one could resist*, he thought lovingly. Even now, dressed in a tattered shirt, a pair of breeches and cocooned in a threadbare blanket, she was uniquely beautiful. With her hair in a tangle, her nose almost invisible under smudges of dirt and her cheeks lined with muddy streaks where the tears had run, he considered her the loveliest, most desirable woman he had ever seen.

"Only God knows how I do love you, Maggie-o," he whispered, leaning down and pressing his lips to her temple. "And only God knows what will become of us now."

THEY WERE ROUSED at dawn and each given a wooden bowl containing a meager quantity of oatmeal gruel. A short time later, they were forced to their feet and marched around the town wall to form a long unbroken line in front of the Duleek Gate.

A heavily built sergeant, his black armor glistening with damp from the morning dew, mounted a table and shouted at them in broken Gaelic.

"We'll be filin' you heathen wretches for dispersal and relocationing now," he explained in harsh, unequivocal tones. "Form one line and step up to this here table one at a time. State your name, age, your place of birth and your religion."

He gazed sweepingly over the upturned faces below him before concluding his speech with a dire warning. "Anyone suspected of being a priest or friar will be shot. Anyone not obeying my orders will be shot—unless 'tis a woman. If a woman disobeys orders, she'll be hanged.''

Climbing down from the table, he seated himself and opened a huge leather-bound book in front of him. The long, seemingly unending process began. All morning Maggie and Conor waited in the damp, chill air, moving forward only a few inches at a time as space was made in front of them.

''Conor?'' queried Maggie.

''Aye, lass.''

''What did he mean by 'relocationing'?'' she asked.

Conor shrugged. ''I don't know,'' he replied helplessly.

The only break in the monotony was provided by carts rumbling through the gate as they carried the dead to communal graves beyond the city walls. Each time one passed, Maggie either averted her gaze or covered her face with her hands. Conor would have liked to have done the same, but he forced himself to search as many of the faces of the cart's gruesome cargo as possible. He still had some faint hope that Patrick might have survived, and the fact that he saw no recognizable face among the dead gave a little more life to that hope.

''Name.... You there, lad, step up here! Name!'' barked the sergeant.

So intent had been his search of the carts that Conor had paid little attention to what was going on in front of him. Now, he suddenly found himself at the head of the line and the sergeant was glaring up at him impatiently. Without thinking, he replied briskly, ''Conor O'Hara.''

The instant the words left his mouth he cursed himself for a fool. His deep baritone voice seemed to reverberate down the line waiting behind him and through the mass of humanity in the courtyard before him. Both his name and his clan were well known among the Irish, even if his face were not, for all had heard the tales of the boy warrior's courage at the battle of Benburb in 1646 and during numerous other confrontations since then.

The sergeant remained unimpressed. "Place of birth?" he growled.

To hell with it, Conor thought, squaring his shoulders and lifting his chin. *'Tis done now, and better to have done with it all.*

"Ballylee," he replied proudly.

"Age?"

"Seventeen."

"Religion?"

"Irish."

"Irish what?"

Summoning all the arrogance he could muster, Conor spat out his reply in ringing tones of vehement insolence. "Irish free man!"

The sergeant sprang to his feet and whipped his gauntleted hand across the table with such speed that Conor was powerless to avoid it. Viciously, it struck the side of his head with a crack like thunder. He staggered under the force of the blow and, for a moment, fought to regain his balance. But it was a losing battle and he quickly found himself sprawled on the ground.

"Conor!" Maggie cried, dropping the blanket from her shoulders and kneeling beside him. "Are you all right?"

"Aye," Conor groaned, as Maggie was pulled away from him by one soldier while two others dragged him to his feet.

With a sharp intake of breath, Conor lunged into one of them with his shoulder and tore himself from the grasp of the other. The instant he was free, he drove across the table for the sergeant, his hands reaching for the man's neck. It was a futile as well as a foolhardy move, for the sergeant simply stepped to one side and brought his elbow crashing down onto the back of Conor's neck. Swiftly, he drew a dagger from his belt, and raising it high above his head, started the downward motion that would silence the insolent Irish wretch before him once and for all.

"Sergeant!" a voice suddenly rang out above the general commotion.

Immediately, the soldier halted the downward sweep of the dagger, as if the word had been a hand arresting his arm from delivering the death-dealing blow.

The harsh call had come from above, and everyone, including Maggie, looked up to one of the gate's two battlements. The man surveying the milling bodies below him was dressed entirely in black. On his shoulders and over his left breast gleamed the insignia of an officer. He was tall and spare of torso but wide across the chest and shoulders. His face in the shadow of his helmet was dark; his eyes were darker still.

He turned his attention to Maggie and she felt herself cringe under the intense gaze of two black beams that seemed to bore into her very soul. Outlined against the smoke-filled gray sky, with his black cloak billowing in the wind and the fire of destruction dancing on his gleaming breastplate, he presented an image that was both awesome and frightening. For one brief moment Maggie was convinced she was staring at Satan.

"Sir!" barked the sergeant crisply, the sound of his voice drawing her back to reality.

The officer ignored him. His cold, impassive gaze remained intent on Maggie. "Your name?" he demanded.

Frightened or no, Maggie had no intention of showing her fear to this murderous English Puritan. Lifting her chin in a gesture of defiance, she forced herself to speak in a clear, calm voice.

"Margaret O'Hara," she declared with pride.

"Are you sister to the lad?" he asked.

"Nay, cousins," she replied. "But we are betrothed. I am of the Antrim O'Hara clan, of Bally-hara."

A thin smile creased the corners of the officer's cruel lips, and Maggie gave an involuntary shudder of fear.

"This lad, Conor," the man persisted. "Is he the son of Rory O'Hara of Ballylee?"

"Aye," she responded with a frown of puzzlement. Why, she wondered, was this Englishman showing such interest in herself and Conor? Surely he cared little whether they lived or died.

Puzzlement quickly gave way to utter despair as he called out once more from above. "Sergeant," he barked sharply. "Put the boy in irons and bring the girl to my quarters."

"Wait...*please—*" she screamed desperately, unable to bear the thought that she and Conor were to be separated once more. With him by her side to support her, she felt she could have borne anything, but without him—

But the officer had already disappeared down the opposite side of the battlement and two burly soldiers were grasping her by the arms.

MAGGIE KNEW how wretched she must look standing before this immaculately groomed officer. The boy's breeches she wore were far too tight, and no matter how she tried she could not keep her breasts completely hidden beneath the torn cambric of her shirt.

She had been standing before his desk for a full

three minutes, and still he hadn't spoken. He simply stared at her, his black eyes evaluating every inch of her. His gaze was bold and appraising, and although it was seemingly lacking in interest, it made her skin crawl nevertheless.

"Would you like to sit?" he asked, breaking the silence at last.

"No," she replied flatly.

He shrugged and leaned back in his chair, placing his hands behind his head. "My name is Robert Hubbard," he declared. "Does that mean anything to you, girl?"

"No. Why should it?" she replied in tones of complete indifference.

He seemed to enjoy her retort. It brought a smile to his face as he leaned his elbows on the edge of the desk.

"You were the girl the point sentries fished from the Boyne," he said, observing her closely. "Who else was on that raft?"

Maggie felt a sudden faint surge of hope. If Kate and Dougherty had not been taken by the English, as this man's question seemed to imply, there was a chance they had escaped after all. Maggie had no intention of betraying them, and thinking quickly, assumed a look of vague puzzlement. "What raft?" she queried blankly. "I was alone. I went for a late-night swim and lost my way."

His low chuckle was mirthless. "You have both spirit and wit.... That is good."

He stood and moved around the desk toward her. She was surprised to find herself looking straight up at him, for she hadn't realized until then just how tall he was. Or how ominous, she added silently, as he stepped forward and stood over her. But there was something else about him, too—something oddly familiar—that sent a ripple up her spine.

Suddenly he smiled, an almost charming smile that increased the feeling of familiarity tenfold. It was as if she had met him before, even known him someplace. . . .

"There is curiosity in your eyes, Maggie O'Hara," he noted shrewdly. "What do you see?"

"The devil," she replied promptly.

Hubbard gave a short burst of laughter. "Aye, girl, well I might be," he remarked in amused tones. "To my men I am a saint; to my enemies I am the devil himself. And that is how I would have it."

Until then, he had been studying her with detached interest. Now, however, his face took on a more thoughtful expression as his gaze wandered over the soft curves of her breasts and down her figure, to return a moment later to her face. She was, he decided, quite the most striking girl he had ever seen. At least, she would be, he corrected himself, once the grime was washed away and she was dressed in a more fitting costume.

"I'll wager you are quite lovely under different circumstances, Maggie O'Hara," he said approvingly, reaching for her shoulder.

Unmoved by the compliment, Maggie gasped and stepped gack, chilled by the black iciness of his gaze as it roamed over her once more.

He laughed at her reaction. "Dear God, girl, do you think I would rape you?" he exclaimed.

"Aye," she replied without hesitation.

"Legally I can, you know," he told her, his smile changing from one of charm to one of cruelty. "Are you Catholic?"

"Of course," she answered, surprised that he would consider it necessary to ask such a question.

"Do you know the penal laws for Irish Catholics that have been passed by Parliament?" he asked.

Maggie gazed at him warily, suddenly struck by the

strange turn their conversation had taken. "I've heard of them," she acknowledged noncommittally.

"You would do well to study them," he said harshly, all mirth and kindness now gone from his voice. "Particularly since one of them pertains to the seduction of a Catholic woman by a Protestant. It is a very easy law to remember, stating that you have no right of redress under such circumstances."

"That's barbaric!" she gasped.

"Perhaps," he conceded with a shrug, moving back toward the desk. "Nevertheless, 'tis the law."

"English law," Maggie hissed.

"Conqueror's law," returned Hubbard swiftly, his tone flat and hard. "To be leveled against Irish rebels."

"No wonder we hate you so!" she exclaimed. Immediately she knew her outburst was unwise, but she hadn't been able to contain herself.

Hubbard continued as though she had never spoken. "General Gromwell has a plan for the relocationing of Irish rebels and Catholics," he went on. "All land is forfeit, and Irish Catholics will be given parcels in barren Connaught or in Clare."

"All Irishmen?" she queried in disbelief.

"Aye," he confirmed. "The remaining three-quarters of Ireland will be parceled out to the brave men of the New Model Army. This brings up the question of us, Maggie O'Hara. You and me."

"You and me," she echoed in puzzled tones. "I don't understand."

"I wouldn't expect you to," he replied, then paused before adding pointedly, "I mean to have Ballylee, Maggie O'Hara. All of it."

For a moment, she simply stared at him in shock and dismay. "No!" she burst out finally, unable to think of any word that would express her opinion more suitably.

"Yes," he countered flatly. "That's why I'm sending you with an escort to the west. I don't want to
arrive at Ballylee to find nothing but burned-out rubble. From what I know of Shanna Talbot, I think it
possible she might destroy Ballylee rather than give it
up."

"She will," Maggie declared unhesitatingly, an
image of the most iron-willed of the O'Hara women
in her head.

"But not, I think," said Hubbard, "when she
learns that the life of both the young O'Hara and her
precious family name depend on her cooperation."

"Conor?" whispered Maggie.

"Aye," replied Hubbard. "General Cromwell has
ordered all combatants put to the sword. O'Hara was
captured in civilian garb, but 'tis no secret who he is.
I could have him shot or hanged—or worse—within
the hour." He paused, letting his words weigh upon
her. When he was satisfied that the emotion he saw
flooding her eyes was true horror, he continued, "As
we finish this conquest of Ireland, General Cromwell
is preparing to offer quarter and exile to those who
forfeit their arms and surrender. I could arrange such
a fate for Conor O'Hara."

Maggie's heart was pounding furiously and her
mind was awhirl with possibilities as she quickly tried
to make some sense of what he was saying. *Lose Ballylee? Exile, probably in France... but at least they
would have their lives,* she thought.

"Does that mean... you'd spare Conor?" she
queried hesitantly, almost afraid to ask in case the
answer should be no. "That he and I could go in exile
to France?"

"O'Hara, yes," replied Hubbard, "but the families, no. At least not for the time being. With no
sword held over them to deter them, these Irish hotheads would raise more armies against us. No,

Maggie O'Hara, the men may go, but until the plantationing is finished, the families stay in Ireland.''

"To starve," she hissed.

Hubbard shrugged and raked her with his icy stare.
" 'Tis the price of rebellion,'' he pointed out.

Suddenly there was more to this than Maggie could
fathom. "But why Ballylee?" she asked. " 'Tis an
odd corner of Ireland for you to desire.''

A slight smile curved his thin lips. "I have my
reasons," he told her unhelpfully. His gaze became
more piercing than ever as he paused for an instant,
then added, "What say you, Maggie O'Hara?"

Closing her eyes and taking a deep breath to steady
herself, Maggie remained silent for a moment. *'Tis
the only way,* she thought. At least with Conor free
in France there was a chance they could be together
again before long. She would simply have to bide her
time until she could join him or he could find some
way to rescue her. "I'll try," she promised finally,
"but Shanna is stubborn, and even Conor's life may
not tip the scales. Ballylee is everything to her.''

"Then I suggest you sweeten the bribe with a second life—that of her son, Patrick Talbot,'' Hubbard
evenly proposed.

"Patrick's alive?" she cried, instinctively coming
forward to the edge of the desk, a smile of joy lighting her features.

Yes, he thought with deep satisfaction. *She would
do quite nicely.* There was unadorned beauty in her
face when she smiled and innocence in the dimpled
cheeks and flashing green eyes.

"He's alive—in chains," he acknowledged briefly.

"I'll go to Ballylee," she declared at once. "But
you must let me tell Conor of Patrick.''

"I am afraid that's impossible," he replied evenly.
"There is no time to lose—you'll be leaving at once.
Sergeant!"

The man must have been waiting immediately outside the office, for the door burst open the instant
Hubbard issued the summons.

"Sir," he answered crisply.

"Have we assigned any of the townswomen as servants?" asked Hubbard.

"Aye, sir, several."

"Good. Turn this woman over to them. Have them
bathe her and do something to her hair, make her
presentable. And find her a wardrobe—a heavy cloak
for riding, some boots, whatever she needs."

The big sergeant frowned. The grand ladies of
Drogheda were being turned into scullery maids, while
the captain desired to make a grand lady out of this
ragged, filthy Irish wench. If he lived to be a hundred,
he would, he decided, never understand officers.

"Female attire, sir?" he queried blankly.

"That's what I said, sergeant," Hubbard replied
impatiently. "Damme, man, in your sack of this town
I'm sure you've unearthed some clothing more suit-
able for a woman that what she's wearing at present!"

"Aye, sir," conceded the sergeant.

"And get back to me as soon as you've seen to it,"
Hubbard added sharply.

"Aye, sir," repeated the man, still mystified but
wise enough not to question his captain's orders further.

Maggie was in a daze. Before she had a chance
either to object or ask another question, she was
hustled from the room. The one thought that kept her
sane during the subsequent madness was the fact that
Patrick and Conor were now safe and would be sent
into exile in France. There would be time enough later
to worry about how she was going to find a way to join
them.

"Sir, the...lady...is being bathed," replied the
sergeant to his captain a short time later.

"Good," remarked Hubbard, well satisfied. "Now here's what I want you to do."

The sergeant became more mystified than ever as Hubbard expanded on his orders, but again, he did not question the man. He knew the captain to be a wily individual. It was the reason he, Sergeant Garner Croft, had attached himself to the young officer in the first place, and he was sure that once this bloody Irish business was over, he would benefit from whatever Captain Robert Hubbard had up his sleeve.

"And sergeant," Hubbard added, just as the man reached the door.

"Sir?"

"The prisoners, Patrick Talbot and this Conor O'Hara...."

"Aye, sir?"

"Put them on the first manifest of slaves to Barbados."

November 1649

CHAPTER THIRTY
NORTHERN IRELAND

THE COUNTRYSIDE TEEMED with frightened women and children fleeing before the invaders. Soldiers without leaders became refugees. Those who had retained their arms took to the hills or hid in the bogs and became reparees.

Colin Dougherty kept his word to Patrick. He stayed with Kate and tried as best he could to see her safely to Ballylee. But it was a great deal easier said than done.

The two of them had barely survived the river journey. Once back on dry land, they had immediately gone into hiding in a smuggler's cave on the rocky coast north of the Boyne. For nearly two weeks Kate shivered in a near catatonic state. Both the younger O'Hanlon children had died during the escape and as far as she knew, only she and Dougherty had survived. Many times each day, memories of the good and peaceful times she had spent at her little cottage or with Patrick on Ballylee would wash over her and she would burst into tears.

"Gone," she would mumble aloud. "Mother of God, are they all gone?"

During these times Dougherty would leave to search for food or more fuel for their tiny fire. He was awkward around women at the best of times. Around one who did nothing but weep, and within shouting distance of an advancing army at that, he was at a total loss.

From peasants he gathered the latest news. The Scots Presbyterians controlled the north. They would not lie down before Cromwell but neither would they march against him. Because of the slaughter at Drogheda, all the soldiers in the garrisons at both Dundalk and Trim had surrendered at the first summons rather than die to a man.

"To a man?" Kate gasped when Dougherty returned with the news of what had transpired at Drogheda.

"Aye, lass, I fear so," he replied sadly. "Ormonde flees south, with Cromwell hard on his heels. A second Parliament force has captured Carrickfergus and moves west."

Kate wailed, "To a man.... That means Patrick and Conor—" She never finished the sentence as the thought of the fate of the two young men became too much for her to bear and she broke into sobs once more.

Awkwardly, Dougherty placed a comforting arm around her shoulders. "Lass," he said gently, "if we're to the west we'd best start now or we'll not stay ahead of the army."

Shoeless, penniless and with only a single dagger between them for protection, they set off toward Ballylee at a pace little more than that of a snail. Autumn rains had either washed away the roads or made of them such sinkholes of mud that they were nearly impassable even for those traveling on foot. Colin and Kate took to the hills, using sheep walks whenever they could or striking off directly overland when there was no path. Before long, their bare feet were raw and bleeding from the rough ground, the scratches of briars and the stings of nettles. Only rarely did they come across a helping hand or receive an offer of food or shelter. Most of those whom they could trust were like themselves, on the move to avoid the army.

It took them nearly two weeks of traveling mostly by night to reach Lough Oughter near Cavan. Dougherty was of a mind to slip into the village to steal food and clothing but was cautioned by a priest traveling in the disguise of a peddlar.

"English patrols, my son," the man warned. "They are thick near here and in Cavan."

His name was Father Hurly, formerly of Clogher. It was from him that they learned that Owen Roe O'Neill had died and that the priest, Heber Mac-Mahon, had been arrested, hanged and his head impaled on the gate of Derry as a warning to other priests.

"Foolish they are," commented the father, "for the people will remember martyrs far longer than they will remember those who martyred them."

Father Hurly joined them on their trek. It was through him that Colin and Kate were able to obtain brogues for their feet and heavy cloaks to ward off at least some of the bitter chill of winter.

They moved north and west to Enniskillen, on the southern tip of Lough Erne. This was O'Neill and Macguire country, but the clans no longer held it and the farther west they went, the more they saw of Irish Catholics being moved off the land. It was a chilling sight and Kate thought fearfully of her brother Timothy and those who were left on Ballylee. What, she wondered, would she and Colin find when they reached Donegal and the west coast?

Yet another fear was added by Father Hurly. Each evening when they stopped for the night he would open his pack and remove the vestments of his calling. As if from thin air, people would materialize around him, emerging silently from their hiding places in groves of trees, from the depths of the marshlands and from mountain caves. And there, under a clouded and moonless night sky, candles would be lit and a Mass performed.

"A fool he is," Dougherty growled. "For one of the very souls he would soothe will one night offer up his head for a reward."

The truth of Dougherty's statement was proved barely one week later. They were camped near Lough Derg and only two days away from the O'Hanlon cottage, Timothy and what Kate hoped would be safety. For several nights running, Dougherty had noticed a harper on the fringe of the little crowds that gathered around Father Hurly. The third night the man appeared, Dougherty's suspicions were aroused. Since they traveled several miles each day, they seldom saw the same people twice. He learned that the harper's name was Maggus and vowed that if he showed up the next night he would find out more about him.

He never got the chance. The following night, in a shadowed glen on the narrow banks of Lough Derg, Maggus did indeed arrive, but not alone. With him

was a troop of fifteen red-clad Puritan soldiers under
Sergeant Garner Croft.

They surrounded the gathering and descended without warning just as Father Hurly began to speak. One
woman and two men were killed trying to escape.
Three others were wounded and all were captured.

Linked together with chains, Kate and Dougherty,
with the others, were marched all night through a driving rain. As dawn approached they arrived near the
seacoast and the temporary command post of the
Puritan army in the west, the ruins of Claymore Castle.

It was the last blow for Kate. Despair was truly her
handmaiden now. In the distance through the winter
mists she could see the cottage's thatched roof. So
close and yet, she knew, a world away.

For a week they were kept in the bawn of Claymore,
herded and fed like the cattle who had inhabited it
before them. Almost hourly there were new arrivals;
tearful women, distraught men, and little children,
their bellies distended from hunger and their eyes wide
with fear.

Other priests besides Father Hurly were found
among the prisoners. They were removed to another
part of the castle and detained separately.

At the end of a week, on a cold, drizzling day, they
were taken from the bawn and marched into Claymore's vast courtyard. Kate staggered along like the
others, her head down, her shoulders sagging with
weariness. Screams and anguished cries erupted from
those in front of her. Startled, she raised her head and
gave a cry of horror as she saw what had caused the
sudden commotion. Swinging from rafters between
the battlements were the bodies of Father Hurly and
four other priests.

For the next two hours she moved as though in a
daze, held up by Colin Dougherty's strong arm and

pushed along by the crush of people behind her. One by one they passed in front of a table behind which sat a black-clad provost who recorded their names in a book. When the ritual was done, he stood and addressed them.

"You are all to be transplanted west of the Shannon, in the province of Connaught," he shouted. "Once there you will be given implements to till the soil as best you can."

Shouts of anger and general mumblings of discord greeted his words. Connaught was said to have been burned and laid waste behind the moving armies, protested some. How could they survive in what was now such a desolate land?

"Once you have arrived in Connaught," he continued, unmoved by their dismay, "you will not be allowed to recross the River Shannon east, on pain of death."

A portly man, his once well-tailored clothes now in tatters, stepped forward. "Sir, I'll not to Connaught!" he shouted in the provost's face.

"Sir, you will to Connaught or you will to hell!" was the only reply he received.

An hour later they started the long march south into Connaught and exile in their own country.

February 1650

CHAPTER THIRTY-ONE
WEXFORD, IRELAND

FROM DROGHEDA Patrick had been taken to Dublin. There he had tried four times to escape. Each time he had been caught and heavier chains had been attached to his body.

His next transfer was overland from Dublin to Wexford. This time, he made good his escape and managed to elude his pursuers for two days before being betrayed by a peasant farmer and recaptured. Taken to Waterside gaol in the town of Wexford, he was once again weighted down with chains and placed alone in a tiny cell in a dungeon deep underground. There he was told he would be held until the next ship was ready to sail for the port of Barbados in the West Indies.

The cell, furnished with nothing except a mattress on a wooden cot, a small iron stove that was never fueled and a night stool, was both cold and damp. Once every twenty-four hours a warder would bring him a pound of moldy bread and a jug of water. Beyond that minimal contact with another human being, Patrick was left strictly alone to contemplate his fate.

Time hung heavily on his hands. Much of it he spent on thinking of yet another way to escape, but at best it was a futile exercise, he knew, and he found himself wondering what was happening beyond the four stone walls of his cell. He had gleaned during his brief period of freedom that the war had gone badly for the Irish and royalist forces. After the slaughter at Drogheda, a similar massacre had taken place at Wexford where, it was said, two thousand had been put to the sword or hanged.

And what of Conor and Maggie and Aileen, he wondered. Was his beloved Kate still alive and, if so, where was she? What of his mother and Ballylee? Had his home been overrun by Puritan forces, or was Shanna still there with O'Higgin. Endlessly, it seemed, these questions ran through his mind and always the answer was the same—he didn't know. So great became his despair over his lack of knowledge concerning the fate of his family that he barely noticed the pain caused by the chains that bound him or the cell's foul dankness. Often, he would be awakened in the night by a nightmare in which he would see a burn-

ing Ballylee surrounded by the faces of his loved ones
frozen in the whiteness of death.

It was almost a relief when at long last he was removed from his solitary confinement and thrown
into a dungeonlike room with twenty other men and
young lads. At least he now had someone to talk to,
something to keep his mind from despairing over his
family. What was more, his companions had news, if
not of the fate of his family, then at least of the fate
that awaited him.

Five shiploads of rebels had already been sent to
Barbados and another West Indies island, Jamaica.
They themselves would be leaving the following
morning on a frigate called the *Nora Ann*. The
voyage was expected to take nearly five months, since
they would be stopping on the African coast to pick
up a number of blacks destined for slavery overseas.

Bound now with fewer chains and knowing that on
the following day the few guards assigned to watch
over them would be too interested in the preparations
for getting the ship under way to pay much attention
to a miserable-looking lot of prisoners, Patrick saw a
golden opportunity for escape. But he would need
help. How many of his companions, he wondered,
sweeping his gaze over the group of disheveled men,
would be willing to risk certain death for a chance of
freedom? More importantly, perhaps, how many
were spies, ready to report any suggestion of insur-
rection to the authorities in exchange for an extra
loaf of bread or one less chain to bind them? He
knew not, but there was only one way to find out.

"Lads," he began, eyeing them all intently, "I
know you're soldiers, but have you ever thought of
being men of the sea?" It was a suggestion, no more,
and for the moment he left it at that. Most of them,
he knew, would need time to weigh his words carefully and if spies were indeed among their numbers, he

wanted to know now, before a detailed plan was worked out.

It took a full day to load the *Nora Ann* with provisions and prisoners. The latter numbered one hundred and thirty men and youths and forty-two women, among whom were fifteen girls younger than twelve. These, the guards jokingly called "breeders," destined to provide pleasure for the island cane workers.

This settled Patrick's resolve once and for all. Spies or no spies he had to take the gamble.

So tightly were they packed into the hold of the *Nora Ann* that he could be heard by each and every one without raising his voice much above a whisper.

"We're Irishmen, not slaves," he railed at them. "But most of you have been near slaves in your own land. Would you now bow your heads and be shipped off thousands of miles, only to be sold into worse slavery?"

Grumblings and mutterings greeted his words, and when his companions finally realized his intentions, a few faces drained white with fear. But many agreed that they would rather die than submit to the fate their captors had laid out for them. It was to these men and women that Patrick made his final appeal.

"We have nothing," he conceded, "but in this place called Barbados we'll have less, for we will have lost our freedom. As for myself, I'd rather become a renegade—a pirate—and take my chances at sea here, near Ireland, than sail like a dog into slavery!"

For another hour he spoke, derided, cajoled and pleaded, surprising himself with his powers of oratory. By the time he had finished, more than half the prisoners had agreed to make a last fight of it. Those who remained too fearful to take such a risk had given their word they would remain silent. Nevertheless, Patrick assigned a few people he felt he could trust to watch over them.

Come dawn the *Nora Ann* would sail with the
morning tide. With fair winds they would be out of
sight of land by noon. With strong arms and brave
hearts, the ship would be theirs shortly after.

Much to Patrick's elation they managed to turn up
between them an assortment of thirty knives, several
picks and a few files. Five of the women even produced pistols that they had hidden under their skirts.
One woman, lifting her skirts proudly, displayed a
short sword bound to her leg.

All night they labored, filing and scraping. Now
and then a chuckle of glee would be heard in the
darkness and Patrick knew that another link had
been broken or a rivet filed through. At the crack of
dawn, they heard the harsh rasp of the ship's anchor
chain as the crew cast off. Using this sound to hide
any they might make themselves, they pulled their
own chains through iron rings, and one by one, stood
up and stretched. In some cases, a handcuff still
dangled from a wrist or a manacle still enclosed an
ankle, but at least they were loose. No one from
above seemed to notice anything was amiss. As Patrick had suspected, the ship's crew was too busy putting the *Nora Ann* to sea to pay any heed to what
went on in the hold beneath them.

The sun was high in the sky by the time the galley
crew approached the three wooden, barred hatches in
the deck with food and water. At each hatch—forward, amidships and aft—a group of men waited in
tense silence.

Patrick's orders had been succinct. "Surprise will
be our greatest weapon and ally. For every one of
them who falls, one of ours is armed. Move fast, and
like Cromwell, be ruthless. They can take the land
from us but they cannot take the sea."

The three hatches were opened at the same time
and the unsuspecting cooks and stewards began to

descend the ladder wells into the dark hold. Armed seamen stood guard on the deck above, but expecting no trouble, none of them was alert. Hardly a one had a blade drawn, and most were leaning on their muskets.

In his right hand Patrick held the one short sword the prisoners possessed. Reaching toward the ladder with his left hand, he took a deep breath and, in one fluid motion, pulled himself through the hatch. At the same time he gave a bloodcurdling yell that was answered by the men now pouring from the other two hatches.

Taken by complete surprise, many of the crew of the *Nora Ann* fell almost immediately. Their swords, muskets and pistols were quickly snatched up by the men and not a few women who had surged up onto the deck. Seconds later, they were streaming along the port and starboard gangboards toward the poop deck, cutting down all resistance in their path. A few prisoners had already reached the quarterdeck and were now heavily engaged with the ship's officers.

Screams, yells and curses, punctuated by explosions of musket fire, filled the air. The acrid stench of burned powder was everywhere.

Sheer numbers alone enabled them to take the quarterdeck in minutes. A huge man in an ensign's jacket expended a musket bare inches from Patrick's head. An expression of disbelief flooded his face when the ball missed. Holding the musket like a bludgeon, he came for the young man with a scream of fury.

Patrick sidestepped the musket's downward arc with ease and ran the man through. Pausing only to withdraw his sword, he retrieved the musket and yelled for three men nearby to follow him.

The master's cabin was empty. Just as Patrick had suspected, gun cases lined one entire wall. Using the thick oak stock of the musket he had retrieved from the now-dead ensign, he went methodically from case to case, smashing the iron locks from their rings. Even as the locks struck the cabin floor, men filled their arms with weapons.

The quarterdeck was theirs, but the tempest of battle was still raging on the main deck below. With a pistol in one hand and the short sword in the other, Patrick searched for the captain, spotting him almost immediately with two other officers. Side by side, they were fighting valiantly in the far stern, their backs against the flag lockers and the stern rails.

Swiftly, Patrick moved to the rear port gun mount. Climbing up onto the cannon, he shouted for the prisoners to back off.

"Sir!" he called when they had done as he directed. "Are you master of the *Nora Ann*?"

"Aye," acknowledged the man in the stern. "Captain Jeffrey Archer."

"Your ship is lost, sir," declared Patrick. "Half your crew is either dead or wounded. I would have you call a halt to the resistance before any more of your men are killed."

"And if I don't, sir?" queried Archer, quivering with indignation.

Patrick leveled the pistol at the man's head and cocked it. "I'll blow your brains out first and there'll be no quarter for your men."

Reluctantly, the captain gave the order and within half an hour the entire ship was secure. Patrick set a course that would bring them back to Ireland at its southern tip near Dunboy Castle on Bantry Bay. He was counting on the fact that Parliament troops would not yet have reached that far south and west. By the following morning, he had complete command both of the ship and of the situation.

Of the male prisoners, fifty-two chose to throw in

their lot with Patrick. He was heartened to discover that eleven of them had more than a passing knowledge of the sea and ships. He became positively gleeful when he was told that two of them were ship's caulkers, one an ironworker and one an amateur helmsman with a working knowledge of navigation. This gave him far more than the raw crew he had expected, and since all fifty-two of the men were seasoned fighters, the risk of their adventure was lessened considerably.

Neither Patrick nor his crew objected when four of the women decided to remain aboard as well and take their chances at sea until they could be landed in France. Indeed, any objection would have been quickly scuttled when it was learned that three of the women had worked in the sailmakers' shops of Drogheda.

As darkness fell, Patrick hove to and anchored the *Nora Ann* near the tip of Bantry Bay. The sea was comparatively calm, and he hoped that the mist would conceal their location.

Boats were lowered and the Irish prisoners who had chosen to return to their homeland were taken ashore first. Hoping to give them enough time to scatter inland before Captain Archer could raise an alarm, Patrick waited nearly three hours before giving the command to release the *Nora Ann*'s crew. Shortly before the captain and his men were loaded into the longboats, Patrick mounted a gunwale and spoke to them.

"Tell Cromwell and anyone else you care to that I've taken the *Nora Ann* in the name of Charles II," he commanded in tones of pride and authority. "As such, I plan to raise a letter of mark from the king and, with it, join Prince Rupert's fleet to prey on Parliament's ships."

Captain Archer cursed and then shouted angrily at

Patrick. "You're bound to be nothin' but a bloody pirate!"

With a wide smile Patrick took a bandanna from around the neck of a nearby seaman and wrapped it around his head. "Aye, captain," he acknowledged, "for I'd rather have my neck stretched as an Irish privateer than as a bloody English slave!"

He paused for a moment and surveyed the former crew of the *Nora Ann* thoughtfully. His grin broadened as he then added, "An' if there be any among you who'd rather sail with an Irish renegade and share in his spoils than live under the Puritan thumb in England or Ireland, step forward!"

Without hesitation, nine men broke rank. A large, broad-faced man with wide shoulders and powerful-looking arms took one extra step and looked up at Patrick.

"Me name's Hooker, sar, chief bo'sun," he declared, "An' we thought ye was never gonna ask!"

"Good man, Hooker!" exclaimed Patrick, still grinning broadly. "You've just become an officer and a gentleman. Move your gear into the first mate's quarters!"

Captain Jeffrey Archer fumed and spluttered in fury as he climbed into the longboat. Before it was pushed off, he turned and shouted up at Patrick, now standing at the rail.

"And who shall I say has pirated my ship?" he demanded.

"Lieutenant...." Patrick paused and looked over his comrades and the *Nora Ann*'s defectors. "Hooker!" he barked.

"Sar?" queried the bo'sun, stepping forward.

"Is there a wood carver among you?"

"Aye, sar.... Harris, there."

"Good." Patrick turned back to the longboat and called down to Archer. "I used to be a lieutenant but

I've just given myself a promotion. You can tell them that the new master of the *Nora Ann* is Admiral Patrick O'Hara Talbot. And if they search for her, they'll be searching for the privateer the *Bonny Kate!*"

July 1650

CHAPTER THIRTY-TWO
BALLYLEE, IRELAND

THEY RODE NORTH from Sligo, keeping the sea on their left and Ben Bulben looming on their right in the distance. At the head of the long column, Lieutenant-Colonel Robert Hubbard rode at an easy canter. With his impressive uniformed figure and his militarily erect bearing, he attracted as much attention as did the magnificent white stallion he rode. Every inch of the horse and rider conveyed exactly the image he wanted—that of the conqueror come to claim his own.

It was nearly over now. In March, Kilkenny had surrendered and the Catholic Confederacy had been dissolved. Some trouble had been encountered at Clonmel but Carlow had been taken with little difficulty. Cromwell had been so satisfied with the Irish situation that he had returned to England at the end of the month, leaving his son-in-law, General Henry Ireton, in charge.

Over half of the Irish population had already been herded into the barren regions of Connaught and Clare. More were being sent each day. Within a year's time most of the land in the remainder of Ireland would be dispersed to Parliament troops or English absentee landowners.

And this time there would be no chance for rebellion.

For Robert Hubbard, it was indeed over. He had completed his tasks and now rode beside the loughs, past the mountains and foothills and through the fertile glens toward his goal—Ballylee. He had meant to keep the march to an even-paced walk, but the closer he came to his objective the harder it was to keep his pace down. He was no farmer, but his grandmother had long ago given him an eye for land. And there was no doubt that this land he saw was good.

Already ideas were forming in his mind. Once this bloody war was completely resolved and power firmly in the hands of Parliament, trade would once again flourish. The key to that trade and the wealth it would bring, Robert decided, lay in linen and wool. He would abolish all these little farms that the O'Haras had allowed on Ballylee and replace them with grazing land for his own purposes. He would have herds of beef and sheep as far as the eye could see.

"Sir," called one of his men, pointing to a castle rising in the distance beyond them.

"Aye," Hubbard whispered. "Ballylee."

For months Maggie had been nothing but a bundle of nerves. Shanna's calm had done nothing to alleviate her state. If anything, it had made her worse. How could Patrick's mother remain so cool and serene when each day could be her last at Ballylee, she wondered in amazement.

The day Maggie had arrived, Shanna had embraced her fiercely, then questioned her calmly and unceasingly about Drogheda until Maggie was sure the woman knew every detail as well as she herself did. When she came to the death of Aileen, and that probably of Kate, Maggie had burst into tears. Shanna had simply crossed herself, muttered a brief prayer and bidden her to continue.

Maggie had done as she was asked, leaving nothing

out. In detail, she had told Shanna of Robert Hubbard and the man's intentions. To her surprise, the name of this captain in Parliament's army had brought a grim smile to the old woman's lips.

"I have often dreamed he would come one day," she had confessed mysteriously. "But I never thought he would come like this."

"You know this man, this Robert Hubbard?" Maggie had asked.

"I know *of* him, child...and from whence he comes," Shanna had replied gravely, and had said no more.

Since then, Maggie, her curiosity aroused, had questioned Shanna frequently on the subject, but each time Patrick's mother had either ignored her queries or had deftly changed the topic.

In early June word reached them that all but a few towns had fallen and a part of the Parliament army was moving north from Connaught. O'Higgin began to send riders out daily to learn more; each day they returned to report that the army continued its northward march unchecked.

A week ago, Maggie had been shocked from sleep in the early-morning hours by the sound of several explosions. Memories of the grim siege at Drogheda had flooded vividly into her mind and she had cried out in terror, convinced that at least one cannon ball was about to hurtle its way through the walls of her bedchamber. A moment later, the explosions had ceased and a deathly silence had settled over the castle.

Jumping out of bed, Maggie had donned a robe and run through the house, questioning servants. None had given her an answer beyond tears and downcast eyes. She had found Shanna on the inland parapets, gazing out over the gardens and down the hill at a pile of rubble that had once been the chapel.

"Why, Shanna? *Why*?" Maggie had cried.

"Because, child," the old woman had explained patiently, "if we the living are to be taken from our land, I would at least have the dead lie peaceful and undisturbed in it."

Silently the two women had watched as workmen swarmed over the rubble. By dusk that evening, only a rounded mound of earth marked the place where the chapel had once stood.

Now the two of them stood once again on the parapets, watching the approach of the reason for its demolition. In the distance, among the hills beyond the heath, they could see the long column of soldiers looming larger with each passing moment.

A shuffling step sounded on the stone floor behind them and then O'Higgin's voice shattered the silence.

"I make out two siege guns, two field pieces and near on eighty men heavily armed, m'lady," he said, his voice heavy.

Shanna attempted a laugh but it came out more as a strange cackle. No humor showed on her face or in her eyes. Her knuckles gripping the two canes she used to support her were white.

"Only eighty?" she queried. "Dear God, the lad is sure of us, isn't he!"

"Do we fight, m'lady?" asked O'Higgin.

"If we did, O'Higgin, how long would we last?" she countered.

He made no reply.

Shanna sighed and her bent figure seemed to shrink even deeper into the heavy folds of her black dress. Slowly, she turned in a full circle, her gaze flowing over every stone, every tower and every chimney of her beloved home.

"When Sir David, Rory and I rebuilt all this, we vowed that it would stand forever," she said softly, more to herself than to her two companions. "My husband stood right here on this spot the night before he went to France to beg The O'Hara to return. He put his arm around my shoulders and told me that only one thing mattered: that there always be an O'Hara on Ballylee.''

"Then we fight?" asked the old bailiff once more.

"Nay, O'Higgin," she replied. " 'Twould be a senseless waste to reduce all this to rubble again.'' She paused for a moment to look around her once more, and as she did so, a tear flowed silently from the corner of each eye. "And, besides," she added in a whisper, "there will indeed always be an O'Hara here.''

O'Higgin and Maggie exchanged quizzical glances but before they could question her, Shanna was moving away, calling over her shoulder.

"Come, Maggie girl, and help me dress, for I would look as regal as possible to greet the bastard. O'Higgin?"

"M'lady," acknowledged the old man.

"I'll meet him in the great room, under the crest," she told him, then added firmly, "alone."

HE STEPPED through the tall oak doors and O'Higgin closed them behind him. Ramrod straight, one hand on the hilt of his sword, the other cradling his helmet, he approached the old woman awaiting him. The leather heels of his shiny black boots beat an ominous tattoo on the stone floor, matching the mood exuded by his black-clad figure.

Shanna was seated near the hearth. Over the marble mantle behind her hung an enormous shield bearing the O'Hara crest. A faint, wry smile at the tragic irony of it all curved the corners of her mouth.

As Hubbard strode purposefully toward her, she examined his face and figure. He was tall, more than a head taller than his father had been, and his body was lighter and less muscular. The litheness and the catlike grace of his movements he would have inherited from his mother, Brenna Coke Hubbard, but the face, with its square jaw, its dark complexion and the coal-black eyes, was all Rory O'Hara. Shanna was surprised that Maggie had failed to see it; until she remembered that much of The O'Hara's face had been hidden behind a full growth of beard by the time the child had arrived at Ballylee

"Madam," he said, reaching her at last and bowing his head slightly.

Even his voice is Rory's, she thought, acknowledging his bow with a nod. *That deep, rumbling bass that could fill a room.* Idly, she wondered if Robert ever smiled or laughed. Somehow she doubted it. There was an odd, almost cruel twist to his lips and an intensity in the eyes that would prohibit laughter.

"I am Lieutenant-Colonel Robert Hubbard—"

"I know full well who you are, young man," she interrupted coolly. "I would have to be blind not to."

"Then you know?" he asked.

"Of course I know," she replied in a voice that suggested she considered his query ridiculous. "The question is, how much do you know?"

"Everything," he answered calmly. "My mother kept a journal. After she died my grandmother gave it to me."

"And the Lady Hatton?" queried Shanna.

"Also dead." His tone was flat and unemotional and his casual acceptance of his grandmother's death chilled Shanna's heart.

Placing his helmet on a nearby table, he unrolled a piece of parchment he had been holding and turned it toward her. "Madam," he said stiffly, "these are my credentials as Parliament's appointed governor of Sligo and Donegal."

Briefly, Shanna dropped her gaze to the paper and then resumed her study of his cold dark face.

"Why are you here, Robert Hubbard?" she asked. "I think 'tis not as governor of Sligo or Donegal."

"I am here, Lady Talbot," he replied, his voice as sharp as the edge of his sword, "to take what is mine."

"Why?" she demanded. "Because having Ballylee will give you revenge? I see no reason for it. The O'Hara loved your mother. You were conceived out of love."

To Shanna's surprise he could smile and did so now. But it was a cold mockery of the real thing, full of rancor and arrogance, conveying not a whit of humor.

"That may well be true, madam," he conceded, "but little of it passed onto me."

"I can see that," she returned dryly.

"My mother wrote in the journal that there was a strong resemblance between you and her," he said. "I see now the truth of her statement. You must have been very beautiful when you were young, m'lady."

His compliment was unexpected and unnerved her. Her surprise must have registered on her face, because he gave a low chuckle, and added, "I have made a great study of the O'Haras. . . all of you. Or, rather, all of *us*, past and present."

"And?" she prompted.

"And you'll be flattered to know that I far prefer my O'Hara heritage over my Hubbard name," he admitted.

Something in his tone, in the slight softening of the coldness in his eyes, struck a chord in Shanna.

"Is that why you're here?" she asked. "Why you sack Ireland and now would take Ballylee? Is your anger so great, your lust for revenge so enormous, because you were denied your father's name?"

"Aye, madam," he growled in reply, his face showing the first true emotion she had seen since he had entered the room. "Indeed it is."

"But it was Brenna, your mother, who made the decision to give you the name of Hubbard," she pointed out. "Why do you wish to take revenge on those who had nothing to do with it?"

The cloud of anger that had disturbed the collected calmness of his features passed as quickly as it had come. Once more he was in complete command of himself. "Whatever decision was made those many years ago was my mother's alone. The decisions now made concerning my future are mine."

"And your decision is to be master of Bally-lee?"

"Totally. As much as possible, I have kept my part of the bargain. Conor is alive—in exile. Your son, Patrick, has escaped."

"Escaped?" breathed Shanna, joy and a faint hope dawning within her.

Hubbard nodded. "He and his fellow prisoners commandeered the ship *Nora Ann*, which was to take them to Barbados."

"Barbados!" she exclaimed, her joy forgotten in sudden anger. "You would have made a slave of Patrick?"

"Madam, they are rebels, as are you," Hubbard reminded her. "By rebelling, you all forfeited any rights of person or property. I saved both Conor and Patrick from the sword. That was all I could do." He paused for a moment to allow time for his words to register fully in Shanna's mind. When he was satisfied that they had done so, he continued on a different topic. "When I came through the gate, I noticed armed men on the battlements. Are you planning to force me to take Ballylee by siege?"

"Would you?" she asked.

"Aye, madam," he replied gravely, "rest assured that I would. For if I am not master of Ballylee by nightfall, there will be no Ballylee."

SHANNA'S EYES REMAINED DRY as she read the proclamation to Maggie and O'Higgin, but she found it impossible to stop her hands and lips from trembling.

Be it known that all undersigned do hereby agree to these Articles of Agreement made and concluded by and between the clan O'Hara of the one part and Lieutenant-Colonel Robert Hubbard of the other part, for and concerning the surrender of the Castle and Lands of Ballylee in the County of Sligo.

Firstly, said clan shall deliver up the said Castle, lands, livestock and all furnishings within twenty-four hours of this document date. In consideration, Lieutenant-Colonel Hubbard doth conclude and agree that all soldiers, tenants and kerns shall be allowed to march away with their baggage as long as said baggage shall have no implements of war.

Secondly, said O'Haras shall have the right to tenant a portion of Ballylee as long as agreed-upon rents are paid to Lieutenant-Colonel Hubbard. . . .

"Damme, I've heard enough," O'Higgin roared. "He'd make you a tenant on your own land!"

"Aye," Shanna acknowledged grimly. "'Tis that or Connaught."

Maggie found it impossible to believe all this was truly happening. As a young girl she had watched her brothers die fighting for Ballyhara. She had wept when her sisters had left and her father had fallen ill and died. Ballyhara had been lost to her, but she had

found a new home and a new family at Ballylee.
Now, they, too, were being taken away from her.

And what of Conor, the man she loved and had
been destined to marry? He was alive, yes, but an indentured slave on an island an ocean away. The one
thing that kept Maggie together now was the knowledge that Patrick, at least, was free. Would he come
to them, she wondered. Would he know that she and
Shanna were still alive? And if he did come, would
Hubbard be waiting to strike him down?

"Maggie."

She looked up as Shanna's soft voice intruded on
her thoughts. "What is it?" she asked.

"Pack, lass," directed the older woman gently.
"We must be off by noon."

Maggie's throat burned and her chest ached as if
her heart would explode. So quickly their lives had
been shattered. She longed to release her despair in a
flood of tears but found she had none to weep.

Part III

August 1650

CHAPTER THIRTY-THREE
BARBADOS, WEST INDIES

CAREFULLY, ELANA REDDING daubed more makeup over the upper part of her left cheek and under the eye. After smoothing it with the tips of her fingers she leaned back and groaned at her image in the mirror. The bruise was just too discolored to cover.

"Damn him," she hissed, unable to stop a tear from ruining the work she had just finished. "Damn him, his drinking, this place and this damnable life!"

With nervous fingers she dried her eyes and applied yet another coat of makeup to the bruise. Satisfied at last that it was the best she could do, she ran a brush quickly through her lifeless hair and stood to smooth down her dress.

The gown was green muslin with a froth of lace at the throat and around the edge of the tiny, puffed sleeves. The skirt fell gracefully over olive petticoats.

The color of the dress showed off her eyes and her sun-darkened skin to perfection, which, she thought, was just as well, since it was the only presentable dress she owned. *It almost makes me look like an innocent young girl again,* she decided, and then laughed hollowly. "Nay, girl, you were never innocent," she told the mirror, "and God knows you're no longer young."

Sadly she surveyed the lackluster hair, the deepening wrinkles on her forehead and around her mouth and the stark vacantness that stared back at her from the depths of her eyes. How those eyes had once burned with life and intensity, she thought with a sigh, and how dull and weary they had become over the past six and a half years.

Six and a half years. Just the thought that she had lived for such an eternity with a drunken madman sent a chill through her body. Wearily, she shrugged it away and moved to the door.

She was emerging from her room, parasol and reticule in hand, when a piercing scream issued from the opposite wing of the plantation house. It wasn't the first time Elana had been startled by such a noise coming from Sir John Redding's part of the house, but she hurried across the sunken great room and up the stairs toward the opposite wing nevertheless.

A young black girl, her eyes wide with fear and her cheeks stained with still-flowing tears, ran headlong into her before she reached the top step. The girl's thin blouse was ripped from one shoulder and down her side. One small breast was exposed and bore an angry welt.

"Onee. . . Onee, what is it?" Elana cried, grasping the girl by the shoulders.

"Massa John, he whipped me," whimpered the young slave tearfully. "Tore the clothes you give me— He hit me!"

Oh, dear God, Elana thought. *Not again.*

"Shh, shh, Onee. . .'twill be all right," she promised the girl. "Why did he hit you?"

"Rum—he wanted his rum," she replied, an almost accusing look on her face as she gazed up at her mistress. "You said no rum in the mornin' for Massa John!"

"Damme— No, no, Onee, not you. I'll take care of it," said Elana. "You go out to the stable yard and tell Tall Boy to hitch up the buggy. Then you have Granny put some salve on that bruise. Then you lie down, you understand?"

The girl nodded, still whimpering. "I'm hurt bad...Massa John mean today."

Feeling suddenly faint, Elana swayed and closed her eyes. Already she could feel perspiration running down the small of her back. Was it from the early morning heat or because she knew she would have to go in and face him?

"Mean today," Onee repeated firmly, in case her mistress hadn't heard her the first time.

How well I know, Elana thought. He was mean every day. "Run along, Onee, do as I tell you," she directed.

The girl needed no further urging and obediently scampered away. Elana moved back into the great room. From a sideboard she took a noggin and a bottle of rum. Squaring her shoulders, she took a deep breath and walked down the hall of Sir John's wing and into his room.

"Ah, good!" he cried, raising himself from his bed as best he could when he spotted the bottle and noggin she carried. "Bring it here, wench!"

"Give me the quirt, John," she said quietly, maintaining her position well away from the bed.

"Damned if I will, woman," he replied rudely. "Give me the rum!"

"The quirt, John," persisted Elana. "You had no reason to strike her."

"I did. The damn wench wouldn't give me rum!"

"She wouldn't because I forbid her to."

"Then I'll strike you!" he cried, suddenly raising the leather whip he held above his head.

Elana neither flinched nor blinked but walked directly to the side of the bed. "Go ahead," she challenged him.

He stopped in midswing, his hollow-eyed gaze riveted on her. "You'd do it, too, wouldn't you, witch?" he demanded.

"I told you I would," replied Elana, her voice calm despite the heavy pounding of her heart. "If you ever hit me again, I'll kill you, John Redding. I'll put a pistol ball right between your eyes. Now, give me the quirt."

"The rum first."

"Nay, the quirt," she insisted.

With a surly growl Redding threw the whip to the floor. Elana poured the noggin half full of rum and handed it to him. Greedily he drank most of the contents, then wiped his lips and gray-bristled chin with the back of his hand. "Leave the bottle," he commanded harshly.

Elana looked at the bottle in her hand and hesitated. "Leave it, damn you!" he shouted.

She shrugged and set it on a rough-hewn wood stand by the bed. "Go ahead then, drink yourself to death," she said indifferently. "I care not."

"I know you don't, witch," he responded, with a cackle of laughter. He reached for the bottle and filled the noggin to the brim.

Elana retrieved the leather quirt from the floor and moved to the window. Opening the shutters wide, she threw the whip as far into the trees as she could.

"Since we have no overseer, I've all I can do to handle the slaves," she observed, turning to face him once more. "Your beating them doesn't help."

"You'd get more done on this place if you'd do some whipping yourself!" he countered.

He swallowed another mouthful of rum, then turned his attention back to her. Slowly, he looked up and down her figure and an evil gleam appeared in the depths of his deep-set eyes.

"Dressed?" he queried, leaving the obvious question unsaid.

"I must to Bridgetown," she acknowledged coldly.

"Oh? And who's the unlucky wretch you'll be writhing beneath once you get there?"

"Oh, how I do loathe you," she breathed, with all the contempt she could muster in her voice.

"No more than I loathe you, my dear," Redding retorted, gloating at her over the rim of the noggin. "But we're tied together, you and I, in this ungodly place, and we make the best of it.... Don't we, my dear?"

She made a move toward the door, but as she passed the bed he reached out and grabbed her wrist in one of his long, thin, clawlike hands.

"I'd best not hear you're flouting your bare breasts in Bridgetown," he warned harshly, "or that you're cribbed up in some filthy hole with another Dutchman—"

"I never was, damn you," she exclaimed angrily. "Let me go!"

"You'd best not be, my sweet. I'll not give my name to another one of your bastards."

Every pore dripped perspiration now, and the skin of her arm crawled where he was holding her. She could barely look at him these days. He had always been thin and his face hawklike, almost gaunt. But he had at least been handsome in a dark, satanic way. Now there were dark caverns around his eyes and his cheeks were sunken, giving him the appearance more of a skeleton than of a devil. His once raven-black hair was almost completely gray, as was the bristly beard that covered his sunken cheeks and sharply pointed chin. The skin hung loosely from his bones, making a mockery of the once virile body.

"There is not a man on this island I would take for a lover and you know it," she said fiercely.

"Even me?" he asked with an evil grin.

"Least of all you," she replied fervently. "Now let me go or I'll slice your arm from elbow to wrist."

When she moved her free arm toward the sash beneath her breasts, Redding released his grip. He knew she had taken to carrying a small knife at all times—had done so, in fact, for the past three weeks, ever since she had ventured too close to his bed when he was in a drunken rage. He had beaten her unmercifully and if Tall Boy and Onee hadn't stopped him, Elana was sure he would have killed her.

The following morning she had come into his room and stood at the foot of the bed, staring at him through swollen, blackened eyes. It was then that she had shown him the knife and a pistol and told him that if he ever struck her again she would kill him. Drunk or sober, John Redding never forgot, for he knew she had meant it.

Elana moved toward the door. Just as she reached it, he called out. "Send the black wench back in here before you leave."

"No. I've given her the rest of the day to rest."

"Damme, I want a bath and shave!" he exploded angrily.

Elana gave the thin-lipped smile he had grown to know so well and to loathe. "Then I'll send in Tall Boy," she replied calmly.

Instantly his face drained of color. His lips quivered and his hands shook as he brought the noggin up to his mouth. As she left the room, Elana heard him mutter, "Never mind."

She walked down the hall and into the great room, the smile still on her face. John Redding hated Tall Boy, but more importantly, he also feared him.

She circulated through the big house, assigning two days' worth of duties to the cooks, chambermaids, washerwomen, coachmen, grooms, gardeners and other personal and house servants. This done, she moved into the great yard and followed a graveled path that would take her by the millpond and on to the stables.

The magnolia and other flowering trees were just losing their blooms, but the hundreds of tropical flowers that blossomed all year long filled the warm air with their rich aromas. It was a cloudless, sunny day and she anticipated no change in the weather until after she returned from Bridgetown.

In the distance she could see the field gangs milling around their huts and in the yard. Since it was market day, the slaves had the day off and would be working in their own plots or resting. That night many of them would seek out an Obeah woman who, after being bribed with stolen rum, would make magic for them with her shells and bones and grave dirt. Some of them would sit drinking in front of their squalid huts, dreaming that they were home and free again.

Free, Elana thought wistfully. How wonderful that would be. For she considered herself to be bound up in slavery as much as any of the blacks she ruled.

She passed the boiling house and skirted the sugar mill until she came to the narrow bridge spanning the small river that led away from the millpond. She was barely halfway over the bridge when her approach was spotted.

"Mama...mama!"

Her sandy blond curls bouncing and her limpid gray eyes flashing, Elizabeth ran into her mother's arms. Behind the girl, beneath a palm tree near the opposite side of the bridge sat an ancient, rotund black woman surveying the morning greeting between mother and daughter with impassive eyes.

"Good morning, my darling," said Elana, picking up the child and carrying her back to the old woman's side.

"Are you off to Bridgetown, mama?" asked her daughter.

"I am, darling. For only two days. Granny?"

"Yes, mum," replied the black woman.

"Watch she does her lessons while I'm gone."

"Yes, mum."

"She can't tell if I do or don't," Elizabeth whispered in her mother's ear. "You know she can't read or write."

"Granny doesn't have to," Elana retorted. "She knows everything."

"Will Tall Boy take me riding today?" asked the child in pleading tones.

"I'll tell him," Elana promised, placing the girl back on the ground. "One hug and kiss now and I must be off."

They embraced and the girl flew back to the old woman's arms. Elana paused before recrossing the bridge and watched the child at play. It was a peaceful scene, with the sparkling water of the pond beside them and the swaying trees above them.

I suppose, Elana thought, *that this really could be a paradise. I am slowly growing wealthy and I have a home that will soon be grander than Claymore ever was.*

But I have no man, she reminded herself bitterly, *and the nights are agony because of it. And the shell of a man I do have makes the days ugly and mean. Yes, it would be a paradise, if only I could share it with him.*

But Patrick is dead, she thought sorrowfully, *and I must forever live with the fact that it was I who killed him.*

Her gaze floated back down to the young girl playing by the millpond.

But I shall make it up to him through his daughter, she promised herself fiercely.

It was so obvious whose daughter Elizabeth was, that Elana had been surprised how long it had taken John Redding to see it. She shuddered when she remembered the changes that had come over him when he had begun to realize the truth.

It was odd, she thought. On the voyage to Barbados, when they had discovered that she was with child, John had been almost gentle, solicitous. So much so that most of the ache and despair Elana had felt at her enforced exile had been soothed.

Elizabeth had been born at sea and Redding had been elated. He hadn't seen what Elana had known the moment the whimpering babe was placed across her belly, its mouth to her breast. She had been both elated and fearful. The knowledge that she would have something of Patrick for all her days had been comforting. But at the thought that her husband might one day discover the truth, a cold hand of terror had gripped her heart.

When they had landed and found that the plantation was not only beautiful but also very profitable and far more civilized than they had imagined, Elana had made up her mind. Although she had been practically forced into a marriage with John Redding, the fact that she was his wife, was a *fait accompli* she could do nothing about, and she had vowed that she would make the best of it.

It had been far from easy, however. She was still a forceful independent woman and Redding, bitter about his exile, had found it even more difficult than she to fit into island life. But in the beginning they had managed to live together in relative peace. Although they never really loved one another, they had accommodated each other in most things and both of them had doted on the child.

Under a young Dutch overseer, Jon Van Horne, the plantation had continued to prosper. The rum and molasses trade had begun to flourish, and at Van Horne's suggestion, a great deal of the tobacco crop on the fertile land had been destroyed to make room for sugarcane. New slaves had been purchased and added to the field gangs. The great house had been enlarged and fine furnishings imported from Europe.

Life became easier and more acceptable. Both Elana and Redding began to forget about the thrill of high adventure and intrigue they had so needed before coming to the West Indies. Much of the spoiled, willful and somewhat bitter young woman that had been Elana Claymore disappeared, replaced by the shrewd and ambitious mistress of a thriving plantation and the loving mother of a beautiful child.

But as the child had grown, she could see that John Redding began to doubt that he was the father. Within a year he had known, and the lines of battle had been drawn between them.

Elana had tried to reason with him, but it had made no difference. Almost daily he had become more morose and bitter. He would lash out at her, verbally abuse her, and when the drinking began, she quickly became fearful for the lives of both herself and her daughter. During many of his bouts with rum he would slyly hint that one day he would wreak his revenge both on her and the child.

It had seemed impossible to her that this man who had once encouraged her to use her body as a means of achieving their mutual ends could now be jealous. But jealous he most certainly was, and became more so with every passing day, until she began to believe that he was bordering on madness for much of the time.

Daily life for Elana became hell. Redding added another wing to the house and moved into it, erecting yet another barrier between them.

Not entirely against her will, she found herself drawn more and more toward the Dutch overseer, Jon Van Horne. It was, perhaps, natural, for he was a giant of a man, young in mind and body, who loved life and laughter—things that Elana found she was sorely missing.

An affair was inevitable. And just as inevitable was her husband's discovery of it. Redding had challenged Van Horne to a duel. The Dutchman was killed but not before he fired his own pistol. The ball had lodged in Redding's spine, paralyzing him from the waist down and making him a cripple for the rest of his days. And Elana quickly learned that life before the duel had been idyllic compared to what he made it now.

Despite his many flaws, Redding had been an independent, vital and energetic man who had enjoyed a highly physical existence before the pistol ball put paid to any movement beyond that of his upper body and arms. Confined to a lonely bed for much of the time, completely dependent on others to bring him what he needed or take him where he wanted, he quickly became an embittered, drunken and highly dangerous madman.

More than ever, Elana began to fear for the life of herself and her daughter. Her only protection from him was her own grit, but she had at least purchased protection for Elizabeth in the form of the towering Cormantin, Tall Boy. Now, gazing fondly at the child whose blond hair and gray eyes reminded her so vividly of the father, Elana was thankful she had.

"Is something wrong, mama?" asked the child, looking up suddenly and surprised to see her mother still watching her.

"What?" said Elana, startled as Elizabeth's voice intruded on her thoughts. "Oh, no, darling."

She gave her daughter a wave, and moving back across the bridge, walked the graveled path around the various sheds and buildings and past the cattle pens to the stable yard. She passed through a railed gate and stood looking around.

"Buggy's ready, mum."

Elana gasped and turned to face the owner of the

unexpected voice. As always, Tall Boy had come out of nowhere to slip up silently behind her on his bare feet. He wore no shirt, and even though he was at present motionless, his well-toned muscles seemed to ripple.

Elana had named him Tall Boy because it was the only way she could think of him. Barely an inch under seven feet tall, he towered over everyone and seemed as broad across the shoulders and chest as he was high.

"Must you always sneak up on me like that, Tall Boy?" she reproached him, the back of her neck already developing a slight ache from the angle at which she had to hold her head to meet his gaze.

"Sorry, mum."

His lone eye gleamed darkly, a solitary beacon of hate in the gaunt face with that oft-broken nose and down-curved lips. During all the years of his slavery, Tall Boy's fierce hatred for the white race that had torn him from his homeland had diminished not one whit.

What Elana hadn't learned about him prior to his purchase she had discovered since from Granny, his only confidante on the plantation. Like many other blacks bound for slavery, Tall Boy would have preferred to die than leave his home country. He had leaped from the ship that was to take him to Barbados and, once in the sea, had forced himself to remain underwater to drown.

But his great size had been his undoing, for he had been spotted almost immediately and pulled into a boat. He had been revived on the ship's deck and when he came to, many of his rescuers wished they had left him to drown. In trying to chain and manacle him, a black gang boss and two white seamen had been killed, literally crushed or beaten to death by his huge, hamlike fists.

In most cases, such behavior would have been cause for instant execution, but once again, Tall Boy was saved by his size. The captain of the ship reasoned that the enormous price he would bring in Barbados would more than compensate for the loss of a few men.

Twice during the voyage the captain had cause to regret his decision when Tall Boy used his colossal strength to break the chains that held him. Two more men died getting him under control.

His violence continued once they reached the island, and the slave traders quickly realized that despite his physical attributes, he was worthless. Nothing could be done with a slave who had "the belief."

Firmly imbedded in the minds of the slaves was the belief that when they died their spirits would automatically return home. Only in death would they once again find freedom, and Tall Boy's desire for freedom was far greater than his will to live as a white man's slave.

Any time you have a slave who is not afraid of death, who indeed welcomes it and desires it, you've got yourself a dangerous slave.

It was decided to hang him.

When Elana had heard of this Cormantin, she became intrigued. Taking Granny with her, she had gone to Bridgetown and made some inquiries.

"Aye, mum, this one got the belief, but he can be gentled and cured," Granny assured her after she had spoken to Tall Boy. "Slave traders don't know how to handle him, talk to him," she added contemptuously.

It was to Granny's great advantage that she spoke the Cormantin tongue. In her talks with Tall Boy, she learned that he had been royalty among his people. He had pride, and he would rather die than lose that pride by becoming a slave. In addition, Granny learned that he had a woman and had every intention of killing her as well as himself if any slave trader so much as suggested he be sold away from her.

Elana had bought both Tall Boy and his woman, Nabob. She made him boss of the slaves who worked the plantation and Nabob head of the great house staff. It was the closest she could come to giving him the position of authority he had been accustomed to.

As soon as Granny had taught him enough English, Elana had sat him down and told him the real reason for his purchase.

"My husband is a cruel and evil man," she explained. "I fear him but what happens to me at his hands isn't important. What is important is that I fear that one day he will go completely mad and that in his madness he will harm my child. If you do nothing else as long as you are here, Tall Boy, I want you to watch over and protect Elizabeth. When there is no more danger to her, I will see that you and Nabob are returned to your own land. Will you do that, Tall Boy?"

"I'll do that, mum," he promised solemnly.

He had kept that promise and Elana had lost no time in warning Redding. "Tall Boy is Elizabeth's guardian as well as her slave," she had told him pointedly. "I have his oath that if anything happens to her you will answer for it."

Redding had tested the child's protector a few times but had quickly stopped, when he realized that Elana had been deadly serious. One wrong move and Tall Boy would have used it as an excuse to kill him with no more thought than if he had been killing a fly. It did not matter to the slave that his killing of his master would be cause for his own death. He still had the "belief" and to him, death would have been a release.

As the months wore on, Elana became more and more relieved. Tall Boy still exhibited fierce hatred for all whites, with one notable exception. With Elizabeth he became a different man, playing with her like a gentle bear and, in general, caring for her as if she were his own child. The only time a smile could be seen on his usually glowering face was when he was around Elana's daughter and it hadn't been long before a genuine bond of love grew between them. Elana had no doubt that she could leave Elizabeth safely in his care for two days while she went to Bridgetown.

Gently he handed Elana into the buggy and passed her the reins. She couldn't help but admire every graceful, supple movement of his strong body. Her gaze lingered for a moment on the powerful muscles of his thighs.

"Mum?" he ventured.

"Yes, Tall Boy."

"He hit Onee.... She's hurt bad."

"I know," she sighed.

"No good hitting a slave for nothin'," he stated. "Sign of a mean man—someday slave hit back."

"It won't happen again," she assured him. "Watch Elizabeth while I'm gone, Tall Boy."

"You know I do, mum."

Elana smiled as she clucked the horse into a walk. Aye, she knew he would.

THE REDDING PLANTATION was approximately six miles from Bridgetown, in the parish of St. George. It was a pleasant ride along the narrow lanes through natural forests and undulating hills, and Elana enjoyed it.

But the land had changed since her arrival on Barbados and was changing more each day. In a few years the forests would be gone, for all the trees were being cut down and burned to make way for cane fields.

She chuckled to herself when she thought of the planter she had become. After Jon Van Horne's death, she had gone ahead with his plans, halving the tobacco, cotton, ginger and indigo crops and replanting the freed fields in sugarcane. She had amazed herself with her ability to supervise the construction of the curing houses and the sugar mill.

She had been one of the first planters to realize how much time, money and work was wasted by the lack of proper food, shelter and medical care for the slaves. Her husband had ridiculed her for "pampering the animals," but she had ignored him and forged ahead with her plans. Both the doctor and the apothecary in Bridgetown were summoned five times as often to the Redding plantation as to any other, and Elana's slave loss quickly dropped to one-tenth that of her neighbors'.

The wisdom of her policy did not go unnoticed, however, and before long the doctor was calling on the huge Drax Hall and Kendal plantations with equal frequency. He was a kindly old man who attended his parish prayer meetings almost daily. He lauded Elana for her humanitarian treatment of the blacks. She would merely nod and thank him, knowing full well that her humanitarianism in this instance, at least, had been strongly coupled with a sensible and highly profitable approach to business.

It was afternoon, just past the heat of the day and siesta time, when she arrived in Bridgetown. Leaving the rig at the communal stables with specific instructions for the horse's care, Elana walked down to the wharf.

It was market day and the pier was crowded with blacks laden with trays and baskets. They wove their way through the narrow streets or sat in makeshift stalls, hawking whatever they had managed to grow on their private plots.

White freedmen and indentured servants, Creoles and a few well-dressed planters added to the general confusion. Two ships, a German merchantman and an English slaver bringing blacks from Africa and Irish indentures, had recently arrived in harbor and their crews swarmed over the wharf and through the great market square as well.

A seaman guard, sword and pistols at his belt and a musket on his shoulder, brushed past Elana. Directly behind him came a long line of men, women and children, all black. The men were manacled at their wrists and ankles with heavy chains. Totally exhausted from their journey, humiliated by their enslavement and bowed by the weight of their fetters, they were no longer the once-proud men they had been.

Behind them came a long line of white indentured servants. Most were young girls. Irish, more than likely, Elana thought, and shuddered at the stark fear evident in their young, wide eyes. *There but for the grace of God,* she thought, *would go my own daughter.*

Elana found the slave trade in the West Indies distasteful at the best of times, but she truly detested the treatment of these young girls. Rounded up in Ireland, many of them torn from their families, they were shipped off to the islands where their indenture contracts were sold to freedmen and planters who would make of them no more than whores and breeders.

It was all a carefully laid plan. By the time these young girls had served their ten years of indenture, they would be too ashamed to return to Ireland. So they would stay on, and watch their children grow up bonded to a foreign land.

As she moved to turn away from the pitiful sight,

her attention was caught for a moment by something unusual. A young white man, broad-shouldered and powerful-looking, with a mane of rusty hair tousled over his wide forehead, brought up the rear of the long line of indentured servants. He was guarded on both sides by armed men and heavily chained with an iron belt around his waist, an iron neck collar, and double-strength manacles on both his wrists and his ankles.

Odd, Elana thought idly, moving toward the shops in the square. They rarely chained a white man. And the last man she had seen that heavily guarded and chained had been Tall Boy.

AT PRECISELY NINE O'CLOCK, Elana left Widow Lessing's where she always stayed while in Bridgetown. She had made most of her major purchases the previous afternoon and evening. Those would be sent by wagon to the Redding plantation the following day. Now, she planned to search the market for a few smaller purchases she could take home with her. She was particularly interested in finding some dress material, thread, shoes and a new bonnet or two.

Since she would be loading these in the buggy, she stopped off at the stables first. Paying the Creole stable hand what she privately considered an exorbitant fee, she climbed into the buggy and drove along the wharf road to the market square. As she passed the slave pens and auction block, the day's selling was about to begin. For a moment, she debated buying the indenture contract of one of the young Irish girls she had seen the previous day. It was a thought she'd often had in the past, and she felt Elizabeth might enjoy the companionship of a young white girl.

But as she remembered what most of the girls had probably already been through, she dismissed the thought with a shudder. No, she decided firmly. So young a girl with such a stormy and unhappy past would hardly be a fit companion for innocent Elizabeth.

Taking her time, she made her purchases and exchanged conversation with the wives of the planters she met. Two of them invited her to their homes for an afternoon visit. Politely she declined, using Sir John's ill health as an excuse.

Both women acknowledged her refusal with solemn nods. Elana flushed slightly at the knowing looks they exchanged. St. George's parish was but a small part of a small island, and not unexpectedly, gossip and rumor abounded. Much of it was fiction, but there was enough truth in the tales that were passed around for the women to guess what went on at the Redding plantation.

Elana was still a proud and independent woman, and although at times she might feel sorry for herself, she loathed being pitied by others. She would rather be without friends than writhe beneath their solicitous inquiries and sympathetic stares, no matter how well-meaning their intentions. Hastily, she bade both women a good morning and left the shop.

By the time she passed the block a second time, the auction of black slaves had ended and most of the indentured contracts had been sold. Elana was relieved to know that she would not be tempted further to buy the contract of one of the young Irish girls.

Nevertheless, she was forced to stop her buggy near the block. The press of people in her way was too great. She was about to demand that her path be cleared, when the trader's strident voice rang out over the crowd.

"Contracts for sale on three indentured servants from the plantation of Sir Thomas Rawlings!" he bawled. "Sir Thomas has sold his holdings and plans on leaving Barbados for the Colony of Virginia.''

Unable to gain the attention of those blocking her way, Elana dropped the reins and sat back to wait. *Only three contracts,* she thought. It wouldn't take long to sell those and then the crowd would disperse.

Idly, she watched as a girl of about sixteen and an older man near his late thirties mounted the raised platform from steps in the rear. And then she gasped and sat upright in the buggy seat as a young red-headed man in chains made his way to the block.

It was the same lad she had seen being marched to the pens the previous day. She hadn't seen his face at the time, but now it was clear in the sunlight. His eyes were a strikingly deep blue in color and his wind-burned face was bronzed to a golden brown. The wide, chiseled jaw was raised in defiance as he looked out over the crowd. That he stood solidly and effort-lessly upright under the weight of his chains was mute testimony to the power of his heavily muscled young body.

It's odd, mused Elana, *but there is something strikingly familiar about him. Built like a young bull he is, much like a smaller version of Tall Boy.*

But why was he in chains?

The contracts of the young girl and the older man went quickly. Then the redheaded lad stepped for-ward, and a low growl rippled through the crowd.

Elana's curiosity was piqued. She leaned from the buggy seat and tapped the shoulder of a man nearby.

"Pray, sir, why is the lad in chains?" she asked.

"Because he's a mean one, he is," replied the man promptly. "Most likely there'll not be a bid for him and he'll spend his ten years of indenture in gaol!"

"What did he do?" she exclaimed.

The man chuckled. "You'd best ask what he didn't do, m'lady. On the sail over, they say he tried to in-cite his fellow prisoners to rebellion. After he was bought by the Lewis plantation in the Scotland district, he did the same thing. When he was whipped for it, he ran off. They finally got tired of him an' sold him to Rawlings.''

"That doesn't seem to be enough to keep him in chains," she observed with a frown.

"'Twas what he did on the Rawlings's place that put him in irons," the man replied. "Sir Thomas had him whipped for discipline. The lad killed the gang boss with his bare hands and then took the whip to Sir Thomas himself. Would'a killed him, too, they say, but for a girl there who finally reasoned with him and calmed him down. He's been in the Rawlings stockade ever since."

Thoughtfully, Elana sat back as the trader once again raised his voice above the crowd.

"Now, here we have a young lad—eighteen, his papers say. Strong as a bull he is, as I'm sure Sir Thomas would testify if he were here!"

This pointed comment brought chuckles and not a few catcalls from the crowd. The lad broke into a grin that displayed his even white teeth.

"I'm sure one of you can find a use for him," continued the trader as the crowd settled once more. "If nothin' else, gentlemen, you could pit him against your biggest slave in wrestlin' for sport!"

"I don't want none o' my valuable ones killed!" came a man's voice from near the back.

"You come up here, sir," challenged the lad, the grin on his face broadening, "and I'll wrestle you for more than sport—and I'll even leave the chains on."

This brought a roar of laughter from the crowd that was quickly silenced by the trader's upraised hand.

"All right now, let's hear a bid for Conor O'Hara!"

With an audible gasp of shock, Elana clutched the

sides of the buggy in an effort to prevent herself from swaying in her seat and losing her balance.

"Are you all right, m'lady?" asked the man whose shoulder she'd tapped earlier. His red, perspiring face was a picture of concern.

"What?" she replied, barely giving him a glance. "Yes, yes...I think so...."

"You look ill, m'lady," he persisted. "Your face is as white as my shirt."

"Yes, yes, I'm all right." But still she swayed in the buggy seat and suddenly found breathing difficult.

Conor...Conor O'Hara.

In her mind she could still see the round face staring impishly up at her from the doorway of her bedchamber at Claymore. Vividly she recalled the bold stare and his quick-witted reply.

Conor O'Hara. The son of Rory, The O'Hara. An indentured servant—little better than a slave.

Patrick's words, once idly spoken, rang in her ears. "Conor? Oh, he's a fine lad, and he'll be a fine man one day. He's like a little brother to me, the brother I never had."

Elana opened her eyes and blinked to clear the sudden moisture from them. He stood proudly even in chains, the arrogant smile daring any one of the crowd to bid for his body.

"Come on now, men, that's a pittance for a lad like this!" the trader protested. "Let's have us a bid here! Got more than nine and a half years left on his contract, he does!"

Elana looked around the crowd. No matter how much the trader harangued them, there was no proffered bid.

Again she tapped on the man's shoulder. "What did you say would happen to him if no one buys his contract?" she asked.

"Gaol, more'n likely."

Elana felt her heart pound in her chest and a huge lump formed in her throat, making it nearly impossible for her to breathe.

No, she thought, *not Rory O'Hara's son!*

She had seen the Breakwater gaol, near the end of the wharf. The rats outnumbered the prisoners twenty to one and did battle with them for their food. Men emerged from imprisonment there after only six months as shriveled, hollow-eyed wrecks.

No! That couldn't be allowed to happen. Not to the son of Rory O'Hara!

She raised her hand.

"And we have a bid," observed the trader with evident glee. "Right there we have a bid!"

"M'lady," said the man beside the carriage. "Beggin' your pardon, but are ye crazy? They call that lad 'the fiery one'—an' not because of his hair. 'Tis his temper—he's a killer, that one."

"I know what I'm doing, sir," Elana said crisply, raising her hand higher.

The smile was gone from Conor's face now, replaced by a puzzled frown as he squinted into the sun to try to see this foolish woman who had bid for him.

"Once. . . twice. . . three times, and sold to the lady in the buggy! What plantation, m'lady?"

The trader was already making his way through the crowd toward her. When he was near, Elana moved the buggy forward.

"Redding," she said in a low voice. "Here's your coin."

"Right enough, m'lady," replied the trader in tones of great satisfaction. "Get you down here, lad!"

Obediently, Conor clanked down the steps. The crowd parted before him like a wave as he walked toward the buggy.

The trader started to shackle him to the vehicle's rear brace. Conor was looking at her with narrowed eyes, but Elana kept her face in the shadow of her bonnet. She didn't want him to recognize her now, not here in front of all these people.

"Remove his fetters," she commanded abruptly.

"But m'lady—" began the trader.

"Take them off," she interrupted brusquely. "All of them."

"He's a mean one, and strong. Wouldn't—"

"Damme, man!" she exclaimed angrily. "Do I have to do it myself?"

With obvious reluctance, the trader removed all the chains and manacles. As soon as they lay in the dirt at his feet, Conor clapped his hands together. With an eerie, wailing cry of fear, the trader turned and made his way back to the block as fast as his legs would carry him. Even the crowd surged back respectfully as Conor stretched and turned in a circle.

"M'lady, are ye sure ye can handle him?"

The speaker stood holding her horse. She recognized him as Hiram Coffey, the overseer at Drax Hall.

"I can handle him," she assured the man, then turned to Conor. "You . . . sit there, on the brace," she commanded. Turning back once more to Coffey, she repeated, "I can handle him, Master Coffey, and if I can't, Tall Boy can. Are you sitting, lad?"

"Aye."

"Then hang on!"

Nodding at Coffey to release the bridle, Elana whipped the horse and the buggy lurched forward. She maintained a fast but steady pace until she was well outside the town and into plantation country, where the dwellings were far apart. Near a bridge that spanned a narrow stream, she halted the buggy beneath a towering magnolia.

"You drive from here," she said, moving over in

the seat and dropping the reins in the place she had vacated. "I'll show you the way."

"What if I decide instead to run?" Conor asked, moving around the buggy.

"Go ahead," she replied, with a shrug. "You'll have to steal to live. You'll be caught and hanged. 'Tis an island, with no place to run. The only way off it is by ship, and no master will give you passage without papers. You'd best climb up here and drive, for you'll fare much better on the Redding plantation than you would anywhere else."

"Redding," Conor mused, frowning in concentration.

Silently, Elana untied her bonnet and removed it. Her sun-bleached hair fell around her face as she turned in the seat to face him.

It seemed that he stared at her for an eternity before his eyes widened in recognition and his jaw dropped open in surprise.

"M'Lady Claymore..." he gasped.

"No more," she said curtly. "I'm Lady Elana Redding, now. Get in!"

Suddenly the handsome features broke into the same impish smile she remembered from his youth. And the sea-blue eyes gleamed with the familiar look of boyish mischief as he threw his head back and roared with laughter.

The laugh was infectious. It brought a smile to Elana's lips and a slight flush to her face, for she suspected what had caused it.

"Forgive me," he said finally, still spluttering with laughter, "but I was remembering—"

"I know," she interrupted stiffly. "The last time we met. Get in!"

"Aye," he admitted, still grinning. "And what an awakening it was for a young lad. Tell me, Elana Redding, do you still have beautiful breasts?"

The flush deepened and she turned away to hide it. But her smile grew wider, and for some unknown reason she felt strangely warm and comforted. Still he didn't get into the buggy, however, and she turned back toward him to find out why.

Gone were the smile and the laughter in his eyes. His gaze was piercing now, and as hard as blue ice as he stared at her with an expression almost of hatred.

"What is it?" she asked in a low voice, shocked by the sudden transformation.

"I was remembering what you did to Patrick," came the cold, grim response.

Elana dropped her gaze and fumbled nervously with the reticule in her lap. She was silent for a moment, biting her lip as she concentrated all her efforts on trying to find the right words to ease the awkwardness of the moment. Finally, with a sigh, she raised her head to look at him once more.

"I have had to live with the fact that I caused Patrick's death, Conor," she said quietly. "For a very long time I have had to live with it. And believe me, I have paid for it."

"His death?" queried Conor, a puzzled frown creasing his brow. He shook his head. "Nay, you cannot claim that."

"What?" she practically shouted, springing to her feet and narrowly avoiding being thrown to the ground as the buggy lurched dangerously.

"Patrick survived Sir John's vile wound," Conor elaborated calmly. "I thought he was killed at the siege of Drogheda, but just before I was shipped—"

But Elana barely heard more than his first sentence. "Patrick is alive?" she breathed disbelievingly, sinking slowly back down onto the seat of the buggy.

"Aye," Conor assured her, "and most likely on his way to this hole."

"Patrick is alive," she whispered. "He's alive...."

CHAPTER THIRTY-FOUR
BALLYLEE, IRELAND

MAGGIE ARRANGED the last of the fresh rushes over the hard-packed dirt floor and straightened to survey the afternoon's labor. She had to admit that it was not very good, but it was the best she could do with what she had and at least it was clean.

The back-breaking labor of hauling the old rushes out of the hut had also served to eradicate from her mind the awful chore that had been forced upon her—and her alone—early that morning. Now, with the hard job finished, she found tears once more misting her eyes at the vivid memory of the tiny, lifeless and shrouded body of the child she had placed in the crude grave she had managed to dig for it.

Night was coming on quickly and the wind had begun to howl. In the brief respite from movement and labor she had just taken, the chill had already begun to invade her bones. She wrapped a heavy cloak around the already thick padding of clothing she was wearing—three old skirts for petticoats beneath a heavy woolen overskirt and knitted sweater.

How different was life on the land than life in the manor, she thought wearily. But she knew she was far better off than the many poor souls who walked the land begging for their daily bread and wearing hardly enough on their backs to ward off the chill. At least she and Shanna had a roof over their heads.

The sudden thought of Shanna made her move to the canvas curtain that separated the two rooms of the hut. Quietly she lifted it and peered cautiously through the opening. She was relieved to see that the old woman was asleep on the room's only piece of furniture, a flock bed. *Thank God*, Maggie thought.

She's breathing evenly. The broth had helped.

Over many weeks now, since the cold winds had begun to hum through the hut's leaky walls and roof, Shanna had grown steadily weaker. The illness had begun as a mere irritation in her throat but had developed into a constant racking cough that shot fear into Maggie's heart every time she heard it.

She dropped the curtain and moved across the first room to the hearth, over which a lamb stew bubbled in a kettle attached to an iron ring secured to the wall. Like the hut, the hearth was a crude mortar and stone affair, hastily constructed, but at least it had a chimney that allowed most of the smoke to escape.

Growing up at Ballyhara and then in the castle of Ballylee, Maggie had never really known how the peasants and the poorer tenants on the land had lived. But over the past seven months, she had learned. Dear God, she thought, how she had learned!

Seven months. Had it really been so short a time? Somehow it seemed more as though years had passed since she, Shanna and their solemn procession had walked under the arch and away from the walls of Ballylee. O'Higgin had led them across the heaths and inland through the bogs, to a corner of Ballylee property that Maggie had rarely visited. The land was hilly, and in the distance she could see the foothills and the looming shape of Ben Bulben.

"'Twas my tenant farm before The O'Hara took me up to the great house and made me bailiff," O'Higgin had said grimly.

The "farm" was no more than a thatch-roofed hut built into the side of a hill. A stone-fenced pen for animals was attached to one side of it, and there was a large portion on the opposite side cleared for a garden. Shanna had accepted it with stoicism. Maggie, however, had been dejected, especially when they had seen the dirt floor and the open hearth in the center of the room.

" 'Tis a far cry from the great house, but, damme, I'll make it livable for ye," O'Higgin had vowed.

And make it livable he had, as fast as his old bones allowed. He had added a second room and built sturdy new furniture for both rooms from newly felled trees. Knocking a hole in one wall, he had built a stone chimney and new hearth. Outside, he had redug the old well and had built a system that would allow the water to be drawn up by animals.

And then had come The O'Hara's former tenants, some of whom had decided to remain under Hubbard, others who planned on leaving. They came from every corner of Ballylee to pay their respects to and commiserate with the Lady Shanna. Each of them had brought what little they could spare: food, clothing, tools and in a few cases, even animals.

It had taken that great show of respect and generosity to break the old woman down. As she gracefully but unwillingly accepted their gifts and their blessings, she had disintegrated into tears.

O'Higgin had stayed with Maggie and Shanna, sleeping outdoors until the winter winds began to howl down from the north. Then he solemnly said his goodbyes and left, never telling them where he was going. But they knew, nevertheless.

He had gone into the hills to join a band of reparee Tories, as the outlawed papists and royalists were now called. Groups of them had been forming in the hills or in the bogs during the day and riding out at night to raid and steal from the Englishmen who now held their land. So successful were their forays that these Tory bands quickly became notorious, and with each new success more outlaws flocked to join their number.

They became so troublesome that Dublin issued orders that classed them along with priests and wolves, to be hunted down accordingly. A reward was placed on the heads of all three categories of these "burdensome beasts": five pounds for the wolf, six if it was a bitch, ten for the priest and twenty for a Tory.

It was a magnificent sum and enticed many an Irishman to turn in a fellow countryman for reward. It had become a time of survival, and there were men to whom friendship—even kinship—meant little when it came to coin. Maggie had even heard tales of brothers and cousins cutting one another's throats for an English reward.

Once each fortnight, O'Higgin had returned to the little hut. Always he had brought something with him—an unmarked lamb, a sack of grain or freshly cut beef.

Every time he had come, Maggie would angrily beg him to stop, to remain at his old tenant farm with them. He was too old, she would declare heatedly, to be riding the roads with an outlaw band.

For the most part, the only answer she had received was a glimpse of a smile beneath the red beard on his ancient, leathery face.

Once when she had pleaded with him almost hysterically, in his fine tenor voice he had answered her in song.

> The master's bawn, the master's land,
>   a surly fellow fills;
> The master's man, an outlaw'd man,
>   is riding in the hills.
> I'll join them there, those Tory men,
>   then one day when I die,
> They'll say he was an Irish man,
>   a Free Man he did die.

Finishing the song, he had looked at Maggie silently for a long moment, infinite sadness in his gentle eyes. "Too old I am, lass, to live under their thumbs again," he had sighed finally.

It had been Robert Hubbard who had brought O'Higgin's lifeless body to them on a blustery day in January.

"It was foolish of him, an old man," had been all he said of O'Higgin's death. Placing the body on their only cot, he had cast a keen glance around the hut.

"Aye, it was," Maggie had agreed sadly, fighting to hold back her tears in front of Hubbard. "But at least he didn't pay you tithes on what he stole."

Hubbard had merely acknowledged her barb with a nod and a shrug, then took Shanna aside. They spoke for a few moments in hushed tones, and then he had left.

He had barely disappeared from sight when a group of women seemed to materialize out of the mists. With them they had brought winding sheets and a canvas shroud. Thirty of them worked as one, their voices raised in cries of mourning. When the bathing and sewing was done, they lifted the body of O'Higgin onto a bier and carried him into the hills. Of necessity, it was a short wake and an even faster burial.

Walking back to the hut, Maggie had expressed her amazement that so many women had come so far to help bury the old man.

"I'm not surprised in the least," Shanna had confessed. "He was The O'Hara's right arm on Ballylee and cared for all the tenants and peasants as if they were his children. He never once stopped looking after them. Do you think you and I were the only ones he stole for to feed?"

Once they returned to the hut, Maggie had remembered the whispered conversation that had taken place between Shanna and the Englishman before O'Higgin's burial. She questioned the old woman on its subject.

"He wanted to know how we were faring," Shanna replied simply.

"I hope you told him well," commanded Maggie.

"I did," the old woman conceded, "but he could look around and see it wasn't true. He suggested we move back to Ballylee."

"He did?" Maggie exclaimed, unable to keep the elation out of her voice.

"Aye, but there would be a stipulation."

"What?"

"You must marry him."

Maggie stared at the old woman in disbelief. "Marry him...marry *him*?" she queried sharply. "Dear God, the man is insane!"

"Nay," contradicted Shanna. "Methinks, rather, he is quite crafty."

"How could he ever think I would marry him?" Maggie cried. "And why, pray, would he want to marry me?"

Favoring her with an enigmatic smile, Shanna replied, "He has Ballylee...and now he wants the name."

There was an English law, Maggie knew, that allowed a man to take his wife's name upon marriage if he so desired. She also knew it was usually used to preserve titles and could think of no reason why the Irish name of O'Hara should be so important to an Englishman. Shanna had declined to enlighten her.

"Maggie. Maggie, lass...."

Maggie jumped now at the sound of Shanna's voice and moved swiftly to the other room. "Aye, Shanna, I'm here," she replied.

"So cold, lass," murmured the old woman. "Could you put new coals in the pan?"

"Of course." Maggie knelt beside the bed. Lifting the covers, she ran her hand along the false bottom until she found the hot-coal pan's handle. "I'll be...."

But Shanna was already asleep again, her face looking fragile and ashen against the pillow.

Then Maggie dumped out the cold coals from the hearth and replaced them with heated ones. As she returned the pan to its position beneath the bed, Shanna awoke once more.

"Maggie, lass...."

"Aye?"

"The wee one, how is she?"

Maggie swallowed hard and averted her eyes as she got to her feet. "Gone," she replied sadly. "I've shrouded and buried her near the mother."

A single tear ran from the corner of Shanna's right eye across her cheek. " 'Tis perhaps just as well," she murmured, and closed her eyes once more.

Aye, just as well, Maggie agreed silently, moving back to the warmth of the fire.

They had found the child in a nearby ditch a week earlier. Less than a year old, she had been wailing pitifully as she huddled against her mother for warmth. But the woman had had none to impart; she had been dead for many hours. Before she had died she had tried to scrape together a mound of earth and make a shelter of leaves for herself and the child.

Her fate was not uncommon, Maggie knew. Women and children such as these were perishing daily. The roads were filled with wandering orphans whose fathers had been sent into exile and whose mothers had died of cold or hunger.

Maggie had taken the child into the hut and buried the mother. For a week she had done everything she could to save the infant's life. Several times Shanna had gotten up from her own sickbed to help. But it had been to no avail.

That morning, Maggie had dug yet another grave, and as she worked, she had thought that all Ireland would one day be a forest of tombstones. Forcibly, she had been reminded of the Puritan God's wrathful words: *And I will make your cities waste, and bring your sanctuaries unto desolation, and I will not smell the savor of your sweet odors. And I will bring the land into desolation; and your enemies which dwell therein shall be astonished at it.*

"No more than I," she had said aloud as she filled in the grave. "No more than I!"

IT WAS SIX WEEKS after the death of the child when Hubbard came again. She heard the horse and without looking out to determine its rider, retrieved from their hiding place the two pistols O'Higgin had given her.

The situation in her part of Ireland had grown worse. Thieves and cutthroats abounded. Only a week earlier, Maggie had caught two rogues making off with a lamb from her pen. Both had been Irishmen, one a neighbor.

Hunger knows no morality, she thought. *Those who were once your friends turn against you when their bellies get empty enough.*

She had had to cock one of the pistols and level it before they would drop the lamb and run.

"Could you?" Shanna had asked. "Could you have shot them?"

"Aye," Maggie had assured her truthfully. For survival—that of herself and Shanna—had become all that mattered to her.

She threw the door wide and stepped from the cottage, both pistols cocked and raised.

"'Tis against the law for the Irish to own implements of war," Hubbard reminded her pointedly. "I'm sure you must know pistols are indeed implements of war."

Dressed in black, his shoulders draped with a heavy black riding cloak, he sat tall on the white stallion. The only color to break the ominous black of his clothing was the traditional Puritan collar of white that lay around his neck and fell part way down his doublet.

He looked, Maggie thought, not unlike the first time she had seen him standing on the battlements of Duleek Gate in Drogheda. And because she now knew the true nature of the man, she found the sight of him more chilling than ever. The cold intensity in his black eyes made her lower the hammers and drop the pistols to her sides. But not before replying, "The laws you constantly seem to quote are always English laws."

"Irish law now," he corrected, his handsome but cruel face expressionless. "For all Ireland is again an English colony."

Maggie said nothing, but the look on her face prompted his next words.

"It seems that the governors will soon meet to sign a formal peace."

"With each other?" she queried in mocking tones.

Her meaning wasn't lost on Hubbard. His lips curved into a semblance of a smile. "Aye," he conceded, "for there's few Irish left to sign. They're all for Connaught or Clare."

"Or Barbados—as slaves," she interjected harshly.

"Indentured servants. There is a difference."

Maggie felt a sudden surge of bitter anger. How calm and cool he was, she thought, just as he had been when he had deceived her so blatantly about Conor. Many times since that conversation she had tried to recall anything that might have given her a clue that he was lying about sending Conor to France. Anything...the lift of an eyebrow, the tone of a spoken word, an expression on his face. She could remember nothing. Hubbard was a true master of deceit.

He swung himself down from the saddle and lifted two baskets from the pillion behind it.

"Food," he said, raising the baskets aloft and walking around her into the cottage as if he owned it.

But of course, she reminded herself bitterly, he did own it.

Silently she followed him, kicking the door to behind her. Wordlessly he set the baskets on a three-legged table in the center of the room and turned toward her. With sure movement he took the pistols from her.

"Where do you hide them?" he asked.

"You mean you'll not confiscate them?"

"Nay. I do believe that two Irish women alone in this barren corner of the land need some protection— if for nothing else than protection from their fellow Irishmen."

His tone of contempt brought a flush to Maggie's face. Not trusting herself to speak, she gestured to a loose, pulled stone near the edge of the hearth. Hubbard replaced the pistols and then leaned against the side of the chimney and raked her from head to foot with a piercing gaze that left her feeling unaccountably embarrassed.

"How is m'Lady Talbot?" he asked abruptly.

"Resting. . .sleeping," she replied with a shrug.

"I suspected that much," he observed dryly, "when no voice came from the other room to inquire who was the intruder. I meant how is the lady's health?"

"Worse—much worse," she admitted, lifting her hands and wearily massaging her temples with her fingertips. Suddenly she didn't care if he knew the truth, if he knew how squalid was their situation or how waning the state of Shanna's health.

"I shouldn't wonder," he declared bluntly. "This place is as dank as a tomb."

"She would get better—perhaps even totally well—if you would let her return to Ballylee," retorted Maggie, dropping her arms to her sides.

"My dear girl, I'm not stopping her," he countered smoothly.

"You mean that I am," she returned, barely managing to keep the despair she felt from her voice.

"Then she told you." With a deft motion he swept the heavy cloak from his shoulders and draped it carelessly over the back of a nearby chair. For some reason he seemed even taller and broader without its shapeless folds around his figure. His presence seemed to fill the room with an aura of command.

"Aye," sighed Maggie, "she told me." Suddenly the curiosity that had been gnawing at her for so long burst forth. "Why, in God's name, do you want me for a wife?"

Hubbard moved forward slightly to gaze down at her more intently, his black eyes boring into hers. "Surely she told you that as well," he remarked, in obvious surprise.

Maggie shook her head. "She said you want the name. But *why*? You have Ballylee and you have the army behind you to keep it. You and your kind have finally done what England has been trying to do for nearly two hundred years—reduce us to dust. Would having me as well give you some kind of final victory over us?"

In the oddly mercurial way he had, Hubbard let drop his mask. His chiseled features took on character and in that instant Maggie could have sworn that she saw a flood of emotions pass like swift-moving clouds over his countenance. And once again, she experienced the eerie, almost frightening feeling that she had known this man before, long before the horror of Drogheda.

"Odd," he said, his voice soft, almost gentle. "I wonder why she didn't tell you the full of it."

"The full of *what*?" Maggie exclaimed, then abruptly lowered her voice to a whisper as she remembered the sleeping woman. "Who are you, Robert Hubbard? What is so strange about you, so mysterious, that she knows but does not tell me?"

But Hubbard, his face once more an impassive mask, dismissed her questions with a quick flick of his wrist. "I'm sure that whatever they are, m'Lady Talbot has her reasons," he said, in formal tones. "I shall leave it at that."

"Dear God, man, let her return to the castle and die in peace!" Maggie cried. "And let me remain here! Have you no pity in your soul?"

"None," he replied flatly, picking up his cloak and swinging it over his shoulders.

"Can't you understand," Maggie pressed on desperately, determined not to let him see the tears that threatened to roll down her cheeks at any moment. "I don't love you, Robert Hubbard—I loathe you! All the love I have in my heart and soul is for Conor."

He gave a low mocking chuckle as he moved toward her. "His indenture is ten years," he reminded her cruelly. "If he survives at all, he'll be a broken man and you'll be an old woman."

"Then so be it!" she flung at him, swiftly turning her back on him.

He grasped her roughly by the shoulders and spun her around to face him. He towered over her like a black cloud. Involuntarily, her gaze was drawn to meet his, and in the gleam of his eyes she saw swirling black pools that mesmerized her, drawing her down into their black depths.

"I will have you, Maggie O'Hara," he declared quietly, in a tone that betrayed nothing but complete and utter self-confidence.

"No—no—" she stammered, using all the strength of will she had to fight the strange spell he seemed to be weaving over her.

"I've bought out many of the English who were granted land. Ballylee will never be as large as it once was, but it will be great again," he promised. "I will make it so."

Blinking, bringing him slowly into clearer focus, Maggie sensed a masculine strength about him. It was similar to the aura she had often felt around Conor.

And yet somehow it was different. How, she couldn't quite fathom. Was it because Hubbard was so much older, more mature, she wondered. No, it went beyond that to something else, something more vital.

Hubbard's face hardened in anger at her lack of response. He drew her toward him until she was crushed against him and her face was but scant inches from his.

"You speak of love, Maggie O'Hara," he charged her in harsh tones of contempt. "How much will you love when your belly is empty? How strong will your love remain as you watch that old woman in there die? Love is for poets and dreamers, Maggie O'Hara, not for soldiers and survivors—and that is what we are, you and I."

Suddenly she knew the difference between the man she loved and this man who would force her into a life she would loathe. There was no heart, no soul in Robert Hubbard. There was only a shell of a man living out a life that had no meaning. And because of it, this man could only create one emotion in her.

Dear God, she thought, *how could I ever give myself to a man I feared? For that is the only thing I could feel for Robert Hubbard.* A sudden and overwhelming anger at his arrogant assumption of his power over her boiled up inside her and overflowed before she had a chance to check it.

"If 'tis a mistress of Ballylee you want," she spat at him, "then buy yourself an English whore. For rather than give myself to you, I would take my life first."

His grip on her tightened painfully, and she could feel the rage ripple through him. "Nay, girl, I want not a Bible-thumping woman from the Midlands any more than I want a painted London jade. And as for your body, 'tis only to consummate the marriage that I would take it. Nay, Maggie O'Hara. I care not for your body—I want your name."

Suddenly he released her and stalked to the door. Pulling it open, he turned and stood facing her, with the wind plucking wildly at his cloak and swirling his raven-black hair around his darkly handsome face.

"And know you that one day I will have it."

July 1651

CHAPTER THIRTY-FIVE
BARBADOS, WEST INDIES

THE ROOM WAS DARK except for a spill of light from the yard torches and the lone taper that flickered on the dressing table.

Elana stripped to her chemise. She laid the dress over the back of a chair and moved to the window. The moon was high in a velvet-black sky. Together with the light from the torches, its silvery beam illuminated the figures strolling around the huts in the slave yard.

Several of the women were moving in a circle, undulating slowly and rhythmically to a faint drumbeat. They wore nothing save for a skimpy cloth, little more than a kerchief, tied at their hips.

Perspiration shone on their backs and arms as they danced in and out of the light. What must it be like, Elana wondered, to be so uninhibited?

It was stifling hot. Not even the trade winds, which usually came up with sundown, were blowing this night. But there was something else, besides the lack of trade winds, in the air this night that made it strangely different from others that had gone before it. Idly, Elana wondered what it could be.

It was, of course, the first night of harvest-end, reason enough to consider it different. For Elana it had been a good harvest and the profits would be enormous. When the sales of her products were complete, she would have more than enough to satisfy Sir John and still have plenty left over for her private reserve.

She called it her "golden escape," to be used if her husband ever went completely mad.

For the blacks, the end of harvest meant a week of rest. For a full seven days they could do as they pleased. With Conor's help, Elana had taken baskets of sweets, meat and rum to the slave yard.

Playing her role as both mistress and master of Redding Plantation, she had sternly rebuked those who had faltered in their tasks during the past six months and praised those who had worked hard. She had toasted them and passed her hands over the foreheads of the newborn children. And although it was frowned upon by whites all over the island, Elana had acknowledged the Obeah woman in whose sorcery and magic ritual blacks firmly believed. She had even stood her ground when the woman had cast her shells and beads in the dirt at Elana's feet. Then she had departed, leaving them to their celebrations.

But Conor had stayed. Even now she could see him, sitting among the others beside Tall Boy.

How odd that relationship had become, she

thought. At first, she had feared that Tall Boy would resent the new young white overseer, but Conor had won him over almost from the beginning. Indeed, he had won the entire plantation over, with apparently little effort.

The handsome young Irishman considered himself just as much a slave as the blacks, she knew, but there was no doubt he endured it better. Despite his lack of freedom and the fact that he had been forcibly shipped to an alien land far from his beloved home, he always seemed to be smiling. Many a time had she heard the sound of his deep, infectious laughter rise above the day-to-day noises of the busy plantation.

Elana had once asked him if he were as truly happy as he seemed.

"Happy?" he had replied with a wry smile. "Nay, 'tis not happiness that makes me laugh, 'tis life. I am alive. I can be thankful of that, so I live each day as best I can. If I were gloomy, the days would go slower!"

"Then you've forgotten Ireland?" Elana asked.

His response had been swift and sincere. "I'll never forget Ireland."

She had to admit that his attitude made a great deal of sense. Ten years of indenture could easily make an old man of him. If he laughed and faced each day with joy in his heart that he had another day to live, he would be forever young. On the other hand, she had been surprised to see that a warrior who had been as a prince among his people was now accepting his enforced servility with so little fight.

But Conor had had an answer for that as well.

"The fact that I enjoy living, Lady Elana, doesn't mean I've given up the battle," he had explained in tones of gentle rebuke. "But I have no choice but to bide my time. I'll not stay here to the end of my indenture and then remain as a ten-acre man, believe you me. One day, when the time is right, you'll see me no more. I'll be for Eire.''

"Methinks, Conor, you'd be better off here," she had suggested. "With each new ship come more tales of desolation and woe in Ireland.''

"Perhaps," he had conceded gravely. "But here there's no Maggie-o.''

Elana had had no desire to mock him but had been unable to suppress a wry laugh at his words. "Conor O'Hara, do you really suppose this Maggie will be waiting for you?''

"Aye, she'll be waiting," he had replied, without hesitation.

And that, Elana had thought wistfully, was what it was like to love and be loved. That night she had awakened from a deep dream-filled sleep, her body racked with sobs.

It was a full ten minutes before the dreams had flooded like ocean waves over her awakened mind, and she realized she had been dreaming of Conor O'Hara.

For a full month she had castigated herself. He was a boy, a young lad full of foolish youthful dreams and ideals. She, on the other hand, was a jaded woman.

He was nineteen. She was twenty-seven.

But would that be so wrong. *'Od's blood,* she had thought angrily, *we are both castaways from the lives we once knew.* Would it be so wrong, if only for a time, to turn to each other for comfort?

She found herself spending more and more time around him. Not that it was difficult to do, for Elizabeth adored him. Every chance the girl had she would search out Conor and beg him to spend time with her. When his work was too pressing to accommodate her, she would follow him around like a puppy.

She sought his approval for everything she did, and it seemed to Elana that the child looked upon him as a replacement for the father who had long since shut her out of his life.

And the stronger the bond of affection between Conor and Elizabeth became, so, too, did the bond between he and Elana. Sir John realized it even before his wife was fully aware of it.

"So, you've bought yourself another lover!" he exclaimed harshly one day.

"Don't be ridiculous," she replied calmly, fighting to hide the sudden feeling of fear his accusation aroused in her. "He's a mere lad."

"A lad, hey?" barked Redding sarcastically. "He's a young bull, he is—could probably handle ten the likes of you!"

"I'll hear no more of it!" she declared sharply, moving swiftly from his bedside to the door to end the conversation.

"Neither will I, wench, neither will I," he returned in threatening tones. "I may be a permanent part of this bed, but I have eyes, I do. And they watch you, day and night you witch. Don't you ever think otherwise!"

The warning rang constantly in her ears. She knew he meant it. If she were to succumb to temptation again, this time with the young Irishman, it would be all the reason Sir John needed to kill both her and Elizabeth.

If, that was, he could. In truth, she doubted he could manage it, but even with Tall Boy and Conor to protect her and Elizabeth, she still feared her husband, bedridden though he was.

Nevertheless, she found herself unable to forestall what she sensed was rapidly becoming inevitable. The dreams had continued, grown worse, until they became far more than the imaginings of a sleeping mind. They became real and alive, a daily yearning for his touch, a gnawing longing to be in his arms, to lie beside him and feel the warmth of his flesh against hers.

Her mind was constantly at war with itself. One half viewed his appeal as transitory, something that would soon pass with familiarity. The other half admitted to an overpowering need to rest, satiated, in his brawny arms, to respond willingly to his every desire and to obey her own amorous instincts.

And now, as she continued to gaze out her bedchamber window at the slaves celebrating the start of a week of rest, she realized with a sudden start what was so strange about this night. It struck her with such vivid clarity she wondered she had never seen it before. For it had been there since the day Conor arrived, in his infectious laugh, his deep voice, his eyes, even in the light dancing off his coppery hair.

In all that time, she knew now, she had been looking not at Conor but at Patrick. Not the physical Patrick she remembered, to be sure, but the nature of the man. From Conor she heard Patrick's laugh, in his eyes saw Patrick's mischievous glint and in his attitude toward life, Patrick's lighthearted gaiety and youth.

So strong was the force of the sudden realization that she knew she could no longer deny it. It was in the heated, balmy air and in the smell that rolled inland from the ocean.

She had been wild with joy when Conor had told her that Patrick lived. The rest of the way back to the plantation she had basked in a glow of euphoria, as if she had been given a new lease on life. The feeling had abated only a little when he told her about Kate.

Patrick was married, and happily so. Conor had told her of Drogheda and Kate's perilous attempt at escape down the river. He did not know if she were dead or alive, but if the latter, he had assured Elana that Patrick would find her in the morass that was now Ireland.

So great was Elana's joy and relief at knowing Patrick still lived that she found herself hoping, almost praying, that Kate did also. In her, Elana knew, Patrick would find happiness, the happiness that she, Elana, in her childish immaturity and callous self-interest had denied him.

Patrick, Kate, Maggie, Elana thought with a sigh. They were miles away across an ocean, somewhere in war-ravaged Ireland. Meanwhile, she and Conor were here in warm, balmy Barbados, where the hot nights, the soft breezes and the sweet scents would stir desire in anyone's blood.

A burst of laughter and shouting voices drew her gaze back to the slave yard. Conor was calling out his good-nights as he moved along the graveled paths through the trees. She could see the broad, tanned expanse of his naked chest and sinewy shoulders in the moonlight. In her mind she could visualize his lips creased in a wide smile and imagine his perfect, even white teeth shining in his sun-darkened face.

The sight of him moving through the moonlight brought an ache to her belly and a quiver to her legs. She could feel her breasts swell against the material of the thin chemise.

You're a fool, she chastised herself fiercely. *A damn bloody fool!*

But it was in the air, in the heat of the night, in the sounds and smells that seemed suddenly richer and more poignant than ever. She saw him disappear into the grove of trees that surrounded the overseer's hut and her heart began to pound so violently that she was sure the sound of it matched the drums that still sounded faintly from the slaves' quarters.

Once, years ago, she had entered that hut and disaster had been the result. Could she risk it again?

From her wardrobe she withdrew a dark indigo gown. It was of a sheer batiste material and cut low. Not a gown designed for outside wear, for a walk on a summer's night, she realized, but it was hot and that would be her excuse, if she should need one.

Belting the robe, she moved to her dressing table and quickly ran a brush through her hair. Was it her imagination or had it suddenly taken on the sheen she thought it had lost forever? She leaned closer to the mirror. Was there more life in her eyes, she wondered, a more lighthearted expression on her face?

She stood smoothing the fragile garment over her hips and thighs. At the feel of the fabric against her flesh, a trickle of perspiration ran down the small of her back. How long had it been since she had cared to stand so straight, with her shoulders thrown back enough to make her bodice appear so full?

Suddenly she remembered and broke into a girlish fit of giggles, that grew into near hysteria.

"Do you still have beautiful breasts, m'lady?" he had asked.

She recalled how she had flushed and turned away to hide the fact from him. She also recalled how warm his words had made her. The memory of them now made her warmer still.

Suddenly she stopped giggling as abruptly as she had begun. Wide-eyed she leaned forward to stare searchingly at herself in the mirror.

Will he still think my breasts are beautiful, she wondered anxiously. *And if he does, what then? Anything?*

She had seen him with the female slaves. It had made her curious, enough to question Granny in private.

"Firehair boy, *naquedamah*," the old woman said

with a shrug that had eloquently indicated her amazement.

It had taken Elana nearly an hour to discover that *naquedamah* meant impotent, that Conor had been offered several girls, the petite, beautiful Onee among them, and had done nothing.

Conor impotent? With his rippling body in the prime of life and his sad but laughing expression in the gaze that Elana had caught more than once flowing over her form?

She knew the look. No, Conor O'Hara was not impotent. He was every inch a man, with the normal desires of a man. And because he was, Elana's own desire, so long dormant, had sprung to new life.

Opening the tall rear windows of her bedchamber, she stepped across the threshold and into the night. Raising the robe to her knees, she moved quickly and quietly along the length of the house and darted into the safety of the trees. Under cover of darkness she waited for a sound, a breath or a footfall that would indicate the presence of the spy she knew her husband kept on her at all times. She heard nothing.

Satisfied at last that whoever the spy was, he or she was celebrating with the rest, Elana made her way to the overseer's hut.

For several moments she stood in front of the door, fighting to cool the fire in her blood. Then, taking a deep breath, she lifted the latch and slipped into the room. Quickly she closed the door behind her and leaned against it. In the flare that had streamed from the torches into the room while the door was open, she had seen his body stretched out on the cot. He was naked to the waist, wearing only a pair of tight canvas breeches.

As the door had closed softly behind her, he had slipped his hand swiftly beneath the mattress and withdrawn a knife. As he sat up, she could see the light gleaming through the hut's lone window and glinting off the razor-sharp blade.

"Who is it?" he growled.

"'Tis me, Conor...Elana," she whispered, gripping the latch behind her with all her strength. Her knees were shaking and she could feel the coolness of her chemise against her sweat-soaked back.

"Elana?" he queried, surprise evident in his voice.

"I—I've come...." She could say no more. The words could not pass around the lump that had risen in her throat. Slowly, hesitantly a step at a time, she moved toward the bed.

"What is it, m'lady?" he asked.

"Not m'lady, Conor," she pleaded. "Dear God, not 'm'lady.' Elana."

She was by the bed now, standing over him. The red-and-orange glow from the window made his hair seem like a fiery halo and played over his massive shoulders and the coppery hair on his barrellike chest.

He knew now why she had come. She could see the sudden understanding in his eyes.

She reached forward and grasped his hands. They felt so strong. The knuckles were gnarled and the palms calloused from working in the cane. Then she stepped backward, to pull him to his feet. Her eyes were closed but she opened them quickly when she felt herself swaying.

"Elana—"

"Shh...please." Placing her hands on his arms, she quivered when she felt his muscles respond to her touch. She moved his arms around her and emitted a sigh of relief when he embraced her.

Awesome, she thought, as his body seemed to engulf hers. His size and the latent power in his broad body completely overwhelmed her senses.

"Please don't think ill of me, Conor," she begged

in a low voice. "There is no wrong or right to this. There is only a man and a woman. Please think of me not as a wanton, but only as a very, very lonely woman. And please, do not hate me."

"I could never hate you...not now," he replied softly. "You've changed since last we met, and I've grown, but I still think you are very beautiful."

"Kiss me...kiss me!" she urged, pressing herself harder against him.

When he made no move to respond, she brought her hands slowly up and over his shoulders. As she rose to the tips of her toes, she drew his head downward toward hers.

Her insecurity, her fears, everything but joy and desire vanished when she felt his lips respond and capture hers. Her body relaxed, became pliant, and she molded herself to him. A passionate need built as the kiss deepened. She moved her hips, seeking him through the thin material that separated them. She was rewarded by his sudden indrawn breath.

Their mouths clung until the kiss became a ravishing exploration of tongue and lips and breasts and thighs. Elana felt a sudden wild exultation of relief. He wanted her, wanted her as much as she wanted him.

Still locked in their embrace, she fumbled with the ties of her robe. When they were loosened, she broke away from him, and stepping back, slipped the garment from her body. Her fingers were sure and deft now as she pushed the small cap sleeves of her chemise from her shoulders. A moment later it lay on the floor at her feet and she stood naked before him, the light embracing every sensual hollow and curve of her body.

Conor's gaze played over her, devouring the gentle slope of her full, still-firm breasts and moving lazily down to her rounded hips and well-molded thighs.

"You're very, very beautiful," he breathed finally.

Swiftly, she went to him. As she smoothed her hands over his powerful back, she pressed against the wiry mat of hair on his chest. But he made no move to embrace her again and Elana's heart fell. Panic seized her. She grasped his hands and brought them to her breasts.

"Love me, Conor!" she begged urgently. "Make love to me and make me feel like a woman again."

She could feel hot tears stinging her cheeks. For one terrible moment, when she looked up into the deep blue of his eyes, she thought she would die from shame. They were filled with sadness and, she was sure, pity.

"I—I'm sorry," she stammered, tearing herself away from him. "You must think of me as no more than a wanton—or worse yet, mad!"

She retrieved her clothes from the floor and began wildly to struggle into them.

"Yes, well, perhaps I am," she babbled on, desperately trying to hide her confusion and embarrassment behind a flow of words.

"Both wanton and mad. Forgive me, I couldn't help it—can't help it. Lord help me, I don't want to. I know I've brought my misery upon myself, but I only wanted a moment...a moment of what? It all seems—"

As she spoke her voice raised in pitch until it approached a scream. Conor moved deftly, grasping her around the waist and placing a hand over her mouth.

His grip was like iron and his huge hand threatened to cut off her breathing. But still she struggled against him, her shame suffusing her entire body with a new kind of heat.

Suddenly she felt faint. Her body went limp and she sagged against his chest. Then and only then did he remove his hand from her mouth and allow her to breath freely again.

"I—I'm all right now," she gasped after a few moments.

With an effort she drew herself erect and freed herself from Conor's grip. As steadily as she could manage, she walked toward the door. She was reaching for the latch when Conor caught her and spun her into his arms.

"I'm sorry, too, Elana," he said softly, cradling her in his strength and warmth.

The dam of her emotions broke like pounding ocean waves against the rocks. Tears stung her eyes and flowed down her cheeks to his chest. Lifting her easily into his arms he carried her over to the bed. Gently he let her down on it and then joined her, cradling her as he would a child with her head in the hollow of his neck.

As quickly as it had risen, her passion diminished, replaced by a gentle feeling of warmth and security. She wrapped her arms around his chest and hugged him to her trembling body with a desperate need. Wordlessly, they remained entwined in each other's arms until at last her sobbing subsided and she was able to speak.

"I truly loved Patrick, you know," she told him, looking up at him anxiously in case he should not believe her. "I just discovered it too late."

"I know. . .now," he assured her simply.

They talked of England, of Ireland. In hushed whispers they talked of the past and the present. Elana's heart swelled for him and at the same time she envied him.

What joy it must be, she thought, *to love another and a land so much.* Deep in her heart Elana knew that she would never be lucky enough to know such joy. It saddened her, but for Conor, at least, she was happy. He was still young enough to realize some of his dreams.

The light of dawn peeked through the window, warning her that it was time to be gone. She slipped from his embrace and stood for a moment by the bed. His body was still beautiful, but she no longer felt an insane desire to touch it. She had everything from Conor that he could give her, and somehow it was enough.

"Your Maggie is a very lucky woman," she said wistfully. "I hope for your sake she loves you as much as you love her."

"She does," Conor replied, warming her with a radiant smile.

Elana returned the smile and whispered softly, "I'll to Bridgetown in the morning and see my solicitor. It should not take more than a month to prepare the papers."

"Papers?" he echoed.

"To release you from your indenture. You can't return to Ireland, of course, but France will have you much closer to your Maggie."

"COME IN!"

Elana's heart sank. From his voice she knew Sir John was drunk but she could put off this visit no longer. He had been demanding to see her since morning and it was now late afternoon.

"Yes, John," she sighed, entering the room and keeping her distance from the bed.

"Good news, you witch!" he cackled, waving a packet of papers in her direction.

"Oh?"

"You're not the only one to visit the solicitor, you see."

An alarm sounded in the back of Elana's mind. Twice during the past few weeks he had ordered that he be taken to Bridgetown. She hadn't cared enough to ask why.

But now there was a mockery in his tone and a return of the old arrogance in his manner that frightened her.

"If you think I've not kept the books honestly, all you had to do, John, was ask to see them," she said, forcing herself to remain outwardly calm.

"Bah, the books," he replied with a dismissive wave of his hand. "I know what you've planned, and you'll not get away with it. I told you I have eyes!"

"If you must talk in riddles, John, you can converse with yourself," Elana told him firmly, moving toward the door.

"Hold up, you wanton jade!" he commanded. "I know you've played the tramp in his cottage, and I know you've given him his freedom."

Elana froze, her hand on the doorknob, her breath coming in sudden gasps. She bit down viciously on her lip to hide her fear.

"I don't know what—" she began.

"Don't lie, damn you," Redding growled ominously. "O'Connor, you called him—an indenture from Munster, you said. 'Od's blood, Elana, how much of a fool do you think I am? It wasn't difficult to find out his real name—Conor O'Hara. He's of the Ballylee clan, and don't tell me you didn't know it."

Dropping her hand from the doorknob, Elana spun to face him. "Aye, I did," she conceded defiantly. "I thought it better to lie than spark your memory and make you more insane than you already are!"

"Mad I might be, but not blind—or stupid," he countered. "I know what you plan, damn you. I'll wager the lad has brought you news that your Patrick is alive. So, methinks you would use this kin of his to take you back to the bastard brat's father."

"No, John, I swear—"

"Swear what you will, I'll not listen," he interrupted brusquely. "Nay, Elana, you'll not get away with it, for I've already stopped you. General Cromwell rules Parliament now, and he's not forgotten the service I once did him. We are welcome again in England, wench, and 'tis to England we will go."

"No!" she gasped, praying she had not heard him correctly.

But she had, and a gleam of triumph appeared in her husband's eyes as he hastened to confirm it. "Aye!" he gloated. "You and I and the brat. I've already arranged for a new overseer to be hired. This wretched place will make us just as rich as it does now if we become absentee landlords in England."

Fear clutched at Elana's heart. At least on Barbados she felt a measure of safety from Sir John's mad rages. In England, she and Elizabeth would have no protection from him at all.

"I won't go!" she declared, her voice and every pore of her body exuding defiance.

"You will, damn you!" he thundered. "I may be only half a man, but I'm still the man in this marriage!" Here he gave a wild laugh and again waved the papers in his hand. "You'd best start readying yourself and the brat. We sail after storm season, the twenty-second of February, aboard the *Bold Venture*!"

ELANA WAITED until past midnight to leave her bedchamber. She knew how dangerous was the game she was about to play, but danger meant nothing when weighed against the fate Sir John was readying for her and Elizabeth. Spy or no spy, she had to see Conor at once—and alone.

Slowly the panic she had felt at her husband's news had been replaced by calmness. It was ironic that the one plan of escape she had never thought of had been given to her by Redding.

Without stopping to knock or even call out, she slid through the door of the overseer's hut and quickly latched it behind her.

"Elana!" exclaimed Conor, startled by her unexpected arrival and rising immediately from the cot on which he had been lying.

"Shh...."

Swiftly, she extinguished all the candles. When the room was lit only by the silvery moonlight streaming in through the solitary window, she took hold of Conor's hand and drew him down to sit on the bed beside her.

Breathlessly she told him of Sir John's accusations and that he had discovered Conor's true name. In a voice tinged with fear and desperation she went on to explain her husband's plans for their departure to England.

"You must help me, Conor," she pleaded. "At first he was insanely jealous of me and...I suppose I have given him reason to be." She paused, feeling a slight flush creep into her cheeks.

"I'll go to him," Conor said immediately, rising to his feet.

"Nay," Elana replied, pulling him back down beside her. "'Tis no longer just jealousy now. The man is truly mad. I'm sure he blames me and the child for everything that has happened to him. He only lives, I do believe, to torment the both of us and in so doing, cleanse his own soul with revenge. In England he can make us both suffer the way he wants."

"You've given me my freedom and coin to aid me, Elana," said Conor solemnly. "I'll help in any way I can."

Elana was silent for a moment as she looked into the depths of his crystal clear eyes, and blinked away the moisture that suddenly formed in her own. "'Tis an...unusual...plan I have, Conor..." she began, her voice low and hesitant.

"'Twill have to be clever to outwit the bastard," Conor chuckled. "Well, out with it, woman!"

"I want you to become John Redding."

"*What?*"

Seeing the look of disbelief on his face, Elana hastened to give him a more detailed explanation of her plan. "He has all the travel and passage papers and has made all the arrangements for the running of Redding Plantation in our absence. He would have the three of us sail for England on the twenty-second of next month, aboard the *Bold Venture*."

Conor looked crestfallen. He could guess what she had planned and could see his newfound freedom disappearing. Free or not, he was still exiled. If he were to land in England and his true identity discovered, he would be hanged without question.

"Nay, Conor, we'll not to England," she reassured him quickly, noting his look of dismay and guessing its cause. "There's a German ship, the *Graf Klammer*, bound for France and sailing on the ninth. I'm going to steal my husband's precious papers and have them changed. You and I and Elizabeth will sail on the *Graf Klammer*."

Stroking an imaginary beard, Conor ran his thumb and index finger back and forth along his jawline as he weighed her plan carefully. "'Tis risky, I do believe," he said finally, in thoughtful tones. "A German ship's captain—"

Sensing doubt, Elana silenced him by placing a finger to his lips. "I have a great many sovereigns hidden away, Conor," she observed, with a smile. "Enough of those pressed into any captain's hand will make him overlook irregularities. Will you do it?"

He looked at her silently for a long moment, and

then a broad grin spread slowly across his handsome features. "Aye," he replied, his eyes gleaming with mischief, "and let's hope for an early end of this year's storm season and fair winds after it."

"Bless you, Conor O'Hara!" Elana breathed with a deep sigh of relief. She brushed her lips lightly across his cheek and left the hut, her spirits soaring.

France...freedom...a new life, she thought joyfully, heading back toward her room on feet that felt as though they were dancing on air. How wonderful that sounded!

"Mum?"

With a gasp, Elana came to an abrupt halt as a giant shape loomed up out of the darkness in front of her.

"Tall Boy!" she exclaimed. "What—"

"This way, mum," he replied, and turning, vanished silently into a nearby stand of trees.

Cautiously, she followed him, her senses alert for the slightest sign of danger. Tall Boy had never given her cause to fear for her life around him, but his great size and strength unnerved her at the best of times. She found him a few feet into the trees, looking down at a dark form sprawled at the base of a huge palm.

"Nacondo," he whispered.

Elana glanced down once and immediately turned away, her face drained of all color. One look at the grotesque angle of the head was enough to tell her the young black's neck was broken.

"Nacondo follow you," explained Tall Boy urgently, anxious that his mistress should understand. He showed her a cane knife he was holding in his hand. "When I caught him, he tried to cut me."

Elana could guess the rest and was deeply saddened by it. Although thankful that the young slave's presence had been discovered by Tall Boy before he'd had a chance to report back to his master, she knew he had had little choice but to follow Sir John's orders. Caught in the crossfire of the battle between herself and her husband he was, like so many other innocent people in this world, a casualty of a war that had been none of his doing and that he'd been powerless to prevent.

"Didn't mean to kill him," interjected Tall Boy with an eloquent shrug of his powerful shoulders.

"I know, Tall Boy," she assured him with a sigh. "And I'm grateful for your help. Thank you."

Satisfied that he had done the right thing, the slave slipped away deeper into the stand of trees. For a moment, Elana stood staring after him, amazed as always that so large a man could move through the bush so silently. Then, sadly, she turned and continued on her way back to her room, her elation at the idea of escape and freedom overshadowed by the thought of how high the price already was.

ELANA CLUTCHED HER RETICULE tightly as the Creole stableman handed her into the buggy.

Done, she thought, thankfully. It had cost a great deal of coin to have the papers changed, and even more to insure that the change would be kept secret, but now it was done.

In the purse were the papers that would take her, Conor and Elizabeth to freedom. When she returned to the plantation, she would pass them on to the young Irishman and he would secrete them with the gold she had already given him. One short week from now, they would be gone.

"Storm, mum," the Creole said, pointing to the ocean. "A strong wind over the sea."

Elana looked to where he pointed. On the horizon, where the azure blue of the water met a cloudless sky, she could see a dark line. It was as if the water had boiled up from the depths of the ocean to form a black indeterminate shape above the glassy calm.

Even as she watched, the mound of water seemed to enlarge. It grew higher and wider as it rolled inexorably toward the island's sandy shore. Ominous and powerful looking, it struck a sudden terror into her heart, yet she could not tear her gaze from it. It seemed to hypnotize her, willing her eyes to follow its path as it continued its way shoreward.

Then it was gone.

What had seemed a towering cliff of water now struck the beach as a gentle wave.

" 'Tis a wind at sea, that's all," she said, exhaling the breath she suddenly realized she'd been holding. Impatient now to be gone, she extended her hand with his payment.

The old Creole seemed neither to hear nor see the coin in her hand. He was still staring out to sea, his eyes wide with fear. Without warning, he suddenly turned and bolted, disappearing into the dark depths of the stable without a backward glance.

Elana stared after him in astonishment. *How very odd,* she thought, frowning in puzzlement. *Usually he overcharges and today he doesn't even take his money!* With a shrug, she dismissed the man's strange behavior and, clucking the horse into a walk, turned onto the road for home.

Time and time again as she drove along the beach road, her gaze was drawn to the sea. Each time, she saw yet another of the dark walls of what looked like water roll into shore. Yet, again, when they hit the beach, they became no more than playful frothy waves licking at the sand. By the time she turned inland toward St. George's parish and Redding Plantation, the ocean was calm and quiet.

Strange, she thought, *'tis the most calm day we've had... not a breeze stirring nor a cloud in the sky. What could have caused those massive waves out in the sea?*

She shrugged and for the remainder of the ride to the plantation put the strange quirks of nature out of her mind. Only when she pulled into the stable yard did she realize that the wind that presumably had been out at sea had now turned inland. And it was growing stronger by the minute, viciously whipping at the fronds of the palm trees and raising swirling clouds of dust in its path.

"Granny say big storm is coming," Tall Boy informed her, handing her down from the buggy.

"Perhaps," Elana nodded. "Have the men drop the extra canvas over the sides of the curing sheds."

"Yes, mum."

Taking a route that would keep her out of sight of the big house, she made her way to the sugar mill. Conor was waiting for her in the doorway. Wordlessly she handed him the papers and the two of them suddenly grinned nervously, like two children huddled over an amusing discovery they wished to keep secret from an adult.

"A week," she murmured.

"Aye," he replied in a low voice. "A week."

She moved on, barely able to suppress a skip in her stride as she mounted the steps to the plantation house veranda. Her hand was on the latch of the front door when she suddenly realized how very dark the day had become. Dropping her hand from the latch, she moved to the edge of the veranda and looked up. Heavy, thick dark clouds rolling in from the sea had turned the calm once-blue sky into a boiling cauldron of ominous gray. In the distance, she could barely discern the setting sun.

It was a sunset like none she had ever seen. In a gap between two seething masses of cloud the sky had become a sickly-looking green and the sun a bloodred ball. Even as she watched, the cloud masses came together, immediately blocking out the light. It was as if the red candle that had been the sun had been extinguished by a sudden gush of wind, plunging the earth into darkness.

And now the wind gained momentum with every passing minute. No longer a strong but playful breeze, it seemed to take on life, becoming a voice that moaned its way across the island. It sounded, thought Elana, not unlike the cry of someone in pain and she found herself unaccountably frightened by it. Instinctively, she thought of Elizabeth and how terrified she must be, and realized that the girl hadn't met her as usual when she returned from Bridgetown.

Worried now, Elana turned and ran into the house. As she ran through the great room to the scullery and kitchen, she called out to the servants.

"Granny...Nabob...Onee! Where are you? Elizabeth!"

"Elana!" It was John's voice thundering down the hall. "Come in here, you witch!"

"Later, John," she called back impatiently. "I shall be there in a moment. Nabob!"

"Come in here *now*!" he roared.

Both the kitchen and scullery were empty. She ran back toward the front door shouting Elizabeth's name.

"I am here, mama...in papa's room." Elizabeth's cry, delivered in a quavering young voice, was followed by an hysterical laugh from Redding.

Barely pausing to change direction, Elana tore down the hall and through the open doorway of her husband's room, not stopping until she reached the center. One swift glance told her everything, and her heart sank.

Nabob and Onee sat like statues against the room's far wall. Elizabeth stood between them, her eyes wide with fear and tears running down her cheeks. The side of her face was already turning an ugly purple, obviously from a blow she had received.

Redding sat in the center of his bed, dressed. Around him he had arranged every weapon in the house. At Elana's horrified stare, a malicious smile parted his thin lips. "Took me hours," he cackled, "crawling from room to room to get them all."

Elana took a step toward him. Immediately he raised both hands from the bed and in each he held a pistol. One, he leveled at Elana's belly, the other he directed straight at Elizabeth.

"They're primed and cocked, witch," he warned. "Best you do as I say."

"You're mad," she declared, then turned furiously on the black women. "I told you never to bring her in here unless I was present!"

"Massa John said he was sick," Onee whimpered. "He said he's sick bad, wants to see his little girl. I get Nabob—"

"'Twas my fault, too, mama," interjected Elizabeth in a whisper. "I insisted."

At Redding's harsh laughter Elana turned back to him. "Ah, isn't she a loving daughter, though?" he derided. "Pity you're not as loving, my dear wife."

"John, why are you doing this?" she cried, her heart racing as she struggled to contain her fear.

Instantly, the cruel thin-lipped smile was replaced by a mask of fury. "The papers, you witch.... My passport!" he snarled. "It had to be you who took them. Where are they!"

Elana felt suddenly sick with despair. She had counted on Redding not discovering her theft of his papers until several hours after her return from Bridgetown, by which time she would have made arrangements to insure that he was watched constantly. But he had been too quick for her, and it seemed as though the weight of the world that had been lifted from her shoulders when she had passed the papers to Conor had now descended again to crush her.

It was useless to deny that she had had anything to

do with their disappearance, she knew, and with a heavy heart, she replied quietly, "Yes, John, I took them."

"Get them," he ordered, "and be quick about it!"

"I will. And Elizabeth?"

"No! She stays here at her loving father's side. And the other two as well. But if you're thinking of sending Tall Boy back in here instead of coming yourself, tell him the first one I'll shoot is his woman."

For a moment, Elana weighed the chances of throwing herself across him to give Elizabeth time to run.

"Well?" he growled.

Reluctantly, she decided that any such action would only serve to get them both killed.

"I'll get them," she said, dully, moving toward the door.

"And have the wagon hitched," he commanded. "We'll to Bridgetown yet this night!"

"But why?"

"You should know that!" Redding shouted. "Bridgetown does have some laws, and the law is on my side. We'll to Bridgetown tonight and wait there 'til sailing."

Elana's heart sank even further. Truly, John Redding had won, and there was nothing she could do about it.

"*Well?*" he prompted.

For a moment she lingered, staring at the caricature of a man sitting on his bed surrounded by an arsenal of weaponry. His eyes, sunk deep in their sockets, gleamed like two pools of black fire. Reflected in their wildness, the flames from the candles in the wall sconces flickered and danced, and in that instant, Elana felt she was looking into the fires of hell. She turned and ran.

Outside it had grown darker still and the sound of the wind, which had now reached well beyond gale proportions, had become a steady, unrelenting roar. The force of the wind took her breath away the instant she opened the door, and she was immediately struck by a heavy, sweeping rain that stung her face and bare arms. It had an odd taste and a seemingly gritty texture, as if it were mixed with sand.

Twice as she made her way slowly across the plantation, the wind lifted her skirts and threw her to the ground as if she were no more than a rag doll. After the second time, when she found herself rolling in the dirt, she reached beneath her skirt and removed her petticoats. Bruised and breathless, she struggled to regain her feet. Forgetting any semblance of modesty now, she tied her skirt up around her waist and, leaning far forward into the teeth of the wind, made her way to the sugar mill.

Rounding the corner, she came to an abrupt halt and gave a gasp of horrified disbelief.

The slave village was gone. Only the yard remained to indicate where it had once stood. Nearby the curing sheds swayed wildly, their cane and thatched roofs long since ripped away.

Suddenly, as if from a great distance, she heard her name being called. It was Conor, motioning to her from the door of the sugar mill. She tried to move toward him, but instead found herself being forced backward by the howling wind. Gasping for breath, she reached out to him and swiftly he moved to her side, wrapping his powerful arms around her. She looked up and stared at him blankly as she saw his lips move but heard no sound. Bending his head over her, he shouted in her ear.

"Granny is in the sugar mill! She says this is a *hurakan*. What is that?"

His words struck terror in Elana's heart. In the years since they had come to Barbados, there had been storms, several in fact, but never a *hurakan*, the killer storm that wiped the earth clean in its path. The earlier settlers had warned her about the *hurakan*, the devil storm. Now she knew why the rain tasted salty and its texture seemed gritty. The powerful wind was carrying spindrift from the sea and sand from the beaches clear across the land.

"Elizabeth!" she screamed in Conor's ear. "Elizabeth is in the great house—"

From his look she knew that her words had been lost in the howling wind. Knowing that he didn't understand her, she screamed again, "The great house! The great house!"

Frantically she wrenched herself from his grasp and fought to make her way up the gravel path toward the house, only to be thrown once more from her feet. Like a doll, she rolled helplessly along the ground until Conor came to her aid, pulling her upright and again wrapping his arms around her.

"The great house!" she screamed again, and this time he nodded.

"They are safer there than we are here!" he cried.

"No! You don't understand—"

"The pond, the pond!" he yelled, moving off in the direction of the millpond and pulling her along with him. "We'll be safe there."

Above them the wind tore at the clouds as if it were shredding a thick dark cloth into tatters. An occasional rent would appear in the seething mass, allowing a quick glimpse of a calm and serene blue sky beyond.

But there was nothing calm or serene about the earth. It was an inferno of whirling destruction. Trees bowed and cracked before the onslaught of the wind. Some were torn from their roots and drawn upward to join entire buildings that were lifted and swept away, in a swirling mass of airborne debris.

The millpond, its surface whipped up into angry, frothing wavelets, hardly looked like a haven. Nevertheless, Elana could see why Conor had chosen it as a place of safety. Beneath its rough surface would be some measure of calm at least and one end was surrounded by land clear enough to insure that they would not be crushed under falling trees or buildings. As he pushed her down into its warm waters, she saw the sugar mill at the far end sway slightly, then topple to the ground, the crash of its fall unheard above the steady roar of the wind.

Time seemed to stand still. Surrounded by dark silence beneath the water, they waited for an end to the wild chaos above it, breaking to the surface every now and then to gasp another lungful of air.

Each time during those brief seconds, Elana tried to see through the grayness to the great house, but it was impossible. All she could do was hold her breath, grip Conor's reassuring hand beneath the water and pray.

It seemed as though hours had passed when at last a deathly silence settled over the land. Soaked and breathless, they crawled from the pond to sprawl thankfully on the sodden earth. It was several moments before they felt strong enough to sit up and stare in silence and awe at the destruction around them. Elana was afraid she had gone deaf, so strange was the eerie stillness after the howling roar of the wind. Not until she spoke and heard the sound of her own voice was she really sure that they were both still alive and in one piece.

"'Tis the center of the storm," she explained in low, almost reverent tones. "It will come again... from that direction, next time."

The atmosphere around them was like nothing she had ever experienced before. In the midst of the storm's havoc, the air seemed to have taken on an unearthly, coppery quality and was almost too heavy to breathe.

They were given no chance to ponder on it, for the

sudden crackling sound of flames brought them instantly to their feet.

"Conor," cried Elana, "the house!"

With Conor at her heels, she leaped forward and
began to run, her exhaustion forgotten in her desperate fear for her daughter. Stumbling and gasping for
breath, they made their way over the rubble of the
curing shed and the sugar mill to the plantation yard.
There they were brought up short by the sight that
awaited them.

What was left of the roof of the great house was a
sheet of flames shooting skyward. Balls of fire
gushed from several of the front windows. Stricken
with horror, Elana barely noticed Tall Boy appearing
as if from nowhere to join them.

"Elizabeth, Nabob, Onee!" she screamed. "They
are in there!"

"Stay here," Conor ordered sharply, and sprinted
away.

Paying no heed to his command, she followed him
into the inferno, Tall Boy at her side. The great room
was full of smoke but as yet appeared to be free of
flames.

"In there!" Elana directed frantically, pointing
down the hall of her husband's wing. "They're in
John's room, and he has all the guns!"

Through the wall of thick black smoke swirling
down the hall they could barely discern the red glow
of flames licking greedily around the door of Redding's room.

"Tall Boy," Conor cried immediately, "the kitch-
en...water buckets!"

The giant black raced to do his bidding, the young
Irishman ripped down the draperies from the tall
windows of the great room.

Gripped now by sheer panic, Elana could wait no
longer. With a cry of anger and frustration, she ran

into the hall and tore toward the door of her husband's room. Reaching down, she grasped the hem of her still-soaking dress, pulled the skirt up and around her head, and threw herself through the wall of flame.

Once in the room, Elana dropped the dress from her eyes but kept the damp hem over her mouth and nose to help her breathe.

"Elizabeth...Elizabeth, my darling," she called desperately. "Where are you!"

"Here...over here, mama!" a young voice screamed from one corner.

Relief that the child was alive flooded through Elana as she peered in the direction from which the cry had come. The smoke was thick and stifling, but through it she could just see part of Elizabeth's body and one of the girl's tiny hands waving to her. Swiftly Elana went to her.

Sprawled across the child was Nabob, the back of her blouse splotched with crimson. Fighting to keep down the bile that rose to her throat, Elana gently rolled the woman's lifeless body from atop her daughter's and gathered Elizabeth up into her arms.

"Mama...papa shot Nabob—" the child sobbed, clinging tightly to her mother.

"I know darling, I know," murmured Elana soothingly, gently smoothing her daughter's tangled hair back from her face.

Conor and Tall Boy materialized beside her, their upper bodies, heads and shoulders wrapped in soaked draperies. The smoke was growing thicker now and stinging tears poured down the faces of all four of them.

"Onee...jumped...out the window," Elizabeth managed to gasp between choking coughs. "I—I think papa crawled out that way, too."

Dropping the drapery from around his body, Tall Boy knelt by his woman's side. Gently he touched the side of her throat, then raised his head to gaze up eloquently at Elana. Rising to his feet, he brushed his hand over Elizabeth's hair just once. Then with a bloodcurdling yell he threw himself through the window.

At the same time there was a deafening roar and the roof in the opposite corner of the room gave way, spewing flame and debris all around them.

"'Od's blood," Conor cried, unwrapping the drapery from around himself and throwing it around Elana. "Hurry—we've little time!"

Retrieving the drapery discarded by Tall Boy, he wrapped it around Elizabeth and scooped her from her mother's arms into his own. Turning swiftly, he plunged through the doorway and tore down the hall with Elana close behind. As they reached the veranda, a roar came from inside the house behind them, followed by the sound of an explosion.

"Jump!" Conor shouted, putting Elizabeth down and taking firm hold of her hand.

The three of them leaped from the veranda. As they did so, the center of the roof lifted and split, releasing a huge ball of orange flame that shot skyward. They hit the ground several feet in front of the house and rolled amid a shower of sparks and flying debris. Without stopping to see if they were injured, Conor dragged Elizabeth and Elana to their feet and ran, pulling them after him. Not until they were among the twisted remnants of a clump of palm trees a safe distance away did he allow them to pause for breath.

Bruised but otherwise unhurt, they sank to the ground, too exhausted to speak. The only sound made by any of them was a whimper of fear from Elizabeth, who was still swathed in the wet drapery.

It was several moments before they realized that the wind and rain had come up again.

"It comes," Elana gasped. "'Tis said the second part is often worse than the first."

"Then we'd best be back to the millpond," Conor said decisively, getting up and gathering Elizabeth in his arms once more. "Come along, little one."

As he turned in the direction of the pond the child's face suddenly drained of all color and she gave a shriek of terror. "Papa!"

With a cry of alarm, Elana sprang to her feet and turned to face the direction in which her daughter was staring. Sir John lay deep in the shadow of the twisted trees, still holding a pistol in each hand. Madness shone from his eyes as he struggled to raise one of them in Conor's direction.

"I'll kill you both," he promised, his voice more rasping than usual from the smoke that had filled his lungs and seared his throat. "But the brat first."

Instinctively, Elana threw herself between him and Elizabeth. Too late, Conor shouted a warning as he turned the child away and dropped to his knees. In that instant, Sir John fired and the young Irishman watched in horror as Elana halted midstride, clutching at her chest. A look of surprise crossed her face and she gave a faint, gurgling cry before beginning to sink slowly to her knees. Putting Elizabeth down, Conor caught her as she fell and eased her gently to the ground. Out of the corner of his eye he saw the giant figure of Tall Boy emerge out of the wreckage of the trees behind Sir John. Redding must have heard him, too, for he rolled over and fired the second pistol. The ball struck the black squarely, but Tall Boy neither checked his stride nor wavered from his path. As he reached out to wrap his huge hands around Redding's neck, Conor turned his attention to Elana.

He knew it was hopeless the moment he looked at her. The ball had struck her directly above the heart and already a tiny bubble of red had emerged from the corner of her mouth to trickle down the side of her cheek.

"Mama...*mama!*" screamed Elizabeth, struggling from beneath the drapery and crawling to her mother.

John Redding was silent, his broken lifeless body slipping from Tall Boy's grasp. Raising his head, Conor watched, mesmerized, as the slave turned, paused for a moment as if to orient himself, then staggered forward until he reached the blazing veranda.

Without hesitation he walked into the inferno of the great house to join his woman.

Deeply saddened by the death of a man he had considered a friend, Conor remained staring after him for a moment before turning his attention back to Elana. Curled up in her mother's embrace, Elizabeth lay close beside her. Elana's lips were moving, but so weakened was she from loss of blood, he had to place his ear close to her mouth to hear her voice above the now-moaning wind.

"Save her, Conor," she whispered. "Take her to Patrick. . . take her to her father."

CONOR STOOD at the rail of the *Graf Klammer*, a white-faced Elizabeth at his side. Hand in hand, they stared in solemn disbelief at the shambles that had once been the thriving community of Bridgetown.

Few buildings remained. None of those that did had roofs and only a few had more than one or two walls.

The huge raised platform that had served as the auction block from which Conor had been sold no longer stood in the market square near the wharf. Picked up by the wind, it had been blown somewhere far out to sea.

But they will build another, thought Conor with a heavy heart. *They will build another.*

"Herr Redding. . . ."

He turned as a smartly uniformed gentleman

came to stand beside him. "Aye, captain?" he replied.

"Your papers seem to be in order," the man said, passing a sheaf of them to Conor. "Your wife...?"

"The *hurakan*," explained Conor briefly.

"I see," the captain intoned gravely. "It was a terrible storm."

"Aye." Conor nodded to the pouch in the captain's hand. "The amount—it is sufficient?"

"Very generous, in fact," acknowledged the man with a faint smile. "My mate will show you to your cabin."

They could hear the anchor being raised as they followed the mate below decks. The door of their cabin had barely closed behind them when they felt the ship begin to move.

Conor picked Elizabeth up so she could look through the porthole at the slowly receding town.

"I suppose," she said sadly, "I'll come back to visit one day."

Conor nodded. "One day you might, little one."

"Is France a pretty place?" she asked.

"Very lovely," he assured her.

"But you won't live with me there, Conor," she observed, looking up at him with a puzzled frown. "Why not?"

"Because I must to Ireland, little one," he explained, "to find a very pretty lady."

"Will you bring her back to France so I can meet her?" she pleaded.

"I'll try, Elizabeth," he promised gravely. "I shall try with every part of me."

"I'm an orphan now, aren't I, Conor?"

He made no reply as he gazed at the innocent young face of a child trying so desperately to be brave and adult in a world gone mad. The gray, fear-filled eyes were brimming with glistening tears. He hugged her tightly to him as he fought the lump that suddenly formed in his own throat.

Nay, he thought, *you'll not be an orphan, not if I can find Patrick.*

December 1651

CHAPTER THIRTY-SIX
CONNAUGHT, IRELAND

KATE TALBOT HAD NEVER SPENT a day in gaol, yet she knew the full horror of imprisonment nevertheless. For they had made of Connaught little more than a prison, a barren stretch of rocks and raped forests where the remains of the Irish people eked out a bare, day-to-day existence.

To the west lay the ocean and on the east the River Shannon. To the south was Clare, now nearly as barren as Connaught. In the north, and beyond Clare in the south, English patrols watched fields and roads, making sure that no Irishman left. Anyone who so desired could enter.

Even inside this bounded prison, the marshals, the army and the provosts of Cromwell were not content to leave them in peace. They had taken the land, and now they would have the bodies and the souls of its people.

Her breath catching in her throat, Kate peered through the crack in the door at the steep path leading down to the sea. A fat, red-faced provost clambered breathlessly up the path between two pikemen.

Inside the crude stone cottage two whimpering young girls huddled together with their arms locked about one another. They were sisters, and their story was typical of the tales of uprooted Irish families everywhere.

They came from a family of twelve. Convicted of

harboring a priest, their father had been given a choice of exile to a foreign land or death. Tearfully, he had bid his family goodbye and sailed for Spain.

Shortly thereafter the mother had died, leaving the children to fend for themselves as beggars and vagabonds. Too young to understand or to tell the difference between those they could trust and those they could not, they became easy prey to the violence of the times. Children, especially comely young girls of twelve and thirteen, were valued by the British sugar merchants for indenture in the West Indies. They paid the provosts a handsome bounty to round them up.

Kate helped the children when she could by hiding them when necessary and sharing her meager rations with them before sending them on their way. It was little enough and did not do much good, she knew, for most of the children were eventually caught. But at least it eased a mind somewhat to know that she had tried.

The many long months she had spent in barren Connaught had hardened Kate considerably. Shortly after her arrival, she had discarded dresses, petticoats and all other forms of feminine attire in favor of trews, heavy shirts, vests and any rag of cloth that would serve as a cloak to keep out the cold. She had joined Colin Dougherty and other men in nighttime forays across the Shannon to raid English bawns. She had plotted with other women to smuggle inland among the people those priests who, disguised as fishermen, had landed on the rugged coast. In short, she had done everything she could to be a thorn in the side of the men who now ruled and raped her land.

Two years of such clandestine resistance had bolstered her heart, but it had sapped her soul and taken its toll of her once kindly nature. No longer was she laughing Kate. Constant worry and a growing hate had etched lines around her eyes and made a thin, clenched line of her mouth. One thing only kept her going, made her persevere and gave her hope that one day she would be free—Patrick was alive.

The only news to come in or go out of Connaught was delivered by the smuggled priests. From them the Irish had learned of the wild and reckless exploits of the *Bonny Kate* and its master, Patrick Talbot.

The balladeers had embroidered the priests' tales until Patrick had become a legend up and down the coast. Twice he had tried a raid on Ballylee from the sea. Both times he had failed, but that the attempts had been made at all indicated to Kate at least one member of the O'Hara family was still there, most likely as a prisoner.

Kate had lost track of the number of appeals she had sent to Patrick through the priests. She had bidden each of them to tell Patrick where she was and that she was counting the days until they could be together again.

For over a year now she had sent messages. Thus far there had been no reply, but she refused to give up hope. In the meantime, the strife and desolation around her, the human condition went on. There were babes to be helped into the world, the dead to be buried, and a helping hand to be offered to those with less sustenance and more fear than herself.

"I hear them!" came a voice full of choked sobs from behind her.

"Hush!" cautioned Kate sharply, closing the door and dropping the latch. Moving swiftly across the room, she withdrew a ladder from a hidden crevice in the cottage's one stone wall that was, in fact, part of the cliff face.

"Up with you now," she directed the two children. "Where the thatch meets the stone there's an opening. Hide yourselves in there, and not a sound 'til they're gone!"

By the time the young girls had hidden themselves and the ladder was again out of sight, the pikemen had started to pound on the door.

"What would you have of me?" Kate demanded defiantly, throwing the door wide open. "I've naught to tax and I've barely enough food for myself."

Without waiting for an invitation to enter, the fat provost lifted the skirts of his black robes and stepped over the threshold, followed by the two pikemen.

"We're here to do God's work," he said, pushing past her and making for the room's only chair. Still breathing heavily from his climb, he sank down into it with every evidence of relief.

"God's work, is it?" scorned Kate harshly. "If I had me a fat bribe, I'd wager God's messenger would move on to do his work elsewhere!"

"Watch your tongue, woman," the man rasped.

The pikemen arranged themselves one on either side of the door, while the provost unrolled a parchment he held in his hand.

"Dougherty, Kate, the rolls list you," he said, his tone conveying complete disinterest. "Widow of Colin Dougherty."

"Widow?" Kate gasped, taking a quick step backward.

"Aye," replied the provost, glancing up to give her a tight smile of satisfaction. "As of three days ago, you are a widow of the hanged reparee, Colin Dougherty."

Tears sprang to Kate's eyes. She had always known it would happen to Colin, as it had to so many of those who had made the raids across the Shannon, but still it was a shock. He had proved himself a true friend, and she would miss him sorely. He had more than fulfilled his vow to Patrick in every way by taking care of her. He had built this cottage and all the furniture in it. On many occasions he had willingly risked his life to help her smuggle the priests out of Connaught so she could try to get her messages to Patrick.

"Or are you?"

"What?" Kate looked up to find that the provost was now sitting forward in the chair regarding her intently. There was an expression of eagerness on his face she found faintly alarming.

"Are you truly the Widow Dougherty?" he enunciated clearly but impatiently.

"I—I don't know what you mean," stammered Kate.

"I think you do. . .Mistress Talbot!" he declared, suddenly getting up and giving a short laugh as he saw the look of shock that she failed to keep from her face. "We caught a priest. 'Tis amazing what we find out from a man who has hot oil bubbling around his bare feet. Bring her along!"

Obediently, the two pikemen stepped forward and grasped her firmly by the arms. They dragged her from the cottage with Kate screaming, "Take heart, take heart!" as if she were shouting to the building itself.

But her eyes had lingered on the thatch where it met the stone wall.

January 1652

CHAPTER THIRTY-SEVEN
BALLYLEE, IRELAND

MAGGIE'S HEART POUNDED as she walked through the familiar rooms of Ballylee. On the surface, they looked the same as they always had, but she sensed a difference underneath. They seemed drab and uncared for. The tapestries on the walls were askew and the rushes on the floors of the lower rooms had not been changed in months. There was a moldy, dank odor to everything that almost brought a smile to her lips.

Robert Hubbard may own Ballylee, she thought, *but he cannot drive the servants to maintain it for him.* Everywhere she could see signs of neglect, and she was sure she knew the reason for it; it was the Irish servants' way of telling Ballylee's new master that he wasn't wanted.

"In here," he called to her from O'Higgin's old office.

The large oak door was open and Maggie entered the room. She had to squint in the semidarkness to see him perched on the edge of the desk.

"Sit," he commanded, indicating a high-backed chair nearby.

Obediently, Maggie sat down, glancing covertly around the office as she did so. It was even more musty than the rooms she had already seen and in far greater disarray.

"Would you like wine?" he asked.

"It has been so long that I fear I have lost the taste for it," she declared, declining his offer.

He gave a shrug of indifference and raised a goblet to his lips.

Beneath the bulky cloak, the dress and several petticoats she had taken to wearing continuously, Maggie was bathed in perspiration. Her curiosity at being summoned so suddenly to Ballylee was such that she wanted to demand an explanation from him immediately. But pride held her back and she remained silent as she gazed up at his darkly handsome face and waited for him to speak first.

"My man Croft tells me that the Lady Shanna is well," he remarked after several moments of silence.

"It comes and goes," Maggie replied briefly, and a hush settled over the room once more.

Finally, just as she thought she could take it no

longer, he rose quietly to his feet and moved to stand in front of her. He towered over her, his very nearness sending a chill of fear through her, and when he reached forward to run the tip of his finger along the fine line of her jaw, she reacted instantly by slapping his hand away.

"Am I still so loathesome to you, Maggie O'Hara?" he asked in a tone that, for him at least, was unusually soft.

Surprised, she looked up at him uncertainly for a moment before replying, truthfully, "No. 'Tis not a question of loathesome.... I think 'tis not even hate anymore. I...."

"Yes?" he prompted.

Still she hesitated, dropping her gaze to avoid his as she sought a way to explain her feelings without giving him cause to mock her. At last she gave up and, raising her head to look at him again, confessed reluctantly, "I am afraid of you, Robert Hubbard. 'Tis as simple as that."

To her great suprise, her words were greeted with neither a laugh nor even a smile of mockery. Instead, he leaned forward and, taking her hands in his, pulled her to her feet and drew her gently toward him. Wordlessly, he stared down at her and as his gaze swept searchingly across her face it suddenly washed over him that this was the woman for whom he had been searching so long. Far from diminishing her beauty, the hard life she had led these many months had in fact enhanced it. In place of the girl whom he had first seen crouched over the lad's body at Drogheda, there now stood before him a woman. He could sense, almost feel, the passion in her body that would match the flame of her hair and the green fire of defiance that flashed so frequently from her eyes.

"Would you believe me, after all these months, if I told you that you are the one person in the world I would not have fear me?" he asked softly.

Unaccountably, Maggie found it impossible to reply. Silently, she met his unwavering gaze, and as had happened so often in the past, she found herself mesmerized by the intensity of his stare. But in the dark depths of his eyes gleamed something she had never seen before. For the first time since she had known him, she saw in them an expression of true emotion and it unnerved her.

Sensing her disquiet, Hubbard let go of her hands and turned slightly away. "Have you and the Lady Shanna talked further since my last visit?" he queried.

"Aye," she replied, grateful to be free of his gaze at last.

"But nothing further has been resolved," he concluded.

"Nothing," she agreed firmly.

"Why are you so adamant, Maggie O'Hara?" he asked, turning suddenly to look down at her once more. "Would life with me, here on Ballylee, be so terrible?"

There was a sadness in his expression she found strangely moving and for a moment she could not trust herself to speak.

No, damn you, she thought bitterly. *Life on Ballylee would not be intolerable, no matter whom I spent it with. And your kindness to Shanna and myself these past months has not gone unappreciated, even though I still mistrust it. You have changed, at least toward me, and mayhap it would be better to be mistress of Ballylee at your side than to spend the rest of my days groveling as a peasant. But don't you see....*

"Don't you see, Robert Hubbard," she pleaded aloud. "Can't you understand...."

But her voice refused to complete the thought that was in her mind.

How can I make you understand that life without Conor would be no life at all?

For a moment, she continued to gaze up at him, then covered her face with her hands in despair as she suddenly realized Hubbard would never understand. How could he when he would remain forever incapable of realizing true love himself?

But Robert Hubbard noticed nothing of her despair. For the first time in his life he found himself looking at the soft curve of a woman's throat, at the gentle slope of her cheek and at the vulnerable lips that had quivered a moment earlier.

"You are beautiful," he breathed, gently removing her hands from her face and tilting it upward with a fingertip under her chin.

Slowly he bent his dark head over her and his mouth closed on hers. Sliding his hands down to her hips, he drew her toward him until she was pressed against the lean hardness of his body.

So long had it been since Maggie had felt the warmth of another's body against hers, the gentle yet insistent feel of a man's lips upon her own, that for a moment she melted against him. Her breath, her mind, her whole body, for that brief moment was swept along on a dizzying tide of desire.

An image swam into her mind, an image of a handsome young man with rust-colored curls blowing in the sea breeze. Her heart leaped as the sensual lips parted in a gay smile and she felt the tug of mischief in the crystal-blue eyes as they pulled her ever deeper into their depths.

I love you, Maggie-o, a voice whispered somewhere in the depths of her memory. *I'll always love you.*

She stiffened suddenly and her lips grew hard and cold. Feeling the change, Hubbard lifted his mouth from hers and gazed down at her with narrowed eyes. Abruptly, he released her and stepped back, the cold, hard mask dropping over his face once more.

"I'll send Croft to fetch the Lady Shanna," he said stiffly. "From this day forth you'll stay in Ballylee—both of you."

"Shanna has said she would rather die of the cold or starve than be the reason that I relent," replied Maggie defiantly.

"Mayhap the Lady Shanna will have nothing to do with it," he countered. "Mayhap the decision will be yours and yours alone. Come along."

Maggie was almost forced to break into a run to keep up with his pace as they moved through the halls and great rooms of Ballylee. As they walked he kept up a steady stream of conversation, his words beating a constant staccato against her ears.

"I'm sure you already know the details through your precious priests, but I shall bring you up to date on m'Lady Shanna's offspring, Patrick Talbot. He has commandeered two more ships to add to his fleet, both twenty gunners.

"This makes him a rather awesome and formidable foe. The amount of Commonwealth shipping he has managed to send to the bottom has become embarrassing. Of even more concern are the huge profits he has sent to aid young Charles in his futile attempts to regain his throne. In short, Patrick Talbot has become a major problem that has been brought to the attention of Cromwell.

"A princely sum of five thousand pounds has been put on his head, dead or alive." Here he paused for a moment, then added succinctly, "I think dead would be preferable."

So saying, he stopped in front of a door and turned to face her, all vestiges of the emotion she had witnessed completely vanished.

"I think I have found the means to force Patrick Talbot to surrender," he declared, his tone flat, devoid of all feeling. "You alone have the means to

save him from the noose and let him live out his days
in Spain.''

With a quick deft movement of his hand and arm,
Hubbard threw the door wide.

''Kate!'' Maggie screamed.

March 1652

CHAPTER THIRTY-EIGHT
CHAILLOT, FRANCE

A TEARFUL AND HIGHLY EMOTIONAL REUNION had followed Conor's and Elizabeth's arrival at the cottage
in which Brian and Maura resided. Maura had won
the child over almost immediately and was now walking with her in the gardens. Brian and Conor had
retired to the cottage's tiny library.

''Maura recognized the resemblance at once,
didn't she?'' Brian observed, pouring a brandy for
each of them.

''Aye,'' Conor replied. ''I'm afraid I didn't at all
until I was told, but then I had a great many other
things on my mind.''

Brian handed his brother a goblet and for a moment the two young men simply stood and gazed intently at one another. Brian, Conor thought, had
grown into a gentle giant. He was still narrow of
frame but more than a head taller than himself.

As they stood surveying each other in silence, the
love they had shared as children flowed back over
them to wash away the many years of separation.

''You've become a bull of a man, like father,''
noted Brian approvingly.

''Aye,'' Conor laughed, ''and you've become very
pretty, like mother!''

Brian grinned and raised his glass in a toast. ''To
the O'Haras!''

"The O'Haras.... May the dead rest in peace," added Conor solemnly.

"And the living have a long life."

They drank and then seated themselves opposite each other on either side of the library's fireplace. So many years had passed, and so much had happened, since they had last seen one another that both of them found it hard to know where to begin. It took Conor more than an hour to give his brother the details of Ireland's defeat and his life since then. By the time he had finished, tears glistened in Brian's eyes.

"Dear God, brother, but I feel so damnably guilty," he confessed bitterly.

"Nay, Brian, you shouldn't," objected Conor gently. "'Twas my own choice to run off and join the wars, remember?"

With a faint smile at the memory of how his brother had jumped ship those many years ago, Brian gave a reluctant nod of agreement. "Well," he sighed, "at least I have been of some good here in France."

He paused and, rummaging in the drawer of a small table nearby, produced several sheafs of papers. These he passed to Conor, and while his brother scanned them he went on to explain.

"Our father was a very wise man. Both before the war and during it, The O'Hara moved great amounts of money to France."

"So I can see," Conor gasped in awe. "And by the look of it, you've been able to manage it very well."

"Thank you," acknowledged Brian modestly. "That's the good news. You and I, Conor, can be considered very wealthy men. Indeed, those of the O'Hara family who remain alive each have a very large share coming to them."

"And the bad news?" queried Conor, looking up from the papers.

"It will never buy Ballylee back for us."

With a smile, his brother replied simply, "Then I'll take it back."

Brian shook his head. "No, Conor," he sighed. "As much as I hate to have to admit it, it's over. There is no more Ireland for the Irish, at least, not in our lifetime, believe me. If Charles II is to gain his father's throne he will have to buy part of it with Ireland. The English who have been granted land under Cromwell will be allowed to retain their holdings, for that is the only way in which Charles will be able to pacify the Protestants. To that end, Ireland and the Irish will always suffer."

Conor had dropped his gaze back to the mass of figures on the papers in his lap while his brother had been talking. Now, as Brian stopped and the sudden silence lengthened, he looked up to find the young man's face dark with anger.

"I have helped Charles in exile," declared Brian bitterly. "I served him at his court in the Netherlands before he signed that damned treaty with the Scots that persuaded him to return to England after his father's death to fight for his throne. I commiserated with him when he limped back to his mother's meager court here in France after he was so soundly defeated by Cromwell at Worcester in 1651. Patrick has helped him as well with a large share of booty pirated from Commonwealth ships." Somewhat taken aback by the bitterness in Brian's voice, Conor nevertheless remained silent as his brother continued.

"I and many others feels that the Commonwealth is doomed. Already Cromwell toys with the idea of overthrowing his Parliament and declaring himself Lord Protector, a deed that would make him no better than the monach he beheaded. Knowing this, I went to Charles and begged him for some sign, some guarantee that all our efforts were not in vain, that if the throne were ever his again, if he were ever again king of Ireland, Ballylee would be ours."

"And what, dear brother, did the Stuart say?" inquired Conor, knowing full well the answer before he voiced the quesiton.

"I think he sincerely felt shame when he denied me," replied Brian.

"But he denied you nonetheless," observed Conor, his voice dripping with disgust.

"Aye," sighed his brother. "And when I pleaded with him for a reason, he sent everyone from the room and swore me to secrecy before saying another word."

"Secrecy?" echoed Conor in surprise. "What in God's name can be so secret about Ballylee?"

"The man who now owns it and who has petitioned Charles in secret to keep it, is a lieutenant-colonel in the Irish army of Oliver Cromwell."

"'Ods blood, man," Conor cried, leaping to his feet. "Then 'tis all the more reason the damned Stuart should return it to us!"

"Aye," Brian agreed wryly. "It would seem so, to be sure, but 'tis not."

"And what reason did Charles give?" demanded Conor impatiently.

Brian shrugged. "None."

"None?"

"No more than to show me a gauntlet with his crest upon it as Prince of Wales, and declare that the giving of a man's life was worth more than all the coin in the realm."

FOR A FORTNIGHT Conor lingered at Chaillot awaiting word from Patrick. The *Bonny Kate* and its two sister ships were expected daily at the port of New Rochelle for minor repairs, rearmament and victuals.

During that time he learned of many smaller items that Brian had neglected to mention. Chief among them was the news of the existence of a Baron Eric Von Wahnfried of Austria, and his sister, Charlotte. Indeed, he heard nothing about them until the baron arrived unexpectedly at the cottage one day to confer with Brian.

Von Wahnfried had long been involved with Brian in matters of business. He had met Maura on numerous occasions and, not unnaturally, had been charmed by her great beauty and gentle, loving nature. Plans were already afoot for a lavish wedding in the near future.

"Please do not hate me, Conor," Maura pleaded when the young man was told of the betrothal.

"Hate you?" queried Conor in astonishment. "Why should I hate you? Because he is an Austrian rather than an Irishman?"

"Aye," she confessed. "And I was afraid you might think I was... betraying the memory of Donal."

"Nay, Maura, nay," he assured her, nuzzling her softly scented hair. "I think it wise you marry him, for 'tis certain Donal would have agreed that we cannot deny the world some offspring from the most beautiful of the O'Haras."

Several days later the diminutive Charlotte Von Wahnfried arrived and to his surprise Conor soon learned Maura was not the only one who had fallen in love.

"'Tis a good choice, brother," he noted approvingly. "She is lovely, with a charming and gracious manner. You will be very happy with her, I am sure. But there is one sad thing...."

"What?" Brian asked in alarm.

"Her Austrian tongue," Conor replied, his face splitting in a wide grin. "She'll never be able to wrap it around our Gaelic!"

It seemed to Conor that he spent the whole of his time while waiting for Patrick in meeting new people. Not twenty-four hours had passed after his introduction to Charlotte when he was summoned to an audi-

ence with Charles II's mother, Queen Henrietta
Maria. Brian warned him of the changes in the
woman before he was admitted to her presence but he
still wasn't prepared for the shriveled, bitter and sick-
ly looking individual he saw. His entire audience with
her was taken up with her railing against Protestants
in general and Cromwell in particular. If she had her
way, she declared emphatically, all those who did not
convert to the Catholic faith would be executed.

When Conor was at last dismissed from her presence he came away more saddened than ever about
Ireland, its people and the lost youth he had spent in
fighting a hopeless war. Cromwell, he thought bitterly, would execute the Catholics, the queen would execute the Protestants; and he considered it more than
likely that the few managing to escape such mass
slayings, would be heretics who would immediately
choose sides and execute each other.

He was sick of it, and vowed that if the day ever
came when he and Maggie were reunited, he would
have no more of it.

Patrick, astride a big bay stallion, arrived unan-
nounced a few days later.

"Conor!" he cried as the young man appeared in
the stableyard to greet him. "'Od's blood, 'tis true,
lad—you're alive!"

He leaped from his horse and the two of them embraced wildly.

"Dear God, man," Patrick exclaimed as he broke
the embrace and stepped back to survey Conor ap-
praisingly. "No longer could I whip you at swords
and arms. You're a yard wide!"

Before Patrick, Conor felt like a young boy again.
As far as he could see, his cousin had changed little.
If anything, he decided, the man looked younger and
every inch the buccaneer in his tight black breeches,
open-necked white shirt and high rolled boots.

Joining Brian, they talked and drank before Conor took Patrick by the shoulder and led him to the window. In the garden, sitting in the shade of a large spreading oak, Maura and Charlotte patiently instructed a bright-eyed beautiful little girl in the art of needlework.

"Patrick, her name is Elizabeth," Conor said softly. "Sit, and I shall tell you."

At the end of Conor's tale, Patrick arose and walked out of the garden. He took the little girl's hand and together they walked the path for over an hour. Tears glistened in his eyes when he rejoined Brian and Conor in the library.

"You'll take care of the lass, Brian, until I can return for her?" he asked quietly.

"Of course," replied the young man without hesitation.

"Good," declared Patrick. "And now, lads, 'tis my turn to surprise you."

And surprise them he did. Conor and Brian were both amazed and elated to learn that Kate, Maggie and Shanna were all alive and at Ballylee.

But they were far from pleased when Patrick told them of the message he had recently received from Hubbard. "If I surrender my ships and my crews," he explained, "Kate and I will be granted safe passage to Spain."

"And if you don't?" asked Brian.

"Kate will be sent to Barbados."

Conor gave a shudder of horror, and Patrick hastened to reassure him.

"Nay, lad, I'll allow no such thing," he promised with a laugh. "I'll have my Kate and you'll have your Maggie, for 'tis not only the English who can play the game of deceit!"

April 1652

THE TENSION AROUND THE TABLE in Ballylee's great room was electric. At one end stood Robert Hubbard, glaring down at one of the many Englishmen seated on either side of him along the table's great length. All landowners, many of them former officers under Hubbard's command, they had been invited to Ballylee to attend his marriage to Maggie O'Hara two days hence.

At the opposte end of the table were Maggie and Kate. Commanded by Hubbard to attend the meal despite their desire not to be present, they sat in stone-faced silence, watching the scene being played out before them with little more than detached interest. The tension grew as Hubbard, one hand on the hilt of his sword, continued to glare down at one of the aristocratic young Englishmen.

His name was Jonathan Conroy. A former captain, he now owned much of the land that had once been Claymore, to the north of Ballylee. All the guests had been drinking, and Conroy too much. Amid the talk of the coming marriage, he had raised his voice above the others to air his negative view of the Irish in general and Hubbard's choice of women in particular.

"For the life of me, Robert," he had declared loudly, "when you can have an Irish slattern in your bed at any time, why in God's name marry one?"

It was as if a cloud had descended over the whole room. Abruptly, the bright chatter and the noise of dining had ceased. Hubbard's face had darkened in anger and he had risen to his feet to glower down at Conroy's still smiling face.

"Conroy, I fear you are a bigger fool than I had

imagined," he had replied, his voice ominously quiet. "I must insist that you stand and apologize to the lady."

"Apologize? I? To an Irish—" Conroy had been about to repeat the word, and everyone at the table knew it.

Four inches of bare steel now appeared above the end of Hubbard's scabbard. "You will apologize, Conroy," he insisted calmly, "or you will answer to my sword."

"Are you mad?" exclaimed the man in disbelief. "Surely you don't mean to challenge me over... her?"

Hubbard's reply was brief and to the point. "I do," was all he said.

Edward Tomlins, seated to Hubbard's right, stood up and placed his hand on Robert's shoulder. "He's right, Robert. Fighting a duel is senseless."

"I'll be the judge of that," said Hubbard curtly, sweeping the man's hand from his shoulder.

"And besides," Tomlins added, "'tis against the law."

"I am the law here," Hubbard rejoined swiftly, his voice matching the icy coldness of his glare. "Conroy."

"Damned if I will!" the man cried, getting up and backing from the table as he drew his sword.

"Then, sir, you are a dead man."

Maggie's interest in the exchange suddenly changed from one of detachment to one of horror and her face drained of all color. She would have liked to have risen to her feet and left the room, but something strangely fascinating about the scene being played out before her kept her rigidly at her seat.

She was being ransomed into marriage as if she were no more than a chattel, for Hubbard was buying her hand by the use of his power to grant amnesty and exile over death. And yet he was now prepared to fight a duel over her honor.

Unless, she thought soberly, it was his own honor he sought to defend.

The room suddenly was filled with the harsh sound of clashing steel as the two men engaged. It was abundantly clear after only a few moments that Hubbard was a master swordsman.

He moved with the grace of a dancer; his feet seemed barely to touch the floor. The blade of his sword was little more than a blur as he steadily moved his opponent backward. It was hardly a fair match, and everyone in the room, including Maggie, knew it.

Her gaze fell on Hubbard's face as he feinted and parried with ease and his expression made her blood run cold. A taunting smile twisted his lips and he sought the perfect opening with narrowed eyes that glinted cruelly in the candlelight. In that instant she knew, beyond a shadow of a doubt, that her husband-to-be sought to satisfy his honor not simply by injuring his opponent, but by murdering him.

She sprang to her feet with a cry of horror, but her voice was lost in the sound of breathless gasps emitted at that moment by everyone else around the table.

Hubbard had thrust half his blade through Conroy's heart, and even now the man was sinking slowly to the ground.

"WHO IS IT?" she called as a sharp knock sounded on the door of her bedchamber.

"Robert," came the reply. "I would like just a moment."

Maggie crossed to the door, opened it and stepped back.

"My apologies, Margaret," he said, stepping into the room, "for the crudeness of my guests."

Maggie's fear of him was now total. The cold and

calculating way in which he had dispatched Jonathan
Conroy had struck terror into her heart.

Nor had his lack of humanity gone unnoticed by
his guests. After Conroy's death, one by one they
had left the great room for the stables. The wedding
would take place without them.

"By your act it would seem that you have alienated
your English friends as much as you have your Irish
peasants," she observed coldly.

"It would seem so," he agreed with a shrug. "I
care little."

"What *do* you care about, Robert Hubbard?" she
asked desperately, wishing she could fathom the enigma of this man.

He moved so swiftly she had no chance to avoid
him. Reaching out to grasp her, he drew her toward
him until she was crushed against the lean, hard
length of his body.

"Woman, are you blind?" he rasped angrily. "I
want you."

"You've said yourself," she cried, struggling
futilely against his embrace, "you want my *name*!"

"In the beginning, that was all," he conceded,
"but in these past weeks I have wished for more.
Damme, Margaret O'Hara, can't you see? We'll be
the O'Haras on Ballylee—the blood in both our veins
descended from Gaelic princes!"

Still wrapped in his arms, she gazed at him with
awe and amazement at the sudden fervor in his voice.
In the depths of his dark eyes she was sure she saw a
touch of madness.

"We'll make a fine O'Hara, you and I," he continued urgently. "We'll rule Ballylee and have an heir
who will pass it on to his sons—all O'Haras!"

"Please," she begged, "let me go! You're crushing
me—"

But he only gripped her more fiercely. "Damme, I
want you," he breathed fervently, "but not by taking

you or buying you. Can't you see that? I want all of you!''

"Never, damn you!" she hissed. "You may buy my body but you'll never own my soul!''

With a growl of rage he stepped back slightly, and grasping her bodice at the neckline, pulled viciously downward. Too aghast and surprised either to cry out or to move, Maggie looked down to see her breasts bared. She stood as though transfixed as he continued to wrench and tear at her gown until it lay in shreds at her feet.

Perspiration bathed his face and his eyes gleamed wildly as he drank in the curves and hollows of her bare flesh.

"You must be the most beautiful creature on this earth," he moaned, curving his hand around her waist.

Inexorably, he began to move her backward toward the bed. Maggie fought in real panic now pounding his face and chest with her fists. It made little difference and in sheer desperation she clawed at his face with her fingernails until blood from several deep scratches trickled down his cheeks.

Still he moved her back, and when they reached the bed, he forced her down into its softness, pinning her beneath his superior weight.

Suddenly she gave up, overwhelmed by the exhaustion and the futility of her struggle.

"Oh, God, why...*why*?" she cried. "What is this madness that drives you?''

Robert looked down at her, his eyes seeming slowly to bring her into focus. "You are everything," he whispered. "You are one with all this." He moved his arm in an arc above him. "Once I have you, it is complete.''

"Then take me," she flung at him in fury. "Take the shell, Robert Hubbard, for 'tis all you'll ever have of me!''

She closed her eyes and waited, then felt him stiffen and lift his weight from her body. With a sigh of relief she heard the door of her bedchamber close behind him and the sound of his footsteps echoing down the hall.

But it makes no difference, she thought dully. *It only postpones the inevitable.*

She lay for several moments as she had fallen on the bed, neither moving nor caring.

And then she heard the sound of his steps echoing down the hall and the door of her chamber close behind him once more. She opened her eyes to find him standing over her by the bed. In his hands he held a thick leather-bound book.

Wordlessly, he dropped it on the bed beside her and strode from the room.

IT WAS SEVERAL HOURS LATER when Maggie, carrying the leather-bound book, slipped quietly into Shanna's chamber and sat on the side of the bed.

The old woman had been sleeping, but opened her eyes immediately when she felt the bed sink beneath the girl's weight.

"Shanna, why didn't you tell me?" asked Maggie gently.

"Tell you?" queried the woman blankly, sitting up.

"I know now who Robert Hubbard is," explained Maggie in a low tone, placing the book on Shanna's lap.

Shanna turned the pages one by one. Each new page elicited a smile, a tear or a muttered comment. "Sweet Brenna," she remarked on one occasion. "She was such a gentle and kind soul. 'Tis hard to believe she and my brother, Rory, could spawn such a devil."

At last she came to the end and closed the book

with a sigh. "Dear God, 'tis as though I've lived our lives over again."

"Each time I was near him I sensed something about him that made me feel as if I had known him my whole life," confessed Maggie. "Now, I know why. At times he does, indeed, look just like his father."

"Aye," agreed Shanna. "He does."

"Why didn't you tell me?" Maggie asked softly.

Reaching out across the coverlet, Shanna enclosed Maggie's hand in her own and gave it a comforting squeeze. "He's a torn and tormented man," she observed sadly. "I fear he has never known love and never will. But he and I have one thing in common—the need for Ballylee."

Here she paused for a moment, and as she turned her gaze on Maggie, the young woman saw that her eyes glistened with tears. Her voice was little more than a whisper as she continued, "I was afraid that knowing how I feel, how I've always felt about the land and the need to have an O'Hara always upon it, you would be swayed if you knew he, too, is an O'Hara. I was afraid such knowledge would make you agree to his offer of marriage when I know you love Conor so deeply."

Once more she paused and choked down a sob before adding, "Even now I am at sea. I fear our family, our name, is soon to be barren. Conor is gone, Brian can never return. Forgive me, Maggie, but in my heart I was almost hoping this wedding would happen, for you are now the only true O'Hara with a future on Ballylee."

Maggie leaned forward and kissed the tears on the old woman's cheeks. She then walked silently from the room, feeling nothing, devoid of all emotion. She knew now she would marry Robert Hubbard, for not only did Kate and Patrick's future happiness depend upon it, but so also did Shanna's.

"DAMME, LAD," Patrick chuckled, "if you aren't a fine looking bridegroom!"

Shaking his head in disbelief, Conor looked down at his attire. He wore an azure blue doublet with breeches to match and knee-high shiny black leather Spanish boots. A gold half-cape rested on his shoulders, and across his doublet was emblazoned the O'Hara crest.

"A groom," he chuckled. "'Tis hard to believe."

Kerns and peasants had crowded into the booley house to welcome The O'Hara home. Now, together with the seamen who made up Patrick's crews, they roared their approval and raised their tankards to Conor.

Tears glistened in his eyes as he looked around at them, at their broad Irish faces and their wide, welcoming smiles. With a pang, he recalled the last instructions he had received from his father as the man lay dying.

Take care of your own, lad, and one day they will take care of you.

Now that day had come, and Conor realized how prophetic had been his father's last words.

One week earlier, he and Patrick, dressed in ragged trews, peasant shirts and brogues, had landed secretly at night on the coast north of Ballylee. For months, Patrick had been planning a raid from within his former home. He knew the peasants whom he could trust, those who were still faithful to the clan.

News of Maggie's impending and forced marriage to Robert Hubbard had reached them almost immediately. Conor's fury had been such that Patrick had had a hard time restraining him from riding directly to the castle and rescuing her singlehandedly. "Nay, lad," he had cautioned his cousin. "'Twould be suicide. But methinks this marriage gives me a better plan than the one I had to gain entrance to Ballylee."

Having extracted from Conor a promise that he

would bide his time, Patrick had outlined his plan. "We'll move into Ballylee through wide-open gates, as the extra servants and grooms that will be needed for the wedding," he had explained simply. "With luck we'll outnumber Hubbard's men twenty to one.

"By the hour of the wedding, we'll have them unarmed, manacled and gaoled in the south tower," he had continued, a gleam of mischief in his eyes. "That, Conor is when you come in."

"I don't understand," Conor had said with a frown of puzzlement.

"Why, Conor, lad, this Hubbard fellow has given us all the makings of a wedding. If we can find us a priest, 'twould be a shame not to use it!"

DRESSED IN A FLOWING GOWN of white silk and lace, Maggie knew that she looked the bride she didn't feel. Nevertheless, she was determined to endure this mockery Hubbard chose to call a wedding with dignity, and her eyes, hidden beneath her lacy veil, were dry. She had cried the tears of a lifetime during the night, and now there were no tears left.

The battle was over, and as far as she was concerned; so, too, was her life. Steeling her heart and mind to accept the fact that she would never see Conor again, she had sealed off all memory of the past and now faced the future with a resigned but calm indifference. Come the morrow Patrick would sail into the bay below Ballylee to surrender his ships to Robert Hubbard. He and Kate would have to leave for Spain, but they would be together and happy.

In a few more moments, she would be married to a man with at least some O'Hara blood in his veins and Shanna would be happy. And she herself. She would be mistress of Ballylee, and neither sad nor happy.

"Are you all right, Maggie?"

As Kate's concerned voice intruded on her thoughts, Maggie suddenly realized that it had been

some moments since they had reached the bottom of
the wide staircase and she had yet to take another step.
"Aye, let's have done with it," she sighed, squaring
her shoulders and walking beneath the high arch of the
entrance to the great room.

During the long walk to the other end of the room,
she saw nothing through the mist that covered her
eyes. Not until she came to a halt before the raised dais
did she become aware of the priest in full raiment.

No, her mind screamed in protest, *that I will not
do. There shall not be a Catholic wedding. Protestant, yes, but not Catholic. I will not be married to
Robert Hubbard in the eyes of the Church!*

She whirled to where Robert should have been
standing—and nearly swooned. For it was not Hubbard who awaited her, but a broad-shouldered handsome young Irishman with coppery hair, laughing
blue eyes and an engagingly mischievous smile.

"Maggie-o, you're the most beautiful bride that
has ever taken the walk."

"Conor!" she gasped. "How—"

The flood of tumultuous emotions that suddenly
engulfed her made further speech impossible. Her
knees grew weak and she felt herself sway against
him. He caught her around the waist and, lifting her
veil, covered her lips with his own.

So powerful was the surge of desire his kiss sent
through her, Maggie felt sure she was dreaming.
After all she had been through, such happiness could
not possibly be real.

"Conor...oh, my Conor," she gasped between
sobs of joy.

"Maggie-o," he said gently, "'twas a big ocean I
had to cross, but loving you made it but a little pond.
I do love you, Maggie-o.... Do you still have the
love for me?"

"Yes...oh, yes!" she cried, throwing her arms

around his neck. "I love you, I love you, I love you.... But how—"

"We've taken the castle," he replied with the care-free laugh she had dreamed of so many nights.

"'Twas not so difficult as we expected. It would seem that the usurping Hubbard has few friends, even among his countrymen, judging by the lack of guests and their guards. His own men offered little resistance when they saw our numbers. They and Hubbard himself now languish under our guard in the south tower. But 'tis only for a time. Come, Maggie-o, we've a wedding to tend to!"

ROBERT HUBBARD STOOD ON THE TOWER, a fine wind plucking at the black cloak draped around his shoulders. Before him on the parapet were set a fine crystal decanter of brandy and a half-filled goblet.

He lifted the goblet to his lips, and as he sipped the liquid warmth it contained he swept his gaze toward the sea and the three sails disappearing on the horizon. When he could see them no more, he took the decanter in his free hand and moved to the inland side of the tower. In the distance, over the rolling hills and heaths he could see the carts and wagons and horses, all leaving Ballylee.

Taking the goblet and decanter with him, he went inside the castle and down the tower's narrow stone steps. He walked the hallways and the rooms, all silent save for the hollow echo of his footsteps on the stone floors.

There was not the sound of a pot or pan being used in the kitchen, not the whisper of a voice in any room. There was not a sound on Ballylee, nor a soul save for himself and his hired guards, now retired to their own quarters. There had been little point in forcing them to remain on duty when there was no one for them to guard him against. For that had been the price extracted him by The O'Hara and the pirate Talbot in return for his life and that of his men; that all Irishmen currently in his service at Ballylee be given the choice of leaving with all their possessions or remaining in their present positions. Without exception, they had chosen to leave.

At last he reached the great room. The log fire that had been lit for the wedding still roared in the gigantic hearth. Slowly he lowered himself into a chair, stretched his long legs and turned his gaze upward, to the mantel and the gold-and-green crest of the O'Haras.

For hours he sat drinking and staring. Dusk was gathering beyond the tall leaded windows when he heard the soft sound of a slippered foot on the floor behind him.

Shanna, a heavy shawl draped around her frail shoulders, moved slowly into his view and stood staring silently down at him.

"I could have you hanged for your part in it, old woman," he said, breaking the silence at last.

"Aye, you could," she agreed calmly. "But you won't."

"They're gone, all of them—servants, peasants, tenants."

"I know."

He laughed harshly. "Don't they know there is nowhere for them to go? That they will be sent to devastated Connaught or Clare—or worse? Didn't they realize how much better off they were at Ballylee?"

" 'Twas their choice," she reminded him quietly.

"Aye," he conceded. "And I doubt not that they'll live to regret it."

"I know."

He paused to take a sip of his brandy before adding in a whisper, "There is no one left."

"Just us," she replied, "you and I. We are the last O'Haras on the land."

"I thought you had left on the ship with your family, old woman. Why did you stay?"

"'Tis my home," Shanna replied, settling into the chair opposite him. "I'll share it with you."

IT WAS A SAD AND SOLEMN FOURSOME that stood on the afterdeck watching the green shores of Ireland and the stark outline of Ballylee recede. None of them had spoken for some time and the only sounds around them were the gentle slap of water against the hull, the cry of the occasional sea gull and the hushed voices of Patrick's crew.

The silence that had grown between them was broken suddenly by the sound of choking sobs from Maggie as she turned her gaze away from the land and buried her head against Conor's broad chest.

"Hush now, Maggie-o," he soothed, gently placing his arms around her. "'Tis not so bad as all that. Brian is right, you know. There is no more Ireland for the Irish."

"'Tis not so much Ireland I hate to leave as Ballylee," she declared, her voice muffled as she remained pressed in Conor's embrace.

"I know," he sighed, and his tone became bitter as he added, "But even that is denied us, now and forever. Would you have our sons and daughters brought up in poverty as tenants of English officers and soldiers? Would you have them become the turf cutters of the next generation just so we could remain on Ballylee?"

Her sorrow overshadowed by indignation that he could suggest such a thing, she raised her head to look up at him. "Nay," she replied firmly. "You know I would not."

"No more would I," he agreed, with a smile of pleasure at seeing his wife return to a semblance of her normal self. "But I have to confess that France, also, holds little appeal for me."

"Nor does it for me," Patrick interjected suddenly.

He dropped a hand on his cousin's shoulder. "What say you, Conor, to the New World—Virginia, or the Carolinas? We'll carve ourselves a new Ballylee."

"The New World...a new life," Kate whispered, her eyes glistening with tears as she continued to gaze toward the receding land. Somewhere in that war-torn country she hoped her brother, Timothy, and his Cathy still lived and she vowed that one day she would return to lead them to a better life.

"A new Ballylee," Conor murmured, gazing down at his wife. "What say you, Maggie-o?"

"I say I love you," she replied promptly. "I will love you anywhere, Conor O'Hara."

"And you, Kate?" asked Patrick anxiously, aware of her concern for her brother.

"Aye," Kate sighed, turning at last from the land to bury her head against her husband's chest. "For there is nothing left for us in Ireland."

"Then the New World it is!" cried Conor.

"Sir?"

Patrick turned from the afterdeck railing as one of his crew members came up to stand beside him. "Aye?" he replied.

"'Tis your mother, sir."

"What of her?" he queried sharply, a look of concern on his face.

"She's not in her cabin," replied the sailor apologetically, "and I can find her nowhere aboard."

As one, the four members of the O'Hara clan turned to gaze once more toward the land and the castle of Ballylee, its towers and parapets now barely discernible against the horizon.

"I should have known," Patrick sighed. "She would never leave."

Clutching one of Conor's hands tightly, Maggie spoke in a hushed whisper.

"There will always be an O'Hara on the land."

An excerpt from the fourth epic volume in

THE O'HARA DYNASTY

*Watch for it—wherever paperbacks
are sold*

The Exiled

by MARY CANON

September
VIENNA WOODS, AUSTRIA

MEGAN O'HARA DROVE the small buggy listlessly,
paying little heed to the mare's pace or direction. In
the same manner she pulled her cloak more tightly
about her to ward off the chill autumn air.

She knew she had stayed in the woods too long and
it would be dark before she reached the manor house.
The family would be worried. How often they had
admonished her about the dangers of being out after
dark. The woods were full of wolves and other wild
animals. The roads and paths were narrow and winding, bounded on one side by precipitous craggy cliffs
down which one could plunge and not be found for
months.

Suddenly her breath caught in her throat. With no
direction from her driver and sensing the nearness of
the stables, the mare had picked up speed until she
was now fairly galloping down the narrow path.
Dead ahead lay a blind curve.

Megan grasped the reins tightly between her slender fingers and pulled with all her might.

"Whoa...whoa!" she cried, but to little avail.
Thoroughly frightened now, she redoubled her efforts to slow the mare when, to her horror, a horse
thundered around the curve straight toward her at a
full gallop. Its rider was hunched low over its neck,
his cloak billowing behind him like a black cloud.

The path was too narrow to allow them to pass and
there was nowhere for either of them to turn.

Megan closed her eyes and screamed as the wheel
of the cart dug into the soft dirt. Lifting from the
ground, the vehicle hung suspended for a brief instant before cartwheeling over and sending her flying. Megan felt her head strike something cold and
sharp, and suddenly she found herself surrounded by
a dark whirlpool, eddying dizzily, pulling her deeper
and deeper down into its depths.

A shadowy face swam into view above her own
and as if from a great distance.

"Fräulein...Fräulein!"

"What...who—ohh!" Megan groaned as she
struggled to sit up, only to be blinded for an instant as
a sharp pain flashed through the right side of her head.

Closing her eyes, she sank to the ground with a
gasp.

"Bitte, Fräulein.... Do not try to move," came a
low, gentle voice.

Megan forced her eyes open, and her breath caught
in her throat at the vision she beheld. Kneeling over
her was the cloaked rider who had caused her acci-
dent. Now, however, the cloak was thrown back
from his face, and as he continued to gaze anxiously
down at her, Megan thought she was looking at the
most handsome man she had ever seen.

His face was deeply tanned and ruggedly constructed, his hair chestnut flecked with gold that tumbled over his forehead and curled around his ears.
His nose was straight and strong and accentuated his

full, sensuous lips. But it was his eyes that made her gasp involuntarily. Crystal clear beneath dark lashes, they were a deep cerulean blue. Bold and unblinking, full of wisdom, intellect and arrogance, they swept searchingly across her face. Megan felt herself being pulled into yet another eddying whirlpool, this one as deep as the ocean.

"Here, this will make a softer pillow than that cold stone," he said, grinning as he swept the cloak from his shoulders and folded it beneath her head. "Now lie back and I will see if you are injured."

Beneath the cloak he wore a uniform of a type that Megan couldn't identify. But he spoke a strongly accented English and she came to the conclusion that he could only be an officer in the Austrian army; there were so many of them in Vienna in the king's guard. Not, at the moment, that she really cared who he was. She sank back and closed her eyes as his strong yet gentle fingers probed her shoulders, arms and ribs, looking for any broken bones.

But as he moved his probing fingers lower, Megan suddenly flushed and stiffened.

"Sir!" she reprimanded him sharply, her eyes flying open.

"Do not be a child, *Fräulein*," he flashed, ignoring her protests. "You could easily have fractured your leg. That was a nasty spill you took."

"Thanks to you!" she bristled.

Abruptly, he raised his head and leveled his piercing gaze on her. "I?" he queried in astonishment. "I think not, *Fräulein*. I had my horse under complete control. It was you who came with too much speed around the curve in the road."

His voice was accusing, almost patronizing, and Megan flushed with both anger and embarrassment. He was right, of course; she had been reckless with the carriage.

"I—I was in a hurry to get to the house before dark," she stammered, making a futile attempt to straighten her clothes and smooth down her tangled hair. "My family...they will be worried."

He raised one eyebrow questioningly. "Oh? And just where is this house that you are in such a hurry to reach? And what family?"

"The O'Haras of Erin Manor."

At the mention of her family name, a dark cloud passed over the stranger's face. His crystal-blue eyes hardened like ice, and his jaw set in a hard line. His abrupt change of mood, from one of carefree arrogance to something much more ominous, made her suddenly uncomfortable—and not a little afraid.

She struggled to stand up. "I'm really all right now," she murmured. "I must be getting back. They're probably looking for me at this moment."

He encircled her slender waist with strong arms and, lifting her effortlessly, settled her gently on her feet. Megan felt a wave of dizziness overcome her, and she found it impossible to tell whether it was caused by the blow to her head or from the nearness of this overwhelmingly masculine and mysterious stranger. She had to reach out and grasp his arm to steady herself.

"Here, *Fräulein*," he suggested, and only now did she notice how deep was his voice. "I fear you are in no condition to travel far by yourself. Nor," he added with a grin, "is your carriage. One wheel has decided to go off somewhere by itself. Come, you will ride with me to the manor house. Your mare can follow our lead."

Before Megan could protest, she found herself swept up in his arms once again and settled astride his snorting, prancing stallion. Quickly he released the harness on her horse, then effortlessly swung himself up behind her on his own mount.

She stiffened as he reached around her for the reins. The nearness of him, his masculine scent, the animal heat she felt as he pressed forward and spurred the horse into a light canter, made her already befogged mind reel even further.

She blinked her eyes and shook her head slightly to clear it. With great effort she concentrated on the path ahead, intending to give him directions. "'Twill be the path on the left—'' she began.

"I know the way to Erin House," he interrupted.

The curtness in his tone again brought Megan up short. Chancing a quick glance at his face behind and slightly to one side of hers, she was struck once more by the grim line of his jaw and the granitelike set of his chiseled features. Why, she wondered, would he react so strongly to the mention of Erin House?

But Megan had little time to dwell on the man's strange response to her family name. He rode like the wind, sure of himself and the mount beneath him. She managed just once more to speak before they reached the huge iron gates that marked the entrance to Erin House.

"I don't remember ever meeting you, sir, yet you seem to know my family."

"We are acquainted," he acknowledged briefly, reining in the stallion. "I apologize for not delivering you to the front door, but—" He paused, his eyes hardening once more with that icy coldness Megan couldn't fathom. "I think it wiser to leave you here."

With catlike grace, he dismounted and reached up to grasp Megan around her slender waist. He eased her from the saddle and into the air, but instead of setting her onto the ground, he tightened his hold and drew her ever closer to him, until she was pressed against his powerful chest.

Megan's breath caught as his gaze locked with hers.

"You are beautiful, *liebchen* . . . the most beautiful woman I have ever seen," he murmured.

And before she realized his intention, he had bent his head over hers and claimed her mouth in a searing kiss that robbed her of all thought and reason. She struggled against him, but he merely increased his grip and his lips became even more demanding, branding her with their soul-searching fire.

After what seemed an eternity, he released her at last and lowered her to the ground. Looking deeply into her eyes, he reached up with one fingertip and traced the line of her trembling jaw.

"A name, *liebchen*. What is the name I should carry in my heart until we meet again?" he whispered.

With difficulty she found her voice. "My name is Megan. . . Megan O'Hara," she managed to reply.

An engaging grin creased the features of his handsome face. "A beautiful Irish name for a beautiful Irish lass," he observed approvingly.

"And—and yours?" she stammered.

"Quite a mouthful I'm afraid!" he replied with a laugh. Abruptly, he assumed an expression of mock seriousness; the grin disappeared and his brows knit in a severe frown over haughty eyes. "Baron Maximillian Leopold Ulysses Von Schyler at your service, *Fräulein*," he proclaimed, sweeping her a low bow as Megan dissolved into a fit of giggles.

In an instant she found herself once more in his arms, his lips burning into her flesh as he brushed them lightly across her forehead and down to rest for a moment in the hollow at the base of her throat before moving up again to claim her eager, unresisting mouth in a demanding kiss.

Reluctantly, she pulled from his grasp. "I must go in," she gasped. "Goodbye, Baron Maximillian Leo—" Suddenly she couldn't remember the rest.

"Max, my lovely *liebchen*. Just remember Max!" he suggested with a laugh. "And we will meet again, Megan O'Hara," he added in tones that left no room for doubt. "That I promise you!"

In seconds he was gone, a mere speck against the gray night sky.

Gone from sight, Megan thought, a chill running up her spine, *but definitely not from mind.*